THE VALLEY OF
THE FOX

THE VALLEY OF
THE FOX

Joseph Hone

St. Martin's Press
New York

Library of Congress Cataloging in Publication Data

Hone, Joseph, 1937-
    The valley of the fox.

    I. Title.
PR6058.049V3   1984   823'.914   83-21125
ISBN 0-312-83609-0

First published in Great Britain in 1982 by Martin, Secker & Warburg Limited

First U.S. Edition

10 9 8 7 6 5 4 3 2 1

For
Lucy and William

'In the Valley of the fox
Gleams the barrel of a Gun.'
Doomsday Song   W. H. AUDEN

'There is a strange land yonder, a land of witchcraft and
beautiful things; a land of brave people, and of trees, and
streams, and snow peaks, and a great white road. I have heard of
it. But what is the good of talking? It grows dark. Those who
live to see will see.'

Umbopa in *King Solomon's Mines*
H. RIDER HAGGARD

Prologue

He'd trapped me. But had he intended to? Had he meant to drive me up against the old pumping shed by the far end of the lake? Or had I carelessly allowed him to do this, moving after him into this impasse where there was no soundless exit, either across the stream ahead or up the steep open slopes behind the ruined building. Either way I couldn't move now. And since the laurel bush only partly hid me I knew that if he moved past the corner of the shed he must see me and I would have to kill him.

There was no doubt about that. I'd kill him just as I'd had to kill his dog. I wasn't going to lose the safety of these huge woods, these three square miles of old oak and beech, with odd nooks and pits in the Cotswold limestone, the heavy undergrowth as well, and great drifts of leaf mould where a dead thing – beast or man – could easily disappear, or as soon decay.

I would kill him because I was angry, too – angry at my stupidity in letting him corner me thus. I thought, in the past weeks, I'd become fairly expert in living wild, in concealment and camouflage. Instead, after I'd first seen the man very early that morning, I'd lost my head and become civilised again – blind, impatient, nervous. And now I was trapped. I had a store of anger within me in any case. And I knew it wouldn't be difficult, now that I was cornered, to let it all explode.

I notched the arrow, eased three fingers behind the cord, drawing it back slowly as I lifted the bow. There was a space of dappled shade fifteen feet from me, by the back corner of the ruined pumping shed. If Detective-Inspector Ross was doing more than just following a hunch – if he actually knew of my existence now in these woods, had seen me at some point that morning and was really following me – then he would surely move into that bright space and he would die for his mistake, not mine.

The sharpened aluminium tip came slowly back towards the knuckles of my bow hand. The long shaft trembled minutely as I made the draw. Then I held the arrow, almost at full stretch, anchored firmly against my shoulder muscles, the aim steady, all movement gone. Ross was the only one who had to move now.

<h2 style="text-align:center">2</h2>

I'd come down for my swim from the top of the great oak tree the usual way first thing that morning – moving across, squirrel-fashion, onto the middle branches of a neighbouring copper beech, set further back against the steep slope of the hill, where one of its great limbs, leaning right over against the bank, made a swaying gangway down to earth. From beneath, at their base, where this line of trees leant over the small lake, it would have been impossible to climb any of them. There were no footholds, no stubble on the trunk of my huge oak until a first ruff of leaves blossomed out in a crown of small branches twenty feet up – while of course the beech trunks were smooth as ice for the same distance.

The only access to my tree-house was via this errant branch. The wood was too old, the trees too high for any other ready climbing. Though there was another branch offering safety, in a tree further along, a few hundred yards away at the south end of the valley – a smaller springy beech branch, which leant across like a parallel bar straight out over the stream just before it ran out of the lake. This was how I'd hidden myself to begin with, on that first evening running from the school, finding the stream and walking down the middle of it, so that the dogs that I expected behind would have no scent to follow.

This other limb over the water had saved me then, when I'd pulled myself on to it, exhausted, barely able to lift the bow and backpack up after me, before climbing higher up, deep into its heart, hidden then by the thick canopy of leaves. For the dogs had come soon afterwards, that same night, led by police with lights, spearing the undergrowth, splashing across the stream. That night and most of the following day they'd ranged back and forth through the wood while I lay up, secure in the leafy sunshine high above them.

It was then that I'd thought of building a tree-house – of how these vast branches and impenetrable summer leaves could save me more permanently. That was almost two weeks ago, passed in growing safety. Since then only one other person had ventured into the steep dell with its small lake, hidden in the forest, which I had made my own. But now Ross had come, a first snake in this Eden.

When I swam I took only the bow with me, two arrows strapped to its belly. I left my clothes behind. It was high summer, a long spell of hot weather, and prudery had no place anyway in this great emptiness. I'd re-discovered the childhood pleasure of swimming naked, pushing gently out into the mist-topped pool just before sun up, the water with just a touch of ice in it after the night, creeping up over my skin like chilled mercury.

It was the best part of my day, this early morning or late evening swim, for I couldn't risk it at any other time. Even though the pool was partly concealed at the bottom of the lake, overhung with willow and cornered off on one side by a fallen tree-trunk, the ripples might have eddied out into the calm central water, attracting some trespassing hiker or fisherman.

As it was, even first or last thing in the day, I had to be careful. There were colonies of moorhen and at least a pair of mallard who had their homes along the margins of the water, in the reeds and by the water-lilies. And careful though I was they never failed to make a fuss when I came down to swim. There were a few deer as well – down to drink now and then, very early or late, strayed from the herd that roamed the great parkland of the estate above the valley. I'd surprised a big antlered buck on my path down to the water two mornings before: it had crashed away through the undergrowth like a lorry. There were pheasants too, much more common in the surrounding bushes: wily, richly coloured old birds who never seemed to fly, patrolling secret pathways instead, beaks to the ground – who, unless you nearly stepped on them, said nothing.

It was one of these splendid cocks who probably saved me that morning. The moorhens had batted away as usual on my arrival, skating nervously across the water, while the mallard, getting used to me I suppose, had swum with more dignity up to the north end of the lake. But everything was finally still as I lolled in the water then, just out of my depth, treading ground, the liquid swirling in chilly spirals round my legs. The early mist smoked about my face as I swam out towards the fallen trunk. But I could see upwards into the morning now, through the ring of great trees that circled the lake – see the growing shafts of gold pushing the night away and the blue that was coming, pale blue now with last stars in it, that would soon form a leaden dome over the hot day. I rested against the moist trunk, digging my fingers deep into the thick moss. There was a sudden damp smell of old ruined gardens as I scratched at it, some memory of contentment.

Then the pheasant sang out, a shriek of outrage across the water, its surprise filling the air with danger in an instant. At first – dead still, with my nose just above the tree-trunk – I heard nothing more and thought it a false alarm. But when the bird cried again and got up in a great flurry of wingbeats and headed out over the lake towards me, I knew someone must have driven it from cover.

Then I saw the man, a hundred yards away, emerging from the undergrowth just above my oak tree. He stood for a moment at the edge of the water by the old boathouse, a big Alsatian dog inquisitively beside him, a shotgun loosely crooked in his arm, looking straight at me it seemed as he followed the bird's path right over my head. At that distance I didn't know it was Ross; the man was dressed like a caricature of an old-fashioned gamekeeper, in plus fours, tweed jacket and cap. He took up the shotgun then, making a pass with it in the air before levelling it straight in my direction.

I saw the brief flash of light, a shaft of crystal morning sun on the barrel, before I ducked behind the fallen trunk, the water suddenly cold all over my body. But when I looked up again after half a minute the man was gone and I glided quickly back under the willow trees and onto the shore. I had my bow and two sharp arrows. But I couldn't get home. The keeper was obviously coming down the lake shore towards me, was already between me and my tree-house. I couldn't get back to the beech branch that leant over the hill halfway up the valley – nor could I risk making for the other smaller branch that would lift me to safety, thirty yards to my left above the stream, for to get over there would be to risk crossing right in his path.

The only escape was off round through the wood on the other side of the lake, making for the old pumping shed – an area which had as much intermittent cover as my own side of the water but where the trees, I knew, had no saving lower branches at all. In any case trees were no real use to me now. There was the dog, who might very soon pick up my scent and then track me to any hidden cover. I had to keep moving and hope to drop the tail somehow as I went along.

For the first ten minutes after I'd made off round the other side of the lake, I thought I'd lost them. The woods were calm behind me, a vast summer-morning calm. The sun had risen in a great arc of gold high above me, the top leaves of the great copper beeches already a deep bronze colour. But among the rabbit paths and undergrowth right at the bottom of the valley, which I kept to, there were still odd patches of mist in dank places. I moved forward, in and out of these swirling blobs of cotton wool very carefully, my skin almost the same colour as the air, a naked ghost.

My plan was to move north up the valley, to the head of the lake and then, to kill my trail, walk down the middle of the stream which ran into it, before doubling back to my tree-house on the far side. The beech forest ran in a thick line here, for nearly a mile along and above the valley, the trees and undergrowth hugging the steep slopes and giving adequate cover before the land opened out at the end of the defile, into rough pasture, dotted with clumps of bramble and gorse. Two or three miles away, beyond these scrubby edges to the manor's home farm lay the northern boundary to the estate, a small by-road that led to the local market town five miles away. But even though there were no farm buildings up there – just a flock of rarely tended sheep – all this open space was out of bounds in daylight to me. The woods I'd come to know intimately; I felt I controlled them. Beyond was the world, a place I'd loved, but a plague-land to me now.

I'd stopped and was crouching right down, my ear almost to the ground, in the middle of a thick clump of old elder bushes. I'd learnt to walk the leaf mould, along hidden paths, almost soundlessly in my bare feet 'uring the past weeks. Surely the man, in his heavy boots, would be unable to move as quietly? I listened to all the natural sounds of early morning that I'd become accustomed to: a blackbird chirruped suddenly and ran away somewhere behind me. Something else moved high above me, scratching the bark of a tree in a small flurry: a squirrel was going up into the light. But the rest was silence.

I was just turning, about to move away, when I saw him. He was standing, absolutely still, hardly more than twenty yards away, just his head visible, as if disembodied, poking out above a patch of mist. He stared at me – straight at me, it seemed –

with his deep-set eyes like holes in a Halloween turnip. He must have seen me, I thought. Or had he? He had the air of a dreamer, of something malign and unreal just emerged from the dying mist. It was Ross, I saw then – the grave-faced dirty tricks man from the Special Branch, sometimes attached to our section: doubtful-eyed, the lids rarely blinking, someone I'd known vaguely in London years before, when I was in Mid-East Intelligence and he'd looked at me over a desk, as he seemed to do now out of the white air, with the same fathomless expression, waiting for you to make the error: the slight lantern jaw, swarthy, the permanent five o'clock shadow: it was certainly Ross, like some more skilled animal, who had caught up with me – Ross, playing the countryman, the man who never gave up. Ross, the hit-man now, who must have been the immediate cause of all my anguish a fortnight before. I'd have tried to kill him there and then except that I'd more to do before I left these woods, a lot more. Besides it was Marcus – his and my old boss – that I really wanted: it was Marcus, after all, who must have sent Ross out into my life to ruin it.

But where was his stupid dog – a police dog, obviously? It must have lagged somewhere behind him for Ross turned and called softly, disappearing back into the cotton wool. I took the chance of moving off as quickly as I could in the opposite direction.

For quite a few minutes then I thought I'd lost him again. I heard the dog whimper, but its excited cries seemed to be disappearing in the distance behind me. What on earth was it doing? My scent must have been clear enough on the ground. I didn't wait to find out, moving onwards, skirting a clearing, making for the end of the lake.

It was on the far side of this open glade, when I'd gone back into the undergrowth of fern and bramble and thought myself safe, that I heard the sounds of some mild stampede on the still air behind me: bushes crackled, dry sticks broke. The Alsatian was whimpering as it ran, and the hungry sounds were coming towards me this time. The dog had found my trail securely at last and was closing on me quickly.

I ran through the bushes now, my skin thorned as I ran fleet-foot, regardless of noise, intent only on putting as much distance as possible between us. But it would never be enough. The dog had four legs and, despite its earlier tracking errors, its training would tell in the end, I knew.

It gained on me as I ran headlong up the valley. And I thought – it must soon be over: the beast will leap on my back in a moment, or tear at my arm, its dark jaws sinking deep into my flesh.

And it was imagining this bloody hurt, and my subsequent death (for that, of course, had been their intention from the start) that made a charge of anger flood up in me, a tingling, like an electric current that brought the muscles tight together, all over my body in a sense of wild supremacy.

A hunted animal, yes, I'd become just that: naked, earth-grimed, bleeding. But such an animal, at the last, can turn and kill too. There was an arrow for both of them, after all, a chance, at least, before they got me.

I ran up the side of the valley, unstrapping the two arrow shafts as I went, and when I thought I was high enough to command the ground beneath, I turned, stringing the first arrow and waited for the dog.

As soon as it saw me, emerging from some laurel at the bottom of the dell, it left the scent and bounded straight up the slope towards me, head high, going very fast, without any whimpering. Now that it was finally confirmed in its purpose, the animal was like a guided missile that would explode viciously in my face within moments. Ross was nowhere to be seen: the dog had run well ahead of him.

The dacron cord came quickly taut against my cheek. I steadied the sharpened arrow-tip on the animal's chest. And since it was coming straight up the slope towards me, without any lateral movement, the dog formed an ever-larger target on the same axis. I thought I could make it.

I let it get to within about twenty feet of me – and just before the arrow sang, cutting the air like a whip for an instant, I knew it was going to strike home. There was that sixth sense that sometimes comes in any physical skill when you know you've got it right just before you do it, when there is a magic certainty of success.

The arrow, without barbs, drove deep into the dog's chest, partly transfixing it like a spit through a pig. It came on another yard or so up the hill. But it was only momentum. It wasn't dead when I picked it up, but there was no bite in it, nor any sound. On. y its eyes remained angry. The arrow must have pierced its windpipe or found its heart. I got it out of the open in a moment, cradling it in my arms towards some cover higher up, and when I laid the animal down on the leaf mould, all my shoulder, where the dog's muzzle had been, ran with foaming blood.

Of course Ross would miss the dog, I knew that. He would look high and low for it now and would surely come back later, with fresh help, to continue the search. But I knew already where I could dispose of the animal, when I had the chance, where it would not betray my presence in the wood and would appear simply to have met with a natural accident. There was a covered well I'd discovered a week before among some bushes, just behind the old pumping shed, with two metal shutters at ground level which opened up, displaying dark water six feet beneath. I would dump the animal there, leaving one of the covers off, so that, if discovered at all, it would be seen as a bloated victim of some woodland error, a town dog fatally unused to country matters.

But I wondered then why Ross hadn't kept the animal on a lead in the first place? Surely that was how they tracked murderers on the nine o'clock news? Perhaps it was his own dog, a pet, not police trained at all? Ross was just the kind to keep such a dog in London. There was a lot of cruelty in him, in his face at the very least; something of the frustrated hunter there, of someone who'd keep just such a big killer dog in his flat or suburban semi, as a constant reminder of vicious life. Or perhaps, simply, no one else had agreed with him at HQ that I could possibly be anywhere in these woods, which they had so thoroughly combed two weeks before, and he'd had to come down from London on his own, unaided, so that with his shotgun to carry, the dog had to be let run free. But whatever the reason, Ross himself was still there to contend with.

He came into the glade beneath me a moment later, his shotgun at the ready now, perplexed but wary. He called for the dog, a soft call on the morning air that I barely heard.

'Karen?' I thought he said. Then he whistled. But only a bird answered in the distance. The sun was rising higher now, beginning to cast long shafts of gold through the cathedral of beech trees round the clearing. The mist had gone. Ross turned apprehensively, as though he felt suddenly exposed in all this brilliant light, and looked up the steep bank towards where I was hidden. I thought – if he comes up I'll shoot him too. But he didn't. He moved straight on, following the path he thought the dog had taken, up towards the head of the lake. And so it was the more careless of me to allow myself to be trapped by him ten minutes later behind the ruined pumping shed. For the shed was in the same direction that he had taken, by the northern end of the lake: if I'd stayed put by the dead beast for a little longer, Ross would probably have left the wood altogether.

Instead, after some while crouching uncomfortably on the slope, I became impatient. I was anxious to get rid of the dog and get back to my crow's nest. So I picked it up again after settling the dead leaves so that no blood was visible, and set off along almost the same path that Ross had taken.

It was when I'd got behind the shed, leaving myself without an exit, and had started to prise up one of the metal shutters with a stick, that I heard something move on the other side of the old brickwork, the faintest sound – but a footfall, I thought, for it was followed almost immediately by another noise, a twig cracking. Peering round the back corner of the building, I saw Ross coming towards me, moving through some saplings, this time with a look of certainty in his eyes, his gun raised.

There was no way out then. The dog was lying in the open, next the well. If Ross came round the corner and saw it, and especially if it had been his dog, I knew he'd shoot me straight away if he got the chance. It was then that I notched the second arrow, drew the bow and waited for him.

One

'All gone again!' Laura sang out in a tone of weary optimism, intent as always on putting a good face on things. We'd become used to the child's intermittent chaos in the cottage long before. But Clare had got so much better lately that this new mayhem, the explosion of moist soil all over the crisp linen Sunday tablecloth, surprised even us. Judy, the postmistress's elder daughter, was nearly in tears. She'd been looking after Clare while all of us had been out to the Easter Sunday service at the church just beyond my cottage.

'I was out in the kitchen, just for a minute – putting the roast in...'

'It doesn't matter.' Laura comforted her, while Minty, our big, over-loving, wire-haired terrier, pranced around in a frenzy of foolish welcome, as though we'd been away for days and this disaster in the dining-room was a carefully contrived homecoming gift which he and Clare had been working on all morning for us.

George – George Benson, a Professor of Anthropology now at Oxford and out with his wife Annabelle from the town for the weekend – moved round the circular table, making odd archaeological surveys into the dirt, scraping it up with his hands, but only making it worse. The clayey soil was moist. Laura had watered the half dozen flowering hyacinths that same morning. And now the table was like a desecrated altar: the dark smudges of this grave soil from the end of our garden, just next the churchyard wall, set against the brilliant white linen cloth, with the conical blue and pink flowers, like little fir trees, smashed all over the place and Clare, still crouching on the table deep about her business, seemingly unaware of us, sorting the soil through, discovering the bulbs, inspecting them carefully, smelling them as a gourmet might ponder some exotic dish.

'Well? What happened?' Laura asked her daughter, not looking at her directly, no hint of annoyance in her voice. Clare didn't reply, though of course she could speak now, very reasonably when she wished. She was nearly eleven after all.

'I expect she wanted to be taken to church,' I said.

I was no great churchgoer. But Laura liked to go, and Clare too, if for different reasons. That was how I'd first met both of them the summer before, high up on one of Lisbon's windy hills, in the Anglican church of St George. We'd all become so much happier people since then, that perhaps Clare had come to identify churches with her new-found contentment, where all three of us were in such buildings together, and had felt excluded this morning – threatened – and had thus taken her revenge.

'But she said she *didn't* want to come,' Laura turned, admitting some of her anguish to me, at least. 'She'd sooner stay at home with Judy and help with the lunch, she said.'

'She wanted to be *made* to come then.'

I disliked hinting, even, at the dry world of psychology, the awful jargon of the child specialists, their arid theories of cause and effect that I knew had done so little for Clare over the years. But even so, we all of us had a need sometimes to be forcibly confirmed in our happiness, to be taken to bed by a woman, or rooted away from the fire by friends for a frosty winter walk.

'Perhaps,' Laura said. And then, more abruptly, 'Though God knows, she's growing up, isn't she? She has to learn what she wants, herself.'

'She wants that as well,' I said shortly. 'She wants it both ways. She wants everything.' I was more upset than Laura, perhaps.

Clare hadn't heard us. She was still totally absorbed in her gardening. Her fringe of blond hair moved into a shaft of sun just then which touched it like a halo. It was midday with the light at its height over the church roof, angled down straight onto the table by the window, and Clare's face beamed as she squelched the soil through her fingers. The room was filled with the smell of fresh earth and hyacinths and bathed with an intense spring light, the child a radiant harbinger of this muddy easter apocalypse. We stood there, the four of us round the table, unable to speak.

At last a log fell off the fire in the next room and I remembered the wine I had to open and set by the warmth before lunch. It wasn't the first time this sort of horticultural explosion had occurred, these wild scents all over the cottage. Clare had a recurrent obsession with nature, with growing things, a thirst for flowers: to touch, to crush, to eat them, a need which died out completely in her at times, like bulbs in winter, only to blaze up again without reason – or none we knew of. She was happy then, so totally involved and happy, all her vacancy gone, that one felt that, lacking appropriate human development, she had instead a perfect bond with nature, alert to all its secret smells and signs, like an animal.

Apart from the hyacinths, Laura always liked to keep a big bowl of lavender on the deep windowsill of the small drawing-room: just the dried stalks in winter, when one could crush their ears at odd moments, gazing at nothing in particular out of the window, kneading them with warm fingers, so that the deep summer smell would live again even on the greyest days. In summer itself the perfume needed no encouragement, the flowers picked fresh from the big clump by the front garden gate.

Clare, on the days when she stayed at home for some reason from the special school near Oxford, found these fresh or dry stalks an almost irresistible source of fascination. This quintessence of English floral life was something new to her, I suppose, something she had not known in London nor, before that, in the desert wadis of East Africa where she had spent the first years of her life.

Sometimes she would take just a single stalk from the bowl and sit with it on the sofa, gazing at it intently for an hour, picking its minute buds out one by one, sniffing it before pushing it up her nose the better to grasp its smell, or turning it round and using the end as a toothpick. Or else she would take the whole bunch out and place the stalks meticulously, lined up in regiments all over the drawing-room floor throughout a morning, before re-arranging them or suddenly stamping on them vigorously, so that even up in the attic study where I worked the odour would rise up the two floors to me, while the drawing-room itself, when I came down to lunch, smelt like an accident in a perfume factory.

Lunch: thinking of our own meals, or those larger weekend occasions with friends: Clare, at ten and a half, nearly two years after her father's death, had learnt to eat properly again at last. The graft had largely taken between her and the new family created around her. To begin with, when we'd first all come down to the Oxfordshire cottage, and before that when I'd first met Clare with her grandparents out in Cascais, she had eaten, when she ate at all, like a savage four-year-old, punishing the food, grinding it into floor or table; or, on her feet then, treating it like mudballs, clenching it up in her fine hands and slinging it all over the kitchen (or the tiled bathroom where she sometimes had to eat) with unerring accuracy. Like most autistic children she had a superbly developed motor system, the physical co-ordination of a circus juggler: she could almost spin a soup plate on an index finger, while hitting you in the eye with a boiled potato across the whole width of a room was child's play to her.

George's wife spoke to her now. How unlike her christian name she was, the sun-tanned Annabelle, a tall, angular, very plain woman with long bronzed tennis-playing limbs, though I doubt she ever played any game. There was a remote, glazed quality about her, of someone always focusing on a matter far away or deep inside her. 'Well,' she said awkwardly to the child. 'You have made a splendid mess!' Clare responded at last. 'Yes.' She spoke without concern, smiling brightly up at us before leaving the table. She said no more. Clare at such times, having expressed some unknown desire or hurt in this dramatic manner, had no memory of the immediate past, or – for hours or even days afterwards – of any time further back. Her life seemed to start afresh on such occasions. She was continually re-born thus, yet one could never quite decide if this was a tragedy or a miracle.

George came with me into the drawing-room as I tended the fire and opened the bottle.

'It doesn't get any easier,' he said sympathetically.

'Oh, I don't know.' I pulled the cork. 'It has recently. She's been a lot better.'

'There's no constancy, though, in the improvement. That must be disheartening. Up, up, and then right back again.'

'Is that surprising? Isn't that very much the evolutionary process?'

George – a palaeontologist, as Clare's famous father, Willy Kindersley, had been – had a haunted face shaped like a large wedge: a long thick flush of greying hair ran sideways across his scalp above a broad forehead. But then the skull narrowed dramatically, down a long nose to a very pointed chin. His eyes were grey too. But they were strangely alert, as if the man was still looking for some vital hominid evidence in the desert.

He and Annabelle had no children of their own. They appeared to be colleagues rather than a married couple, a pair devoted exclusively, it seemed, to man's past; for Annabelle, an ethnologist by profession, worked in almost the same line of country as her husband. Yet George had a longing for a more present life, I felt, where the bones were clothed with flesh, and Clare for him was a living mystery, a deviant hominid species more strange than any skeleton he had found while delving through millions of years in the sub-soil of East Africa.

He saw Clare – as we all did, for it was so obvious – as someone physically supreme: a beautiful, blue-eyed child, peach-skinned, ideally proportioned with marvellous co-ordination, balance, grasp – a body where human development, over aeons, had culminated in a sensational perfection: yet a form where there was some great flaw hidden in the perfect matrix, black holes in the girl's mind that defied all rational explanation. George regarded Clare with awe, his scientific mind touched, even, with fear. Indeed, I sometimes wondered if, with his evolutionary obsessions, he looked on her as evidence of some new and awful development in humanity; if he saw Clare and the increasingly numerous children like her as precursors of a future race who, though perfectly built, would look into the world with totally vacant eyes.

George had been a colleague of Willy Kindersley's before his death, and before George had settled down in Oxford. They had worked together three years before, long months beside the dry streams running into Lake Turkana in northern Kenya and before that on other prehistoric fossil sites further afield in the Northern Frontier District and on the Uganda border. For many years out there they had sought man's origins, found small vital bones casually unearthed by the spring rains, a piece of some early hominid jaw or cranium, picking them out of the petrified old river beds with dental probes, Laura had told me, dusting them with fine paintbrushes before setting these part-men in patterns, jigsaws that gradually displayed proof of some earlier Eden by the lake shore, earlier than a nose bone found near the same site the previous season: earlier by a million years.

Theirs was a job with the long view, pushing back man's past before first vaguest speech into a time of signs, and before that to a moment when these small, hairy quadrupeds, down from the trees, had first stood up, erect, on two feet. It had been their ambition to date more exactly this miraculous change, this moment between animal and human life, when one had finally given way to the other and man had first set out on his long trail of upright destruction.

And here Willy Kindersley had apparently succeeded, his career among old bones in East Africa ending in great celebrity. For it was he who, nearly three years before, way up near the Kenya–Uganda border, had discovered the sensational bones of 'Thomas', as the part skeleton had been named: the fossilized remains, nearly four million years old, of a young man who not only walked on two feet but had used the sharpened animal bones found along with him to hunt and kill.

An irony never mentioned more than once (when Laura had first told me all about it) was that Willy, the victim of a hit-and-run accident, had been killed by a direct descendant of these men whose haphazard graves he had so painstakingly disturbed, by a Kenyan, an African (the man had never been traced), who had run over Willy, his car mounting the pavement out of control apparently, just as Willy had left a news conference at the Norfolk Hotel in Nairobi two years before.

Though I'd never met Willy, I always felt very much as if I had: as though, through my subsequent close association with his friends and with his wife, the informal name they used for him belonged to me as much as them. Willy was always Willy, alive or dead: a small dark-haired man, as I'd seen from photographs, verging on the plump; a good deal of the professorial in him, by all accounts (he'd held a chair at London University), arcane depths which were decorated, though, with many surface conceits. He had a sharp wit, I'd been told, which often strayed over into the practical: as when he'd successfully offered his students an early hominid skull and jawbones, elaborately mounted on some snapping mechanism, a research project intended, as he explained, to pinpoint man's first sense of the comic in life – for here, with micrometers, carbon dating and suchlike, they would at last isolate that initial earth-shaking guffaw . . .

Of course such academic drolleries can fall very flat for those outside the magic circles. And Willy, these scholastic jokes matched only by his intellectual depths, was perhaps an unlikely person to have married the more balanced, outgoing Laura who shared few if any of his professional concerns. But then she shared few of mine, and our marriage subsequently had been as happy as theirs had apparently been.

Willy was greatly missed of course. But his memory was never oppressive about the house. Laura and I, or their old friends down for weekends, would talk of him, when we did, almost in the present tense, as if he were upstairs and would come down in a moment to correct or comment on some opinion we had ascribed to him.

He wouldn't, of course, ever come down or drop by in any shape or form now. But we didn't mention this. Clare had ready ears everywhere about the house, and it had been enough of a business, Laura told me, explaining Willy's death originally to the child, who had then relapsed for months into fearful outraged traumas. She had almost recovered since, we had thought, in the ease and security of our Cotswold cottage. But she had not yet come to see me as she had her father: as the miracle man, digging up old bones all over the splendid wilds of East Africa.

I was a duller thing by far: a schoolmaster of sorts, taking junior English at a pretentious minor public school five miles away. It's true Clare had once paid me really startled attention: when she'd come round to the school one afternoon with Laura and found me involved with the archery club there, which Spinks, the games master, ran with some senior boys.

Spinks was absent that day, I remember: he sometimes was, suffering dire after-effects of the bottle. I was in charge, in any case, and Clare had watched the sport intently, eyes out on stalks, as the arrows thumped into their straw targets away on the far side of the games fields, where the fields gave out onto a rise with a beech coppice on top, only the empty Oxfordshire farmland beyond.

Clare had stared at me then, as I let off half a dozen shafts on the 40-metre range, as though the modern recurve bow in my hand had some profound old magic for her.

As indeed it had. Laura told me when I'd finished shooting. 'In the Northern Frontier District once, in the very wilds on the Sudanese border we were on a fossil search, looking for some dried-out stream up there – and we came on this tribe, a lot of nomadic woolly-haired people with thin cattle, and butter in their hair, and some of the men had these old smoke-black bows with them, small bent things, like toys really. But with poisoned arrows, Willy said. Clare remembers, even though she was hardly four. One of the old men showed her how to hold it.'

Clare had been happy in East Africa, apparently. I'd heard tales of this sort from Laura often enough, memories of wild adventure. Clare had lived with her parents all the time then, wife and child out of town and up country for months on end, following Willy across the bush, through long hot days to evening tents under the stars; travelling by Land Rover or, in the great desert stretches to the north, moving by camel, even, to distant waterholes.

Animals shimmered on vast horizons for Clare in those years. Flamingoes had paddled in pink waters, hippos rose from crystal pools – and she'd become as much a part of this natural landscape then, I gathered: an animal herself playing beneath the thorn trees. Her world, for the first three or four years of her life, had been a world before the fall: literally, in fact, for there is another painful irony here, in that Clare's malady, her complaint, that strange mix of frenzy and vacancy which is autism, never shows itself for the first two or three years of its victim's life, when the child appears perfectly normal. And thus with Clare it happened to emerge only after she had left the plainslands and the deserts of the Great Rift Valley, when she had returned with her mother to London.

Her freedom out there was suddenly over. Walls replaced the tents, stones the grass, the sun was mostly put away – and Clare fell down some deep hole in herself. Of course, it seemed to Laura at least, as it did afterwards to me, that Clare's problem might have come as a direct result of this deprivation as much as through the death of her father. But the experts had denied this. Autism, they said in their typically equivocal manner, had a physiological, psychological, or parental, but not an aesthetic, cause. It was something deeply inherent in any case, implicit from before birth perhaps, and not brought about by a change in landscape. Clare's arrival in London, they said, had no bearing on her illness, which would have occurred as readily in Timbuctoo as Hampstead.

Laura had thought, she told me, to take the girl back to East Africa and see if a return to paradise might work a cure in her. But the images of her latter unhappiness there were too much for her, and certainly I, when I married Laura, had no skills which would take me to, or fit me for, those wild parts. Besides, we thought, surely the Cotswolds might work instead as a natural remedy, the high sheep pastures beyond Woodstock where we lived, lost in the hills: was this not an equal grace, a balm of classic English fields and trees and dry-stone walls which would set Clare free at last from whatever bound her, release her soul from the tower of silence where it was so often imprisoned.

We had hoped the Windrush valley and a Welsh pony through the autumn stubble might form a cure. And gradually, it's true, under Laura's intensive care, helped by Judy from the Post Office, and with her special school when it opened, she had seemed to get better. The tantrums, the silences, diminished and Clare had found threads again to lead her back into life.

Yet it was clear from her behaviour that Sunday morning that her progress might always be subject to dramatic collapse. George had been right: it was disheartening. One foresaw all the possible years ahead, the pain that lay in wait, forever on tenterhooks over this child, who would become a woman, still carrying the hidden plague, which might erupt again at any time, in a bus or in a marriage bed, or which might eventually lead her permanently to an institution.

Clare's brightness, her beauty seemed so provisional that Easter morning, a wonderful light threatened with extinction – now or ten years hence. And I suppose it was this that made me short-tempered at lunch with the Bensons on that Easter Sunday, angry at life, taking too much wine with the meal, so that the others had to rescue me afterwards, force me away from the fire for a tingling afternoon walk.

Ours is a manorial hamlet, set quite on its own, high on the wolds, isolated near the top of the western escarpment, without shops or even a pub, largely owned by a celibate aristocrat, the last of a long line, a recluse who lives in the manor at the far end of the single street. My cottage, once the sexton's, which I bought from the Church Commissioners eight years before when I was 'retired' from the Mid-East section of the Service, is not part of his honey-coloured empire. A quirky red brick neo-gothic affair beside the churchyard, it looks out over the narrow road in front with a small lawn and vegetable plot behind, bounded by a dry-stone wall and beyond that a great empty expanse of typical rolling Cotswold country, most of it still open sheep pasture, but lined here and there with high ridges of beech, sunken laneways and crossed in part by an old Roman road, now largely overgrown, but which, if you manage to follow it correctly, takes you near to the school I teach in, four miles away. I knew this landscape intimately, and quite often in summer, even walked to work through it.

We set off in this direction across the fields that afternoon along a bridle path, Clare on her pony which we'd saddled up for her in a garden outhouse made over into a stable. It was bright but the wind was cold, whipping up the valley to the west, long wispy streaks of mackerel cloud running high above us. From the back windows of our cottage you could see out over most of this great stretch of open sheep pasture, divided only by a few dry-stone walls, gently shaped here and there by small folds in the land.

Apart from a stand of beech on a rise half a mile ahead and lines of dead elms, old windbreaks dotting the western perimeter, there was little immediate cover. And since the bridle path led only to a farm a mile away, there were rarely other people to be seen out in this pasture. A local farmer took hay to his stock in winter and once in a blue moon a trail of serious city hikers, with maps and bobble caps, thick socks and ostentatious boots, would wind their way impudently across the landscape. So it was that Laura, who saw the tall man first, was surprised.

'Look – down there.' I couldn't see anyone. 'There, just by the corner of that wall. I can't see his face – he's got a pork-pie hat on. And something round his neck.'

We saw him then. But only because he was moving quickly away from us, at right-angles to our bridle path, climbing a wall, heading out from the village. He had field glasses and a streaky, mud-and-green army type anorak, which was why we hadn't spotted him at once against the spring grass.

As far as I knew there was no footpath along the direction he was taking. Yet he wasn't the local farmer, who was a burly man, and the hikers always went in groups. He didn't look back, just scuttled expertly away, a query in the placid landscape. We never saw his face.

Now I can see him well enough, though. He was one of Ross's henchmen, sent down by Marcus to spy my land out, and the same man, in the same pork-pie hat and old army anorak, was responsible for the subsequent disaster. But then, on that bright spring afternoon with our friends, after nearly a year of such peace, we took no more notice or thought of him. He disappeared from our minds completely as we strolled away down the pasture, Clare trotting a little ahead on the pony, Laura with her arm in mine, the Bensons behind, talking about Cotswold long barrows and Iron Age forts.

'On that rise there.' George pointed ahead. 'With those beech trees. I'm sure that's one. You can just see the vague shape still, a ditch like a crown all round the top. There'd have been stakes above it as well in those days of course. They'd have brought the animals in at night. Wolves, other predators, rival tribes. A different world.'

'Do you find artefacts?' Annabelle asked in her neat scientific voice. 'In ditches? Implements, pottery?'

'Or bones?' George added with interest.

'I haven't,' I said, clutching the flesh of Laura's hand for a moment. How pervasive the sense of happiness was that afternoon.

Later, when we got back, we burnt some old elder branches and trash, making a bonfire in the corner of the garden. The days were lengthening rapidly now. It was light till nearly eight o'clock, a violet sky, streaked with red on the horizon. The wind had died and the smoke went straight up into the air, but there was cold in the twilight and we warmed our hands on the embers before going inside and eating again, in the kitchen this time, a sort of Spanish omelette which Clare had always liked: she was quite calm now after her earlier distress.

Afterwards, when Clare had gone to bed, we finished most of a bottle of port, all of us together chatting by the fire, and I was glad I'd already corrected the fourth form's English essays, due next morning.

I found this school work something of a drudge, taken up nearly three years before, back from Yugoslavia, in desperation for some activity, some money. But I still had my slim academic qualifications, last used in Egypt twenty years before, and the Headmaster at this school, a naïve Anglican cleric, had liked my face; and more, I suppose, the evidence in my *curriculum vitae* and some formal letters that I had worked for several years in the information department of the Foreign Office.

I didn't, of course, tell him that in fact I had been with British Intelligence, a clerk, if not exactly a spy, thumbing through Arab newspapers in the old Mid-East section in Holborn, and afterwards unwillingly involved with David Marcus, now Head of the Service in a wild goose chase through Europe that had ended three years before in every sort of folly and disaster. But I'd left all that nonsense then, had returned to my cottage, and was in bed now with Laura. That past was largely forgotten. In my early forties I was living again at last, as Laura was after her own tragedies, five years younger than I.

I said to her 'Remember all those old books and magazines the villagers left in with us for the book stall at the church fête, which got all damp out in the garage?'

Laura was sitting up in bed still, arms behind her head letting her hair out. It wasn't that long but in the daytime she usually wore it up in a small knot at the back of her head, where it splayed out in wisps over her neck. She nodded now, some hairgrips in her mouth.

'I was burning some of them today, a lot of old useless books, all soaked through. They smoked a lot. But then I saw one by R.M. Ballantyne in the flames – do you remember him at all? Marvellous Victorian, sort of *Boys Own Paper* author.' Laura shook her head.

'*The World of Ice* it was called. Some polar adventure. I'd never read it as a child. *Coral Island* yes, but not this one. I'd have rescued it from the fire but it was no use, all charred and the pages mostly stuck together. I just managed to see the beginning of one page: "The men gathered round the huskies for the last time..."'

'Well?' Laura broke the silence at last, the grips out of her mouth.

'I don't know really. But you remember George was talking about that Iron Age fort this afternoon? "A different world" he said. And I suppose he meant adventure: hunting, basic survival and all that, like that *World of Ice* story.'

'So?'

'I was thinking, it's only children who have that sort of instinct now, when they play Red Indians and games in trees and hide and seek and so on – '

'Men too,' Laura interrupted sharply, 'when they go to war or play those silly spy games like you used to do. It's all still there, isn't it? Just under the surface. Why? Do you think it's a valuable instinct?'

'Not valuable – it's vital, surely.'

'But we don't have to survive that way any more.'

'No. So we fight just as badly – between ourselves – in more subtle ways, all those natural instincts frustrated.' I didn't say any more.

'*We* don't fight,' Laura said.

'No.'

'Well, le voilà...' She turned the light off, and settled down for the night.

I thought afterwards that I didn't know quite what I was trying to tell Laura, that I hadn't really told her anything in fact. But much later I woke in the pitch black and heard Minty barking downstairs. And later still, just before dawn, I dreamt of dogs racing across an ice floe, where I was a helpless, terrified child again pulled by them wildly on a sleigh going headlong towards some frozen water, where I couldn't control them, where I knew we were all about to be drowned. And yet there was a tremendous sense of excitement in the ride, a thrill of sheer pace where we seemed to be airborne, the dogs and I gliding like valkyries towards disaster.

Laura told me how I'd tossed and turned in bed unusually that night. I told her of the dream, explaining it as a common mix of repressed fear and longing, where the two are inseparable. Later, before anyone else was awake, we made love first thing that Monday morning, and I was no longer alone then, but in the midst of life again after the nightmare.

Now, a month later as I write this – certainly alone perched in this oak tree – I remember the dream again, and the book, *The World of Ice*, burning in the fire. I remember the afternoon, Clare riding away over the pasture: the Spanish omelette, the evening's port, next morning's love. The nightmare and the reality were so utterly opposed then. Now they are one; indivisible, inseparable.

Still, I have escaped. have remained free so far, cradled in these branches. I am alive up here in the air, living what many would describe as a perfectly childish existence. Well, with this licence, I may at least freely plot my revenge. What would be unthinkable in ordinary, adult circumstances is now constantly on my mind: revenge, to kill, to make brutal amends.

As someone liberal enough in the old days, who certainly hated any kind of physical threat, I find it difficult to understand the depth and breadth of this violence within me: at Marcus, at Ross, at the world generally perhaps. Even on a philosophical level my reactions may seem extreme, for one can say that, in any case, an end is implicit in even the greatest happiness and to have had such at all, even as briefly as I had, is to have had a sufficient share, in a world where many have none. One could argue that quality, not duration is the significant thing in love. But I can't argue that, not at all, not for a moment.

And the question remains: why, once reasonably human, am I living up a tree now, back in a savage state, worse than an animal in that I seek vicious retribution, no matter how long it takes, certain that I am right? The only way to account for the strength of this anger, perhaps, is to remember the depth of that earlier peace.

Two

'Bom Dias!'

The vague old man who ran the lifts in the Avenida Palace Hotel bade us good morning as we came down from my bedroom that afternoon.

'"Bom Dias" indeed.' I turned to Laura afterwards. 'It's nearly four o'clock.'

That was the first time we made love, in August, almost a year ago in the heavy, gilt-decorated room I had in the old *belle-époque* hotel, at the bottom of the Avenida da Liberdade, Lisbon's Champs Elysées, which ran straight through most of the city, like an arrow, down into Pombal's magnificent eighteenth-century town by the waterfront, with the hills all round, climbing into the summer winds, where you could follow the breeze up in street lifts, ancient trams or along steeply rising cobbled alleyways.

'Shall we have some tea?'

'Shall we walk?' I said.

'It doesn't matter what.'

The city was an open invitation. We had no appointments. Clare was at home with her grandparents in the suburb of Cascais. Laura looked at me, still with bedroom glints in her eyes as we passed through the lobby, and I had that sudden sharp feeling, in the pit of my stomach, of youth, when age doesn't push any more, at least, and there is no end to things in the air.

The hotel was being redecorated that summer. There was a smell of paint everywhere downstairs and sawdust where they were cutting out the wood from an old cloakroom, carpenters sawing away like animals in dark corners.

'The *Retournados*,' Laura said. 'There were nearly a million of them, ex-colonials back from Angola and Mozambique: the government put them up for months in all the luxury hotels in town. Now they're "refurbishing" them.'

'A million of them?'

'Well, the lucky ones. Four in a bed, I suppose.'

'The beds are big enough.'

'Yes.'

We remembered. We'd had lunch that day in the great panelled dining-room, with its mirrors and canopy of chandeliers, on the first floor, the lifts just down the corridor outside, the old man off duty, so that no one had seen us go upstairs afterwards. Not that they'd have cared one way or the other, I fancy. The Portuguese, I'd found in over a month's stay in the country, had a classic restraint, a politeness in almost every matter; the last people in Europe, it seemed, with such old-fashioned virtues.

But perhaps the old liftman not being there made things easier for us, in our own minds at least, for we were both of us old enough ourselves, with similarly formal backgrounds, to remember all such ancient prohibitions.

Laura wasn't a prude. She just had a lot of out-of-date manners. She liked to do things in an acceptable way. Despite, or more likely because of, her obvious beauty, she presented a cool anonymity to the public. She tended to hide in the light of the world, her face immobile; her stance, her walk or gaze things calculated to deceive; so that they would not draw attention, at least, either to her body or her soul.

In private, with her parents, her friends – or with me in bed – she was something different. We all are, of course. But with Laura this change, though not schizophrenic, was much more extreme. There was a natural barrier in Laura, which Clare's fate and her husband's death had helped increase, between the public and the private person. She could be very formal, even cold on the surface. So that when I'd first met her, more than a month before, she had struck me as the last person in the world I was ever likely to sleep with. Yes; before I knew her, she seemed far too haughty and beautiful for me. She was, I imagined, one of those idle Tory women living abroad, remittance women in the sun, on permanent holiday, rich enough, no longer young, probably divorced, with loud-voiced horsey friends back in the English shires, one of the skin-deep people herself, all floating on gin and tonic.

When I first saw Laura, three pews ahead of me in St George's Anglican church with Clare fiddling strangely at her side, I thought she was someone merely decorative, those wisps of blonde hair down the back of her neck too carefully tended, with a spoilt child in tow that she had not bothered to bring up properly. Even her name – 'Mrs Kindersley', when she was introduced to me at the church's sardine barbecue afterwards – seemed a perfect suggestion of old upper-middle-class hauteur, impregnability, respectability, foolishness.

But Laura wore all these marks of her tribe as mere camouflage. They were not her real colours at all. When you knew her you found everything different in her mind: strange furniture in what had seemed, on the outside, so conventional a house. And when you loved her, it was different again, for her clothes were formal too, even her casual ones: pleated skirts and blouses – and when she took them off, as she had an hour before, there was another landscape, other attitudes which one could never have anticipated.

She had said, quite suddenly half way through lunch, just after we'd done with the mountain trout and the *vinho verde*, her hands neatly in her lap, leaning across to me with a look of amused confidentiality, 'Afterwards, Peter?'

'What?'

'Make love.' She paused. 'Won't we? Upstairs. Where better? Don't you – '

'Yes,' I said. 'I've forgotten most of the tricks though.'

'So have I.'

But we hadn't.

Her face was very long as she lay flat in the light from the bedroom windows. The shafts of afternoon sun, slanting on her cheeks seemed to exaggerate the natural distance between her eyebrows and jawbone, just as, in this position, it emphasised the slight turn up at the end of her nose, the equal snub at the tip of each breast. Her long body angled across the sheets, toes almost poking through the brass rails at the end, she had an air of vastly settled comfort about her that afternoon – nothing feverish at all, as if she'd just found exactly the right spot in a garden and was sunbathing there. Her lovemaking had the same calm: no rising storms, no vast passions or alarms, simply a firmness, a clarity, something open-eyed where she did not want to forget herself but rather, to remember everything.

Laura, I soon discovered, had a great gift of sharp consciousness. Continually alert behind her cool façades, anxious to invest something in every waking moment, it was sleep she feared. Once you had fallen through her outer reserve, and, beneath that, the layers of the familial or the workaday, when you fell into Laura most truly herself, you were in a continually busy place, a mind always on the move, ever concerned with sights and thoughts and tastes, kingdoms in the sun. She was something of a daylight atheist, I suppose, for the nights were different. Then she fussed and cried in the dark, accused herself of non-existent crimes, murmuring incoherently about her earlier life in Africa, for sleep she feared – the dreams, the panic it brought.

In Portugal certainly, living out in the marvellous light and heat of Cascais by the Atlantic with her parents for a year, she had found what she needed: long dazzling afternoons in their big garden overlooking the bay with Clare, or days down on the beach swimming, constantly involved with her daughter: activities in any case which left her exhausted by bedtime, so that there would be few moments in the dark to fill . . .

Laura clutched me on the bed then, the only time she hurt. She said 'Since Willy went, and Clare, too, in another way, I've had this thing about not sleeping, as if I at least have to remain fully conscious. Do you know?'

'Yes.'

'To stay alive. If I sleep – I mightn't.'

'It's a fear, naturally. Especially since you sleep alone.'

'It's as bad sometimes as not putting your hand out under the bed as a child.'

'Yes.'

'I want to stay awake, all the time.'

But she didn't that afternoon. She drifted off ten minutes later, in my arms, before going out like a light, released at last from fear, at peace. Loving thus was one part of our content.

But there was living, too, the whole city outside the bedroom window: the summer wind, always from the south, whipping the rubbish along the mosaic pavements beside the cafés on the downtown boulevards; the ferry klaxons out in the bay, sliding into my own dreams as I dozed beside her then; or on other empty afternoons when we returned to my bedroom – the great white cruise liners, indolent dreams which materialised in the harbour in the space of a siesta, between lunch and tea. The city had been a marvellous promise for me in any case right from the start. Now, with Laura, its gifts were guaranteed.

She said when she woke, startled, surprised that she had slept,

'I've survived . . .'

Most things discourage us from love these days. The omens and confirmations are commonplace: it will not survive, it will crack up on the rocks of liberation, impatience, infidelity, so that we embark on it half-heartedly in any case, if at all in middle life.

Laura had had her chances since Willy's death, she'd told me, vague hints from London friends and other less subtle approaches during her year in Portugal. But they had not convinced her of anything. She felt a great fatigue about all that side of life: it hadn't tempted her at all, lying fallow as she had, with Clare absorbing all her energy.

I must have been simply lucky, I'd thought, in my timing, in meeting Laura at a moment when things began to stir in her again. Or was it, in fact, something special which we had for each other? One tends to play this sort of idea down nowadays as well. It seems presumptuous to imagine there is anything so unique between two people, especially among the middle-aged; especially with me, who had seen a first wife go and lost several other women since.

I'd loved well enough, but the knack of permanency wasn't there. In twenty years I'd gone through three women, that was the fact of the matter, and I'd told Laura so one afternoon a few weeks before when we'd gone down with Clare to the little beach at Cascais.

We'd had lunch under the canopy on the Palm Beach restaurant terrace, set right over the sand Clare playing near the small frothy waves almost immediately beneath us.

'Yes,' I'd said to Laura, the prawns dismembered on our plates, gathering the soiled paper napkins up. 'It seems like blind man's buff, looking back on it: me and women.' I made the point lightly, flippancy a ready balm to failure.

'Surely it was your job?' Laura asked. 'That intelligence work you told me about in Egypt, America. You were living all sorts of lies then. And so were these women you were with too, apparently.'

I nibbled at a last bit of prawn. 'Perhaps. Though that's a convenient excuse. It was probably just me.'

We were hovering on the brink of love that afternoon. We were likely to think the best of each other in any case. So I put myself unduly at a disadvantage, wanting Laura to forgive my

past as well as love me now. Age only sharpens the plays we
bring to courtship. After forty we know too well how best to
present what's left of us.

But Laura understood all this that afternoon, I think. She was
nearly forty herself, after all. She leant across, taking the soiled
napkins from me, touching my hand at the same time.

'Every failure, or success, is both people, surely? One as
much as the other. Each of us is to blame – as much as we are *not*
to blame. I don't see men and women as unequal at all in such
things.'

'If you bothered to count up the score, though: men – '

'Well, if you'd killed your first wife, or the other women, that
would rather tip the balance, certainly. But otherwise you can't
run things on a profit and loss account between people.'

She paused, tidying up the paper plates before looking out
over the deep blue sea.

'Do you have – secrets?' she said at last, still gazing out at the
ocean.

'Professional secrets?'

'No. Wife-beating, drink?' She picked up the nearly empty
wine bottle, offering it to me gently. The sun was just beneath
the canopy now, settling down in the sky for a blazing
afternoon. 'You peep through keyholes?' she went on shading
her eyes. 'Read other people's letters. What is it?'

'Worse. I tend to be possessive.' I poured myself a last glass.

'Ah! The heavy paterfamilias?'

'I've not had children.'

'Perhaps that's why. The women were everything.'

'Possibly.'

I looked down at Clare then, playing in the sand beneath us,
or rather obsessed with it, running it endlessly through her
fingers, from one cupped hand into another, then back again. As
I watched she stopped suddenly before starting off on another
manic pursuit, spinning a plastic bucket round by its handle,
with great dexterity, on the very tip of her index finger.

I said, 'With you there'd be children, wouldn't there? Clare's
half a dozen in one.'

I was rushing my fences. But age as much as youth can have
its sudden fevers, its imperatives. The sky was lead-blue all the
way down to the horizon. And yet the sea glittered, the waves
capped with froth, for there was still that summer wind from

the south, flapping the canopy gently above us. The breeze cooled my cheeks.

One day all this would be lost to both of us: the marine vision, the soft airs, lunch in summer. The cliché struck me forcibly, of loss, an end of things. Pain came then, just as strongly as hope arrived two weeks later as we left the lobby of the Avenida Palace Hotel. Laura must have seen it in my face.

'We'd share the burden, you mean?' she said, looking down at Clare. 'Or do you want to marry me?' she added brightly, almost mockingly.

'Both. They'd go together wouldn't they?'

'*Marriage?*' She looked at me quizzically, suddenly serious.

'Well, that's too grand, perhaps. Sounds too formal. I suppose – I'm too old,' I went on, backing out, piling up the excuses. 'I'm sorry.'

'Oh don't be! Not at all. That'd be fine. If you think – ' She leant across, pausing.

'What?'

'Clare is more than a handful. A big commitment – to me, I mean.'

'That's fine.'

'You see, I think she can get better, with a lot of love, attention, effort. Oh, not the child psychologists, the quacks. We've tried that. Just me.'

'Or us. You said it was Willy dying that had put her back so much.'

Laura smiled. 'You can't just pick new fathers up off the street though, can you?'

'Or wives.'

'It's barely six weeks, since you came out here.'

'You count the weeks?'

'Yes,' she said candidly. 'I have.'

'Well then?'

'Oh, I love you. That's not the problem.' She looked down at Clare again.

'Nor that either, then,' I said. 'Unless you think she's taken against me. Or would do, if I took Willy's place in that way.'

'I don't know. She likes you now, I know that. But if we lived together . . .'

Clare herself answered the problem later that afternoon, when we'd all swum out to a wooden raft, anchored fifty yards from the shore. She and Laura were up on the platform, I was still lolling in the water, my arms on the edge.

'Come up!' Clare said urgently. 'Come up! Please!'

Yet there was nothing imperious in her tone. She was simply worried, frightened that I might sink or disappear or swim back to shore on my own. She put her small hands out, gripping my wrist, tugging at me strongly. I joined them, heaving myself out of the water and onto the burning wood so that the whole raft pitched and the water boomed and belched among the drums beneath.

We lay in the sun for five minutes, the light too bright in our eyes to look at each other for more than odd seconds. Clare knelt over my back, scooping up the sea beside her, trickling it through her hands so that it fell in little cool points all over my skin. I could just see Laura, the line of her body like a run of small golden hills against the light, stretched out in front of me, lying on her back, one arm across her eyes, the other barely six inches from my nose. I could see the fine hairs like a forest on her wrist.

The ocean warbled all round us, the sounds from the small beach drowned in the afternoon heat. Without looking at me Laura moved her hand, blindly searching out the features on my face, before finally letting her fingers come to rest on my lips. She spoke then – but softly, her voice lost in the sea murmur.

'What?' I looked up.

'I said "Yes",' she said.

The ga.den in Cascais had some strange trees round its edges – strange to me at least: like overgrown olive trees, the branches extraordinarily twisted, with heavily crusted bark, the whole blown sideways from many years in the south wind. They were old cork trees, last remnants of a time when this slope that led down to the sea had been part of an estate attached to a large house on the hill immediately behind Cascais.

The big house was long gone and all the open land, too, cut up years before into half-acre plots and filled now with expensive villas, ranch-style bungalows, ugly hotels, or tactless modern apartment buildings.

But Laura's parents, Captain and Mrs Warren, when they'd left England more than thirty years before, had bought one of these empty plots intact and kept it that way, a last completely rural garden, a largely overgrown retreat amidst the vulgar glamour all round. Their house had originally been a farm building on the edge of the old estate and, apart from a new terrace looking out over the little harbour, they had left the property as it had been, a simple two-storied whitewashed house with thick bright umber slates running down a single sloping roof above.

The house was comfy in a chintzy, old-fashioned British manner. But the garden beneath the terrace was something quite original, far from the shires, a range of scent and dim colour on that first evening a month before when I'd first come out here with Laura to meet her parents. A great purple bougainvillaea and a tree like a weeping willow but with tightly packed yellow flowers festooning its branches, formed a centrepiece in the middle of the long coarse sea-grass. A path wound its way through the exotic undergrowth, with a table and chairs halfway down almost hidden beneath the flowering branches. A swing hung from a cork tree to one side and Clare was out there now, pushing gently to and fro in the warm half light, where the colours were smudged together in a strange, blue tinted luminosity.

Thomas Warren's wife, Laura's mother, was almost crippled with arthritis. She lay out, a long form in a heavily cushioned steamer chair on the sun-baked terrace, greeting me faintly, a rather disordered, nearly old lady, her face lined with long pain and discomfort. She wrapped a loose straggly woollen cardigan round an old print dress as if she was cold; a crumpled copy of the *Telegraph* lay at her feet like a faithful dog.

'Mrs Warren,' I said. She could barely lift her hand. 'Don't move,' I went on.

She humphed. 'I'm not likely to, I'm afraid. Bring up a chair – give him a drink, Tommy – and tell me all the news from home.'

'I'm afraid I've been away some time, over two months,' I said. It seemed, in fact, like a year, and England as distant as a childhood memory. That summer I'd been trying to live again, longing for anything new.

'Been away, have you?' Tommy asked. 'Travelling?' he added hopefully, bringing me over a drink, a perfectly prepared, fizzing gin and tonic, though I'd not asked for that, with just the right amount of ice and a delicate sliver, not a chunk, of lemon, all served up in a cut-glass tumbler from a Georgian silver tray.

Tommy, very unlike his wife, was a small, sprightly man in slacks and a navy blue blazer, impeccably dressed, his hair so meticulously cut and groomed that it seemed almost a theatrical creation, something got up with glue and bootblack.

'Yes,' I answered. 'I've just been wandering round Europe rather. Since the school term ended. Places I'd not been to before. The Rhine, Provence, Spain . . .'

'At a loose end, eh?' Tommy seemed enthusiastic about this idea.

'Yes. I suppose so. Though perhaps it's age, too. One wants to see the sights before – ' But I left it at that, realising I must have been nearly half their age.

'See the sights indeed!' Tommy said with relish.

Laura had joined us. 'My father – I told you – he was in the Navy. Given him itchy feet. What were you? Practically an Admiral,' she added affectionately.

'What do you think of Mrs Thatcher?' Mrs Warren suddenly interrupted us, bright-eyed, looking up at me. Her eyes alone seemed to have escaped the encircling pain in her face, clear, bright blue pools in the threatening landscape.

Mrs Thatcher? I don't know. She seems to have – '

'She's an abrasive woman.' Tommy came in sharply. 'She won't do. Simply not on.' I was surprised at his vehemence. He seemed so quintessentially Tory himself.

'Oh come now,' Laura said. 'Isn't she going to resurrect the Navy? A new aircraft carrier?'

'Just the opposite. It's all too late,' Tommy said.

'Too late for you, Daddy.'

Daddy humphed now in his turn, before leaving us to gaze out over the bay. I saw a big brass naval telescope then, mounted on the edge of the terrace. Tommy was a typical old naval buffer, I thought, retired to warmer climes. But how wrong I was about him too, in the beginning.

'Why didn't you join the Portuguese Navy?' Laura asked mischievously. 'After all you're a Portuguese citizen now in any case, aren't you?'

'I should have done,' Tommy shouted back to us. 'Damn good sailors.'

'Daddy retired early,' Laura explained.

'I see,' I said. Though I didn't.

'They took our house away,' Laura went on. 'The land, everything.'

'The Navy?' I was surprised.

'No. The War Office – the RAF I suppose. During the war, in Gloucestershire, the village where we lived. They took the whole village over and the land all round for some secret aerodrome. They were developing something very hush-hush. The jet, wasn't it? And they never gave any of it back. Compulsory purchase.'

'It's all still there?'

'Yes. Ruined now though. The village, the church, our small manor. It's still secret, out of bounds. We've never been back. And Daddy's never even been back to England. He hates the place, the way they treated him over his house.'

The Warrens said nothing. It seemed a painful enough subject. 'I am sorry,' I said, getting up, awkward in the silence. Tommy was over by the far side of the terrace now, looking through the telescope at something in the bay. The light was dying fast. He couldn't have seen much, I thought.

'How's the ship?' Laura asked brightly, changing the subject.

'Ready and willing,' her father answered promptly, still looking down the tube.

'A *ship*?' I asked.

'Yes. Go and look, if you can.'

I went over and Tommy offered me the lens. It was getting quite dark now. Bats were flipping about. I was doubtful if I'd see anything. So it seemed a miracle, in the great magnification, like a fairy tale coming up on a nursery wall from an old magic lantern, when the lovely blue and white ketch suddenly appeared at the end of the glass, moored to a buoy in Cascais harbour, bobbing gently in the violet light.

Laura stood behind me, putting an arm on my shoulder as I crouched down. 'His toy, his dream,' she said. Tommy had gone away to recharge the drinks. There were lights on along the hull, I saw, a row of portholes glittering in the blue haze.

'That's Jorge, first mate, deckhand, general factotum. He looks after it. Cleaning up I should think. We'll go out on it. Tomorrow perhaps.'

I took another look at it. The long white boat, since one couldn't see it at all with the naked eye, was certainly a dream, with its necklace of lights dancing on the water in the gathering dusk.

'What's it called?'

'She's called *Clare* – now,' Laura said.

The graceful bow cut the Atlantic swell, flowing through it at a steady ten knots so that the spray jumped in the air over us, spitting in our faces as we dipped in and out of the big waves a mile out from Cascais.

Clare, in a lifejacket, was next me on the prow, her hair pasted back against the side of her head by the wind. She seemed totally absorbed by something, her eyes fixed on some point on the horizon dead ahead of her. But there was nothing there.

Then, above the wind, I heard a sort of keening noise, a low-pitched whistle almost, as if some strange bird was hovering immediately above the boat. But again there was nothing there. But, bending down, I realised it was Clare beside me who was whistling into the wind, half whistle, half hum, her face alight, an unbroken, unconscious sound of pleasure, elemental itself among the other elements.

Tommy was behind us at the big brass-tipped wheel, with Jorge, master-minding things. They were some way back, their heads bobbing about behind the sails, for it was a large enough ketch – a fifty-footer, with a Croxley marine auxiliary diesel, which Tommy, angrily abandoning his country, had sailed out from Southampton forty years before. His wife, never a sailor, wasn't with us. But Laura was there, joining us on the bow a minute later.

'Have you ever done this before?' she shouted against the wind. I shook my head. A turreted castle rose up on a promontory ahead of us, a kind of Martello tower suggesting old adventure. The sea lost its sheer blue further into shore, where bands of moving aquamarine, like green oil slicks, shimmered in the great light beneath the Atlantic cliffs. None of this sort of life had been mine before.

Laura kissed me briefly then, on the lips, putting an arm round my shoulder for a moment to steady herself. Salt ran down my throat as I swallowed afterwards, breathless suddenly. Her father must have seen us, I thought. And I felt a childish guilt, as though discovered in some shared mischief with a companion behind the laurels thirty-five years before.

But I'd had no juvenile companions at my home in north Wales then. All this, even the guilt, was quite new.

Laura had younger friends in Lisbon outside her parents' circle: one or two families from the Embassy, other British expatriates, but mostly a number of Portuguese acquaintances. She got on very well with the natives. She met them sometimes for mid-morning coffee on the Chiado, the Bond Street of the city which ran up the hill behind my hotel: at the Brasileira café or the Pastelaria Marquês, the last of the city's old baroque tearooms. I began going with her on these occasions, carrying her parcels as she did her errands about the city. I had little else to do, after all. We were slipping into marriage, I suppose, before either of us was ever aware of it.

One of her friends – a suitor, indeed – was a prominent young Portuguese general back from Angola, a Socialist officer prematurely elevated in the army coup six years before, an olive-skinned, volatile bachelor, a member of the Revolutionary Council, who strode about town eccentrically in combat boots and green battledress, followed by a monkey-faced chauffeur batman in a small broken down army car, which, against all regulations, he would park right outside the Brasileira while his master went about his business in the crowded interior.

He burst in there one morning like a knight errant, moving easily among acquaintances, before seeing us at the back where I was surrounded by parcels, for all the world the hen-pecked husband. He joined us, a small, decisive, humorous figure, the gossips in the café hanging unsuccessfully on our every word.

'How is the President?' Laura asked him straight away. They had met originally at a reception in the Palace for the British community and press corps given by President Eanes.

'Fine. Excellent. He is proposing a bill shortly requiring all unmarried foreign women to take Portuguese husbands. May I present myself?'

'No. You may not. But have a coffee though.' They started to chat. The man didn't take the slightest notice of me. Perhaps, with all my parcels, he thought me an Embassy clerk or servant. I was tempted to disabuse him.

Yet afterwards, when he left, I was determined not to appear possessive.

'He's rude. He's pushy,' Laura said, mildly excited. 'But I do like him.'

'Yes.' But my silence then was an admission of my hurt and Laura noticed it.

'Apart from your first wife – and the other serious girls – how many women have *you* had?' she asked abruptly.

'I never bothered to count.'

'So many? Or so few?'

'Why? Have you slept with him? Is that it?'

She looked at me quizzically then, distancing herself, seeming to leave me, merging into the busy anonymity of the crowded café behind her.

'You have a thing about fidelity,' she said at last. I didn't reply. 'So do I,' she added, standing up, smiling. We had lunch afterwards in the Avenida Palace – mountain trout and *vinho verde*. That was the day we first made love.

Clare had started to fidget badly. Then she said in her fractured, incomplete English, 'Why do you be with us all the time?'

I hadn't answered at once, the question taking me by surprise, so that she looked at me now, doubtfully, out of the corner of one eye.

I'd been pushing her quietly to and fro on the cork tree swing out in the Cascais garden one afternoon, pushing her back and forth like a metronome for nearly half an hour. It was one of the few balms in Clare's life then, this calm, endlessly repeated movement.

But now, since I'd been trying to read to her, we were sitting at the table beneath the bougainvillaea tree and Clare was twisting about, embarking on a quite different sort of restlessness, common to autistic children, Laura told me afterwards, where they become violently, inexplicably possessed.

Clare had much improved, I gathered, from the time a year before when her father had been killed in Nairobi. But she could still be a vastly difficult child, prone to deep silences or just the opposite, to bouts of frenzied, ever-increasing movement, which struck her now, as she tried to twist a screw out from the side of the table with her thumb nail, bloodying herself in the process, so that I moved to stop her. But then she started to kick the table legs, viciously, repeatedly, bruising her shins and toes.

'Why? Why?' she said over and over again, so that I leant across trying to take her hands, to calm her.

'Because I like you – and your mother. That's why I'm here,' I said.

She seemed not to hear me and certainly wouldn't be appeased. 'Why? Why?' she shouted to herself, her thumb bleeding badly now as she attacked the screw again. I got a handkerchief out. But she pushed it away. She was lost, unreachable, her eyes quite vacant, seeing nothing, but her body electric with violence. She was punishing herself, kicking and tearing her flesh, trying to dig into herself, deeper and deeper, as if looking for some ultimate hurt.

Laura came out then. I thought she would stop the child – physically stop her, take her up in her arms and end this self-destruction. But she didn't. She let Clare go on kicking the table, let her thumb bleed, standing away from her: so that I moved towards her myself.

But Clare avoided me in a flash, running away then with great speed back to the cork tree, climbing it like a rocket, where she perched dangerously among the top branches.

'It's no use when she's like that,' Laura said calmly. 'You have to leave her. She has to be allowed to test us. "How much do you love me?" All that.'

'But she'll kill herself.'

'She won't. Not unless you push her.'

We were at the bottom of the cork tree ourselves now, whispering, Clare above us swaying defiantly, precariously on a top branch.

'It's crazy – she'll fall!'

'It seems insane, I know. But it's the only way. I *know*. You'll see.'

Laura had brought out a first-aid box with her and she showed it to Clare now, lifting it up, flourishing it under the tree. Then she put it on the ground, leaving it there.

We went back to the table and waited. 'Surely you can't let her do these things?' I asked.

'She drove a nail right through the palm of her hand a few months ago,' Laura said easily. 'You have to leave her. She stops at a certain point. Oh, I thought just the same as you to begin with. These fits, they were worse then, I was terrified, mad with worry. But then I realised these children, like Clare, they have an extraordinary need to guard their separateness; not like most children at all in that way. If you force yourself on them, or use force, you're lost: they clam up altogether then. You'll never reach them. It's an endless tightrope for them: care on one side, freedom on the other. They want both. And you have to give them both. By just waiting beneath.'

Them. They. Laura spoke of her child as of a stranger, another species. And it was exactly so, I thought then. I saw Clare perched up in the branches against the blue Atlantic sky, her back to us, gazing like a look-out into another world, a girl in the crow's nest of a ship, as she had been on the ketch a few days before, blonde hair running in the wind, absorbed in some secret voyage. Yet was she going anywhere? A branch swayed to and fro beneath her as she pushed it with monotonous regularity. And there was the first sense of hurt for me then – about Clare: I felt she would never really accept me, that I was an enemy, a sane stowaway rudely discovered now aboard her mad ship.

She came down an hour later. And we saw her in the twilight, kneeling by the first-aid box, rustling among the Band-aids and ointments before expertly tending her dry wounds.

I said to Laura, 'She asked me why I was with you, with her, all the time. That was what started all this, I think. It's probably a bad idea, my being here. I'd better leave.'

The evening had come on very suddenly and the bats were on the air now, big bats, malign shapes swirling round against the crimson sheet of sky.

'She wanted you on the raft in Cascais,' Laura said.

'Perhaps. But I don't understand her, Laura. She's really miles away from me.' It all seemed too much for me then. I was no rock of ages, no child specialist, no surrogate father.

'You're wrong,' Laura said. 'You're part of her life already. If you weren't she wouldn't test you like this. She'd just ignore you completely.'

'I see,' I said, pondering this sudden commitment.

'And if you leave she won't forget about you.'

'Like Willy, you mean?'

'A bit. She loves you – quite a bit.'

'That's why she hurts herself like this, is it?'

'Partly. She's frightened of losing you, that's why, I think. So she punishes the thought.'

We rarely embarked on psychological theory about Clare after that, the cloudy jargon of the specialists. We had no need to. We were her specialists by then, on a permanent basis. Laura and I were married at the Lisbon Embassy when I came out there during the following October half-term. There was a small party afterwards at the Warrens' house. The young Portuguese General attended, still in battledress. He spoke to me this time, jocularly, a hand on my shoulder, commiserating with himself: '*Ah! Fortuna cruel! Ah! Duros Fados!*'

'What?'

'It's from Camões – our greatest poet. "Cruel fortune – hard fate."'

'Oh,' I said. 'I'm sorry about that. He sounds like a tragic poet.'

The little General was like a soothsayer when I think of it now. But I try to think more of the happier things when I look back. I know now, for example, what made me so change my mind about Clare, about taking some responsibility for her. It was seeing her that evening in the garden, after her fit, kneeling by the first-aid box, under the cork tree in the twilight, patching herself up with Band-aids. A strong sense of independence has always appealed to me in women.

Three

Spinks, the games master, was sacked a week before half-term in my school that summer. And since no reason was given to the other staff by the naïve Anglican cleric, phrases such as 'gross indecency' and 'unnatural vice' echoed wordlessly in our minds.

In fact, as one of the all-knowing school prefects told me privately later, it had been a simpler, entirely natural matter. The worse for drink one night Spinks had forced himself upon the school housekeeper, a pneumatic divorcée known by the boys as the 'Michelin Woman', down near her room by the garages.

There was, indeed, a decidedly motorised air about the whole business, since, as the boy explained to me, the assault had apparently taken place not only in one of these lock-up garages, but in or about Spinks' own car, a small, ill-conditioned MG two-seater, the lady in question forced over the bonnet or some such. Though Spinks had vehemently maintained, the prefect who knew him went on, that the event had occurred with the lady's full co-operation, while the two of them were actually seated in the passion-wagon – a proposition which, given the housekeeper's girth and apparent decorum, had not convinced the Headmaster.

However it was, this matter, a farce in one way, turned out a blessing for me in another. Spinks had packed his bags at once and left. And since I had some athletic inclinations I was immediately given his job, pending a replacement. Yet Spinks, in his blind hangover, hadn't taken everything with him. Going alone into the sports room the next afternoon I saw that he'd left a big backpack of his behind in a corner, hung up in a slovenly way, but complete with sleeping bag, a small camping gas burner, some iron rations and a lot of other jumbled-up camping equipment I didn't bother to look at.

Spinks had been in charge of some senior boys on a mountaineering trip in Wales during the Easter holidays, and this was the unpacked remains of their week in the hills. I left the bag where it was, assuming that Spinks, when he'd sobered up, would return for it.

In the same room, behind a locked metal grill, was the school's archery equipment, half a dozen junior flat bows, with arrows to match, and the same number of more powerful, fibreglass, recurve bows, 25- and 30-pounders, for the seniors. One of these, the biggest of them, belonged to Spinks, a 32-pounder which he used on the longer ranges and which I'd come to shoot with fairly well myself over the past year. I had duplicate keys now, both to this archery equipment and to the sports room itself. So it was that Spinks' alcoholic and sexual excesses led directly to my own survival a week later.

But before then the headmaster had asked to see me.

'About Spinks,' he said, getting up suddenly from the big mahogany table. His study, the best front room of an older Georgian building in the school, looked out over the playing fields. A house cricket match was in progress on one of the far pitches, the white clad figures distant moving spots on the green sward. The headmaster, at the window now with binoculars, gazed at the players lovingly. He'd been something of a cricketer himself, apparently, in his youth, playing for his county.

'Yes,' I said. 'What about Spinks?' I had things to do, indeed I should have been out umpiring one end of the cricket match at that very moment. I liked my cricket, too.

The headmaster turned. 'I don't want it voiced around: that he was . . . drunk in charge.'

'Oh, was he? I didn't know.'

'Yes. That wretched car of his.'

'His car? I understood it all had to do with Matron – *in* his car.'

The Head looked at me quickly. 'You heard that?' he said, alarmed.

'It's a rumour.'

'Worse still.' The head pulled at one of his long earlobes mournfully.

'I liked Spinks,' I said suddenly. 'I'm sorry he's gone. He was very good with the boys, even when he was drunk.'

'No good at cricket, though.'

I didn't point out – and I should have done – that the Head himself, fanatic that he was, normally tried to deal with most of the cricket, certainly with the seniors, leaving Spinks and me to manage all the unwilling or incapable other boys. Spinks himself had told me he'd never been given a chance with the cricket.

I hadn't respected the Headmaster much before. Now I suddenly disliked him. Spinks had had to do with life, at least, drinking and copulating and thumping most arrows into the gold at fifty metres on a good day. This man and his third-rate school were both concerned only with appearances.

I said to Laura when I got home that evening. 'The Head's a fool.' She was out in the back garden by the stable, helping Clare with the pony.

'And his school is worse,' I went on. 'If you can't get into Eton or Winchester why bother with any of these other tatty sort of places at all?'

She said nothing. So I added, with a touch of annoyance, 'I'll have to get another job.'

'Yes,' she said at last. 'What?'

It was the old story. Apart from the nonsense of espionage

and now fourth-form English, I was unemployable. Oh, I might have held down some awful job in London in advertising or some such. But in the middle of the country?

'You've almost finished that book, haven't you? About your time in Egypt,' Laura said.

'Yes. But they don't publish books like mine any more: colonial memoirs, amateur history. There's no market. Only for sex or violence – or Edwardian country diaries.'

I looked out over the pasture behind the cottage, the fine, early evening light piercing through the great lime tree next the church, edging all the fresh green leaves with gold. More than forty I thought, with nothing, professionally, to show for it. A feeling of disappointed ambition came over me. But for what, I wondered? What had I ever really wanted to be? A taxi driver, yes, when I was a frustrated, motor-mad boy during the war and had noticed that, besides doctors, only taxi drivers could get petrol and drive freely all over the place. But apart from that, afterwards? I realised that I'd never wanted to do very much in the world as it had become. I'd fallen into my few jobs or, as with my work in British Intelligence, they'd been forced on me.

I'd seen behind the curtains of British political power – seen the moral vacuum there, the casual mayhem, the violence to no end. And since then I'd compromised with the public face of our morality, too, in the minor public school where I worked, and I saw that now in all its pretentious hypocrisy.

There weren't any more dashing people left in England, I suddenly decided; only crafty ones. The idealists, the witty drunks, the eccentrics, they were all gone. Decent fools like Spinks, for example, they got the chop every day, while the cunning, the dull and the vulgar prospered. The small men had come to rule.

And since I wasn't a crusader, lacking the heroic almost entirely, there wasn't much left for me to do in England, I realised. Without Laura and Clare I would have sold up and gone out to the south somewhere, France or even further afield. But with them I had everything, I saw that then, and the school didn't matter.

Laura said, 'Well, you'll have to stay where you are then, won't you? For the time being.'

Our lazy Welsh pony leant against the stable door, dozing in the sunlight, almost asleep even though Clare was using the

curry-comb, working it vigorously down its flank. She talked
to the animal as she combed out the last of its winter coat. He
was called 'Banbury'.

'Blueberry, Bunbury, Bellberry,' she chanted with each
stroke. She named him differently almost every day. Minty, our
wire-haired terrier, had joined us and was lying out now,
knowing it to be quite safe, in a sunny spot right beneath the
pony's belly.

Laura said, 'Why don't we have a drink when I'm finished
here – and forget about the stupid school.'

With happiness, how easy it was not to care a damn in the end
about failed ambition or the state of the nation. 'For the time
being,' Laura had said. And that, certainly, I knew now, was
everything.

Of course, what I've asked myself since is why David Marcus
should have suddenly decided to kill me more than two years
after I'd finished all my dangerous business with him. So why
take so long to move against me?

I can think of only one answer: as Head of Service now, he'd
got wind that I'd started to write about my chequered career in
British Intelligence, and thought that I was about to join the
ranks of those little sneaks, as he would have seen it, who told
tales out of class. Yet there must have been more to it than this:
many others, in fact and fiction, had thus publicly betrayed the
faith and survived. And especially so, since I'd only written
about the very beginning of my career in Cairo, as a
schoolteacher, when I'd first become involved in the old Mid-
East section there, more than twenty years before. I'd sent a few
sample chapters about this to a London publisher some months
before. I'd thought it was innocuous stuff, those early days in
Cairo, the life of that burnt city just before Suez: how I'd met
my first wife there: before she ended up in Moscow a few years
later working for the other side. A broken marriage – as well as a
smashed and betrayed British network in Egypt. But it was all
very old stuff.

Well, it struck me that some publisher's reader or editor must
have seen this autobiographical material and chatted about it, in
a London club, to a friend still in the game, who in turn had
mentioned it to Marcus or someone close to him.

And that was the rub. If I'd started to talk about my wife,

Marcus must have thought, I must one day talk about the other agents and worse, the double agents I'd dealt with. There were other horses from the same stable, later recruits still active, apparently in Moscow's cause, but in fact serving the west – or what was left of the 'west'. I knew at least one of their names and even though I'd no intention of ever actually writing about them, I suppose Marcus had decided he couldn't trust me and my entirely quiet life had to go. Of course, as I see it now, I should never have sent those few chapters of my memoirs to London in the first place. It's the only time I ever had enough vanity to betray me, for they weren't very well written anyway, I see that too, now.

Clare was downstairs with us that evening, a Friday, just at the start of our week's half-term. It was nearly eight o'clock. Had she gone to bed at her usual time she would have been saved some of the pain. But as it was we were all there together, Clare between us, on the big sofa in the drawing-room.

The record-player was on, which was why Clare was late going to bed. She loved music, all sorts, as long as there was a melody, however faint, or a rousing tune to hang on to. It calmed her. Instead of the smell of flowers or lavender stalks, it was the pure sound here which she absorbed in rapt silence, like a fastidious critic, her eyes quite still but alert, as though she was looking backwards into herself, opening channels into the blocked confusion of her mind where the music could flow, miraculously easing the congestion.

She withdrew deeply on these occasions. Indeed the child experts had previously forbidden her music for this reason. What fools they were: she went back into herself, yes, but only to find herself, to make amends, where the line of music could connect the broken circuits, and give her a good vision of herself which was what she most needed. Like all autistic children Clare lacked a sense of self. *Oliver!* could give this to her, or a good thumping, swirling version of 'The Blue Danube'.

Our sofa backs onto one of the drawing-room doors, which leads out through a small corridor into the kitchen. Thus we were facing the wrong way. Indeed there would have been no warning at all but for Minty in his basket under the fire canopy, where he slept in summer.

He growled suddenly. I hardly heard him over the saucy duet between Mr Bumble and the Widow Dorney on the *Oliver!* LP.

I was involved myself in any case, correcting an essay by one of my fourth-formers, my mind on the laboured banalities of his 'Great Experience', the theme which I had given the boys to write about the previous week. This one had chosen to discuss a rainy, scoreless football match he'd been to during the Easter holidays between Oxford and Banbury United. I remember wondering if his vision wasn't a bit limited.

Then Minty growled again. I heard him properly now, since the music, at the end of the track, had stopped for a moment, though the others still took no notice. Laura was sewing and Clare was sucking her thumb, looking meek and absorbed, hoping to postpone her bedtime indefinitely. I turned and looked round.

Our drawing-room door has a habit of swinging wide, silently, unexpectedly, if someone opens the back door out of the kitchen and lets the draught through. And it opened now as I watched, as if touched by magic, giving me a clear view down the small corridor into the kitchen.

A thin, tall man was standing there at the end, surprised at his sudden exposure, holding an automatic in a gloved hand. He had a stocking mask pulled over his face, and the collar of an old mud-and-green army anorak rose about his neck. He lifted the gun.

There is always that first moment of total disbelief in a catastrophe – a sense of high farce almost, before one's stomach drops like a rock and the gut turns over when you know it's all going to be absolutely real.

But this latter knowledge had barely come to me before the man fired the gun and I could see at once how it had missed me and hit Laura, next to me, in the back, for she hadn't turned, had never seen the man. She slumped forward, her round sewing-basket spinning like a broken wheel across the floor, just as I stood up, trying to protect her. For I knew, even in those first instants, that it was me the man wanted, not her.

Not her. Not her. My next thought was for Clare. But several seconds must have elapsed, for I don't remember exactly what happened then. I can just see all the jumbled cotton-reels on the floor – and Laura on all fours like a dog sinking into them. Clare was nowhere. She was no longer on the sofa. She'd disappeared.

I remember it all clearly then – I was over by the drawing-room door, slamming it shut and flattening myself against the brick work. Laura had sunk right forward now on her stomach, lying straight out, her head almost touching the fireplace, and Minty was barking round her, in a panic, as though to wake her. The music was still on – some rousing chorus from the orphans. Then I saw Clare. She'd hidden between the wall and the sofa arm on the far side of the room by the window and was peeking out at us looking at her mother's fallen body, amazed.

In my arms, I thought Laura must be dying. She couldn't see me, though her eyes were wide open – eyes fresh as ever, but not seeing now, like a flower that appears to live as beautifully as ever the moment after its stalk is cut. She couldn't see me and though her mouth was open too, she couldn't speak; there was blood on her lips, no longer any words.

But I hadn't the time to watch her die – or die with her, for the door opened and the calm tall man was there again, standing high above us, raising the gun once more.

I rolled out of his aim and kicked the door violently. It caught his arm. I stood up again, rushing the door, throwing all my weight against it, pinning half his body to the jamb. The force I brought to bear on the wood was incredible; the force of murder. The gun fell from his gloved hand as he pulled his body away. I tried to hold him. But I lost.

I could hear him running back through the kitchen. In a moment I had the gun in my hand and was after him out into the back garden with Minty at my heels. It was still twilight, so that I saw him vault the small dry-stone wall to the side of our garden, over into the back of the churchyard. I fired once, as I ran, but the shot went wild.

In the churchyard I could suddenly see much less. The shadow of the building blocked the last of the evening light. The old tombstones cut my shins as I ran. I thought I heard the church door open. But it wasn't open when I came to it. I went in anyway and switched on all the lights. There was a dry smell of old wood and lime wash. The door leading into the vestry was open. I fired into the black space again as I ran. But I couldn't find the switch inside and soon I was caught in the dark, surplices and vestments choking round my neck.

I was running then, down the village street – firing the last shots in the revolver wildly about the place, at anything that seemed to move, like a madman.

Laura was dead when the police came. I'd turned her over on the floor but hadn't the strength to lift her. I was shaking violently, my head jerking about uncontrollably in a state of wild animation.

There was just one young constable, in a police van, who had come first – on his way home, in my direction apparently, when the call had come to him. Together we got the body up onto the sofa and I explained what had happened.

'Well, go and look for him!' I shouted at the man then, who did nothing but just look at me warily. 'After him – in your car. Don't just stand there!' I started to clear up all the cotton-reels and buttons and thimbles off the floor, suddenly obsessed that the room should be meticulously clean. But when I came to the blister of congealing blood where Laura had been lying on our green carpet I stopped tidying up and started to shout again.

'For God's sake! Someone's emptied the tea pot all over the floor. Look at this – the filthy pigs. Look at it. *Clean it up!*'

I remember the expression on the constable's face then. It wasn't one of sympathy or understanding. It was more a frightened enmity. And I realised for the first time: he thinks I'm mad. I've had the automatic in my hand. He thinks I've just killed my wife.

I turned to Clare, who was still crouching behind the arm of the sofa, immobile, her eyes firmly shut now, but her thumb still working furiously in her mouth.

'Tell them,' I said. 'About the man who was here, with the gun, who shot Mummy.'

But Clare said nothing. And when I went to pick her up, to hold her in my arms, I found that her body, though quite unharmed, was absolutely rigid. She remained exactly as she had been against the wall, her legs up against her chest, one arm round her ear, thumb in her mouth: frozen solid.

I turned to the policeman. 'He was here. In the kitchen, a tall man with a stocking mask. This is *his* gun. I don't have a gun. Don't you see?' He didn't.

I heard the ambulance coming then and other sirens behind it. The constable came towards me, diffidently, but with ice in his eyes. 'Now, if you'll just put the child down,' he said. 'Take it easy and come with us.'

I found calm then, out of the blue. I stopped shaking. I realised my own fingerprints were all over the gun now, that the man with gloves on had escaped and that Clare couldn't speak or move. Laura was dead and I had killed her. What else could they think?

On impulse I put Clare into the man's arms, edging round towards the door as I did so. As he took her I pushed the little frozen weight into his body so that he stumbled a fraction. Then I ran, out through the kitchen and into the deeper twilight that had come up all round now. I was across the back garden, over the wall into the pasture before I heard the first shouts behind me. But I knew my way here, the old Roman road leading four miles across country to the school, where the police, men from the bright lights of the local town, would be lost in the gathering dark.

Why did I run? To begin with, at least, I had doubts. It was an added admission of guilt. Besides, even though the man had gloves on, the police must surely have been able to find some other evidence of his presence in the cottage: the marks of violence on the door, fibres from his clothes, a footprint obviously not mine in the back garden.

It was the look on the policeman's face at first: I knew he didn't believe me. And in that moment I saw the whole thing clearly as a set-up, by British Intelligence, against me. I'd been framed by them once before – and that had taken me to four years in Durham Jail. Now it was my death they wanted. I was sure of that. And so, despite Clare, I had to run.

I hated doing it, leaving her – but my years involved with David Marcus and his various hit-men and 'persuaders' had told me, even in that shocked state, that unless I went, they would see me dead in any case, one way or another: a 'scuffle' in some local police station, or an 'accident' later in the cells beneath Scotland Yard. There were half a dozen ways. I'd witnessed one of them myself: a Soviet agent they'd taken in London once, whom they failed to 'turn'. They had worked on him with black bags and wind machines – leaving him mindless at that point, with vomit marks running down the *back* of his jacket. Later they had put him completely out of his misery. And so, that night, I'd run to avoid any similar fate.

I hadn't regretted it for long. The next morning and during the days afterwards up in the tree, I'd heard the news on the transistor: they never caught any tall man in an ex-army anorak. They were after me from then on, a brutal wife-killer, starting out then on a vast manhunt through the Cotswolds.

Of course, as I saw at once, that suited Marcus's book just as well: they would never find his hit-man, so Marcus could now leave me to the ordinary police, the army, allowing them to think I was no more than the commonest sort of criminal. At best, they would kill me; at worst, Durham Jail would claim me again, but for much longer this time. Either way my 'memoirs' would not be continued.

But as I ran that night across the dark countryside I remember thinking: I must tell the truth. I must make these notes, as I have done. Thus, apart from Clare, it's essential that I survive for the time being, which is the only curb on my anger at the moment. I want to get all these basic facts down before I start looking for Clare and before I see what I can do about Marcus and Ross and the others. 'What I can do.' What do I mean by that? I want to do to them what they did to Laura. It's quite simple.

I made for the school because I knew it would be empty during half-term. I'd decided even then, out on the old Roman road, that this was the best means of survival. I thought of Spinks's sleeping bag and backpack as I ran; I would lie up in the countryside somehow. I'd friends in London and there were other friends of ours in the immediate neighbourhood. But none of them would be any use. The police would see to that. However, if I moved fast, I thought I could get to the deserted school and then away into the more remote open land on the high wolds beyond, before the police thought of going there. And if I was careful, when they did arrive at the school they wouldn't find any evidence of my visit there, and might perhaps never know I'd gone to ground in the country further afield. It was Spinks's backpack after all, which wouldn't be missed when school started again. And Spinks's 32-pound fibreglass recurve bow as well. I thought of that, too, as I ran.

But the school wasn't deserted when I got there, breathless, half an hour later. The housekeeper, seeming now to justify all Spinks's earlier protests, was entertaining. Lights were on in her rooms down by the garages – and the sports room, next the gym, was just beyond her accommodation. An asphalt driveway led past her windows, which were curtained, but as I tiptoed by I could hear the nature of the party well enough: laughter, music, little shrieks, the tinkle of glass. Of course, it might have been the housekeeper's sister or her maiden aunt inside, but the smart little Renault by one of the garages suggested otherwise – as did the giggling couple who came towards the sports room when I was inside it ten minutes later, just as I was about to leave with Spinks's equipment and his bow.

I put my foot sharply against the bottom of the door and the rest of my weight against it – hoping they'd no intention of even trying to open it. Why should they in any case? What could these merrymakers want in the sports room?

They wanted something. A key was thrust into the lock and the handle turned an instant later. I lay against the wood, praying I wouldn't slip.

A young voice spoke, north country, one I knew. 'That's funny. It's stuck.' It was Ackland, who took junior science, a vastly bearded, recently qualified, north-country youth who, it was rumoured, actually slept in the lab, so keen was he on his job. But he had some other job in mind now.

'Won't be a jiffy. You'll see.' He tried the lock again.

'Come on then! Either in or out. Let's not hang around.' The young woman was impatient, bossy, with a slurred, partly cultivated voice I'd not heard before.

'There's a sleeping bag in here I'm sure. You could use it,' Ackland whined, pushing at the door with some desperation now, I felt. One of my feet slipped a fraction. I was damp with sweat.

'But I'm *not* staying anyway, I *told* you,' the woman said, changing her tune. 'No more one-night stands, thank you. Let's go back.'

Ackland, like Spinks, was trying to have it away. I cursed him. If Spinks's lechery a week before had offered survival, Ackland was now about to ruin me.

'Come on, Ruthie, I'd break the door down, if you wanted me to. I'm sure there's a bag inside.'

I held my breath. Ackland was a heavy fellow, a lot of puppy-fat beneath the beard. Luckily virtue, if such it was, prevailed. 'No,' the bossy woman's voice came again. 'No, not with you, in or out of any bag. You think I'm any Tom, Dick or Harry, don't you, for your pleasure? Let's go back.'

'No, Ruthie, only trying to help . . .'

'Only trying it on, you mean . . .'

Their voices faded as they walked away. I realised they must have been pretty drunk, the two of them, which was what made me risk stealing the transistor radio I saw on the top of the dashboard of the Renault as I passed it a few minutes later. The cock-teasing woman wouldn't miss it until next morning, and when she did she probably wouldn't bother reporting it. It was worth the risk anyway. Leaving the world, I knew I needed to keep in touch with it. I was coming back after all, I thought, as I made off fast across the school playing fields into the deep countryside beyond.

There was no moon, but with few clouds and approaching mid-summer, it was never completely dark that night. There was still some light away to the west, a fan of dying colour, and I knew my way in this direction, too, from school walks and cross-country runs I'd been in charge of with the boys the previous winter. Beyond the beech coppice where the archery range was, at the far side of the playing fields, I took a line north-west moving through open pasture at first along the top of the eastern ridge of the Evenlode valley. Soon there was a farm lane which sank slightly between hedges, making the going easier: part of an old ridgeway, it ran for several miles towards Chipping Norton, with the farm itself half way along, set high on the wolds.

I gave these buildings a wide berth when I came to the first of them, a big dutch barn looming up in the half-light, bearing off to the left down the valley, through sloping pasture, skirting the long dry-stone walls, streaks of crimson right down on the horizon which still just lit my way.

A flock of sheep stirred uneasily somewhere ahead of me. And then I walked right into them, losing my bearings at the same time. The light in the west disappeared completely and I seemed to be in some dell halfway down the valley, enclosed by the land or by trees, I couldn't see which, as I moved blindly among the sheep, bumping into their great woolly backsides. They started to bleat and then to move; and then they seemed to mass in great phalanxes about me in the dark, going this way and that, as if increasingly hemmed in by something which I couldn't see. Their own panic was as great as mine now as I thrashed about among them, trying to find the rise in the ground which would take me back up the valley and give me my original vantage-point. Suddenly the animals seemed to rush me in the dark, all together, pushing and butting as they went, and I went with them, thrust along, upwards at last, where the sheep scattered away all round me and I saw the west again, the dying smears of colour on the horizon.

I ran across the great field, keeping north this time, moving away from the dying light, and within minutes I could see the greater lights of Chipping Norton, isolated like a great ship, moored across the valley ahead of me. I was coming to the end of the ridge at last. The parkland I was making for wasn't far now; I knew that. It lay a few miles to the south-west of Chipping Norton. There was only a small by-road to cross at the bottom of the valley.

I'd seen the great estate many times from this road, some thousands of private acres rising up to a plateau on another hill, run through with great stands of beech and oak, so thickly wooded, indeed, that it was impossible ever to see the house itself which, though on a rise, was shrouded, even in midwinter, by the huge trees.

This Beechwood Manor and the lands had been bought a few years ago, I'd heard, by some American shipping magnate with a great collection of pre-Raphaelite paintings, paintings which the public were never allowed to view. I'd not been there. But I'd noticed these thick woods – and remembered, too, the little eighteenth-century bridge, the balustrades decorated with stone pineapples, which the road crossed as it ran along the borders of the estate. One of the most attractive streams in the Cotswolds rose somewhere in the vast privacy beyond. When the tracker dogs came after me, as they would, I could put the beauty of this brook to an entirely practical use, moving up the water so that the dogs would lose my trail.

A dog barked, several sharp yelps somewhere in the night to my left in the distance as I crouched in the ditch near the bridge. The road was strangely white, an almost luminous ribbon in the last of the light. Water gurgled over stones on the other side of the road, the stream coming from somewhere in the great cavern of trees beyond. Otherwise there was silence. The backpack, with the radio which I'd put inside, had been no trouble; nor had the quiver of arrows on my shoulder. But the long recurve bow, which I'd clutched in my fist all the way, was now an awkward weight in my hand.

I thought: what nonsense – a bow and arrow in this day and age. I saw the innocence of my plan then. England was no wild country now, nor was this Sherwood Forest. I felt the pain of a child suddenly, out too late at night, hopelessly astray, whose dare had failed, who could look forward only to punishment, to foolish disgrace, a loss of innocence.

But another sound came then, behind me from the hills, other dogs faintly calling, the noise hurrying down the still night air towards me.

Without thinking I ran across the road and stumbled into the water on the other side beneath the bridge, and then I was splashing madly up the stream through the canopy of dark trees, my shins bruised and cut once more as I fled. At first I thought it was water from the stream wetting my cheeks. But after a minute, when I'd gone some way into the twilit forest, I realised I was crying. They were tears of anger, though: not regret nor uncertainty any more: anger and annoyance, so that even the tall, closely meshed barbed wire fence that crossed the brook, and which I crashed into twenty yards further on into the woods, didn't deter me. As soon as I realised it wasn't electrified, I pushed my way under the lowest strand of wire, ducking right down into the water to do so, soaking myself completely, but wriggling through in the end like a fish escaping up-stream. So much the better for this great fence, I thought. It would deter, if not prevent the police from following me – while tracking away from them, keeping in the water all the time, would kill my scent for the pursuing dogs.

Four

Apart from fear and my soaking clothes, it was cold as well by the middle of the night, so that I barely slept at all, wedged in the branches halfway up a big copper beech that had saved me a few hours before, one of its lowest limbs reaching out horizontally over the stream.

The police with their lights and tracker dogs had passed close beneath me some time before midnight and they were likely to return, I thought, when the dogs found no further scent as they went on up into the woods. I didn't know about the lake then, or the fact that the little brook which fed it rose several miles beyond it to the north. They must have followed this stream right to its source, perhaps thinking that I'd swum across the lake in the night, for they didn't return until just after sun-up, when I was well awake and could hear them stomping about almost directly beneath my tree.

The dogs whimpered. I thought they must have smelt or sensed me high up in the leaves above them. In the morning light the police would surely see the branch over the water, put two and two together and would be up after me in a moment.

But they were tired or I was lucky, for after a few minutes they left, the sounds dying away as the men went back down the wooded valley to the road. That was where my scent ended, just by the bridge: finding no trace of me in the forest they would think, for the time being at least, that I'd stopped a car and got a lift out of the area the previous night.

I was safe. Or was I? I couldn't be certain. So I stayed where I was, halfway up the tree, sitting astride the stem of a big branch, my back wedged into a fork of the smooth trunk. I tried to relax and the first of those nearly silent, very early summer mornings started for me, living in a green world, in a capsule of leaves, where every smallest movement in the air about me was registered by an equally small rustling in the foliage. But this noise seemed strangely loud that first morning, almost alarming, as if some great hand were dusting the tree from outside, shaking it, searching me out.

To begin with the light that filtered through was grey and indeterminate. After ten minutes, as I let my head lie back against the trunk, the leaves above me turned gradually to a lighter shade – faint green at first. But soon they were edged with sunlight at the top, odd bright points dazzling my eyes, as the morning breeze moved them.

Gazing upwards, I wondered again if the whole business was worth it. I could hardly live in this tree for the rest of my life. I'd escaped: I'd proved something. Perhaps that was enough. If I climbed down now and went to the police I could surely explain everything in the calm light of day: my behaviour had all been an aberration, a brainstorm. They would hold me for a week or so. But the presence of the tall masked man in the cottage would inevitably come to light and I would – I paused in my thoughts here: yes, I'd pick up the threads of my life again with Clare. But what life, without Laura?

Her loss struck me then, a series of hammer-blows in the calm morning, a vast shadow over all my future that first was sad but then brought a fury to me which I felt could only be eased by revenge. Indeed, without this thought of retribution, I couldn't think of Laura for very long at all. I know now that one of the reasons I decided to stay in the woods was that I felt that, for as long as I remained an outlaw in this manner, I could freely contemplate such violent amends. And in another way, by not returning, I could avoid facing the actual fact of her death, avoid the place, the circumstances, the whole memory. In short, if I stayed outside the real world completely, I could imagine Laura still alive. It was I who had gone absent, was missing somewhere, and so long as I remained free in these woods I could plot her rescue, a return to her, she whom I had temporarily left behind in civilisation.

Or so I persuaded myself. But perhaps there was something else, deep in my character, which made this persuasion an easy matter. At more than forty, with so little behind me other than Laura, I was tempted now, with this forced change in circumstance, to go on and change my life completely: to leave my ruined past where it was, leave the pretentious school, England, too, in effect, with all its squalor, its whining, lazy compromises, to clear out, let it all die and take on some new life. I was tempted by vast change, a leap into the blue, just as a child sees the world simply as a place of limitless opportunity, each new day nothing but a space for adventure.

For me, the mould of my existence was already broken, however I looked at it. I could only die myself, or create some quite new way of life. It was all or nothing. I could return: to prison or at best to a familiar life in the cottage that would soon become unbearable without Laura. Or I could set off in a new direction, self-reliant, master of my fate.

Yes, that last phrase, so redolent of some Victorian adventure yarn, comes easily to me, as an emblem of youth, ambition unachieved when I was young. So that what I really felt that morning was that the chance had perhaps come for me to find my roots again, find that lost way back into real life. Apart from anger, apart from the need to get Clare back, I had a purpose of my own then. Not just to escape but to create: to change everything, to risk everything, to win at last.

But when I opened Spinks's backpack I wondered if I had sufficient or appropriate equipment for the crusade. For the first thing I came on, in an outside pocket, was a quarter-bottle of vodka that had smashed somehow during my journey in the night. The liquor had soaked into a small book that had been stuffed in with it. It was a copy of Baden-Powell's *Scouting for Boys*, but an old edition, thirty years old at least, for the youths were drawn in brimmed felt hats and there was mention of doing one's duty to a King, not a Queen.

I thought kindly of Spinks again: evidence here of the amiable rogue once more – vodka soaking through the precise plans of how to lay a fire: the saloon-bar jokes impinging on all that long-ago Empire idealism. How like Spinks not to bother with anything up to date, going off into the wilds of Snowdonia with just his own tipsy goodwill and commonsense to preserve him: that, and a quarter of Smirnoff and scouting instructions a generation out of date.

If he could survive on so little, then so could I. On the other hand, his had been a legal enterprise; mine was not, and with these fairly useless objects found to begin with, I feared that Spinks might not have much more to offer me inside his bag.

But he did. I took the stuff out carefully, draping most of it on the branches about me. Apart from the sleeping bag and the small blue gas burner, there were a variety of other outdoor survival necessities: a first-aid kit, a tin mug and plate, a billycan, an imitation Swiss Army knife, complete with assorted files, probes, blades, bottle openers and a magnifying glass; a canvas waterbag, a lightweight mountain hammock, a folding pocket saw (two rings at either end of a flexible line of minutely serrated steel), a packet of half a dozen assorted Woolworth's fish-hooks with leaders but without any line, a small mountaineering axe, unused, with half a dozen aluminium pitons still strapped to it, together with a coil of quarter-inch nylon rope and a small pair of green Army surplus binoculars, old but functional.

The food line wasn't so good: just half a packet of Lyons Green Label tea, one of Ritz biscuits, some bone-hard cheddar and two crumpled packs of Knorr Spring Vegetable soup. There were other personal odds and ends, some likely to be of use, but most not: an old dark green Army pullover with leather epaulettes, an unopened pack of 'Fetherlite' French letters, and two soiled paperbacks: *Hot Dames on Cold Slabs* by Hank Janson and last year's *Good Beer Guide to Great Britain*. Spinks, obviously, had thought well of Baden-Powell's maxim: 'Be Prepared'. He had followed this injunction to the letter.

There were also two maps: a large-scale Ordnance Survey of the Snowdonia area and, much more usefully, a smaller-scale one of the north Cotswolds, from Woodstock south-west to Winchcombe, which included the school and the big estate where I now was. In another outside pocket I found three emergency distress flares, a compass and a torch. But the battery was nearly done for. There were no matches.

I checked through my own possessions then, feeling about the pockets of my grey-green cord suit. I had a box of matches, a little damp, less than half full; eighteen cigarettes, my red felt-tip pen that I'd been correcting the fourth form's essays with, and the keys of our car. Nothing else. No money. I rarely carried my wallet or cheque book.

But there was something else, I felt it now, in my other inside pocket: it was the boy's exercise book I'd been correcting the previous evening, folded up and stuffed in there without my remembering: his 'Great Experience', the rainy soccer match between Banbury and Oxford United. But it was the first and only essay in a new book – the rest a hundred blank pages, which I use now to write this.

I put Spinks's stuff carefully back into the bag. Yes, I thought, there was enough here to make a go of it: a start at least. But then it struck me: apart from the previous night I'd never spent twenty-four hours entirely out of doors alone in my life. I'd lit picnic fires and barbecues as a child, and years later had done the same with Laura and Clare. But nothing more. And what of the elements, the damp? It was fine now, in this last week of May, but it would surely rain soon and it was still cold at night. The tea and the Ritz biscuits and the lump of cheddar would suffice as a snack. But when they were gone, what then?

I realised I was as unfitted to life alone in the open as I had been to life among most people in the ordinary world, a stranger, really, in both places. A walk in the woods, yes, I'd done that. But I'd never lived in them. I'd never been a boy scout either. The whole thing seemed ridiculous once more. My legs hurt now, too, the cuts and bruises I'd suffered climbing the dry-stone walls and my face and hands and back were scored with little scratches from the barbed-wire fence. My feet were cold; cold and damp.

I took my shoes and socks off and let them lie in a pool of sunlight out along the branch. I opened Spinks's first-aid box. There were antiseptic ointments, bandages, a lot of Band-aids – and using them on my hands and legs, the pain easing after a while and the sun warming my toes, it struck me how much of a lucky gift all these things were, that Spinks's backpack had been something meant. Fate was on my side, had given me a chance, at least, and I had better take it.

A police helicopter flew over the woods at about midday not far above my tree: the downthrust from its rotors blew the leaves about above me like whirlwind for a few moments. But the storm didn't penetrate to the foliage where I was. I was still safe. The news – which I heard later on, a local bulletin from Radio Oxford, describing me in some detail and the precautions people in the area should now take – made me more resolute. I was free here. Even with tracker dogs and a helicopter they hadn't found me The copper beech tree had saved me. I was invisible, from beneath or above. The next thing to do was to make or find some more permanent hiding place. And I thought then: why not a tree house?

The beech-tree I was in wasn't suitable. The leaves thinned out too much towards the top while the branches halfway up, where I was now, would never have allowed for any platform of logs or planks such as I had in mind. I'd have to find another tree. But in the meantime I strung up the lightweight hammock between two branches, ate some of the Ritz biscuits and cheese and slept afterwards for several hours. I listened to the radio again, the volume turned down, close to my ear: the local news and the 'P.M.' show, which talked about me, too: a wife-slayer on the run. I had gone nationwide. The police might be back, I thought, sometime in the daylight, with fresh men, fresh dogs, so I waited until well into the evening before I climbed down carefully from my perch. I was surprised the day had passed so quickly: those early days all did. It wasn't until a few weeks had elapsed that the problem of boredom arose.

I came on the lake first, upstream, barely half a dozen yards beyond the overhanging branch I'd found. If I'd gone tramping up the brook that previous evening in the failing light I'd have fallen right into it. The equipment in Spinks's bag would have been soaked, most of it ruined. I was lucky again.

The lake, more large pond than lake, was about 300 yards long and 70 wide, a slowly moving sheet of dark, copper-coloured, leaf-filled water, shaped like an hourglass, the heavily overgrown banks narrowing in the middle, leaving two channels on either side of an even more heavily encrusted island covered in wildly rampant rhododendrons with a huge yellow-leaved willow at the centre whose branches drooped out over it all like an umbrella. The water in these two channels moved quickly enough on one side over the fallen supports and arches of a small wooden footbridge. Elsewhere, along its margins, this lower part of the lake was choked with duckweed and flowering waterlilies vying for the light, beneath the circle of great beech trees which leant right over the water, completely surrounding the whole area. And above these lakeside trees were other copper beeches, rising straight up from the steep sides of the little valley, so that I had the impression, as I stood there that evening, of being at the bottom of a vast, dark, leafy well, with the dregs of water about me, where to get in or out one would either have to fall or climb.

Besides the waterlilies there was the long gone to seed, and sometimes exotic, evidence of other cultivated plants and bushes, sprouting wildly here and there in the choked banks, while up by the ruined footbridge I found the remains of a covered boathouse in the overhanging trees, the rotten timbers in the roof collapsed over a small inlet, with a jetty that had sunk into the duckweed leaving only a chunk of dressed stone and a rusting metal bollard above water.

The lake had probably been an artificial creation and its borders must once have been a carefully tended water garden, a pleasure-haunt many years before, where people from the great house, I imagined, must have come down for boating afternoons, with parasols, when liveried butlers had served them hamper teas on the small island afterwards. I supposed the money had gone long before, with the previous owners, to keep it up, while the American magnate had yet to bring his cash to bear on this secret Arcadia. It remained now, with this overgrowth of the years, a deep wilderness where yet one could just make out all the bones of an airy formality beneath: eighty, ninety years before the great beech trees would not have leant so overpoweringly over the water; there would have been order and reason then, clearly imposed by the many contrived effects: the willow-pattern bridge, a Gothic folly on the island perhaps, a boathouse in the same mode. Now this hidden landscape, long since freed of all such impositions, grew apace, forgetting the world, by whom it was forgotten.

Leading away from the ruined footbridge, the remains of a stepped path rose sharply up the angle of the valley, through the trees to the top of the ridge, which must have been a hundred and fifty feet above the water – though when I got to the top, the lake was quite invisible hidden somewhere below me. I had managed to move up the slope here quietly enough. But I realised that anyone coming directly down into the valley would almost certainly slip and make a fearful commotion in the process. Already I saw the place as an ideal retreat: and more than that, as my domain.

At the top of the ridge the beech forest thinned somewhat. There were great clumps of flowering blackthorn here and there, but otherwise the undergrowth was less severe. Soon there were odd clearings in the wood and then I came on an old metal boundary fence, with open parkland beyond, open in the traditional eighteenth-century manner, informally landscaped with clumps of chestnut and oak dotted here and there, a few cows, and a flat, roped-off space to one side, near the estate wall – a cricket pitch, it seemed, with a strange thatched log-built pavilion facing it.

The house itself was visible now, or at least the east-wing, hardly more than a quarter of a mile away, on a slight rise in the parkland, with elaborate, almost castellated terracing above the meadow grass, fringeing the house like a stone ruff.

From what I could make out in the fading light, it seemed a huge Victorian creation, probably high Gothic, for I could see the tall brick chimneys and spiky towers against the sunset, the variety of different roofs and roof levels, as well as the steeply sloping slates and pinnacles and gable ends that jutted wildly about the crown of the house.

I was surprised. The north Cotswolds, I knew, contained a few Georgian and other earlier masterpieces in mellow stone. But I'd never heard of any Victorian pile in the area, and certainly of nothing like this place, seemingly vast as a railway terminus: a house which, even in the bad light, clearly had a lot of mad character and a confidence to it, bristling with the busy confusion of half a dozen architectural styles.

But then, as I've said, it had been impossible ever to see the house, either from the roads or hills about. From the outside the whole estate was entirely enclosed by its tall belt of beech-trees and I could see these now, from the inside, forming another complete circle round the parkland, leaving the house at the centre inviolate, unknown.

I had Spinks's Army fieldglasses with me, but the sun was low in the west behind the house and I could make few other details out except the thorny pyramids and spirals of masonry all about the top, the clusters of elaborate chimney stacks. It was just a soft charcoal silhouette on the hill, a fantasy like a Rackham drawing as the light waned behind it.

There was, I could just see, a huge conservatory jutting out from the end of the wing nearest to me, two storeys high, a graceful glass arch over the top and what looked like a walled vegetable garden to the right of this, at the back of the house, where there must have been a big yard as well, together with a lot of other outbuildings. There was no sign of life and no lights on anywhere, though it was nearly dark now.

And then, just before I moved away back down into the woods, a lot of surprising light did suddenly occur – in the big conservatory. It seemed as if a series of bright spotlights were being moved around inside as I put the binoculars on to it. Shafts of light illuminated great vague dark fronds, climbing plants, and even whole trees beneath the great crystal arch. I was too low on the ground to see anyone inside. There were just these mysterious lights, coming from beneath, playing up over the foliage, rhythmically patrolling the greenery, crystal fingers moving slowly up and down and around, as if someone was conducting some kind of horticultural theatre, or creating a mysterious ballet, a dance of white lines against the gathering dark. I watched it steadily for ten minutes or more, but could find no rhyme or reason to it, to these questing searchlights in the night.

I had Spinks's torch with me, going down the hill into the valley, hurrying back to my tree before total dark. But its beam was feeble and I didn't want to use it anyway. And thus I fell, missing my footing about halfway down the steep hill – falling headlong at first, then slipping madly through the undergrowth as I tried to pull myself round and get a grip on things. But it was no use. I thundered down most of the last part of the valley, cutting and bruising myself all over again.

A root or branch had caught me as well, I found, when I got to the bottom, hitting me somewhere just over the eye, a solid blow that I didn't really feel at first but which made me gasp with pain, almost crying out, when I came to a final halt near the lake. I lay where I was, not moving. I found I couldn't move in any case. I was practically unconscious – though I'd heard the racket I'd made coming down through the undergrowth clearly enough. And I hoped then that someone else had heard me, up at the house perhaps, that I would soon be found. For all I wanted at that moment was some sort of professional attention, a warm bed, comfort. My forehead was damp, there was blood there and the cloudless night sky above the lake moved round and round in my eyes when I looked up, with the trees forming a spinning margin around it: I was at the bottom of a dark whirlpool. Then I passed out.

When I opened my eyes again it must have been the middle of the night, an hour or more later, for the stars were clearly out now, in the circle of sky above me, quite still in their courses. I was alive. The blood had caked over my eye. No one had come. I was still free. I found I could move myself a bit; no bones seemed to be broken.

The woods about had resumed their nocturnal calm, an almost total silence, except, when you listened very carefully, after minutes on end, for odd sighs and crackles in the undergrowth that might have been the breeze. Then something definitely moved, a little way along the lake edge. Was it a water bird or some small thing fleeing from an owl on soundless wings? Was it a fox, a badger, a mole? I lay where I was for another ten minutes, wondering, letting the peace sink into me. A moon had come up, I saw then, which explained the gauze of faint white light in the air, a broad scimitar just above the trees on the other side of the water.

I stood up at last and hobbled painfully to the edge of the lake where I could see the ruined footbridge to the island in the moonlight. Next to it was the old boathouse and the half-sunken jetty. Moving out along this I found a place where I could kneel. I bent out over the water and washed the blood from my face, trying to leave the scab intact, and then, cupping my fingers, I drank great handfuls of the liquid. It was cool, cool on my face and in my throat, with nothing brackish about it.

In luck again, I thought. I might have been blinded, with a broken leg: instead, just a few more cuts and bruises, a bad graze on my head and my legs feeling as if they'd been shot out from under me once more. Yet I was certain I didn't have the strength to get back to the beech tree at the far end of the lake, least of all pull myself up into its middle branches where my hammock was.

But then, as I leant back from the water, wondering what I might do, I saw something man-made rising up from the edge of the island in faint silhouette against the moonlight: man-made because it rose upwards, in an exact straight line, from beyond the branches of the willow, at an angle of 45 degrees. It was the edge of a roof, I thought. Was it a folly or a bower, some Gothic summer house that I'd imagined the island supported earlier in the day?

When I had come this same way earlier in the evening I had seen nothing on the island other than the rhododendrons and the willow flowering out above it like a yellow fountain. But here, certainly, was a building of some sort. I could see it more clearly now: the edge of a roof jutting out over the water.

The channel was about ten yards across at this point. The ruined footbridge wouldn't bear my weight. But by walking out into the stream and using the old wooden piles and arches for support I found I was able to wade across onto the island without too much difficulty. The channel had silted up here and the water never came above my waist.

Pushing up through the bushes on the far side I first stumbled on some steps: a rise of half a dozen moss-covered steps. Beyond was a bramble-shrouded doorway, I saw, with a stab of Spinks's torch, covered by a metal grille like a tall garden gate. When I touched it the rust came away in great flakes in my hand. But it opened readily enough.

Inside I found myself in a small octagonal space, with cut stone all round in the walls, well made originally, but cracked in places now, I saw by the faint torchlight, where the ivy had come rapaciously in, ivy and bramble that had crept in from the door, and ferns that had risen between the flagstones from the earth beneath. In front was a small terrace, edged by a stone balustrade looking out over the water, and the sloping roof which I'd seen from the shore above that.

It was indeed some kind of summerhouse, a little pleasure-haunt, contrived, it seemed, in rather the same eccentric Gothic manner as the house in the parkland above. And since the island was set in the middle of the lake, with few trees to cloud the sun, the place was still almost warm inside, the stones retaining the heat of the day. I took off my trousers and finding a stone bench of some sort at one side of the summerhouse I laid myself flat out on it and was soon asleep.

When I woke there was a faint smell of roses in the air, the bright morning light reflecting off the lake making queer watery patterns on the white stuccoed ceiling immediately above my head. It was a conical roof, built in a series of stuccoed fan arches, the delicate Gothic tracery partly crumbled away and the paint badly flaked, though I could see it had once been blue like a sky, with the remains of flower garlands and cornucopias and cherubs here and there in the corners. There was a faintly ecclesiastic air about this heavenly tracery above me. And when I at last got up from the stone bench I saw why: I had spent the night sleeping on the flat top of a large raised tomb.

On the other side of the chamber, I saw then, was another identical tomb, with a stone base, but with a white stucco surround on top, elaborately carved along the edges allowing for an inscription beneath in heavy Gothic lettering: 'When the wicked man turneth away from his wickedness...' I couldn't see the rest of it. The biblical admonishment ran right round the corner of the stone.

I didn't shiver, even when I saw the skull and bones at one end of the other tomb, where part of the stone casing had caved in, for it was nearly warm already in the little mausoleum, the sun well up above the lake. I stood there instead, between the bodies wondering who they were, or had been, as if I'd spent an intimate night with two strangers who'd disappeared unaccountably at daybreak, companions who had given me vital sanctuary and warmth, whose names I had to know...

I looked on top of both tombs and along the sides. But apart from the old-testament inscriptions there was no other writing. Then I saw the ivy-margined tablet set in the wall above the doorway. I brushed a few leaves aside, displaying the whole stone, woodlice and earwigs caught in the light suddenly running madly now, escaping from crevices in the deeply cut inscription. There was no religious or other preamble, it started in straight away.

George Arthur Horton, Kt., M.P., J.P.
1830 – 1897
Formerly of Harrisbrook House, Nottingham,
and of Beechwood Manor in this parish.
Rose Horton (née Blumberg)
1840 – 1914
Of Brompton Gardens, Kensington, and of Beechwood.
This Avalon, on the waters they loved,
made over into their final resting place.
Together Again.

The tablet had an admirable simplicity, I thought, so happily lacking in the usual verbose and grandiose pieties expected in such Victorian inscriptions – this almost Arthurian legend applied to some Midland coal-baron, as I imagined, who had bought Beechwood estate, built himself a Gothic pile in the middle of it as a sort of re-created Camelot, perhaps, and had lived here with his Jewish wife, disdaining an appropriately Christian resting place in the local churchyard, choosing instead this lesser Gothic folly where, in due time, his wife could join him, passing eternity together in the middle of their lake, which the two of them had probably created, far from the prying, gossiping eyes which would otherwise have found them in some public burying-place.

For I sensed at once a clear attack on convention here, in the inscription as in the lives of these two people. The Jewish maiden name need never have been so bluntly included, after all – nor, indeed, in those severely Christian times, could it have been an expected marriage in the first place. The words here were an affirmation of something, a confirmation, in life, of some social disregard in this man who, with his traditional industrial honours, seemed otherwise so conventional. I admired what seemed such forthright deviations.

Something had changed George Horton, with his dour Midland background: a snub to his wife, perhaps, among the county gentry where he had come to live – the fault of 'new' money compounded by a Jewess. Or perhaps, more simply, his wife had changed him – softened the puritan industry, his hard familial ambition, had ironed out the rough nature of his soul.

So that halfway through life he had changed course and they had built themselves a water garden, a pleasure-haunt where they were indeed together again now. It was all conjecture... But I could at least, with certainty, admire their love.

Then I saw the vase of flowers. It had been placed outside on the small terrace, shielded from the wind just beneath the stone balustrade that gave over the water: a dozen fine red roses, which had been the smell, I realised now, that had wafted in on me as I woke that morning in the faint breeze. They were fresh blooms, early hothouse roses I thought, most of their petals still firmly sheathed around the bud, a sheen of moisture on the deep colour. I was not the only person to have been here recently.

I turned quickly, involuntarily, searching the empty space behind me as though some fourth person had crept in with these flowers during the night while I slept, and might still be there, somewhere on the island, who would come on me through the bramble-filled doorway at any moment. But there was nothing: only the morning sun slanting directly on the tombs now, warming them once more.

Five

I returned to my beech tree at the south end of the lake and with painful stiffness managed to pull myself up the branches to my hammock. Lying back in safety at last I saw that the valley beneath me was not so inviolate as I had imagined.

Someone else had been in the little mausoleum within the last few days. Yet how had they gained access to it? Had they waded across the channel, as I had, with a vase of roses held high? Difficult. But how else? The footbridge would have held no weight, not even a child's. They must have come by boat, I thought suddenly, from the other, northern end of the lake perhaps. And if they had come by boat, they must, too, have come from the big house above me, for the boat would have to be kept somewhere along the margin of the water. I was nervous about this strange intrusion, and yet curious, so that having slept again for most of the middle of the day, I climbed down from the tree later in the afternoon and set out along the eastern shore of the lake to see if I could find such a boat.

I took Spinks's bow with me for the first time, with a single arrow tied to its belly. Later I always brought two arrows with me, for a second shot. But these were early days. I don't know what I expected to shoot with it. I hadn't even sharpened the arrow tips yet. The bow, I suppose, was simply an emblem to begin with, an earnest of something I intended to achieve in the way of protection or pursuit, I didn't know quite which then.

My legs still ached, and my back too, so that I moved slowly, pausing behind every tree and bush for a minute, as I moved round the lake edge in the late-afternoon sunlight. Again, in those early days I moved almost too cautiously, before I found the rabbit and other woodland paths, where I could travel faster and more securely, well back from the lake, hidden by the thicker undergrowth.

The lake shore on this far side had less cover in any case than on the western margin which led up to the parkland. And the hill that rose from the valley here was not so steep, a more gentle rise, with the beech trees even taller, their branches less accessible.

At the far end of the lake on this side I found the old pumping-shed some yards back from the water, overgrown with elder and bramble: a stone shed, roughly built many years before with the roof largely collapsed. But the wooden rafters here, protected from the weather by the heavy canopy of trees, were nearly all sound: more than a dozen 8-foot lengths, 6 inches by 2: ideal material, I saw at once, for the tree-house I had in mind. There were even a number of old nails which I picked up before realising that, in hammering them in, the noise could give me away. I needed twine, and there was none of that. Nor was there much else of use to me in the place apart from some broken lengths of old lead piping and a huge monkey-wrench, a kind of steel shillelagh. I put these potential weapons aside for possible future use.

Immediately beyond the shed the lake narrowed quickly to where the brook fed it from the north. Here the trees and undergrowth thinned, and the steep sides of the ravine gradually gave way to easier slopes which led out to more open, and thus to me more dangerous country. But I had to move into it. I had to see how the land lay, how far the safety of this valley went.

There was a rough path out of the beech trees to begin with, an old, hard deeply rutted cattle path which wound its way along by the stream through clumps of furze which gave me reasonable cover from the more thinly wooded hills above me on either side. After half a mile the stream narrowed, then became a broad, flat trickle filled with watercress, which finally spread out, losing itself in a delta of marshy ground which was its source. There were clumps of marigold and yellow iris here, a still, airless place, like a cavern, overhung by a semicircle of sheer limestone walls, the remains of an old quarry, it seemed. And there, running along the top of the quarry, was the great, ten-foot-high barbed-wire fence, the same that I'd crashed into on my first evening in the woods, here again, obviously circling the entire estate, making me a prisoner.

Retracing my steps, and then walking round onto the top of this limestone bluff, standing just inside the fence, I saw the long lengths of much more open pasture beyond, with sheep everywhere, some of them within a stone's throw of me, many with lambs, the great fields dotted with winter feeding troughs. A mile or two away to the north, down this long gentle slope, a car windscreen flashed in the slanting afternoon sun: there was a small by-road there leading to Chipping Norton. To my left, on a rise half a mile away, I could see what must have been the home farm at the back of the estate, some big dutch barns and a straggle of other farm buildings. This was the end of the hidden valley: the end of my world.

I came back round the other side of the quarry and here, shrouded in elder and blackthorn, I found a much older Cotswold stone barn, with the stump of a metal wind-pump next to it that had once drawn water up for the animals from the spring below. But now the whole place was unused, except for storing animal feed in winter, for there were several broken hay bales scattered about on the earth floor. And here I found any amount of strong red baler twine, along with a dozen or so yellow plastic fertiliser sacks, the discarded remains of some previous attentions to the big pasture beyond. I left the sacks where they were but took as much of the twine back with me as I could, stopping on the way to pick great bunches of watercress in the flat shallows of the stream, stuffing this salad into all my pockets.

Back at the lake, I looked along its margins for a boat. But I could see nothing. I hid near the island then, on the eastern side of the water, and gazed out at the roof of the little mausoleum. I waited till it was almost dark and fish had begun to jump in the long twilight, watching. But no one came. No barque, no mysterious passenger, set out on the still waters to comfort the dead. And yet I hadn't imagined the vase of fresh roses.

That evening I needed the watercress. The cheese and Ritz biscuits were gone and I ate it up like an animal, stuffing it into my mouth in great ham-fisted bunches. Yet when I'd finished it all I realised I was still starving. On the other hand the news on the radio was more encouraging: the police were definitely looking for me elsewhere now, in London, in Oxford. It was thought that I had managed to get a lift out of the Cotswolds that night. Car drivers travelling in the area at the time were being asked to report any such movement. The chase for the time being seemed to have passed over me.

I contemplated lighting the gas burner and cooking up some of the Knorr Spring Vegetable Soup in Spinks's billycan. But the light might have given me away and in any case the branches about me allowed no firm base for any such cuisine. I went hungry. And it was cold again too that night, even in Spinks's Army-surplus pullover and sleeping-bag, wrapped up like a cocoon in the hammock. But on the plus side, having left my few matches out, the box half opened – tied to a branch to dry in the sun for the past two days. I found they worked now. I had a cigarette, which was marvellous. I now had seventeen left. I counted the matches. There were only twelve of them.

And I thought, in the time it takes me to build a tree house, in order to make a firm base for the gas burner, in order to cook the soup, in order to survive, I may well have used up all the matches, tempted by the smokes, so that the gas would be no use to me in any case. Never mind, I thought for a moment: I can pop down the road to some local village shop and replenish these vital supplies.

And it was then that I realised that I hadn't yet faced up seriously to the problems of survival in the open at all, that I still viewed the whole business as something of a game. For, after all, even if I did risk going to any local shop, I remembered then that I had absolutely no money with me. I slept in a wind that came up that night – waking distractedly three or four times, hearing the branches rustle about like witches above me. What if it rained – a long spell of English summer rain? I'd pack it in then. I'd give myself up.

But it didn't rain. The hot sun was there again at daybreak and later on I found the tree I thought I needed – one of several very old oaks in the valley, with a big collar of twigs and leaves about twenty feet up its trunk which completely hid the centre of the tree, if anyone looked up into it directly from beneath. The foliage in any case was much more dense than that of the beech trees. And the branches, I could just see, were thicker and more numerous. It was a vast tree, almost in full leaf, set about five yards back from the water, a little below the island and ruined footbridge, in the southern end of the lake. The only problem was to climb it. From beneath that was obviously impossible.

After ten minutes moving about it, I saw the beech tree, on the steep sides of the valley above the oak, and noticed how its branches interlocked in places with the other tree. If I could climb the beech I might be able to cross onto the oak. And so it was. I found a long sloping limb on the beech tree, running down to within a few feet from the ground, near the top of the valley, which gave me ready access, like a gangway, up onto the main trunk of the tree. And from there, moving carefully out along one of its great central branches, I found that I could cross over onto the oak fairly easily getting into its middle, about thirty feet above the ground.

Right at the centre of the oak, higher up, the trunk splayed out, like an upturned hand, into half a dozen smaller limbs, forming just the kind of support I needed for the old rafters in the pumping-shed on the other side of the lake. It seemed ideal. I could see nothing of the outside world at all here. Yet by climbing upwards another fifteen feet or so, to where the branches thinned, I found I could peek out over the whole northern end of the lake – and by moving outwards horizontally along another thick branch lower down I found myself looking straight down into the smooth, coppery water forty feet beneath me.

With some lengths of baler twine attached to Spinks's canvas water carrier, and with a stone to weight it in the bottom, I could then lower it into the lake and ensure myself a constant supply of drinking-water without ever leaving the tree. With some long single strands of the same twine, attached to the nylon leader of one of Spinks's Woolworth fishing hooks and a worm, I might even have fish for my supper with no more inconvenience. With such thoughts, some hidden boy scout emerging in me, I forgot about the vase of roses in the little mausoleum on the island.

I built the tree house right in the heart of the green oak. It took me all of three days, pushing the rafters out one by one late that evening from the old pumping-shed and letting them drift down the lake in the current during the night, so that next morning they had all arrived by the island, lodged against its shores or caught in the ruined footbridge supports.

From there I hoisted them up into the tree with Spinks's nylon mountain rope, and fastened them securely with the baler twine, like floorboards, across the cradle of branches. I had to cut some of the smaller oak branches out of the way so that the rafters would fit, and prune some of the beams themselves as well. Spinks's flexible pocket saw made this a possible, if laborious, business. Later I'd set other planks or branches upright round this floor, tie the fertiliser sacks to them and build a roof, too. I'd make a proper house out of it all. Why not? For the thought had come to me even then: if this tree-house was successful, if I remained free, I'd somehow rescue Clare from wherever she'd been taken and bring her to live with me. I didn't think about how exactly I'd manage this. At the time, since things were going well, I took only the broad view. I was filled with mad optimism.

But for the moment at least, in actual fact, I had an almost flat space – about seven by five feet wide, where I could lay the sleeping bag out, where I could cook and eat and listen to the transistor in some comfort. The only trouble was that by the time I'd finished the house I'd nothing left to cook. The packet soup was all gone and I couldn't face another mouthful of watercress. I thought of mushrooms, but there weren't any: and nettle soup, but that appealed less than the cress. There were fat pigeons flying in and out of the trees. But how to catch them? I'd heard of setting out lime for the smaller birds. But where was the lime and how did you set it? There were the wild mallard, too, on the lake which I fancied. But I could never get to within fifty yards of them before they clattered away. I'd made some snares and put them along some of the rabbit paths. But the wire that I'd taken from an old fence by the quarry must have been too stiff or rusty. I'd tried to fish as well from the big branch:

tying long single strands of baler twine to Spinks's Woolworth leaders and hooks, with a piece of oak bark as a float, letting the line sink into the dark pool from my perch far above in the great tree. But I had no success. Perhaps the fish didn't fancy worms. The old cheddar would have been more to their taste, but that was long gone.

On the morning of my fifth day in the open I was literally starving. I'd sharpened the steel tips of the six arrows on the stone jetty meanwhile, and practised long hours with them against a rough target, the end of a fallen beech branch near the old pumping-shed. So I suppose I'd already taken the decision subconsciously, without admitting it yet. But I did then: there were all those lambs just beyond the rim of the quarry, so many that one, surely, would never be missed. I thought about it for a while. It was a risk and I was no butcher, though the various blades of Spinks's knife were sharp enough, I thought . . . All the same, how did you gut a sheep? Would you let the carcase hang for a bit, like a pheasant? And what about the blood? I didn't think about it any more then. But by late afternoon I was thinking about nothing else.

I'd never understood before how hunger could cause actual pain, an ache in the belly that spread everywhere else like a wasting disease. But I understood then. I took two of the sharpened arrows with the bow, as well as the knife, and climbed down the tree.

Passing the ruined footbridge and old boathouse, I moved up the western edge of the lake, back from the water, along the hidden paths I'd found there. There was only one danger spot – almost at the end of the lake, where some days before I'd found another path that led away from the lake at right angles, up a much gentler slope here, through the trees towards what must have been the back of the great house.

There was a big clump of flowering hawthorn here just before you reached this path, and I always stopped behind it, hiding in its cover for a minute, before crossing over the open space and going on up the valley. But there were no sounds that afternoon in the sunlight, no sign of any movement among the sloping trees to my left or on the path that ran through them. I moved from cover and I was several yards out into the clearing before I froze: there was a woman coming straight down the hill towards me now, only about a hundred yards away.

I don't know how she failed to see me. The hawthorn immediately behind me must have served as camouflage – or else she was just preoccupied, with a big bath-towel wrapped round her folded arms, held in front of her like a muff. I got back behind the bush again in an instant. But I could still see her through the flowering branches as she came nearer: not tall, but with a lot of wavy black hair that made her seem tall, rising well forward on her brow and combed straight back so that it looked like a helmet, glistening in the distance: a bouncing helmet, for she had a strange jaunty walk, putting little skips and steps into her pace, as though merry over something, wearing smartly cut cords and a blouse wide-open at the front for it was muggy hot down here by the water in the late afternoon heat.

Crouching down, I crawled into the hawthorn bush and, working my way gently round inside the cavern of branches, I got almost to the front of the tree where I could just see out the far side through the snowstorm of white twigs.

I saw the boat then, a little blunt-nosed fibreglass dinghy, which must have been hidden in the bank. Leading back from the lake at this point a rough clearing had been made in the long grass. And the woman was there, too, her back towards me now, less than fifty yards away, getting undressed. She must have been in her late thirties, not muscular, but compactly built, with a great neatness about her, the neatness of a young girl: not an inch spare or wasted in the body. I couldn't see her face, just her naked back, and this was unusual: a long slim back, very long, out of proportion with the rest, which splayed out dramatically just below her waist. She was deeply bronzed everywhere, without any strap marks. She was so sunburnt indeed, so dark-haired that I thought for a moment, irrationally, that she might be a Red Indian. She swam then, calmly, easily, yet with a kind of powerful athleticism – out into the equally bronzed water.

She swam for ten minutes or more, vigorously, up and down the lake, ducking her head right under now and then, kicking her legs back high in the air, diving deeply, only to emerge in a fountain of spray a few yards further on, vertically like a missile, shaking the water out of her eyes, the skein of dark hair twirling round her face now like a whip.

She swam like someone who had just discovered the trick, finding water a marvellous pleasure for the first time. Yet there was something spiteful, wilful in her pleasure, too – an unnecessary determination, as if she were challenging the liquid, wanting to fight it, punish it. She was bullying the water, that's what it was – as if taking out some great frustration on it.

I noticed, though, that she never went further than the island halfway down the lake, never swam on through the small channels on either side of it, down to my end of the water. This lower half of the lake, where I had my tree, she never visited. It was, indeed, invisible from the northern end where I was then hidden.

When she got out she lay flat on the great bath-towel for five minutes in the sun, letting the heat dry her, for she couldn't have wanted any more tan. She stood up at last and looked out over the lake into the trees on the other side, arms akimbo. I thought she was going to get dressed. But instead she did a curious thing: putting her hand to her mouth she let out a series of loud war whoops – yes, war whoops – letting her fingers fall rapidly on her lips like a drum. The surprising sounds spread over the water, echoing round the small valley. She stopped and listened intently, as if waiting for a reply – and I was petrified, fully expecting one. Then she did it again, in a slightly higher register, but more a question than a threat in the tone now.

I looked around wildly, peering through the branches of the bush to my left, first over to the far side of the lake, then right, looking up the steep side of the valley. And it was then that I saw the other woman – hidden, as I was, behind another clump of hawthorn, near the old pathway here that led up from the lake towards the house. She was a big woman, middle-aged, dressed in what looked like a white housekeeper's coat. Or was it a nurse's uniform? There was the sense of an overseer – a wardress almost – something powerful and malign in this huge woman as she stood dead still, a threat in the warm valley, observing the antics of the other younger girlish figure, standing by the water now, naked, bellowing and whooping like some lovely savage.

Finally she got dressed then and when she walked back up the path not far away from me – the other woman had vanished by now – I saw that she was smiling, an almost too radiant smile, like someone in a toothpaste advertisement.

I forgot my hunger, watching her disappear in the distance up the path. War whoops and that bronzed skin – *was* she a Red

Indian? I began to doubt my senses, before I remembered the actual timbre of her whoops, sharp, light, a tremulous excitement in the tone, a voice that cut through the muggy afternoon air like a romantic announcement. Was it this woman, then, who had brought the roses to the long-dead pair on the island? It seemed very possible. Yet could she be forty, middle-aged? Her acts were more those of a child or some dream-filled adolescent girl. Or was she just a madwoman, simply deranged, someone from the big house, a relation, a visitor, a servant?

But then I realised suddenly how nothing she had done was actually mad at all. Working too long in the pretentious school, among dull or frightened people, in a country that had lost all its confidence in sharp personality or adventure, I had come to think of such behaviour as extreme, whereas the spirit of fun and energy which she had expressed just now was in fact quite natural. It was I who had gone sour, hemmed in by too many formalities and compromises. And it was I who was mad now, if anyone was, I who had gone to such unlikely extremes, up in my oak tree, running away from the world, almost a crazed hermit already. So that after the woman disappeared, I longed to throw it all in, to follow her – up the path back into civilisation. Instead, an hour later, I was up on the rim of the old quarry, behind the barbed-wire fence, wondering how I might kill a sheep: or a lamb.

But even if the fence had not been in my way the sun was in my eyes, slanting down across the long green fields from the west, and the animals were much too far from me in any case, way out of bowshot. I thought of waiting till dark, climbing the fence somehow and then taking the sheep by surprise, storming them, wrestling with one of them before cutting its throat. But despite my hunger this idea didn't appeal.

I began to wonder about the vegetable garden behind the great house. I'd seen this more clearly the previous day through Spinks's binoculars, from near the top of the beech tree that gave me access to my oak, from a spot very high up in its branches that I'd made over into a look-out post, which gave me a good view from the top of the valley right over most of the parkland, together with the side of the house where the great conservatory was and all the yard buildings behind. The kitchen garden, I could see, surrounded by a large redbrick wall, was the last stonework attached to these out-buildings. Beyond it was an orchard and then the thick cover of beech trees. The path down to the lake, which the woman had taken, obviously ran through this orchard and then into, or near to, the vegetable garden. It was worth the risk; there might be some early carrots or late cabbage. Even an old onion would do. Anything would be better than the watercress or cutting a sheep's throat.

The moon was less of a scimitar and more of a bright gas globe at about twelve o'clock that night. But there were clouds too, now and then, which suddenly darkened the sky, when I had to stop completely or grope my way forward along the path up from the lake. However, by the time I'd come to the end of the orchard and saw the garden wall rearing up immediately ahead of me, there was a long cloudless spell and I could see as much as I needed. There was a door in the wall here. I waited behind it, listening, for five minutes. A dog was what I feared, or worse, some electrical device, a burglar alarm set against all the precious pictures, even this far away from the house. But there was no sound. A totally still, white, early June night. I lifted the latch and pushed. Inside I found myself not in the garden but in a long greenhouse, sloped against the wall on the other side. Small tomato plants were tied with string to overhead wires down almost the entire length and there were trestle tables next the wall crowded with petalled shrubs and flower pots. The moon shone down directly through the glass. At the far end was a workbench piled with trugs, with a stack of garden implements to one side, very old garden tools by the look of them. There was a faint smell of iodine and some booklets on the bench. I picked one up. It was a seed catalogue. Suttons. I could just see the name on the cover. But this must have been pretty old, too, for the paper was thin and dry, crumbling in my fingers. But there was nothing I could see anywhere to eat. Leaving the greenhouse I moved up a path next the garden wall. Again I could see nothing on the beds. It was too early in the year, I realised, and I certainly couldn't risk digging about, pulling things up.

I saw the figure then, in some sort of slouch hat and long, old-fashioned coat to my right, arms wide, suddenly menacing me. And there was a second's blind terror before I saw it for the scarecrow that it was. It got me out of the garden, though, sooner than I intended. There was nothing here for me in any case. It was just the wrong season.

Since the moonlight was still good when I left the garden, I decided to move along the outside of the wall, through the end of the orchard, and take a closer look at the house itself. A hundred yards further on there was a thick beech hedge and beyond that, as I'd seen from my look-out post, the pleasure gardens which ran down in a series of grass terraces from the great conservatory.

As soon as I'd pushed through this hedge I saw the strange spotlights piercing the dark fronds in the conservatory again. I was much closer to them now, of course. But still, since the pleasure-garden rose above me here in a series of shallow herbaceous borders, I couldn't see anything or anyone beneath, at ground level in the glasshouse: just the hidden lights again, moving gently to and fro, caressing the greenery inside. I was drawn to them like a moth.

Keeping close against the rising beech hedge, I moved slowly up one side of the pleasure-garden until I reached the castellated stone balustrades which surrounded the house. There was a gravel walk behind this and then the conservatory itself, less than ten yards away. Peering through an arch in the balustrade now I could see right inside the glass building at last. And I saw the woman then, a moment later: the Red Indian woman by the lake.

The space beneath the exotic shrubs and trees had been empty at first, before she had moved into it from the shadows, moved into the light, carrying a silver goblet in one hand, talking over her shoulder to someone apparently right behind her.

Her face was lit then, with almost theatrical effect, as she stood for several moments in one of the hidden spotlights: a startlingly white face in the brightness. Or perhaps she was made up. The narrow, perfectly arched eyebrows seemed too good to be true, while her wavy dark hair was precisely parted in the middle, no longer a helmet against the sun but a discreet Victorian-style cowl, set carefully out over her temples, just touching her high cheekbones. She had changed: no longer the carefree outdoor girl by the lake, she seemed involved now in something contrived, even forced. Her face showed the strain: the huge smile by the lake was long gone. She wore what looked like a sort of Camelot outfit: a long, loose-fitting flimsy white dress with brightly patterned Etruscan borders, held tight, right up beneath her breasts and flowing out from there in folds of silken sheen. Her lips moved. She was still speaking, though no one had yet joined her. She turned then, swirling round in her thin dress, to greet someone at last as I thought. But instead she simply gazed up at the lights wandering about in the air above her.

A classic Italianate fountain played in the background and just beyond that was a tall slim tree which rose up almost to the roof of the conservatory, a mimosa I thought, whose branches cascaded out in long feathery streamers. Wire baskets fell from the roof, little aerial gardens trailing long green anchors beneath them, while the walls were smothered in creeper. The whole place was a delicate jungle of blooms, with a minstrel's gallery to top it all, jutting out from what would have been the first storey of the house, a sort of Juliet balcony with slim Gothic pillars set high above all the other natural effects.

The woman moved to a table to one side of the conservatory, which I hadn't seen, where a meal of some sort had been laid out. She lifted a heavy gilt platter. My attention was painful now, the more so when she took a chicken leg from it and, moving back towards me, started to pick at it fastidiously.

I was so taken with this, imagining the taste, salivating, that I still didn't see the discrepancy: that though she had continued talking, no one had yet joined her. She was talking to herself. The conservatory was empty. And it was only then that I recognised something eerie in the whole tableau: the woman's pre-Raphaelite dress, hairstyle and appearance, the old goblets and platters: her general performance. For performance it must have been, I thought, just like the war-whoops by the lake, for herself alone, in the empty glass hall: a courtly picture, against this backdrop of Gothic stone and glass, here brought to actual life with medieval props and dresses.

An act? Perhaps she had an audience somewhere behind her which I couldn't see. Was there a house party, a late night of amateur theatricals in progress? If not, then she must be mad, I thought. Or was I still being too quick, too shallow in my judgement? Was there some other rational explanation?

There was. The coarse-featured man moved into the light a moment later, dressed in a dark business suit, a drink in his hand, but held in an ordinary glass this time, not a handsome silver goblet: in every way a complete, even an appalling, contrast to all the woman's lovely airs and graces: a tall, long-faced almost elderly man; dank tufts of hair carefully tended over his broad collar, American smart, expensively dressed, attentive. But the care in his expression was for himself, I thought, not for others. The face was carefully composed so that it would give nothing away; it was essentially sour, grasping.

The woman must have been talking all the time to him, I realised then, where he had been invisible to me, hidden somewhere at the back of the conservatory. They were together now, though, facing each other. She was telling him something, speaking at some length. He was listening, nodding from time to time, as though engrossed. But when she stopped talking he said nothing in reply, just stared at her for a long moment before turning quickly and walking away. And this last expression of his stayed with me, as it must have done for the woman: a look of hatred, of wordless, contemptuous dismissal.

Six

If I'd not been so hungry the following morning I'd have thought more about the events of the previous night. As it was, other than assuming that the two people in the conservatory were the American couple who owned Beechwood Manor, I thought of nothing but food. I still had a few spoonfuls left of Spinks's Green Label tea and I was able to brew up one of these in the billycan for breakfast. There was some old cress left, too, and I forced myself to eat it, only to feel an even worse hunger afterwards. I realised I had to find something substantial to eat that day, or give myself up. But what? And where? It was obvious I had no talent for living wild. It had all been in the mind.

I went back into the sleeping-bag when I'd had the tea and lay there like someone in a famine photograph, knees up in stomach, dead still, eyes wide open but unseeing. I was aware of the sun, though, bright again, filtering through the leaves. But there was a sharp wind as well, blowing from the west, coming in long gusts, rattling the top of the old oak like a storm at sea, and I imagined a change in the summer, a spell of rough weather approaching this calm centre of England, rushing up the Bristol Channel at that moment, bringing rain, which would soon catch me, drench me. I'd pack it in then...

But it didn't rain. I listened to the news on the transistor which never mentioned me now, and the weather forecast, which talked of high pressure away to the north by Iceland, but with bad weather doing battle with it, a depression moving in from the Azores. The man thought the rain would win, but not until tomorrow. I had another day to fill before I could use climate as an excuse for throwing in the towel.

Today was Saturday. I'd been a week in the valley. The world outside had become like home when one is in an ugly foreign country. After the news there was news of sport: football in Italy, tennis at the Queen's Club, cricket in Nottingham, seventy miles away, against the West Indians, events as distant to me now as things passing on the other side of the world. I felt a touch of shocking loneliness then, of self-pity, which overcame me almost to the point of tears, like a great luxury; a warm, pathetic feeling. But even that didn't last; the hunger was a sharper pain. I lit a cigarette and saw that my hands were shaking. I thought the tobacco would dull the starvation; instead it only made me feel sick. I put it out.

I had three and a half cigarettes left – but only three matches. There was always the small magnifying glass attached to Spinks's scouting knife. But that would need strong, direct sunlight, and there was little of that in the valley, except on the water and out on the island, away from the overhanging trees. Should I move to the island, as an answer to my hunger as well? For, perhaps, since the woman had brought roses to the old tombs there, she might, like the other Indians in their religion (or was it the Chinese?) come to leave bowls of milk out there, and sweetmeats too...

Such wild thoughts came and went, the result of a mild delirium, as I dozed the morning fitfully away in a green limbo, the tree shuddering in the wind. I hadn't even the energy to dream when I finally slept.

But a little after twelve o'clock I stirred myself. If I was to get some food, it was now or never. Soon I'd be too weak to get up or down the tree. I climbed the tall beech first, next my oak, going up to the look-out post I'd made there, which gave over the parkland and the side of the manor. I went up because I'd heard a hammering noise faintly through the trees, and the thump of an engine droning from the same direction.

I could see now, even without Spinks's glasses, what was going on: Saturday. They were preparing the cricket pitch, near the bottom of the parkland, about half a mile away from the house: hammering boundary pegs in while a gang-mower moved slowly round the outfield. Some local team must have used the place at weekends. There was only one man that I could see, on the mower, with a car parked near the curiously thatched, log-built pavilion.

Then, looking more carefully through the binoculars, I saw a woman leaning into the back seat of a car. She emerged holding a big covered tray, taking it into the pavilion. She returned for a second tray a minute later – and then some cake tins and a big carton. I could just make out the legend on the side: 'Walker's Crisps.' Crisps and cakes and sandwiches no doubt – for the cricketers' tea. But for me as well, me too . . .

My spirits leapt like a child's. The man finished cutting the outfield and five minutes after that he left with the woman in the car, driving away from me, along the side of the cricket field and out onto what must have been a back drive into the estate. It was lunchtime. Just after one o'clock. The match wouldn't start until 2.30 perhaps. No one would be there for another half hour or so. If I was quick, if I was lucky . . .

I'd seen part of a field of young corn immediately to the left of the cricket pitch, beyond a post-and-rail fence which formed the boundary. The corn wasn't high. But it was deep enough to duck down and hide in, I thought, if anyone appeared while I was in the open moving towards the pavilion. And if I followed this fence, it led directly behind the strange building.

Ten minutes later I had left the steep side of the valley, moved down through the cover of the beech wood, and was out on the edge of the cornfield. The pavilion was on the other side, a few hundred yards away, with the wooden fence for cover as well, if I could get safely across the field to it.

I did, and after that it was relatively easy, skirting along, with my head well down behind the fence, until I got in behind the back of the pavilion. There was a door here, next some rough latrines, which led through into a small open kitchen with a circular counter beyond. The trays were on top of it, covered in tea-towels, together with the cake tins and the crisps. When I lifted the towels my hand was shaking again.

And then the sandwiches were suddenly there, like a stupendous conjuring trick. They struck me with the greedy force of some great restaurant display; moist, luscious, neatly cut, lightly buttered, in brown and white bread with all the crusts removed. There was ham; there was beetroot and grated cheese; there was egg; there was egg and tomato; there were some with a sort of spam filling which I didn't fancy and others just filled with plain watercress which I left entirely aside.

I gobbled one up there and then, unable to resist it, like a madman, scattering crumbs on the floor which I had to clear up. But from then on I was more careful. I took eight half-rounds from the two trays, carefully rearranging the rest so that the gaps wouldn't show. I looked in the cake tins then: one was filled with flour-dusted scones, the next with raspberry-jam and lemon-curd tarts, the last with small, fluffy cream cakes. I took a careful selection from all three tins. There was a big plastic bag filled with sausage rolls. I took four of these, stuffing the lot into every pocket. The big carton of crisps hadn't been opened so I had to leave them.

I looked round the rest of the cricket pavilion. There was a nice smell of linseed oil and leather and old grass in the air. The main room beyond the kitchen was lined with trestle tables covered in red check cloths; old team photographs ringed the rough log walls. Though so quintessentially English in purpose, the place had somehow the air of a Swiss mountain chalet. There was a small bar at one end, with soft drinks and tins of shandy on shelves behind. I tiptoed across the room and pinched a bottle of lemonade. And then, on my way out through the kitchen I saw the box of matches by the Calor-gas ring, where they boiled up a great urn for the tea. I took the matches, too. The box was nearly full. I was saved.

And yet, I thought – a last whiff of leather and old linseed oil in my nose – I thought how much I'd like to have stayed on that afternoon and had a game of cricket. But as I left through the back door I saw my face in a mirror by the gents for a moment: there was the scar across my forehead which I'd forgotten. And I had a beard now, which I hadn't seen before, a nasty half-growth about the jowls. My hair, since I'd no comb with me, was a dirty, tangled mess, while my rust-green cord suit was caked in streaks of different-coloured mud. The idea of my playing cricket seemed suddenly laughable then. I was a world away from those smart, crisp white clothes. But I didn't laugh. Instead, I realised it was no fun at all being a savage.

I managed to watch the cricket, though, for most of the sunny afternoon, up in the top of the beech tree in my look-out post, a bottle of pop in one hand and a succession of sandwiches and squelchy cream cakes in the other. It wasn't a bad match either. One of the teams, the visiting team I thought, had several West Indian players, and one of these, a small, wiry, afro-haired fellow, clouted the ball repeatedly for fours and sixes over the boundary, straight driving them in huge arcs into the cornfield.

I played his game for him, vicariously, enjoying it all more than anything since I'd arrived in the valley. A few huge plum-bruised clouds ran in over the ground after tea, and the wind increased, with a slight chill in it now. But still it didn't rain. Instead, great slanting shafts of sun pierced the tumbling clouds, apocalypse-fashion, brilliant beams low in the west, spotlighting odd parts of the parkland, setting the small white figures on fire. And I was happy again, seeing the match out, and happier still that I was fed at last, with energy once more to think, to move, to plan a future.

I lit a cigarette when I'd finished half the food, keeping the rest for later. The sickness was quite gone now. I drained the lemonade bottle. It was like school, years before: behind the cricket pavilion taking a quick drag before first prep. Then I saw the flash of light, where the late sun had caught something moving in front of the manor away to my right.

Training Spinks's glasses on the building I saw that a huge Mercedes had just drawn up in front of the house. A man in a chauffeur's cap got out of the car and a minute later he was carrying luggage, several heavy suitcases, down the porch steps. Finally the well dressed, dank-haired, middle-aged man that I'd seen in the conservatory appeared. There was no one with him as he hurried with a briefcase into the back seat. Then the car was gone, the dust rising, as the great hearse-like vehicle sped down the front drive away from me. And now I thought about this man and the woman and what had passed between them the previous night.

The food, at last, had revived my interest in such things. And yet, after a few initial points had struck me, I realised there wasn't all that much to think about them. The woman wasn't mad – just high-spirited, immature perhaps, with something of the actress in her, remembering her sudden change from merry outdoor girl to sorrowing pre-Raphaelite maiden. The man – her husband I presumed, the American business magnate – had appeared wary, world-weary and perhaps he was cruel. Certainly it was obvious they weren't getting on together. He had just left, as a result of their row maybe, with sufficient baggage to suggest a prolonged absence. What more was there to say? Even the very rich had their domestic agonies.

But then it struck me, a wild, faint thought: perhaps, where he had failed, I might succeed. I put it out of my mind at once, watching the end of the cricket.

But later that night, as I leant over the darkening waters of the lake from my oak branch, some bread paste and cheese instead of worms on two of Spinks's Woolworth hooks, I thought about it all again. The wind had dropped completely. Bats whipped about above the water; there were flies and midges up in the tree and the fish were moving, jumping, splashing in the deep silences beneath me. I had time to think. And I realised then that, if I was ever properly to make use of my freedom in these woods, to get Clare back, to clear myself, to take the various sorts of revenge I had in mind, I would have to have some help. I couldn't do what I wanted all on my own. And what better help, perhaps, than that of a high-spirited, immature, theatrical woman?

If I continued as I was, without moving from the valley, I could only arrive at a dead end. At best I might survive till the bad weather came in the autumn. But meanwhile, on my own unaided, I could never break out of this fenced prison and do something constructive: or destructive. I had no money, no shaving gear, my clothes were filthy, my hair appalling: I looked like a savage. Even if no one was looking for me, I'd be noticed at once in any local town or village, bus or train. However successfully I managed to survive in these woods, I was stuck in them. And it was not my purpose just to survive: I had ambitions... That was why I'd run in the first place: in order to fulfil them. And if I never made the effort to fulfil them, well then, I might as well give myself up now. Yet I couldn't achieve them, I saw, without help. Thus all these factors in the equation led to a neat answer: if, in some fashion, I managed to persuade the woman to help me, and she refused, then I had really lost nothing – for without such help I had no future. She would phone the police and that would be that. If on the other hand she agreed to help . . .

I smiled then. It was so unlikely: an American woman, living abroad, perhaps quite alone in the great empty house now, surrounded by priceless paintings. She'd be terrified out of her wits in any confrontation with me, a bearded wife-killer, as she would probably have heard, from the manor woods. Besides, how would I meet her? The house would have servants, alarms, perhaps a permanent security staff. But then I realised that meeting her might be simple enough. I had only to wait behind the hawthorn bush when next she came down to swim, or better still, surprise her when she came out to the island again, where she could not so easily escape, when she next brought her grave gifts. The roses would have faded by now. She might come soon.

I had some hope then, and more still when, later that evening, just before real dark, I caught a fish: a perch, I thought, nearly a foot long, as I looked at it squirming in my hand after I'd pulled it up, its scales still reflecting a little silver in the last of the light. It had run and tugged excitingly in the water beneath me, but the strands of baler twine had held. And having got it up in the branches successfully I felt for a moment that I could now live in these woods for ever.

But cooking it next morning for breakfast wasn't so easy. In the end I had to chop the fish up with Spinks's knife and poach the bits in the billy can, where in the end they disintegrated on the surface without being properly cooked inside. But it still tasted of fish, and I had the floury scones to go with it. All I needed was some lemon. I was living again, I thought. Yet I needed a proper cooking-pan, I realised – and I needed to lay in more food now that I was fit and eager enough to try and get it. I thought of the sheep again, or rather the lambs, though I avoided that precise description of them in my mind.

I'd swum then, in the hidden pool at the bottom of the lake, cleaning myself as best I could. The wind had gone entirely now. The day looked like being sultry and oppressive. There was thunder in the air, I thought. I practised with the bow and six arrows afterwards, taking them over to the undergrowth on the slopes above the old pumping-shed. I didn't shoot for long. I had neither a bracer nor finger-tabs, so that the loosed string hurt the inside of my bow-arm after a dozen shots. But it was long enough for me to see that my aim had deteriorated in the past few days, when I hadn't practised and hadn't eaten. The arrows were nearly all short, dropping low beneath the target. I wasn't strong enough to make a full draw and maintain it, quite still, for those few vital moments. I was still too weak. I'd had plenty of carbohydrates with the sandwiches and cakes. But I needed protein now. I needed some meat.

A squirrel appeared as I was shooting, a quizzical little animal, flat out against the trunk of a beech behind me, about thirty feet up. I was about to test a shot at it when I noticed, above it, two other baby squirrels, running up and down like toys along another branch. I didn't fancy shooting the animal then, possibly the mother, so I left it, frustrated. And then I thought: if I wasn't prepared to shoot a squirrel, how was I ever going to kill a lamb? And, given this squeamishness, what did I really think I was going to do with David Marcus? Kill him too? It seemed an unlikely idea, in truth, even if I ever got the chance. I saw then that I was entirely unfitted for killing, unless, I suppose, my own life was at stake. But wasn't it now? Without food, one died.

I set out, up to the top of the lake and then on to the old quarry beyond, considering my inabilities. There was a strong smell of cow-parsley or elderflower, both come to rampant bloom now in the hedgerows along the cattle-path that led out of the valley a strong yet delicate, slightly tangy smell somehow, hanging everywhere in the silent, heavy air. The thunder rumbled in the distance, but a closer distance now.

I supposed one could stew up cow-parsley, make a sort of soup out of it? Though possibly, through boiling, it became poisonous? It was bound to be pretty unpalatable in any case, worse than the cress. There was the elderflower, of course: I knew you could make elderflower wine. Laura, in fact, had been planning to make some later that spring, from the crowd of old elder bushes that ran along one side of our garden...

And then, quite suddenly, as if touched by some violent hand out of the air, the sense of being able to kill came back to me, came like a physical thing, so that I could feel the muscles contracting all about my body. And I could have killed anything, man or beast, there and then, had it appeared at that moment.

I hadn't thought about Laura recently. I'd kept her out of my mind on purpose; it was too painful. And my hunger in any case had made me think about nothing else but food. But then, thinking of the elderflower wine she might have made, thoughts of her broke through me like water smashing a dam, and the bitterness and enmity filled me again, as it had at the beginning, a frightful, uncontrollable violence which made me shake almost as I stood in the path, the thunder above me now, the first raindrops falling.

By the time I got to the top of the old quarry by the barbed wire fence the rain was pouring down in long straight rods, the drops so close together it was like a solid grey curtain, the clouds massing low down in huge folds of dark velvet all over the long pasture running away to the north. And I was in luck: it was almost too easy. Half a dozen of the lambs had somehow pushed their way through the fence from the pasture and were flocked together in one corner of the field, near the old stone barn. I drove them through the open doorway, where once inside and trapped they began to panic, terrified, bleating above the thunder which crashed about us immediately overhead, the rain falling like pebbles on the broken slates. I herded the lambs into a corner of the old barn, where they pushed and shoved madly to and fro, a great mass of wool, their coats smoking in the damp air. I could have killed as many as I wanted, I thought at first.

I chose the fattest of the lambs and, raising the bow, aimed for its neck. The arrow struck home all right: in fact it transfixed the beast, going right through its neck, without apparently doing it any other harm. It charged up and down in the corner of the barn, shaking its head wildly, rising up on its hind legs and dancing for moments, trying to rid itself of the arrow, pawing the air in a frenzy. And it was difficult to get in a second shot as the other beasts stampeded round me, escaping back out into the storm. I was left alone with the single wounded lamb.

Now the panic spread to me, as I didn't know what to do to stop the animal's pain. I loosed another arrow but it missed entirely. Finally I rushed the lamb, caught it, straddled it and tried to cut its throat with Spinks's knife. But this didn't have any effect either: the blade wasn't sharp enough or the fur was too thick. Or both.

The lamb started to career around the barn with me on its back like a rodeo rider. Finally it threw me and made for the door. If it escaped away into the pasture or back towards the Manor with an arrow through its neck I was done for. So I dived after it, just catching it as it ran outside by a back leg.

In the end I stoned it to death, hitting its skull again and again, smashing the life out of it, without looking at it, as the rain drenched us both in the doorway of the barn. After five minutes I had a dead lamb in front of me, bleeding, cut about, which I never wanted to see or think of again, let alone eat. Yet I couldn't leave it there, and there was no point now in throwing it away and hiding it. So, with even more distaste, I had to consider how to chop its head off, bleed it, gut it . . .

I found another stone at last, a loose Cotswold stone with a fairly sharp edge along one side; it served its purpose, with a second stone as a chopping block beneath. The head came off. I tried to hack the legs off as well, but with less success. The gutting was even more difficult. Again, though I managed to open part of its stomach, I couldn't get any of the woolly skin off. The knife wasn't sharp enough. I hung the animal up with some baler twine on one of the beams and let it bleed for ten minutes or so while I sharpened Spinks's knife.

In the end, even though I got the blade pretty sharp, I made a fearful mess of the butchering. When I'd finished the beast looked as if it had been mutilated, torn and stabbed about by a madman. All the same, I had managed to roughly skin and gut it and the blood was washing away now in the doorway as the rain fell less heavily and the storm passed on. I wrapped the entrails in the wool coat and stuck my hands out the door, letting the rain wash the blood away. The carcase lay in the mud behind me. I held that out to wash it in the rain as well. But my arms were so weak I had to let it drop after a moment.

I put the skin and guts to carry away in one of the old fertiliser sacks and tied the rest of the sloppy, still-warm animal round my waist with baler twine. The storm had cleared now. But the land was waterlogged outside. And down by the source of the brook, as I went back, the marshy ground smoked, risen in a small flood, so that I was up to my ankles in running water as I walked through it. I was soaked again. But halfway to the lake the sun returned suddenly and warmed my back, and the horror of the last half-hour faded. Indeed, by the time I got back to the lake, I had so successfully put it out of my mind that the violence appeared the act of someone else, not me.

It wasn't until the next morning, when I inspected the carcase, hanging from another branch in my oak, that my feelings changed again: the fatty, bruised blue colour of a butcher's-shop lamb was beginning to form on the inner skin as it dangled, as if from a meat rail, by its back legs. I had a sense of strange achievement then, of having unearthed some long-forgotten, essential gift in myself. Unpleasant the killing may have been – but necessary: yes, necessary, I reminded myself. I had killed for food after all, for survival. I would eat the beast. And yet, at heart, I knew I was lying to myself, was secretly disgusted by the whole business. I would never kill another animal in such a way, I thought. And from then on I kept a continual eye open for the woman from the manor. Much as I had come to dislike the world outside, I was going to have to save myself and ensure my future through some other more civilised means.

The weather was cool and showery for the next few days, and the woman didn't come down to swim, though I kept a sharp look-out for her each afternoon from the top of my oak tree. The bunch of roses had quite faded out on the island. She had not returned there. Perhaps, after the disagreement with her husband, she'd gone away herself.

I kept a watch on the house, too, twice a day, from my look-out post on top of the beech tree. But again there was no sign of the woman anywhere. Indeed, for such a big place, there was a strange lack of activity about the manor, even when I looked over it carefully with the binoculars. It seemed almost deserted. No one came and no one left in the hour or so, each morning and afternoon, that I kept an eye on it.

There was a gardener, I saw, quite an old man with a younger colleague, at work in the vegetable beds to one side of the kitchen garden. They seemed to work very slowly and conscientiously, with a rake and a hoe and an old-fashioned high-sided wooden wheelbarrow. They repaired the wire netting over a clump of blackcurrant bushes and laid out strawberry nets and refurbished the scarecrow, which I could see now wore what looked like a Victorian frock coat together with a stovepipe hat. Surely it had a slouch hat of some sort the other night? There seemed to be a lot of dressing up of one sort or another going on up in the Manor.

The younger gardener mowed all the front lawns and grass terraces one morning, including a croquet court at the bottom of the terraces with a little wooden summerhouse at the end of it. He fixed the hoops and sticks out on it afterwards. But no one played on it, then or the next day. There were no animals about the place that I could see. No one except the two gardeners appeared anywhere in the open, and the lights didn't come on again at night in the conservatory. The whole place, both Manor and estate, had an air of life suspended now. The great Gothic pile brooded over the parkland, impervious, empty. And in the evening, when the light sank in the west and the troubled, showery skies let great washed beams of sun suddenly flow over the manor, the brick took on a fairytale aspect again, but this time more powerfully when, from the height of the tall tree, I could see the whole house now, its slim turrets and long chimneys dark pencil-strokes against the rain-bright sunsets. There was an air of sheer enchantment about it then. But the woman must have migrated, gone south for the summer, or to London, or perhaps back to America. I was disappointed.

I let the lamb hang for several days before I cooked it, living on the stale remains of the cricketers' tea meanwhile. I'd decided in advance to roast the animal whole, if I could, in the old pumping-shed. And I managed to build this up with a collection of stones and a few bricks, making a kind of three-sided barbecue pit hidden at the back of the shed. I skewered the carcase right through, with a steel fencing-post that I'd found, and placed this across the top of the stones, bending one end into a vague handle so that I could turn the meat as it cooked. There was plenty of dry wood about; that was no problem.

I prepared this grill throughout the evening and waited until it was quite dark before lighting it, so that the smoke wouldn't show. The flames would be invisible in any case, hidden by the shed. Some of the dry branches crackled to begin with, that was my only fear. But once the fire settled down there was hardly any sound. And soon the bigger logs began to glow, red at first, and then with an almost white heat, and the stones got very hot and the carcase sizzled, the fat spattering in the brilliant embers, the meat blistering, then darkening as I turned the spit.

It took almost three hours to cook properly. But in the

meantime I cut little slivers off to test it and soon had a meal going out of the tit-bits, sharpening my hunger as the night wore on. These nutty little *hors d'oeuvres* were magnificent. And at the end, when I'd taken the whole carcase off the fire and let it cool, I rather gorged on it, demolishing nearly half a whole leg down to the bone. It was very good indeed, burnt on the outside, tender as a melon in the middle, juicy.

Afterwards I dismantled the brick walls and scattered all the ashes and slept nearby, along one side of the old engine, the meaty, woodsmoke smell all over my skin and my lips tasting long afterwards of cinders and burnt fat. I slept warm, content, replete, the sleep of the just. I slept well, except for the dream in the early morning, when I dozed in and out of sleep, turning on the fire-warmed earth.

I dreamt of a sardine barbecue, on top of one of Lisbon's windy hills, in the graveyard outside the Anglican church of St George. I had experienced just such a barbecue nearly a year before when I'd first met Laura and Clare out there. But now, in my sleep, neither of them was present. It was a summer party of complete strangers. I could hear the ferry klaxons out in the bay, honking and moaning, but much louder than they would have done in fact. I asked someone why they were so loud, so continuous. 'The King has died,' the stranger said. 'They are carrying him here. He will be buried here in a moment.'

'What King?' I asked in surprise. 'There's no king now in Portugal.' But the man had hurried away, leaving me isolated, alone. The barbecue party broke up then and the guests all formed two long ranks on either side of the graveyard. And beyond them, in the distance, I saw a procession heading up the hill towards me. They were carrying nothing, no coffin, no cross. Yet they were all dressed formally, in black frock coats and tall stovepipe hats...

I saw they were heading straight towards me, these grim mourners, that I was standing right in their path between the two rows of barbecue guests, who had all bowed their heads now, their earlier merriment quite forgotten. I moved to join them to hide myself. But of course I discovered that I couldn't move. My feet were stuck, rooted to the ground. I struggled to free them. But it was useless. And I knew with certainty then, without looking round, that there was a great freshly dug grave right behind me that had not been there before, which had mysteriously opened up for me just at that moment.

The dream annoyed me for a long time when I woke, even after I'd brought the rest of the lamb back to my tree and come down again to swim in the calm of the hidden pool at the end of the lake. It struck me as some kind of symbol of failure in my life here in the woods, or of some vast egoism within me, for where had Clare and Laura been in the dream, both so much part of that Portuguese landscape in reality? Had they ceased to exist, even in my unconscious? And was the open grave my punishment for that?

I'd stopped thinking about Laura because of the pain that brought. But I hadn't thought of Clare, I realised now, because I'd left her, betrayed her, had pushed her into the arms of a stranger to save my own skin. I'd no idea where she was. And so, indeed, I'd not cared to think about her. For she must have been in some home or institution for disturbed children now, and that made it worse.

I saw the cruel folly of my behaviour then, as far as Clare was concerned at least. And as I swam I very nearly got out of the water there and then to give myself up. How could I have left this already disturbed child, my daughter in all but blood, to the mercies of some institution? Now that I was properly fed at last, rested, fit and clean, I saw the full horror of my situation: a dead wife and a child that I had inexcusably deserted. I would have to start making amends that very day. This time I would definitely give myself up.

It was then that I'd seen the man in the early morning sunlight, dressed in a gamekeeper's outfit, with a gun and an Alsatian, on the other side of the lake, coming out of the undergrowth up by the ruined footbridge. He'd raised the shotgun, making a pass with it in the air; then he'd levelled it straight in my direction.

Of course, as I have already explained here, the man was Ross; Ross, the grave-faced, dirty tricks specialist once attached to our section in Mid-East Intelligence; Ross, one of Marcus's hit-men, who, on some hunch perhaps, had come to this hidden valley to search me out. And from then on that bright morning, I stopped thinking of Clare and Laura again and thought only of myself, as I ran from Ross and his great dog, up and about the lake, until, having killed his dog, he came to trap me behind the old pumping-shed, where I had no escape. I moved from the useless cover of the laurel bushes then, the dead beast at my feet, drew the arrow on the corner of the shed where I expected him to appear at any moment, and waited.

But he never appeared. I thought perhaps he'd smell the remnants of the cooking fat inside the shed. His dog certainly would have done. But Ross moved on, past the other side of the building, whistling softly, calling out for the animal.

'Karen?' I heard his voice clearly. 'Karen?' The tone was fainter now in the still air as he moved away, up towards the brook where it came into the lake, and on up the valley towards the old quarry after that, I supposed. I gave him fifteen minutes before I dumped the big Alsatian into the covered well behind the shed, leaving one of the metal covers off, so that when Ross or his colleagues returned to look for the dog, and if they ever found it, they would assume that it had had an accident, had been drowned, running headlong into the watery pit.

The well was deep in any case. The water level didn't start until more than six feet down. They might never find the beast. I was pleased once more, rubbing any fingerprints I might have left off the metal cover with handfuls of dry leaves; pleased that I'd survived again, given Ross the slip and killed his fearsome dog, too. Yes, I was pleased with killing again. Perhaps I'd found a taste for it which I didn't want to admit. But in any case, I thought with some pride, I was really learning to live in the wilds at last. I had beaten the system.

I tidied up the ground around the well, throwing leaves about and brushing away the remains of the dog's blood from my shoulder. And then suddenly, without any clothes on, having escaped from Ross straight away from the bathing pool an hour before, I was cold in this dank, shaded spot by the laurels next the well. I shivered, before turning quickly to get out into the sun again, back to my tree. And when I turned I saw the woman, watching me from the sunlit space where I'd expected Ross to appear, by the corner of the shed.

It was the woman from the Manor. She looked much taller, close to, dressed as the outdoor girl once more, in an open shirt and cords, with her long dark hair running straight back over her head. And I could see her thin, finely arched eyebrows clearly now; they weren't made up. She looked at me solemnly, as she must have been doing for some time while my back had been turned: a serious face, quite immobile, intent, as if she were studying, trying to interpret a difficult canvas in an art gallery. Then she moved, but only a fraction, lifting the old pump-action Winchester .22 she was pointing at me a little higher, so that it covered my heart.

Seven

I raised my hands automatically, feeling more awkward than frightened, stupid in my nakedness.

'Ah,' she said slowly, looking up at my arms. 'There's not much need for that, is there? Unless you've got something hidden up there in all that nest of hair. A little gun, a knife?' she added quizzically, smiling a fraction.

She spoke carefully: an American accent, East-Coast, New York State, Connecticut? New England, at least. And yet somehow it wasn't absolutely convincing East Coast. There was a touch of somewhere else, something harsher and more natural, lurking behind the over-educated consonants, a breath of the Mid-West perhaps. There was money and there was culture in the voice, but it wasn't certain that both came from the same place. The timbre was fine, though, a thing beyond background, only of nature: distinct, resonant. Like a small bell, the tone stayed on the air for a moment at the end of each sentence. She said nothing more then, just went on examining me carefully, with that same studied concern: a curiosity, almost a surprised welcome, as if for some rare species she had long sought and had now stumbled upon in this least expected of places.

'Well,' I said at last, feeling that one of us had to break the silence. 'You've caught me. Clever of you. You're the Lady of the Manor, I suppose?' My voice, as well as this latter phrase, sounded forced, very formal, as if both came from some other man, a stranger who stood beside me. I felt I should be shaking hands with this woman, accepting a cocktail from her, perhaps, in some fashionable American drawing-room. Yet I had no clothes on.

'Yes. I'm Alice Troy. And all this,' she gestured round the

thick circle of trees, 'all this is my property. You're trespassing. Where are your clothes? You've been swimming, I guess?'

'Yes.' Was it conceivable that the police hadn't visited her, that she didn't know who I was, a wife-killer on the run: that she thought I was just some lone eccentric camper poaching on her preserves? But that rifle? She had come prepared.

All the same, I decided to pretend for a moment. 'Yes,' I went on innocently, 'I was just having a swim.' I spoke casually, naturally. But of course I couldn't see myself – my wild hair and half-beard, the scar on my brow, the savage I must have appeared to her.

Her eyes smiled first, then her lips, as she considered my innocent response. Like her naked back, that I'd seen a week before, her mouth was unusually long; long, well-bowed lips beneath a straight nose and above a chin that ran out very firmly from sharply cornered jawbones, ending in an equally firm point. Though her body was muscular and compact, her face was thin, finely chiselled, every bone, each line carefully angled and distinct, like an anatomical drawing. Below her neck she was an athlete; above it there was a contrary, quite unexpected refinement, a questing distinction of some sort; the face of someone who has thought about life more than they needed to, who had hounded the conventions.

'Just having a swim!' she said rather mockingly. 'With that bow on the ground there. And looking like Robinson Crusoe. You're something of a shot, aren't you?' she went on, looking at the recurve bow on the ground next the well. 'You killed that German Shepherd with it, didn't you? – the dog I saw you tipping down that hole.'

'Yes,' I admitted.

'Curious,' she said, appraising me carefully once more. 'Curiouser and curiouser.'

'Why?'

'You're the teacher, aren't you? That boys' school near here: the one who killed his wife ten days ago.'

'Yes. I'm Peter Marlow. But I didn't kill her.'

'Of course not.'

'No, I didn't.'

'They all say that, don't they?'

'It's true,' I said wearily.

'Well, maybe it is,' the woman replied after another long

pause. 'That's what's curious you see. That's what makes it really *very* interesting,' she went on with sudden enthusiasm. '*Why* you should choose to lie up in the woods here for ten days and how you managed it. You must be an educated man, after all.' She said this with a touch of admiration or mockery in her voice, I couldn't decide which. 'Books and chalk,' she went on. 'Grades and all that. I wonder you managed to survive at all out here in the wilds.'

'I haven't survived so well. Not really.'

'What have you been doing? To eat I mean. Shooting the pigeons or the duck? You must really be a fine shot – '

'Look,' I interrupted. 'What does it matter? We're not here to talk about survival or the wild life, are we?' I started to move. 'Why don't you just call the police. I'm tired of standing here like an ass. I'm cold. Let me get some clothes.' I moved again. But she raised the rifle.

'Not so quickly, *please*,' she said. She had a genuinely polite, concerned tone in her voice now.

'Look, you think I killed my wife,' I said. 'Well, call the police then. You'd better not take any risks.'

'I'm *not* taking any risks.' She lifted the rifle, holding it up in one hand now, finger still on the trigger, cowboy fashion. 'I can use this as well as you seem to be able to use that bow.'

I relaxed. 'All right,' I said. 'Yes, I'm sure you can. And you can track people just as well, I've noticed. Without a sound. I never heard you come up behind me here. Like an Indian scout.' I stopped, thinking then of her own strange behaviour the past week. 'You know,' I went on, taking the offensive now, 'You're an even more curious mixture than you think I am. I've been watching you recently. You don't add up somehow. Oh, I've seen you without your knowing it, I've become something of a scout myself: those strange lights on all round you in the conservatory in the middle of the night. And bringing that bunch of roses out to the tombs on the island. And those war-whoops you let out the other day, when you came down to swim here, that afternoon when it was hot, when the midges were about. I thought you were a Red Indian, I really did: so bronzed, that long brown back, all that dark hair.' I looked at her now, straight in the eye, then up and down, moving over her body, appraising her minutely as she had me, undressing her with my eyes, taking visual revenge on her as she stood in the pool of sunlight by the corner of the old pumping-shed.

Her face changed, a whole new expression, forceful, amused. She smiled at me intently, just as she had that afternoon coming back from the lake: a huge smile, almost too radiant, so that I wondered again if there was, after all, a touch of madness in her.

'So you saw all that did you?' she asked, a hint of excitement in her voice.

'Yes. And heard it, too: those war-whoops. I liked that. In fact,' I went on, filled with sudden enthusiasm myself now, 'The way you behaved ... it made me feel ... I was going to ask you to help me.'

'You were? About what?' she said with interest.

'About my daughter, my getting out of here. I'm not that good at living rough, I've found.'

'Funny. It's the opposite with me. I'm not that good at being civilised,' she said. 'Perhaps we're in luck: we could change places maybe.'

'No, I meant – I thought if I explained things you might understand how I didn't kill my wife. It was the people I once worked for. I used to be ... with British Intelligence.'

She nodded her head as I spoke, too readily, as though agreeing wordlessly with a child's preposterous story, as I told her a few brief details of my recent history, my present predicament. But I stopped quite soon.

'Why should you believe it?' I said. 'It sounds nonsense enough just in the telling.'

'Maybe I do believe it. You'd hardly have spent ten days lying up in the woods here if it wasn't true, would you?'

'Why not?'

'A real wifeslayer,' she said with some relish. 'Well, you'd have kept on running or given yourself up at once. They nearly always do.'

'Are you a detective?'

'Only of myself. That's what I'd have done. One or the other. I wouldn't have hung about if – '

'If you'd killed *your* husband?' I said to her pointedly. 'I saw you both the other night. I was watching when you were in the conservatory together, very late. You were eating a chicken leg. I saw the way he looked at you.'

She didn't say anything for a moment. 'Was yours a good marriage?' she asked finally.

'Yes. Very.'

She pondered this. Then she said suddenly. 'I'll listen to you then. You'd better tell me all about it, properly. Though all the same...' She thought about something, undecided. Then out of the blue she threw the old Winchester across at me, so that it came at me very quickly out of the air, slap into my hand. I only just caught it.

'What?' I said. 'What's this for?' I held the rifle, completely at a loss.

'Just to see,' she said. 'Well? Go on!'

'To see what?'

'If you're really being honest.'

'How?'

'Well, you'd shoot me now, if you weren't telling me the truth, wouldn't you? Or at least, you'd run away. No?'

I stood there, doing nothing.

'You see? You're telling the truth,' she said with satisfaction. I handed the rifle back to her.

'Yes, but what if I hadn't been?'

'I'd be dead. Or you'd be gone. That's all.'

'But why take the risk?'

'My! Why do you think? I had to know *now*, not later. If I'm going to help, I had to know at *once*, don't you see, if you were lying? Well, that was the best way. The quickest. I hate wasting time, if I can help it. There's so much to *do*.'

She paused in her staccato rush of words, looking round her at the empty lake, the empty woods, as though she was in the middle of Bond Street, surrounded by all sorts of marvellous choices and conflicting temptations. Something nervous had overcome her in the last minutes as she spoke; impatience had replaced the calm to such an extent it seemed as if a whole different person had crept into her skin without her knowing it, a frustrated, vehement spirit.

She looked at me much less clinically now, with a candid restlessness, looking just at my eyes, enquiringly, as though we were old friends, school friends perhaps: children suddenly, contemplating mischief, both now trespassing in someone else's woods.

'I say,' she started up again, 'before you come up to the house, why don't you finish your swim? It's hot already. It's going to be another scorcher.'

Her language, I noticed, was sometimes curiously archaic, Edwardian almost. 'I say, it's going to be a scorcher.' The accent remained American but some of these phrases were from an England of long ago, again as if some completely different character, a different nationality indeed, had come to possess her.

'Well,' she said. 'What about swimming?'

'That dog,' I said, pointing down the well. 'The man, the policeman who owned it, he'll be coming back this way most likely, to look for it. It's hardly worth the risk.'

'He won't be back. I met him before I got round to you here. He was trespassing too. I moved him off,' she added proudly, a childish rashness in her voice, as though Ross had been no more than a snotty schoolboy whose unwelcome attentions she had repulsed.

'How did you know I was here? It couldn't have been a surprise: you had that rifle with you.'

'I knew someone was here. The police were all up at the Manor ten days ago, warned us. Then we heard they thought you'd got clean away. But I wasn't so sure of that. Someone had been out on the island.'

'But I didn't touch a thing out there –'

'No. But I found an old Band-aid on the floor.'

'You've been back there? I never saw you go.' I was surprised.

'I can move about these woods as well as you can.'

'Apparently.'

'I live here. This is all mine,' she added, again with that sharp proprietorial air. But again it wasn't so much a tone of serious adult possessiveness as that of a child holding onto a doll in the face of a rival. And I thought once more that perhaps she was touched, if not mad. But touched by what? I couldn't say. All these woods, this estate, the house itself – perhaps they did actually belong to her. There was certainly money in her voice. She need not have lied or exaggerated.

And yet . . . She wasn't a child, clearly: she must have been in her late thirties. But she had the insistence of a ten-year-old, that was it: of someone craving recognition, fair play in some nursery cause that had been unjustly denied her.

I'd moved across from the dank shade by the well into a patch of sunlight now by the corner of the shed. Yet I was still cold. I shivered again. And I thought of the other woman, the big woman in the white housecoat or nurse's uniform, who I had seen spying here, hidden in a bush, down by the lake, a week before.

'I don't think I'll bother swimming,' I said. 'I'd prefer some clothes.'

'Yes, where are your clothes?' she asked casually.

I was just about to tell her where they were – back up in my tree-house in the oak. But I stopped myself at the last moment. It might have been a trick of hers to discover my hideout. She saw and understood my hesitation.

'Of course, you're still hiding out somewhere here, aren't you? Why should you trust me?'

I'd picked up the bow and the two arrows and was close to her now, following her slowly, walking behind her as we left the undergrowth and came down towards the lake. But even though she was in front of me I was nervous, wondering if she might be leading me into some trap.

'That rifle,' I asked her. 'You said it was loaded. Is it really?'

She turned quickly. 'Why should I lie? I *don't* lie,' she added emphatically, with anger almost. Then she pumped the mechanism violently, holding back the firing pin, so that a stream of little bronze-coloured bullets dropped all over the woodland floor. 'You may have to lie. But I don't.' She seemed genuinely angry, hurt.

'I'm sorry,' I said, bending down to retrieve the bullets. There were so many questions I wanted to ask this woman that I didn't know where to start. Not having spoken to anyone for ten days I realised that I was as starved for words now as I'd been for food before, that I was as desperate for communication as she appeared to be. And yet I still didn't trust her somehow. Was there a trap?

But then, I thought, if there was, what had I to lose? If she didn't help me, I had no future hidden alone in this valley in any case, and the worst she could do then would be to hand me over to the police.

It was warm now out in the full morning sun by the edge of the lake: the start of another real scorcher, just as she had said.

'All right,' I suddenly decided, not caring now who might be watching us. 'I'll finish my swim. Why not?'

I was halfway out across the water, enjoying the wider, open spaces of this northern end of the lake for the first time, when I looked back to the shoreline for a moment. She had got undressed herself now and was standing on the edge, naked again. Then she dived in and swam towards me with just the same punishing vigour that I remembered from her aquatic antics a week before, doing a racing crawl, arms flying, her head half-beneath the water like a hidden prow butting the waves ahead of her.

She dived down again then, into the coppery depths, swimming completely under water now, passing close to me, several feet beneath the surface like a great fish, before she emerged ahead of me suddenly, exultantly, as she had a week before, like a missile from a submarine, exploding vertically, her body rising right up into the air almost as far as her knees. She might have been showing off, I thought.

'You're something of an athlete,' I shouted over to her.

'Once,' she called back to me. 'Once I was!'

Her eyes gleamed with excitement, reflecting the stark sunshine out in the middle of the lake. And the water falling down her cheeks, glistening on her dark skin, made her look much younger, fresher, almost adolescent. And I was reminded then of something by this face: an old photograph perhaps, of a face seen somewhere before, at least. But I couldn't place the memory. It might just have been an advertisement from an old *New Yorker*: some chic woman in that magazine promoting a classic cotton summer dress or a select Park Avenue hotel.

'I swim – a lot – all my life,' she went on. 'I love it.' She was still gasping for breath. 'But – the sea – mostly. The Atlantic,' she shouted across to me. 'I like this fresh water better – when it's warm enough. Much more, really. You sort of swim *in* it somehow. It's so much more *watery*. And the salt isn't there. Your eyes don't hurt. Do they?'

She looked at me enquiringly, intently again, as if her last question, far from being conversational, had some great importance for her and she expected some equally considered reply. We both of us trod water now, a few yards apart, the sun a great torch almost directly above us, dazzling the lake, turning all the copper shades to blue.

'No. There's no salt,' I said. 'And the sharks won't get you.'

'Did you catch fish here? Is that how you survived?'

'Yes. A perch, I think.'

'You came prepared, with a rod, hooks?'

'No. Just with some luck: a man at the school, the sports master, he left a lot of camping stuff behind, in a backpack. I took it.' I didn't tell her about the sandwiches and cream cakes in the cricket pavilion.

'You're used to living outdoor then, living rough? With bows and arrows.'

'Just the opposite. I'm a great stay-at-home. A roof and four walls, I love that.' And saying this I was suddenly reminded that I had no home now, that I was on the run, with my wife dead and a child that I loved gone away. Then, in the bright light, the water pliant as blue mercury, with a woman splashing happily a few yards away from me, I remembered the horrors of the last ten days; I didn't belong here among these easy pleasures. I was from a world of disaster and loss.

I felt giddy, even faint. The sudden fun of this meeting, the surprise of swimming together, this no longer meant anything, and the sadness must have shown on my face, for she was concerned now, in her eyes, in her voice.

'Are you cold?' she asked.

'No. Just – as you said yourself: I suddenly felt I've got so much to do.'

'Come home and tell me about it, then. Why not?' She swam a little closer, ever the concerned enquirer.

'I'll have to get my clothes,' I said.

'There's plenty up at the house. You can use them. Arthur left a lot.'

'Arthur?'

'My husband. Or he was.'

'The man I saw going off the other day? In a big Mercedes?'

'Yes. He's gone back to New York. The divorce should be through by the end of the summer.'

'But I can't just walk up there with nothing on.'

'Why not?'

'What about those two gardeners I've seen? And you've probably got friends up there. Or a cook, servants.'

'I live alone. There's a housekeeper, yes. Mrs Pringle. And her husband Tom, Arthur's driver. They live in one of the gate lodges. But she's out for the day. Gone to Stow. She has a sister there. And Tom is still up in London, since he took Arthur to the airport: something to do with the car. And the gardeners are thinning the trees right over the far side of the park. There's no one there right now.'

We'd swum back to the shore. Alice had climbed out and was dressing on the bank. 'I know,' she said. 'There's a towel I keep in the little boat over there. You can use that. I'll get it for you.' She moved away.

'Why do you bother?' I shouted after her, exasperated, suddenly unsure of everything. 'Why do you make it all so easy?' She returned with the towel, throwing it at me as I came out of the water.

'You expect people to be nasty to you, do you?'

'Yes. Recently.'

'I think you're honest. I told you. But even if I didn't . . . Well, I could hardly leave you to spend the rest of the summer stuck out in these woods, could I?'

'You mean, you're going to phone the police in any case. Is that it? Do me a favour, before I know it – '

'If you want me to. But I'd prefer not to. I'd really prefer – ' She stopped.

'What?' I was even more abrupt, angry.

'It's childish,' she said finally.

'I'm sure it isn't,' I said, thinking that an open admission of this quality from such an unconsciously childish person would surely offer something vital.

She said, 'I've often wanted to disappear myself and live away in the woods. Oh, for some *real* reason, like you, not just for fun.'

'I've touched the romantic in you?' I asked flippantly.

'Yes, you have,' she said, with an openness that surprised me even in her. 'That's why I bought all this – the house, the park, all the trees. "The Romantic in me." I've had the money to pander to that instinct,' she added rather bitterly. 'But Arthur, of course, he finally thought I was just playing games. "Arrested development," he said.'

'It was his money, was it?'

She humphed then, the first trace of the cynical that I had noticed in her. 'Oh no,' she said. 'It was all my money: Troy Shipping. Troy Meat Packaging and Refrigeration. Troy Hotels. Troy Leisure Incorporated. Troy Chemicals. Troy Everything. I'm the daughter.'

And now I remembered her: a face, a photograph, an article I'd seen a year or so before in the leisure section of *Time* magazine, or was it the *Sunday Times*? Alice Troy, of course, with her chiselled, Red Indian features, her fortune – rich beyond the dreams of avarice – her good taste, her interest in interior decor and pre-Raphaelite art: Alice Troy who had come to live in England, buying some half-ruined Victorian Gothic folly in the Cotswolds, and doing it up: a rich Manhattan socialite I'd thought then, a world away from me, from my simple, rather penurious cottage life with Laura: a woman I would never know – who yet stood in front of me now.

'Of course,' I said. 'I should have realised. I read something about you, a year or so ago: what good taste you had, your Victorian paintings. And an interest in courtly etiquette – what was it? Yes: the Arthurian legends: Glastonbury, Camelot and the Knights of the Round Table. You were going to finance another archaeological dig, weren't you? In the Vale of the White Horse, wasn't it? Or was it the Red Bull, looking for the real Camelot?'

'That was another me, another person,' Alice interrupted sharply. She spoke with great finality and confidence – as if such various and totally assumed personalities had been as freely available to her as her family's money had obviously been, as though a profligacy in both had not yet begun to satisfy her.

We walked up a laurel-bordered path, which shut out most of the sun, towards the back of the house. It was gloomy here even at midday, the thick green branches arching, linking completely overhead.

'A typical Victorian idea,' Alice remarked as she walked easily ahead, pointing upwards at the greenery. 'This laurel-covered way was so that the household wouldn't have to see the tradesmen or the servants coming and going. It leads to the back sculleries and kitchens. I left it as it was. Some Victorian houses actually had stone tunnels underground for the lower orders to come and go by. This was a compromise, a refinement on the part of the Hortons who built the place, because they were great horticulturalists, too, planting things everywhere – laurels, trees, shrubs, bog gardens.'

'Yes. And burying themselves out on that island. They seem to have been eccentric generally.'

'Eccentric? Hardly. Little family mausoleums somewhere on the estate? It wasn't uncommon then, especially after the Queen had Frogmore built for Albert. It was quite the fashion.'

She pushed the latch down on an old, heavily studded, red door that led into the back of the house, and my bare feet were suddenly chilled on the big flagstones that led away up a dark passage, with similarly heavy, red-painted doors leading off to either side. A big, black old-fashioned woman's bicycle, with cord skirt-guards forming a fan over the back wheel, stood propped against one wall. A patent gas cycle lamp of the same Edwardian period, with a bulbous magnifying lens, rested on the handlebar bracket. The whole thing looked in exceptionally good order. Yet it was no museum-piece. It had been used recently. There was mud on the front tyre, which had splashed up onto the fresh, gleaming black paintwork.

'We found several of these in one of the old coachhouses,' Alice said casually, taking the bike up. 'I had them put in order.'

She got onto the machine suddenly and rode away up the long stone passage on it, before trying to turn back by some steps at the far end. She nearly succeeded, losing her balance only at the last moment. 'Sometimes I can get right round and back again in one,' she said joyously, the child working in her again.

As she wheeled the bike back towards me I noticed that it left an intermittent trail of white tyre-marks on the flagstones. Then I saw that each of the half-dozen steps leading up at the end of the passage had a bright rim of whitewash along their edges, and that the front bicycle wheel, pushing against the lowest step as she'd tried to turn, had then repeated the whitewash in a series of broken lines back down the passageway.

'It's to make sure they cleaned the steps every day,' she explained, when I asked her about the fresh paintwork. 'They painted them first thing every morning, so that all the dirt would show up quite clearly at the end of the day. Though of course the official reason was that it made the steps stand out more clearly at night, in the lamplight.'

'Yes,' I said. 'But why do you still have them painted? There's plenty of light here now, isn't there?' I looked upwards then, along the roof of the passageway. There were no light fittings anywhere and no switches on the walls.

'No,' she said, 'All this part of the house on the ground floor, I've made it over, exactly, I think, as it was. Just with oil lamps. Here, I'll show you.' She opened one of the heavy red doors leading off the passage. 'This is the lamp room.'

And so it was, as I could just see now in the faint light. There was a sudden sharp breath of paraffin oil, and on the dim shelves inside I saw a considerable collection of old Victorian oil lamps, of every shape and sort. Some were merely serviceable, kitchen lamps, with pewter-coloured metal oil reservoirs and sensible white globes. Others were much more elaborate, cut-and-coloured glass affairs: tulip-shaped red shades perched on top of fretted brasswork; or heavy brocade cloth pierced through by delicate clear-glass chimneys. Some were small and easily held, the sort to light you to bed with. But a few were very large indeed, three and four feet high, formidably decorated Gothic illuminations, made to stand on pedestals, lighthouses for a baronial hall.

'But you don't use any of these now,' I said.

'Oh yes, some of them. Why not?' Alice looked at me in surprise. 'We have electricity, of course. But this sort of light, lamplight, it's far nicer, softer. Isn't it?'

My feet were getting cold on the dark flagstones of the lamp room. I shivered now, with just a towel round my waist.

'Come on up to the kitchen and get warm,' she said.

She closed the door behind me and we walked up the steps at the end of the passage.

By now I almost expected it, I think, the big room we entered next, with its half-dozen arched clerestory windows along either side, high up; and the white scoured wood of the ancient cloth dryers, anchored far up by ropes to the ceiling; the long double lines of heavy cast-iron pots and pans on the shelves above the immense, black-leaded kitchen range which ran along most of one wall, with the legend 'Waste Not, Want Not' picked out in Gothic-lettered tiles above it. A coal-fired range, I assumed, with projecting hobs and brass hot-water taps, hummed softly, warming the whole room.

Yes, I had half-expected this Victorian kitchen, with its vast scrubbed pinewood table down the centre; an oak dresser eight or nine feet tall, filled with heavy old kitchen crockery at one end; a huge flour-barrel with a wooden scoop in a corner; the high-backed chair with its patchwork quilted cushion by the grate where Cook might have relaxed after a hard day's work; a kitchen complete in every Victorian detail as far as I could see, right down to the heavy cast-iron meat mincers on the shelves and the rectangular wooden kitchen clock, each corner crosshatched in the Gothic manner. There was, I noticed, some modern equipment: a big refrigerator, an expensive Moulimix, a long line of contemporary glass spice jars, an electric toaster, a waffle grill. But these were just incidental scratches on this Victorian masterwork.

'Warm yourself by the range.' Alice seemed terribly out of place in the old kitchen, in her smart blue cotton jeans and open shirt, like a guide in a museum.

'Arrested development': I remembered the phrase she'd told me her husband had used of her. And I thought now how he might quite easily have left her, at first impatient and finally contemptuous of her decorative Victorian obsessions: this apparent need she had to translate each of her fantasies into exact fact, and the fortune she did this with. It was enough to bemuse, and finally annoy any spouse.

Yet I didn't want to leave this woman, who seemed just about to help me, though I was wary of her again now, standing in this perfectly restored kitchen, looking at her. For it was obvious that she saw nothing unusual at all in so meticulously recreating the past in this manner – old Edwardian bicycle lamps, whole Victorian lamp rooms and kitchens – and using these things, quite casually, it seemed, as if time had not moved forward at all in the intervening years.

She seemed to be living in the past of eighty, a hundred years before, and yet she seemed quite unaware of any contradiction: a sort of Queen Canute, I thought, defying time, living alone in this vast house, moving backwards into the years, not forwards. There was something eerie about it all. And yet there was nothing the least sinister about Alice herself: she was no Miss Havisham. Indeed she looked as fresh and contemporary just then as a woman in a telly commercial for some space-age kitchen. I couldn't follow it.

'Come upstairs. Get shaved, washed if you like. There's all Arthur's stuff. He had rooms to himself.'

Beyond the kitchen was another brighter, cream-painted passage leading into the body of the house, with doors, open this time, leading off into various smaller service rooms on either side. There was a butler's pantry, with row upon row of perfectly carpentered silver drawers beneath a green-baize worktop; there were wine coolers, a partly filled bottle rack with the necks of some old vintages up from the cellars poking out; there was an old brass cork-puller screwed to a table-top, such as pubs had on their counters long ago. Further on was a footman's room, with two braided uniforms on a pair of tailor's dummies, white waistcoats, navy-blue cutaway jackets with tails and gold buttons, knee-breeches and white stockings hanging beneath them.

At the end of this corridor, to the right, giving out through a hatch into an invisible dining-room, was a serving pantry, with long silver-gilt plate warmers, methylated-spirit chafing dishes and two huge carving trolleys with great half-globes of brilliantly polished silver closed over the tops. On shelves behind, someone's family dining plate was stored – heavy crested dishes with a green pattern, rimmed in gold, in every shape and size, for the most varied foods, on the most formal occasions.

Immediately in front now was a sombrely panelled Gothic Baronial Hall, which ran for a hundred feet or more at right-angles to the passage we had just travelled along: a dozen tall, indented windows, hung on either side with great brown plush curtains, gave out onto the front of the house, with the parkland and cricket pitch, brightly green, just visible beyond.

In the middle of this vast space, immediately opposite, was an inner hall door, two wooden half-arches, glass-paned, so that one could see out into a large porch beyond, with formal columns and steps leading down to the gravelled drive beneath. Between each of the front windows, in a long line, were Corinthian pedestals, and on each of these was a white marble bust: Victorian worthies, all of them, to judge by their beards and mutton-chop whiskers, but here masquerading as Roman noblemen, each with a creamy stone toga thrown casually over one shoulder.

The floor was polished wood throughout the long hall, except at one end, where there was a thick, rather grim Aubusson carpet, and on it a vast horsehair sofa together with a collection of equally large high-backed brocade armchairs, all of them camped like an invading army round a fireplace as big as a tunnel-opening. Around and above the grate here, to a height of ten feet or so, a most elaborate stuccoed mantel frieze had been set in the wall. It told a story of some kind, I could see: there were figures active in various pursuits, carefully moulded in the plasterwork.

Standing in the middle of the huge hall, I turned about and then looked upwards. On the long high wall behind me, beneath a row of stag's heads, interspersed with shining swords and breastplates, to either side of the last flight of a great oak staircase, were the principal pictures in the house, I thought, eight or nine of them, in recesses, large canvases, all from the pre-Raphaelite school. I looked at them more carefully. One of them was the romantic figure of a young knight, in dark medieval armour, kneeling at the feet of some quite ethereal woman with long, golden tresses, holding a haloed chalice: Sir Galahad or Sir Launcelot, I thought, reaching for the Holy Grail. A second picture was of a shepherd in a smock with a wispy but minutely rendered red beard, on a hillside filled with highly coloured, almost photographically real wild flowers, walking towards another kneeling woman in the foreground. She had just laid out some bread and cheese for him on a red check handkerchief. The food was painted in such detail it brought my own hunger back as I gazed at it.

'That's a Ford Brown,' Alice said. 'It's called "Noon".'

'The food's real enough. But were wild flowers ever as colourful as that, in England?'

'Of course. Why not? Before all the pesticides, before they ploughed everything up and tore the hedges out. And do you see?' she went on, with sudden sparkling enthusiasm, 'Look! Down here in this corner: he's painted in a Ghost Orchid, right behind where the woman is kneeling. Look! She's almost sitting on it, as if she hadn't seen it. It's the rarest of all the wild orchids in England. It's only been sighted fifty times or so in a hundred years! And only by women, for some reason. So he put it in there. As a bit of spite, I think.'

She was smiling radiantly once more as I turned to her. 'I see,' I said. 'You know about flowers, English wild flowers, do you? Past, present?'

'Yes,' she said, surprised at my surprise. 'I've always known. But then I've had a thing about England.'

Above us, on the first-floor level, heavy banisters ran right round three sides of the hall, forming a gallery. And above that, very high up, was a dark hammer-beam roof, the beams picked out in faded circles and diamonds of colour, like old Red-Indian totem poles. To the left, at the opposite end of the hall from the great fireplace, was an intricately carved wooden screen, completely dividing the space, with a Gothic entrance arch in the middle, that led to a library beyond. And further on were stone arches in an identical style, but with plateglass screens set between them, and a glass door that led into the tall conservatory beyond where I could just see a green jungle of shrubs, small trees and hanging plants dangling in the bright sunshine coming through the glass.

The hall was warm, almost breathless, filled with a dry smell of old wax polish and the remains of great log fires burnt here long ago. It was calm, dark, heavy. Yet for all its impeccable tradition, there was something antiseptic about it. The space here had been filled once, or waited for fulfilment. But meantime, in the present, there was no life in it. With a few tactful signs and velvet ropes it could have been turned into an art gallery or museum straight away.

'You don't seem to do much here,' I said, 'do you? It's as big as a football pitch. Or a tennis court.' And then, thinking of such games, of youth, the question suddenly struck me, and I wondered why I hadn't asked her before.

'With all this space,' I said. 'Do you have children? It's the sort of place, ideal . . .'

'Yes, a son. He's nineteen. Touring Europe now. In Italy, I think. But that was an earlier marriage.'

'He's not interested, in all this?' I looked about me and then out the windows, thinking of the great parkland, the home farm beyond.

'Not very,' she said, turning away, moving over to the fireplace now, looking up at the great plaster frieze above her. She touched one of the little figures. I joined her.

'It's a moral story. Do you see?' she said, her voice regaining an interest which it had not had in speaking of her son. 'It's called "Art and Industry". Full of good works.'

I could see now how the frieze was divided into a series of intricately linked rectangular and diamond frames, with inset stucco figures: a group of men scythed corn in one; barrels rolled from a warehouse in another towards where a fully-rigged clipper lay at unlikely anchor in a third; in a fourth a half-draped woman, ample as a pastrycook, cradled a lyre. It was all executed in the most literal manner and the conjunctions were absurd. But as a piece of madly idealised Victoriana it was superb.

'It was specially commissioned for the Great Exhibition in 1851,' Alice said, admiring it with loving surprise, as though seeing it for the first time. 'We bought it from another house. But it suits. Don't you think?' Again she made the enquiry as if something vital hung on my response.

'Yes,' I answered. 'It's ... splendid. A bit overpowering perhaps, if you were just sitting here trying to read the paper.'

'Of course. But this isn't the library. Of course it's showy, pompous, self-righteous. But it's practically the ultimate in all that, isn't it?'

'Yes.' I had to agree with her. It was.

'And do you see this man down here?' She touched a little bowed figure down to one side of the frieze. 'He's dressed as a footman, or a waiter, I can never be sure which.' She fondled the plaster man lovingly. 'Well, he's a bell pull. If you pull him – ' she pulled him – 'he rings a bell!' I heard a bell go off somewhere faintly in the back regions. She laughed then, another joyous laugh. And I thought how much more at ease she was among these purchased, inanimate objects, these figures in plaster relief or pre-Raphaelite paint, than she had been in the matter of her own nameless son, flesh and blood that really belonged to her.

I pulled the little man myself then and heard him tinkle away in the distance once more. 'The whole place is wired up, I suppose,' I said. 'With all these ... valuables. Alarms, I mean?'

'Yes. What had you in mind?' She smiled. 'I think you'd need a truck to take anything out of here.'

'It rings in the local police station, does it?'

'It can do. If it's turned on that way.' There was a moment's uneasiness between us. But Alice didn't let it last.

'Anyway,' she said brightly, 'You'll have time enough to see the whole place. Why don't you come upstairs?'

I'd wandered away from her as she spoke and gone over to the great hall door. Idly I turned the big plaited metal ring that formed one of the two handles. But it wouldn't turn. It didn't move. I realised the great doors were locked.

'Of course,' she said, seeing my attempts, 'I keep it shut. As you said, with all these valuables here.' She stood in the half gloom on the other side of the great hall. Was she staring at me? She might have been. In any case, hands on her hips, there was something impatient in her stance.

'Well?' she said, seeing me hesitate. 'I'll show you to

your...' she hesitated herself then, 'your quarters!' She smiled, making light of a description that might otherwise have sounded ominous. And I wished then that I'd never met this woman, never come into this great closed house of hers; that I was back safely hidden among the leaves of my tree-house. But instead of my oak tree, I climbed the great oak staircase behind her.

Upstairs, in Arthur's suite of rooms, and what I glimpsed of her own room through an open door across the corridor, the fixtures and fittings were rather different. Indeed they could not have been more opposed to the meticulous Victoriana of the ground floor. Alice's large bedroom, looking inside briefly as she pointed it out to me, was sparsely white; light and airy, with cushions on the floor and a very few bits of delicately modern furniture: a low bamboo, glass-topped table, and a dressing-table even lower, so low down by the big French windows looking over the formal gardens that a person, I thought, would have almost to kneel down to see themselves in the glass.

Arthur's rooms were even more contemporary, but in a much heavier mode, which included unbearable chrome-plated easy chairs, mirror-topped table, a futuristic bureau and a chest of drawers in some highly polished, deep-veined hardwood, edged in brass, with counter-sunk brass handles, an old portable Indian Army officer's travelling chest gone very wrong.

I was surprised. 'You lost heart with the Victorian, I see,' I said, looking about me. 'When it came to the essential creature comforts?'

'In a house this size,' she said, 'you've got the space to make a lot of little theatres, haven't you? Different rooms. Different settings, whole new backdrops, that you can walk into. And out of. A variety. Lots of new parts,' she added with excitement, like an actress reflecting on some unexpected recent successes, where she had broken out of a previous typecasting with a vengeance.

'And the attics?' I said. 'Are they *belle-époque* – or Louis Quinze?'

'A lot of the rooms up here are a little different,' she admitted. 'Only the ground floor is all in the original Victorian period. Change,' she added with the sudden excited stridency of a dancing mistress, 'Change! Variety! Why not? You didn't think the *whole* house was a sort of Victorian mausoleum, did you?'

'No,' I said, lying. For I had expected exactly that. It was obvious that she saw this house, this whole estate as some kind of personal theatre, woods and rooms made available, made over, each in a different fashion, in a manner that would enhance or fulfil her in some way. And I didn't mention this thought to her either.

The bed in Arthur's room was slightly raised on a dais, a huge affair, covered in a snowy white counterpane: it was like a remote sacrificial tomb or an Emperor's sarcophagus. I knew I would never sleep in it. A dressing-room led off to one side filled with hanging cupboards and beyond that a large bathroom, with showy gold and marble fittings. Two unopened boxes of Roger & Gallet soap, one of carnation, and the other cologne, lay to either side of the twin washbasins.

'Two basins?' I asked. '"His" and "Hers"?'

'That was the idea. To begin with.'

'I'm sorry.'

'It was the second time round for both of us.'

'Yes. It was the same with us. I expect we shouldn't have hoped for so much.'

I looked up then and saw myself properly for the first time in the big triple mirror. My beard, even in ten days, was no more than a half-hearted, unsuitable thing. The scar above my eye had healed well enough. But the half-beard and the red wound together gave me an ugly, even a frightening, piratical air. And I noticed, too, how scratched and torn my skin was, particularly behind my shoulders and down my back, red welts, as if, a martyr to something, I had been scourged recently. I wondered what Alice would have thought of me had she met me in any ordinary circumstances, dressed and shaved, the dull pedagogue smelling of chalk. She would never have noticed me. But, obviously, in the guise she had found me – naked, hirsute, scarred – I must have seemed an ideal player for her repertory company. I would be costumed soon. But what was my role to be?

Back in Arthur's dressing-room Alice opened out half a dozen drawers in the deep-veined mahogany wall cupboard. There were formal and leisure shirts, from Turnbull and Asser, and Hawes and Curtis, in every shade and material; silk, sea-island cotton and winter wool, sky blue, red pin-stripe, casual olive.

There were classic and tropical suits, from Benson, Perry and Whitley in Savile Row, tweed sports jackets from Dublin and Edinburgh, together with tail suits, formal grey morning wear and smoking jackets with scarlet cummerbunds, all meticulously, expectantly tucked into the big press. There were casual Bally shoes, more casual multi-coloured sneakers and traditional bespoke brogues from Ducker and Son of Oxford; silk ties by Gucci and silk socks from someone else – and sporting wear, too, I saw; jogging suits, tennis clothes, shorts, swimming trunks, patent white cellular cotton shirts, and even cricket flannels.

'Does he play *cricket*?' I asked.

'He's tried. Out in the Park. It's the old Beechwood estate team. I'll give him his due: he tried as well.'

The dressing-room was an emporium of very expensive male attire, all of it tasteful, to certain tastes, but not to mine. And I prayed that none of the clothes would fit me, that here would be an excuse, a first reason to make it back to the woods. But Alice flicked one of the sea-island cotton shirts out of its neatly ironed shape, and held it up against me. The chest width and length, the arms exactly matched my own. And the shoes, I'd noticed before without admitting it, were exactly the same size as mine.

Yet she sensed my lack of enthusiasm, how I held back.

'You said you wanted help, remember, to get out of here, didn't you? Well, you can't get out of here without clothes. And your own clothes out in the woods must be pretty filthy by now. So what had you in mind? Running naked?'

'No,' I said. 'Thank you.'

'So go on, then. Have a hot bath, a shower, a shave. It's all here. Choose whatever you want. Then we'll have lunch. And you can tell me ... whatever you want to tell me. If I can help ... You did *ask*. Remember?'

It was warm in the dressing-room, with a smell of expensive carnation soap, good cotton, old leather and fine worsteds: tempting smells that I had missed in the woods. She laid out the short-sleeved summer shirt and some casual trousers. But she put back one of the formal silk ties that had fallen on the floor.

'You won't want this, I think. Not yet, anyway.'

'Yet?'

'Unless we have guests in,' she smiled, leaving me.

Eight

'My!' she said when she saw me transformed half an hour later outside Arthur's bedroom. 'I wouldn't recognise you.'

'No.'

She looked at me in her carefully appraising manner again. 'You're a whole different person. It all fits, doesn't it? Even the shoes.'

She looked down at the pair of hand-stitched moccasins I'd found in the bottom of the press.

'A bit tight round the toes,' I said.

'Yes. But you're not the same man at all.' She considered me, a distant look in her eyes, like a casting director giving nothing away.

'Maybe the beard was better,' she said at last.

'I can always grow it again.'

'Maybe.' She thought about this intently, so that I became impatient at her too careful consideration.

'Or I could black up,' I said. 'With burnt cork and one of your husband's cutaway morning suits and play a nigger minstrel.'

'You could,' she said shortly and decisively, as though she really believed this. 'There's an awful lot of clothes in this house one way or another,' she went on. 'Even old ones. We found a lot of Victorian clothes here, in one of the attics.'

'Yes. I think I saw some of them on the scarecrow out in the kitchen garden. And that Camelot outfit you were wearing the other night in the conservatory,' I added pointedly.

'I *like* dressing up,' she replied with equal point. 'So did the Hortons. Why, they even had a theatre here. Oh, just a little stage they rigged up at the end of the real tennis court at the back of the house. But that's where all those old clothes must have come from, including the Camelot outfits.'

'What?—the Hortons had Medieval Pageants here, did they? The Death of Arthur? That sort of thing? They took the Gothic Revival that far?

'Yes, they did indeed. That's one reason why I bought the

house. They had pageants and jousting tournaments and all sorts of Gothic things. Rose Blumberg was an actress, of sorts, before she married.'

'Was she? I wondered about her. Jewish, marrying such a worthy-sounding Victorian, some provincial coal baron.'

'He wasn't so worthy, or provincial. They were lovers, to begin with. He was already married. There was quite a scandal before they came down here and built this place. I found out quite a bit about them.'

Alice walked away down the long corridor. 'So they produced themselves, did they?' I called after her. '"Life as theatre"; I thought the great new psychology was *not* playing games?'

'What a bore!' she called back over her shoulder. 'I'm hoping to get the stage going again. I've had the curtains fixed and talked to some of the local people. They weren't mad about the idea. But then maybe that's just because we're a little too far out from Stow,' she added optimistically.

Alice had changed herself meanwhile, into just such a classic cotton summer dress as I'd imagined her advertising in the *New Yorker*. And her hair, parted in the middle now and quite dry, had been combed to either side in a long wavy flow so that it came out like a black fan covering her neck and most of her shoulders. She wore no jewellery. But then of course, with her almost over-dramatic beauty, she didn't need any. The two of us walked downstairs together, both of us quite different people.

But Arthur's unaccustomed clothes had already begun to itch by the time we got to a small drawing-room beyond the great fireplace in the hall. My skin, though enclosed only by the lightest cotton, prickled in the heat. My face itched, too, the beard gone. I wished I was naked and bearded again.

'Please, help yourself.' Alice said. 'Can you get me a lime soda?'

There was a generous Georgian silver drinks tray incongruously placed on the turned-down leaf of a Gothic lacquered desk in one corner. A heavy Victorian tantalus with three cut-glass spirit decanters stood on top. I gave Alice her lime juice and had the same myself, but with a good measure of gin thrown into it instead of the soda. The ice, I noticed, was already there, in a silver-lidded chalice adapted as a vacuum bowl, with a beautifully coloured enamelled kingfisher as a handle on top.

'You were expecting someone?' I asked. 'With the ice.'

'No. Mrs Pringle or it may have been Mary – she comes in most mornings to help – one or other, they fill it up every morning. It was a thing of Arthur's. He was always expecting people.'

'You don't have any cigarettes do you, by any chance?'

'Yes, somewhere. I don't, but there are some.' She found a silver cigarette-box behind some social invitations on the mantelpiece and handed it to me. There was a message engraved on the lid, cut as in sloping longhand. It said: 'Arthur – with love, Alice.'

When I opened it there was another message, engraved on the inside of the lid, a verse:

> 'When I die in the long green grass,
>   Death will be but a pause.
> For the love that I have is all that I have,
>   Is yours and yours and yours.'

Alice saw me looking at it.

'It's nice.' I handed her back the box and lit the cigarette. 'He didn't take it with him?'

'Arthur's very busy.'

'Yes. I suppose so. Everyone's very busy these days. It's the curse of the age.' It struck me then how strange it was that neither of us had anything to do, becalmed in this great warm empty house, detached, suspended, waiting. It made me uneasy. 'I'm sorry – about Arthur.'

I repeated the sympathetic phrase, but with an emotion now in my voice that had not been there before. And then a much stronger flood of feeling came to me, that I couldn't account for at first, until I realised I was thinking of Laura. I walked away from the fireplace, looking round the room, my back to Alice so that she wouldn't see the pain of this memory. There was a picture, an exquisite ink and pastel drawing, on the far wall, of a woman, a little like Alice, just the head and shoulders, with long wavy black hair. But the eyes were much bigger, the neck thicker, the lips even more bowed than Alice's.

'That's a study of Jane Burden, by Rossetti. Dante Gabriel.

For his *Queen Guinevere*.'

'It's beautiful.'

'Yes. Though people say she wasn't really so ethereal at all. Bernard Shaw thought she was quite a frump. Only talked about pastry-making when he met her.'

'Yes?' I turned back to where Alice was standing by the fireplace.

'Yes,' she said. And she was smiling; one of her radiant explosions, almost mischievous, so that the whole mood changed and the sadness in the air quite disappeared.

The drawing-room, built at the corner of the house, had long windows looking both south and west, over two sides of the open parkland, but with the thick line of beech and oak as usual all round the horizon blocking out any further view. The room was a little more cheerful than the great hall, with a daisy-patterned Morris wallpaper and some fairly easy chairs covered in a heavy matching chintz. Yet, like the hall, with its great Victorian bracket lamp fittings and slightly fusty smell, the little drawing-room felt barely lived in. The desk where the drinks were had no other clutter; nothing poked from any of the pigeonholes at the back. There was a large engagement diary and a fine leather address book next a telephone by the tantalus. That was all. Elsewhere a few copies of the *Field* and *Country Life* were stacked too neatly on a small drum table by the window.

I said, 'You hardly live in this room either, do you?'

'Oh, I've a room of my own up in the tower, where I keep my things. This was where the ladies came after dinner. While the others had their port.'

'You led a . . . a pretty formal life, you two, together here?'

'Sometimes. Americans often like that more than you British. We even had place names in the dining-room, on little bamboo easels.'

'I thought you'd have liked all that: courtly manners, formality, etiquette. Isn't that one of your things? That article I read . . .'

'Yes. I do like it. But I didn't like the little bamboo easels. That was Arthur's idea.'

'You had a lot of dinner parties here?'

'Yes. To begin with . . .'

'A busy social life? Out among the county folk?'

'To begin with. But that rather faded, thank God. People have somehow . . . died for me, recently anyway.'

Alice sat down by the fireplace, not at all the social failure, the rich American drop-out but poised, confident, beautiful. And I thought suddenly that despite her isolation here, how many other friends she must have, this very rich, attractive woman. And the more friends, surely, at just this moment in her life, on the brink of divorce: girl-friends, old flames, relations, sympathetic confidantes, or just scandalmongering nosy parkers. Where were they all? Surely the phone would go at any moment, long-distance from New York: or a big car from London would sweep up the drive, hell-bent on some mercy mission.

I said, with as much hidden nervousness as curiosity, 'With Arthur gone, where are all your friends? Surely . . . just being alone here?'

'Yes,' She drank deeply from her glass. 'I've not been so good with my friends. It wasn't just a question of Arthur.'

'How?'

'Oh, coming over here in the first place. They didn't understand that.'

'You mean the Edwardian bicycle out in the back hall? And all this, the Gothic restoration?'

'Perhaps. Some of them said it was "cute". They were being polite. But most said nothing. They thought I was out of my mind.'

I smiled then. I very nearly laughed. But I stopped just in time. 'Are you?' I said.

'Do you think so?'

'I wondered. But,' I hurried on at once, 'all this – it's nothing so crazy as my lying up in the woods out there for ten days, running about naked with bows and arrows.'

'No. That's really strange,' Alice said, looking at me, genuinely surprised once more. And indeed it was, I thought. By comparison her life in this Gothic folly was almost conventional. There was something of an agreement between us now, I felt: a wordless contract that we shared against the world. We had somehow touched each other without touching.

'Besides, about friends,' she went on. 'I've always asked too much or been too honest or had too much money. The usual things.' She rubbed her chin. 'Friends were difficult. Loving –

or hating. That was easier.'

'Of course. But – '

'The friend thing, you know,' she interrupted with enthusiasm. 'It's like this: friends prepare themselves too much for you. Oh, that's exactly what they're not supposed to do. But it happens: it *becomes* prepared, a role you or they take on: "I'm your friend." But I've never been completely sure about that.'

'They might just have wanted something from you – in your case?'

'Possibly. But much more it was the feeling of their coming a long way out of the past, into an equally long future. It all seemed *endless*,' she added lugubriously.

'But isn't that the whole point about friendship: that it *is* the same, that it is always there?'

'Yes,' she admitted. 'It should be. But, I told you, I just haven't been good at it. I had a great friend once – oh, I didn't see her that often. But when I did, well, it was like living suddenly, when you realized you'd just been getting by before. I met her in Florence, at the design school I went to there. An English girl. She did silk-screen printing, beautiful scarves and things. She was very bright and funny: original – *outré*, you'd say. And talented. So I offered to back her myself, with my money, to go into partnership. But she wouldn't. Said it was taking the easy way. In fact she thought I was patronising her, or trying to get in on her act. Either way I ... I found in the end I simply couldn't *explain* myself to her at all. And I wanted to. I wanted that very much because I knew it was the real thing.'

'The real thing?'

'Yes: what you *have* to do, the real thing, whatever it is, with the one person you can really do it with. The rest is just – inconsequential chatter. Friends are great for that,' she added derisively. 'The world is full of "friends",' a sudden extraordinary vehemence rising in her voice. 'They're almost as bad as the others, the enemies, the vulgar fourth-raters most people are today: thugs and gangsters when they're not mean-minded little schemers. I *hate* them, hate them all.'

Vulgar fourth-raters, I thought: Alice had lapsed into her Edwardian archaisms again, an embattled Duchess, where the bourgeoisie were storming her gates.

'You rather narrow your field though, don't you?' I said. 'Seeing life that way. Making it all – or nothing.'

'That's exactly what Arthur told me. Like everyone else, he loves compromise. Arthur Roy. Funny name, like a king. But he wasn't. He's a New York attorney. He loves his friends, too, down in the Century Club. They mean a great deal to him. But then his whole life is a kind of Club. And I couldn't join it in the end. And it's too late anyway now. We're not actually divorced yet. But as far as I'm concerned I'm Miss Troy again.'

I thought of telling her how all this struck me as pretty childish, how the problems in her life seemed largely of her own making; of telling her how she just lacked the necessary abilities to compromise, to understand, perhaps even to settle for less; of saying to her, in short, that she had simply failed to grow up.

But then I thought how, like Alice, I, too, had cut myself off from wider life and friendship in the past few years; with what perhaps childish derision I too now looked on the contemporary world: a dull place filled with duller people – the churlish, the crass, the ignorant, the cunning. And I thought how an innocent sot like Spinks stood out in such a world, as Alice's girlfriend obviously had. Like her, Spinks in his way, with all his beer-laden enthusiasms, Spinks was the real thing, too. I knew how rare such people were. And how much one could miss them.

Besides, in criticising Alice for her immaturity, I would surely be doing no more than Arthur had apparently done. She would have heard it all before. Criticism wouldn't cure her at this late stage. But finally I said nothing because I saw how, if Alice had been a woman of any ordinary sense and convention, I wouldn't be here, in Arthur's fine clothes, drinking ice-cold gimlets in her warm drawing-room. I'd have been in Stow police station by now, waiting on a murder charge.

'I've tried to make my own life,' Alice summed up, in a confident, a happy and not at all a disappointed tone.

'But why all this very *English* life? Why so much of that? The pre-Raphaelite paintings, the Gothic decor, the old kitchen; British wild flowers.'

'Oh, I've loved all that ever since I was a child: I had an English nanny, she was always reading to me. Scott's novels and the stories of King Arthur, the search for the Holy Grail, and that sort of thing. The Knights of the Round Table... I had a book then. I used to read it myself oh, so many times, I *lived* with it. I must have been about ten or eleven: a big story book, *In the Days of the King*, it was called, with wonderful line drawings by Walter Crane: a Knight going through a thick, evil, brambly sort of wood on a white charger with a beautiful long-haired maiden, up sidesaddle in front of him: a dark wood. But there was an extraordinary brightness about their heads, I remember, like haloes, like a fire in the dark. They were going to *win*.'

'Yes. I wonder if the Knight was Launcelot, taking Arthur's wife away. He certainly won.'

'Maybe. But I was never cynical.'

'No. I can see that. It's a fine quality: to believe the best.'

'All right, maybe it was a little crazy, this Anglomania. But I told you: I had the money to do what I wanted. So why not?'

'And your parents? What did they want?' I must have looked doubtful.

She smiled, her eyes narrowing happily. 'Oh you can't blame them for anything. I get on pretty well with them. My father's just retired. My two elder brothers, Teddy and Harold, they're in charge now. Along with one of my uncles. It's very much a family business.'

'Don't you miss the family?'

She hesitated here. 'I do and I don't,' she said finally, equivocating over something for the first time.

'You're the only daughter?'

'Yes. The youngest.'

She spoke with the slightest tone of regret here, so that I said, 'Poor little rich girl, were you?'

'I went to a lot of costly private schools that I hated, if that's what you mean. Boarding schools. I hated being cooped up. I spent a lot of my time trying to run away. The riding; that was the only thing I liked about them. That and the running.'

'Literally running?'

'Yes. Athletics. Apart from escaping school. I loved running and swimming and climbing and tennis, all those outdoor things. I hated books and pens and pencils and indoors. That's what I loved about the Hamptons: everything was outdoors and summer. My father bought one of those great, spooky, Charles Addams houses out on Long Island. That was the Atlantic. I remember thinking one day I could just swim on and on straight out into the ocean and get right across to England and never come home. We lived there every summer. Then there was Vevey in Switzerland, a smart place for rich brats. I hated that, too. Then there was the design school in Florence, and that was something good, at last. And then New York, when I first married. My husband,' she smiled remembering. 'Well, he was something of a man-about-town. In fact, that's all he was. We spent most of our time in the Russian Tea Rooms or at some smart disco till four in the morning. I got tired of that fairly soon. So I started a company, making fine cloths. Weaving. And big patchwork quilts, you know, designed with Red Indian motifs. Reconstructed. I specialised in those. You see, you were right: I am part Indian. An eighth or so. My mother's mother, she was from one of the Michigan lake tribes.'

She stood up then, put her glass back on the desk and looked out over the hot parkland. 'I suppose I was the golden girl,' she said lightly, looking back on her life. But now there was another slight hint of disappointment in her voice. The memory, or the present fact, of some loss creeping into her tones. And I was sure I knew what it must be: Alice Troy had everything except what was really important: a husband, children, family. Those were the vital things she lacked, the permanency, support, the continuity created through love or blood. Something wilful or even disastrous in her character had withheld those gifts from her in the end. Some considerable flaw in her emotional make-up had prevented her ever maintaining such familial ties satisfactorily. And she wasn't going to tell me now what this might be, even if she knew what it was herself.

'Do you still weave?' I asked.

'Yes. I've several looms upstairs. For tweed. From Cotswold wool. I'm trying to revive that. We have our own special flock.'

'I see,' I said, fearing a sudden onset of Gothic Arts and Crafts talk, thinking that this might be Alice's real problem: an obsession with woolly sheep.

'Yes,' she went on, going over to the window. 'Out there. Can you see? Some of them are on the other side of the park, over there, by the chestnuts. Are you interested?' She turned from the window, looking round at me sharply, suddenly intently quizzical again, as if the fate of the whole of the British tweed industry hung on my reply.

It seemed churlish to say 'No.' And besides, I did like good tweeds, even if I preferred the soft Irish Donegals to any of the tougher Scots varieties.

So I said 'Yes. I am interested,' and she smiled happily in

return. Like a child rewarded.

We took a salad lunch on a trolley out to the conservatory where we sat in the shade of a great mimosa tree under the hanging flower-baskets, with the Florentine fountain splashing and warbling to one side of us. In this heat, the ventilating windows high above had all been opened, so that every now and then fronds rustled and the long green trailers from the baskets swung minutely in the little eddies and down-draughts of summer air.

Tomato and potato salad and Yorkshire ham cut straight from the bone, with watercress and mustard and cheese and bottles of chilled Guinness to go with it. Apart from the cress I ate everything, down to the bone, to the last rind of cheese, telling Alice my story from start to finish between mouthfuls. I left out nothing, not even my theft of the cricketers' tea, or her Cotswold lamb that I'd killed and barbecued. And it was hard to tell her this, knowing how she valued the flock. At that point in my story I thought she might turn on me, divorce herself from my violent affairs: I thought she might see how far I'd gone into mad ways, stoning defenceless animals, gutting them, murdering them in the rain.

But instead my shamefaced account of this seemed to draw an increased interest and sympathy, a sort of happy wonder from her, as if I had returned to her something of great value which she had once prized and lost.

Sometimes she interrupted or interjected a query, sitting across the table from me, hoping to clarify something I'd said. She was not a passive listener. She listened like a military commander hearing vital news from the front, news upon which he would soon have to make even more vital decisions.

The thing that surprised her most was my handing Clare over to the policeman.

I said, 'At the time I felt there was no alternative. Laura was dead. If they'd taken me I would have been dead for Clare as well, with ten years in gaol or worse. As it stands, well, at least I can do something now. I'm free.'

'Yes. You mean we can get her back?'

'We?'

'You asked me to help.'

'I didn't mean personally. If I could just use a few things from the house: clothes, a car, money. I'd pay you back.'

She laughed. 'And if you did manage to rescue her, all on your own, what then?'

I had, in fact, already roughly thought out what I'd do then: try and get Clare and me back to Portugal, to Laura's parents in Cascais. It was the only thing to do, I thought, since I felt that Laura's father, Captain Warren, would understand, would give me sanctuary. He hated the British authorities already, the War Office and the secret men generally in Whitehall who had dispossessed him of his land and home in Gloucestershire forty years before. And if I could get to Portugal, David Marcus and his hit-men in MI6, as well as the police, would have another problem altogether. And even if they eventually got me back to Britain, Clare would be able to stay out there, with her grandparents. She would be safe from any dreadful institution. I told Alice all this.

'And how would you get yourselves to Portugal?'

'A plane. A ship. The usual way.'

'With false moustaches and so on? They'd be looking out for you, you know.'

'I haven't thought it all out. And anyway, it depends first on whether I can get Clare away from wherever she is.'

'I could probably find that out for you,' Alice said, leaning forward, a sudden sparkle of adventure in her eyes. 'The regional Committee for Autistic Children held a wine and cheese party here last winter, to raise money. I know the secretary – '

'I don't want you to get involved personally. There's no need.'

'Why not, for heaven's sake?'

'I'm sorry, you shouldn't.' I stood up. It was getting too hot, even in the shade of the mimosa tree. 'If you help me directly it can only make it worse for you.'

'You mean, you'd just like me to pretend that you came up here, for example, and *stole* a car and some clothes and some money?'

'Yes. That's exactly what I thought.' I stopped over by the Florentine fountain and splashed some cool water from the great Carrara marble bowl over my face. 'There's no point your getting involved. You mustn't.'

I turned to Alice. She was sitting, rather hunched, over the table, her head down, hair falling over her cheeks, fiddling with a napkin, dejected: like a child just denied a treat.

It made me angry that I seemed to have upset her so. 'Good God, Alice, you've got better things to do. You could find yourself in gaol as well!'

She looked up. 'Why? Why should either of us find ourselves in gaol? You're telling the truth, aren't you? Well, they're bound to find out you didn't kill your wife in the end. And find that other man ... And what's wrong with regaining control of your daughter? You're still her legal father, after all.'

'Nothing wrong, if you do it legally. But this is taking the law into my own hands, to put it mildly. I've gone too far to do otherwise. Besides, as I told you, it's really British Intelligence who are after me. I know too much, about various people. They want me stopped, put away, killed. Not the police. So even if I were proved innocent about Laura, that wouldn't stop the others still coming after me. Look at what happened this morning: that man with the shotgun. That was Ross, the head of our dirty tricks section. Well, he's somewhow got onto my track. They're working hard. They're out to kill me. It's obvious. So I can't do anything "legally" in this country. I have to get out if I can, with Clare. But you mustn't get tied up in all this. If they killed Laura by mistake, why, they might do the same for you.'

Alice stood up and started to clear away the lunch. 'That's all theory. You could be wrong. In any case, one thing is fact: you won't get Clare out of any institution, or either of you away to Portugal, without help. Without me,' she added decisively.

'Why not? I had some training when I was in the service. With a car, some money – '

'And passports? You'd need them. And one with Clare's name on it.'

'She's on Laura's passport. It's back in the cottage. Or I could buy one. There are places in London ... I'd pay you back.'

'Yes, of course. I need the money.'

'Besides, if I need help, I've friends in London. One of them could help. They're my friends after all. You don't have to be involved.'

She saw at once that I was lying here. It was a stupid thing to say. We were already closer than I realised.

She said sharply. 'I don't believe you have such friends in

London. If you had, you'd have gone to them in the first place, instead of lying up in the woods here for ten days. I think you're probably as bad as I am about friends,' she added with some defiance. 'Anyway,' she went on, 'I'm here to help . . .'

But she didn't finish the sentence. We both of us heard wheels crunching over the gravel surround in front of the house just then. And we both saw the police car a moment later, a big white Rover streaked in orange and black, pulling up by the porch. Alice didn't hesitate for a second.

'Quick! Over there,' she said. 'Don't go through the hall. There's no time. Get in under that big shelf at the back, where the pots are. The other plants in front will hide you completely. I'll get these dishes out of the way.'

I ran over to the back of the big conservatory where a profusion of brilliantly coloured potted plants and shrubs lay along a broad shelf against the wall. On the stone floor in front were other taller shrubs in pots and urns. Pushing my way in behind these from one end, I found myself beneath the shelf in a kind of greeny cage, hedged in by the exotic plants, with just the odd spyhole through the leaves and crimson petals out into the conservatory.

I heard the great hall doors opening in the distance. Alice would surely take the police into the drawing-room at the far end of the great hall, I thought. So I was surprised – no, I was angry – when a minute later I heard the footsteps coming through the library and on into the conservatory. What the hell was she doing bringing the police in here, unless to have done with me, to betray me? She'd probably fixed it all on the phone, when I'd been changing in Arthur's rooms.

A bluff, nice, west-country voice rang out not far in front of me. '. . . I shouldn't, Miss Troy. But I couldn't resist asking you – just another look at your conservatory? I only glanced at it last time I was here. I'm not really a hothouse man myself, and I don't get up to Chelsea now. But this! This is really wonderful. You don't mind if I take another look, do you?'

'Of course not, Superintendent. Go right ahead.'

'These camellias, Miss Troy. They're quite extraordinary.' I heard the heavy policeman's footsteps coming straight towards me. 'Never seen anything like them. Even in Chelsea. This one . . .' The Superintendent had stopped right in front of me now. I could see his black trousers blotting out all the light. The camellias were obviously all along the shelf immediately above me.

'Yes, I'm proud of that. Marvellous, isn't it? So dramatic. Those crimson petals on the little narrow bush. "Anticipation", it's called. Yet it's ideal for small gardens. But my favourites are these, over here, these single-flowered ones: "Henry Turnbull". They're so delicate, the petals, like some fantasy Ascot hat. Just a breath of air and you'd think they'd disintegrate. In fact they're quite robust.'

'Beautiful. Just beautiful. Of course they don't really do at all up here on this soil. Outside, I mean.'

'No. Not enough acid. You have to pot them. And then pot on, and re-pot as they get bigger. It's a bit tiresome, and you have to have the right kind of mulch every year and a good loam compost: acid loam if you can get it. Or add some sulphur. But once you get your compost right there are really no problems, they're quite trouble-free. You have to watch the watering, though. Not too much, that's the great thing. I use rainwater. The softer the better.'

'Yes. I'd heard that.'

'Or you can sub-irrigate, with a sand base and a water drip, if you're really doing it grandly. But I prefer the old watering-can: the personal touch.'

'Of course. That's what plants are all about anyway, aren't they? The personal touch.'

'Would you like a cutting? Here – this japonica hybrid: "Tinkerbell". There's no problem.'

'I wouldn't think of it, Miss Troy – '

'Not at all, Superintendent. Here, I'll get my secateurs. Put it in some damp moss peat, you know, cover and seal it with a thin polythene, a little warm water now and then and you should have something in six or eight weeks...'

Their voices drifted away as they went out to the far side of the conservatory. But they were back again in a minute, right in front of me again while Alice took a cutting.

Then she said, 'Coffee, Superintendent?'

'No thank you, Miss Troy. As I mentioned in the hall, I really came up about this man who's escaped.'

'You think he's still somewhere here, do you?'

'Well, I don't. But some people from London do, from the CID there, that man you told me about down by your lake this morning. They think he may be still hiding out somewhere on your estate. So we're going to have to go through the whole place all over again, if you don't mind. In fact, Miss Troy, I have to admit it, the man from London, well, he went back through the little valley down there, after you'd moved him off your land. He came to us then. You see, he found some things.'

'Oh?'

'Yes. You see, he'd brought a dog with him: an Alsatian tracker. He lost it earlier in the morning. But he found it when he went back. It had fallen down a well behind that old pumping-station you have on the far side of the little lake.'

'Yes?'

'It seems the dog was speared by something, a piece of metal, through the throat, before he drowned. Well, that's not so important – probably ran into something, an old bit of wire fencing. But then inside the pumping-station we found the remains of some cooking: warm bricks, a few bits of meat, ashes.'

'Oh, that was me. Yesterday. I'm often down by the lake, bathing. And we sometimes make a barbecue in that old shed. Gets you out of the wind. That was me, Superintendent! Not the man you're looking for.'

'Well, that explains that. But then, Miss Troy, another thing: our dogs picked up a scent, just by the shed, of someone, possibly this man, and it led right up to your house here, to the kitchen door in fact. I have some of my men out in the yard now.'

'So? I was down by the lake myself this morning. That trail must have been mine: I was right at the pumping-shed, then walked straight back here, to the back door in fact, about two hours ago. So that was my trail.'

'Of course. I'm sure it is. But just possibly not. You see, with our own tracker dogs, we'd given them a scent start with one of this man's socks. And this seemed to set them off. Took off at once, straight up here. Of course, it's probably nothing. But we ought to make sure.'

'You mean?'

'Well, how long were you out of the house this morning?'

'An hour. Not more.'

'And your domestic staff? They were in the back of the house all the time. In the kitchen?'

'No. Not this morning, now I come to think of it. My housekeeper went to Stow. And her husband's away. And Mary, the daily help, she leaves before midday.'

'And your gardeners? They were in the yard?'

'No. They were thinning wood on the other side of the park.'

'So there was no one in the house, or the yard, for more than an hour this morning?'

'No. I suppose not.'

'Well, I think we ought to make sure then, Miss Troy.'

'You mean he could have come in *here*?'

'You didn't have your alarm on, did you?'

'No. I don't bother. Not during the day.'

'It's just a chance, then. You don't mind us looking round the house? It's a big place. He could have come up to steal something, and then hidden somewhere. It's better to be sure. He's dangerous, Miss Troy. Especially if you're here on your own.'

'Yes, I've heard. And what happened to his poor child, by the way?'

'Oh, the little girl is quite safe. Being looked after, in the Banbury hospital for the moment.'

'Well, of course, if you think it necessary, take a look round. But are you *sure*?'

'I'm sure we should take every precaution, Miss Troy, every nook and cranny...'

The Superintendent's voice faded as they walked out of the conservatory, back into the library, and by then I was out from my hiding-place and moving over towards the big glass doors that opened from the conservatory onto the garden terraces and the parkland to the east beyond. It was time to get back to the woods if I could, I thought. But in any case I had to get out of the house.

Luckily I never opened the door. As I touched the handle I saw two policemen in gumboots coming towards the Manor along the beech hedge which divided the terraced gardens from the yard area behind. I drew back quickly. I couldn't leave the house by way of the library and the great hall, I could hear people moving out there already, and I didn't dare stay cornered, with my back to a wall hidden behind the camellias.

I looked up at the Juliet balcony with its slim Gothic balustrades high above me. And then I saw, just to the side of this, a dozen cast-iron rungs that had been set into the wall of the house leading up to it – part of some old fire escape, I imagined. That was the only answer.

I climbed up fast, pulled myself over onto the balcony and opened a glass door that led onto the Minstrels' Gallery that ran all round one side of the library and the hall, but which gave off immediately to my right into a long corridor I'd not seen before. And then I was running soundlessly, in the soft moccasins, down the carpeted landing of this unknown house, wondering where to hide in such a vast place – yet a place whose every nook and cranny was about to be exposed.

This first-floor bedroom corridor ran northwards, towards the back of the house, before turning left and giving onto a small half-landing, part of the back stairs which led up from the kitchen area. From a window here I saw the two policemen again, out in the yard. But this time they had a tracker Alsatian with them. If they brought the dog in I was done for. But in any case I would have to go upwards – to the second floor, the attics? Perhaps I could hide behind an old water-tank beneath the eaves – or better, get out onto one of the many haphazard roofs that, given the generally bizarre design of the house, could well hide me completely from the ground below. I heard the tramp of feet on the lower floor; doors opening, furniture being moved. There must have been half a dozen men combing the place beneath me. I ran on.

This servants' staircase led up from the half-landing to the second floor into a narrow twisting badly-lit corridor. And here the elaborate restoration of the house had come to a full stop. The landing was in considerable disorder and there was a slightly musty smell in the air. The heavy varnish had been stripped from the panelling, and whole panels removed, leaving damp patches, old water-marks on the rough plaster behind. Repairs had been started here and then abandoned. And now the corridor had been turned into a long storeroom, it seemed. It was littered with expensive Victorian bric-à-brac of all kinds, like a room in Sothebys before some important sale of nineteenth-century effects. There were pictures stacked against the walls: lesser pre-Raphaelites, nude slave girls and piping Grecian dancers. There were great, elaborate cast-iron fireguards and fenders, magnificent brass telescopes on huge tripods; early, but essentially decorative, scientific equipment, wind gauges and strange mechanical devices beneath great glass domes. And there were Victorian display-cases everywhere, of butterflies, moths and wild flowers; and larger boxes filled with stuffed fish and animals: a huge pike, two wildcats fighting, a golden eagle. It was more a museum than a corridor, where the objects had all been assembled but not yet put together.

I had to move carefully now, in this crowded gloom, clambering over half-opened packing cases, coming towards a sinister shape: it was a magic lantern, I found when I squeezed past it, set on a tall stand that looked at first like a man with one great Gorgon's eye, wearing a stovepipe hat. And then straight in front of me – I couldn't avoid stepping on it – was a crocodile, ten feet long, lying out along the floor, its snout raised, teeth bared below two beady eyes. My heart thumped like a drum as I veered sideways trying to avoid it. But I couldn't, and as my foot touched it I waited for the searing pain as its teeth sank into me... Of course it didn't move. It was dead, perfectly preserved, some Victorian memento from the Nile.

The landing got darker as I went further along it, pushing myself slowly and much more gingerly now through this strange debris. Without more light I couldn't safely or soundlessly go much further. I opened a door to my left. It was a nursery. Or at least it was filled with a lot of old nursery toys: a wooden steam-engine big enough for a child to sit on, with two canary-coloured carriages linked behind; a rocking-horse, prancing wildly, front feet splayed out dramatically on the long runners. A collection of Victorian china dolls in lacy dresses and red ribbons stared at me with big blackberry eyes, sitting neatly, mutely, all tight together in a line along a miniature sofa, and there was a vast dolls' house, sufficient almost for a child to live in, over by the window.

But it was the window that I really noticed. It gave out onto a lead guttering with an interior slated roof rising up to the left a few yards away. I opened the small sash. But just as I did so my heart bolted again: there was a sudden, terrifying, unearthly shriek from immediately outside. A great bird rose up right in front of my face, its wings brushing my hair: a huge, mythical thing, it seemed, a multi-coloured nightmare in shimmering blues and greens with a long tail. Peacock-blue. It *was* a peacock, I saw, as it flew off the ledge down towards the flat top of a great cedar tree in the garden below.

But at least from here, I saw now, I could get out and look around for some completely hidden part of the roof. Or perhaps I could even get down to the ground from the big tower which I could see now, too – Alice's tower where she had her rooms – which rose above another taller roof near the centre of the house.

I closed the window behind me after I'd stepped out onto the narrow ledge, and after that I managed without difficulty to pull myself up the side of the roof in front of me. The tower lay immediately ahead. And sure enough, there was a fire escape, or at least some wooden steps, leading up to a door at the top of it. The only problem was reaching the tower, since, from my perch on top of this small gable end, I found myself looking down into a large glass-covered well in the centre of the house, the sloping top lights set above the big dining-room, on the ground floor, I imagined. And there was no way across this wide gulf, other than by three narrow stone bridge-buttresses that linked and supported both the interior walls of the house, at this point a good twenty feet above the glass.

I could stay where I was, of course. But on looking back I saw that, on top of this roof, I was no longer hidden from the ground. And if I returned to the ledge outside the nursery window, the police – perhaps having heard the peacock's commotion and coming into the room to investigate – had only to open the window to find me. I could at least test the stone buttresses beneath me...

I slid gently down the edge of the roof to the first of them, nearest to the front of the house and thus almost completely hidden from the overlooking windows. The stonework was at least a foot wide to begin with, and firm as a rock as I straddled it. But the buttress narrowed gracefully as it rose to a bridge in the middle, and I wasn't certain that it would support my weight at that point. On the other hand, since it was built in the form of a bridge, with a keystone in the middle, I thought it should quite naturally take the increased strain.

I moved very slowly out over the glass, legs soon dangling in space to either side, edging forward along the buttress inch by inch, never looking down. The sun was suddenly very hot on my neck and shoulders and I started to sweat, unable to move a hand to mop it up. The salty moisture soon came down in beads in front of my eyes, over my nose, into my mouth.

Towards the apex of the buttress, when I was riding up it, my head and shoulders hunched down over the bridge like a·man on a galloping horse, I thought I heard a stone shift, the minute sound of something giving, beginning to crack. I froze for a minute, sensing the sharp glass beneath, a great pit opening in my stomach. But nothing moved; there was no other sound and I inched my way down the far side without mishap.

And now it was an easy journey up the corner guttering of the roof opposite and down the far side to where the big square tower with its pagoda roof rose up into the dazzling summer sky like an irresistible Victorian command, pushing its way imperiously through the other fantastic Gothic excrescences, the eccentric roofs and turrets, the miniature spires and stone pineapples which covered the top of the manor like barnacles.

The railed steps down from the tower, though, I saw now, didn't lead to the ground. They were part of some interior fire escape, if anything, and led straight to a small doorway in one of the gable ends, which of course would only lead me straight back into the house again. Perhaps I might be safe in the tower?

I climbed up the steps, unseen from the ground below since they faced inwards, and the door at the top opened at once. There was quite a large, perfectly square room inside, with four expected Gothic arched windows – but with a quite unexpected domed ceiling covered in blue-and-white tiles, an eastern mosaic of turbanned gentlemen smoking hookahs with camels in the background, and Arab lettering picked out in long scrolls that ran right round the circumference. The view was stupendous from this height, right across the rim of beech and oak which normally hid the estate, giving out over half the North Cotswolds.

A big wooden loom stood in the middle of the room, skeins of variously coloured wools to one side of it and lengths of lovely finished tweed on a day-bed in one corner. There was a telephone on a small but this time well-cluttered desk. I saw an open diary – another large engagement diary, but again with no engagements in it. Glancing at the top of the page I read: '... awful thing – that he won't let me touch his hands even...' There was some crockery, cutlery and a small fridge filled with tubs of yoghurt, pots of honey and a half-bottle of champagne. I could have done with a cold beer. Even though one of the windows was open it was very hot, with a hot, baked smell of wool and dried pine from the floor and wooden loom. It was a marvellous retreat, a hermit's eyrie, high on the land, quite cut off from the world. And indeed, that was the problem. There was no access to, or escape from this tower as far as I could see other than the steps I had come up. It seemed a wilfully inconvenient place to have a workshop.

But then I saw what must have made it much more habitable. In one corner was a heavy, ecclesiastically carved panel with a wooden handle beneath carved in the shape of a big cigar. I lifted it up. There was a dumb-waiter behind, the serving shelves presently in position. And then I realised: of course, the cigar-shaped handle, the desert Arabs smoking hookahs on the tiled dome of the ceiling. This turret retreat had obviously been built as a smoking-room originally, where the Victorian grandees, the more agile of them, the youngsters perhaps, could get well away from the ladies and freely indulge their fumes, their vintage port, their risqué jokes. And if this was so then the dumb-waiter would certainly lead down to the dining-room, or to the pantry, and perhaps below that to the cellars where the butler could the more readily load cargoes of Fine Old Tawny on board for the bloods on high.

I could get right down to the bottom of the house in this way, I thought: it was worth the try. The opening into the lift was quite big enough. The ropes inside were new. If I lowered the serving box down a few feet I could get inside the shaft, stand on top of the box and then, working the return rope, let myself down to the ground floor or basement.

The police were searching upwards through the house, I knew. But if I doubled back on them in this way, and got into the cellars which they'd have checked out by now, I might finally be secure.

As I thought about it I heard a sound on the roof beneath and, looking out the window for a second, I saw the door in the gable end which led out to the tower steps beginning to open. The police had reached the top of the house, but still weren't finished. I needed no further prompting.

I pulled the lift down to below the level of the floor and, gripping fast onto the return rope, I levered myself quickly into the dark hole, closing the serving-hatch behind me. The shaft was hardly more than two feet square. But everything had been perfectly built and carpentered here and I slipped down gently, soundlessly, through the guts of the house, down this dark gullet, without any problems.

I passed a chink of light in the wall, where the dumb waiter gave out onto the kitchen or dining-room or pantry. But there was still a further drop in the shaft; it went deeper. Eventually the lift came to a halt in complete darkness. I must have been at the bottom of the house, in one of the cellars. I felt in front of me with my fingers. There was nothing but open space. The sleeve of wooden panelling which all the way above had enclosed the lift shaft must have been absent in the cellar at least in front of me, for I found then that I was still hemmed in to either side. But in front I was free: sitting on the serving box: free, but in complete darkness. Lowering myself very carefully, my feet eventually touched the floor. And then I saw a very faint crack of light ahead. It came from beneath a door and I groped around the sides of this looking for a switch. Finding one at last, I turned the light on.

I was in a cellar, certainly, a big cellar with arched stone alcoves all about me, filled with pyramids of dusty claret, fine brandies, vintage port. But the cellar door, naturally enough, was firmly locked on all these riches. And there was nothing I could see inside that would help me open it.

Nine

Of course, I was safe enough now, I realised, in the locked cellar. The police, if they'd bothered to check it at all, must have done so some time before. On the other hand, unless Alice came to fetch some of the fine wines, which was unlikely, I was incarcerated here. Letting myself down on the dumb-waiter had been easy enough: the pressure on the mechanism had not been extreme. But tugging the whole thing upwards would be another matter altogether: the ropes and pulleys would probably take the strain on any return journey, but I would hardly have the strength for such continuous effort.

I looked around me more carefully in the light of the single dim bulb. On a table by the door was a cellar book, together with several empty decanters, a few tulip-shaped wine glasses, a candle for checking the vintage colours and another of those old pub-counter cork extractors, a mate to the one I'd seen upstairs in the butler's pantry. And, of course, there was the wine itself, carefully but generously chosen, with champagnes, ports, sherries and brandies to go with it.

I looked in one of the stone alcoves: Tättinger. Blanc de Blanc, 1967. The bottles were held in a metal rack here, given their bulbous shape. Further along was a great pyramid of Haut-Brion, 1961 – and beyond that there were a lot of Burgundies: Chambolle Musigny, 1971 and Les Charmes from the same year. There was some superb drinking here, I could see that, with all the necessary decanters, glasses and a most suitable corkscrew to start things moving. But there was no one to share it with...

And then, to one side of the dumb-waiter, I noticed two bell-pushes that had been let into the wall. One was marked 'Pantry' – the other 'Smoking Room Tower'. Of course: having loaded the clarets and vintage port into the serving-hatch in the old days, the cellarman would thus warn the staff on the floors above to expect the lift's arrival.

If I waited here for an hour or so, until I was sure the police had left – and if the bells still worked – I could write a message on a page of the cellar book, put it in the lift, haul it up and sound the alarm. There was a good chance that Alice would hear it, either in the pantry or up in her tower.

I tore a page out of the back of the cellar book. There was a ballpoint next to it. 'Am locked in the wine cellar,' I wrote, and then to make sure she saw the piece of paper I stuck it onto the partly released wire surrounding the cork on a bottle of Tättinger. Then I added a P.S.: 'Come on down and join me!'

I was rather pleased with myself.

About an hour later I sent the lift upwards, straight up to the tower first, and rang the bell. I couldn't hear if it sounded or not, that high up. Nothing happened in any case. So I brought the lift down then, to the pantry level on the first floor, and rang the 'Pantry' bell. Now I heard the sound, quite clearly, not far above me. And a few minutes later, after I'd rung a second time, the hatch doors opened and I heard the champagne bottle being taken out.

'Alice?' I called up the shaft. 'I'm here!'

But there was no reply. She was obviously coming down to me straight away. I was saved.

I stood by the cellar door, waiting expectantly. Some time passed. Eventually a key was pushed into the Yale lock outside and the door finally opened.

'Alice!' I said.

But it wasn't Alice. It was a very large, almost gross, woman in a pink twin-set and tight skirt, smartly got up, with too much powder and lipstick, who held the door open for me. Her size made her seem older. But she couldn't have been more than forty. Her face was quite creased in fat, but the brown eyes were sharp and small and set close together, like chocolate buttons on a big sponge cake. She was large . . . Of course, I realized then: she was the same woman I'd seen spying on Alice down by the lake a week before.

I said nothing. I was speechless.

'I'm sorry,' the woman said entirely self-possessed. 'Miss Troy must have gone outside. I'm the housekeeper, Mrs Pringle. I just got back. I heard the bell ring.'

'Stupid of me,' I said, for want of anything better to say. 'I – I locked myself in.' I thought I might bluff it out. 'I was looking . . .' I turned and gestured vaguely at the wine behind me.

'Yes, of course,' the big woman said easily, sympathetically. 'You're not the first person to get locked in here: the door, it swings to without your noticing.' She had a London, not a Cotswolds voice; not Cockney London or South Kensington either, but the voice of someone trying to rise from one of the grey areas in between. Then to my great surprise she said, 'You'll be Mr Conrad, from London. Miss Troy said you'd be coming down some time this week. She must have shown you your room already. I don't know where she is at the moment, out round the park looking for you, I expect. She wasn't here when I got back.'

I followed Mrs Pringle along the basement passage. She clipped along the flagstones in her high-heeled shoes, with the neat-sounding rhythms of a Guardsman on parade, though she looked, on her small feet with her body rising out dramatically above, like a ninepin upside down. She seemed a very competent, authoritative woman, almost too familiar with her employers, I thought. But I assumed this might just be a reflection of an American domestic equality imposed on the household by its new owners.

We walked up some steps and round into the big kitchen. A kettle was already singing on the great black range.

'Yes, Miss Troy can't be very far away. I'm just getting tea ready. Perhaps if you'd like to take a look round the gardens? I'm sure you'll find her. I'll serve tea in the small drawing-room.'

'Thank you. That's very kind. I'm sorry to have bothered you.'

'Not at all. It's no trouble at all. And I hope you enjoy your stay here.' She turned and took some cake tins from a cupboard. A big currant loaf was already out on the pinewood table, several slices cut and gone from it. Mrs Pringle obviously liked her tea early, I thought.

I left the kitchen and went out by the back door and through the yard into the parkland to the west of the house. I was dazed, light-headed. Did Mrs Pringle really think I was Mr Conrad? And who was this Mr Conrad?

The grounds to the west of the house sloped away in a series of formal Versailles-style herbaceous terraces, enclosed with box hedges. Romantic, mythical statuary – the Muses, the Four Seasons – lined a broad flight of steps leading down to an ornamental pond at the bottom, where a big Neptune fountain sent rainbows of fine spray from the mouth of a dolphin up into the dazzling summer sky. Alice, her back to me, was walking slowly round the circumference of the pond.

I surprised her with my footsteps. She turned, twenty yards away, and I'm sure she would have run towards me, full of relieved welcome, had I not whispered across the space to her: 'Be careful! She's probably watching.'

'What happened? What *happened*?' Alice was like a child again, a desperate child whose companion in some frightful mischief has just returned from a visit to the headmaster's study.

I told her all that had happened. We walked slowly round the pond and then moved further away, almost out of sight of the house, towards the croquet and tennis courts beyond the formal gardens. There was a dry-smelling wooden summerhouse here, with steamer chairs, where we sat down, completely hidden from any view.

'Well,' I said, when I'd finished my tale, 'what do you think?

About Mrs Pringle?'

'It's true, of course. We were expecting Harry Conrad. He's more Arthur's friend than mine. But Mrs Pringle doesn't know that. A lawyer in London. He was to have come down here this week. But Arthur cancelled it just before he left.'

'Did Mrs Pringle know he'd cancelled it?'

'No. I'm sure she doesn't. Arthur left in such a hurry. And I forgot to tell her.'

'So it's possible she actually does think I'm him?'

'Yes.'

'But she must be perfectly well aware . . . of this hunt for me around here: the police all round the place this afternoon, for example.'

'She may know about them. I was out when she got back. I thought you might have hidden somewhere in the garden. But she probably didn't see any of the police here this afternoon. They left almost an hour ago – full of apologies.'

'*Has* anyone ever locked themselves into that cellar?'

'Yes. Arthur did, only a week or so ago. The door swings to. There's a breeze along the corridor, if the back door out to the yard is open.'

'Well, maybe she does think I'm Conrad,' I said.

'Why shouldn't she?' Alice asked hopefully. 'She's always been a perfectly reliable, sensible, honest person.'

'I wondered . . . Is she really just a housekeeper? Those eyes: I'm not so sure she's honest. And that puffy face.'

'Oh, that's her only problem. But it's just physical. She's overweight, got a frightful sweet tooth. Always eating candy and baking marvellous cakes, and eating most of them herself. But she's not calculating, I'm sure. She'd stop feeding if she was, since she likes to look smart. I've tried to help, given her several diets. But she'll never stick at them.'

'And her husband? The chauffeur? Of course she'll tell him about me.'

'Tom? Yes, but why should he bother about you? It's true he's more calculating, maybe. He's thin, wiry. Just the opposite of her. A real Jack Sprat. He was in the army here, before they came to us. But he's *totally* honest.'

'Well, if so that's what worries me: if they think I am . . . who I am, well, they're going to let the police know at once.'

'They *won't* think, I'm sure. They're not like that.'

'What happens if Mrs Pringle finds I have no luggage, in the guest bedroom? If she goes up to turn the bed down or something?'

'We'll go back now. And I'll put some luggage in the room. There are plenty of suitcases in the house she's never seen. And plenty of Arthur's clothes. I can fix that. You'll see.'

Alice had regained all her confidence and enthusiasm. 'I told you,' she went on, 'I *told* you, when you first changed into Arthur's clothes: you're a completely different person. You're free! The police found nothing up here. The Superintendent said he was quite convinced that you'd got a car out of here that first night. He told me before he left how this whole new search for you was just a wild goose chase. It was only that man, with the shotgun – Ross wasn't it? – from London who thought you might be still here.'

'Yes. And that worries me too.'

'Well, don't let it,' Alice said lightly. 'Ross won't be back; he's not going to bother the local police a *third* time. Don't you see? You can stay here quite openly now, for a bit anyway. You don't have to go back to the woods like a savage. And we can start thinking about Clare. I asked the Superintendent – '

'Yes, I heard you. In Banbury hospital. Her grandparents obviously haven't been allowed to collect her yet.

'But I told you at lunch: it was in the papers. Laura – your wife: they sent the body back to Lisbon for burial. And the child, well, she must be in some state of shock. Unable to move yet, maybe – '

'It's all nonsense,' I suddenly interrupted. 'Running like this, pretending to be Harry Conrad, thinking of kidnapping my daughter. I don't know what I'm doing. I wanted – just wanted revenge, when I first got away that night. I wanted to kill Marcus. Or Ross. Or anyone. But now it's different. All this childish plotting. If you hadn't encouraged me,' I said angrily, confused and annoyed at my predicament now that I recognised how that first wild need for revenge had died in me. Revenge wouldn't bring Laura back, which was all I wanted just then, for Laura had gone back to Lisbon for ever. They had probably buried her in the Anglican graveyard by the Estrela gardens on that windy summer hill where I had first met her.

And it was the thought of this and the state I was in generally, exhausted and overwrought, that made the tears prick my eyes, so that I turned away, unable to stop them.

But Alice confronted me the moment I stood up – her arms suddenly around my shoulders, kissing me, kissing me.

They weren't the kisses of a lover, I thought then. They simply represented the concern of a close friend whose sympathies could no longer be restrained and whose artless nature it was to express them in such a way. Of course, I was still in love with Laura. And I hadn't yet realised that Alice had already started to fall in love with me.

She drew back from me, perspiration, hers and mine, smudging her long, angular face. It was too hot again now in the little pavilion, exposed all day to the glare of the sun. Sweat had come to mark both our shirts beneath our arms and where she had pressed against me her breasts showed through the damp of the fine material.

Oh, I liked Alice; I was attracted by her – that would never have been difficult, God knows. But I held back. It all seemed too convenient. It was nonsense, really.

'It's not nonsense, you know,' she said at last, as though listening to my thoughts. 'You'll see. Everyone can start again. You'll see.'

I thought she was simply invoking the American right to happiness here, that hopelessly optimistic amendment to their Constitution. I have never had such expectations. On the other hand, I could not but be drawn forward by her optimism, by what she offered me, both spiritual and material. Certainly I couldn't go back. In the space of six hours I seemed a part of Alice's life already, as though I'd known her for years. I was responsible for her now, just as she, almost from the beginning, had so clearly meant to take charge of me. And I thought: such a sense of responsibility belongs as much to friendship as to love, especially with her, who lacked friends. I was a friend at last for Alice, I thought.

So I kissed her myself then, briefly, but just long enough to sense the ache in her lips, in her body, which I should have known had little to do with friendship.

'I'll put the luggage and some clothes in your bedroom,' she said. 'We can have some tea then.'

We walked back up to the house, the great Gothic pile shimmering in the afternoon light. And the thought first brushed across the edges of my mind. What if I was ever free again, if they caught the man who'd really killed Laura and I had Clare back with me? What if Alice and I ever came to love and marry? Would we all live together here, in this great place, the scheming, mean-spirited, penny-pinching world outside well forgotten? Would all three of us live happily ever afterwards? I let the thought die at once, unlikely as a fairy story: or a medieval romance.

But I was wrong here. The same thoughts soon crossed Alice's mind. She was quite an actress, of course. More than most of us, she saw inviting, if quite unlikely or unsuitable parts ahead of her in life, which she had but to choose to fulfil. But that's no excuse. I should never have encouraged her in this role of courtly damsel with me. On the other hand I encouraged her by my very presence. She was in love with me – if not that very afternoon in the summerhouse, then very shortly afterwards. The only way I could have changed things was by going back, there and then, to my oak tree in the woods. And of course I didn't do that.

Instead, as I soon realised, we embarked on a world then, that afternoon, where everything seemed possible at last for us, where we had both miraculously been given a second, a third? – but certainly a last chance in life: she to make amends for that social and emotional failure which had apparently so plagued her and I to find some hope, some renewal, out of my own disasters. Thus, alone together afterwards in the empty house, we took to each other with the sharpest sort of appetite: our very lives came to depend on each other. Each could save the other. But could we be saved together?

I changed into some more of Arthur's casual clothes in a guest bedroom along the corridor from Alice's room. Mrs Pringle hadn't come to turn the bed down and one of Arthur's large leather suitcases now occupied a prominent place on a chair.

Mrs Pringle gave us tea in the small drawing-room afterwards, an elaborate tea, of scones and cakes and sandwiches. If I'd not been told of her own gluttony I'd have thought she must have known all about my starvation in the woods. When Mrs Pringle was in the room with us, bringing the tea or taking it away, Alice and I talked about London and New York – about friends she and the real Harry Conrad had in common. I knew London and New York well enough, so I was able to reply convincingly in the same coin. But I watched Mrs Pringle's face out of the corner of my eye. It was impossible to tell anything from it. The extreme plumpness hid almost all facial movement and thus any change of expression.

Then she said to Alice, 'I hear the police were up all over the place here again this afternoon. Looking for that man.' She gathered the tea things up onto a tray as she spoke.

'Yes,' Alice replied easily, 'we were just talking about that. They found nothing of course.'

'Oh, I'm sure the villain left the area weeks ago,' Mrs Pringle said, confidently putting the silver lid back on the strawberry jam pot. 'I'm sure of it.'

She never so much as glanced in my direction either then or as she made her way out of the room. I was just going to say something to Alice when suddenly Mrs Pringle was back, putting her head round the door.

'For supper, Madam, I've done a salmon mousse. It's in the fridge. And there are the lamb cutlets you ordered afterwards. Five minutes under the pantry grill should do them. And I've made a salad.'

'Thank you,' Alice said. 'Thank you, Anna. I don't know what I'd do without you.'

And in that instant, just as Alice spoke to her, Mrs Pringle looked at me directly for the first time from the doorway. Her expression had certainly changed now. She smiled at me. But was it simply a polite courtesy, or a smile of connivance? I couldn't tell which. It could quite well have been either. Its meaning remained buried somewhere beneath the pumpkin of flesh, behind her little dark eyes.

Alice and I ate supper next to each other at a large round table set in an embrasure at the head of the great windowless dining-room in the centre of the house. Mrs Pringle had laid the two places complete in every high Gothic detail: gleaming fern-handled cutlery and old plate, with chased silver goblets and all the other accoutrements of a feudal dinner in time to go with them. I felt I should have been dressed in one of Arthur's dinner-jackets, though this, of course, would hardly have suited the Arthurian mood of the surroundings. I would have needed a doublet and hose to match the Camelot outfit, the almost diaphanous, high-waisted silk dress which Alice wore again that evening.

'We could have had all this in the kitchen,' I ventured.

'Yes. But Mrs Pringle likes to do it all properly. And so do I.' Alice looked at me almost severely. 'So why not?' Then she smiled. She liked having this formal dinner with me, I realised then, the huge candelabrum in the centre of the table, the flames casting steady shadows in the warm, still air, the long silver-strewn sideboards running away from us, down either side of the dining-room walls: a ghostly, summer dinner-party, with just the two of us at a table made for a dozen.

Alice liked entertaining me in such formal circumstances – as a prelude, perhaps, as she had hinted in Arthur's bedroom, to even more elaborate occasions, to the 'real thing': dinner parties with real guests, honourable, courtly people like ourselves, parties we two would preside over from opposite sides of the great round table.

Behind us, running right round the curved wall of the embrasure, was a rather faded Victorian mural of a medieval jousting tournament. Heavily armoured knights, bearing different coloured plumes and shields, charged at each other across the length of the wall while women in high toque hats and veils gazed at them with saintly rapture from a candy-striped pavilion in the middle. The whole thing had an air of idealised unreality.

'That's by Walter Crane,' Alice told me, noticing my interest. 'The Hortons had it done, after they'd staged a jousting tournament here when they opened the house in 1880. And do you know, we're going to do just the same thing later this summer. It's a hundred years since they built the house. There's to be a two-day fête: a jousting tournament, a medieval costume ball, an 1880s cricket match. The Victorian Society are helping me.'

Alice's face shone with something of the same rapture as the damsels on the wall as she spoke. It made me want to tease her a little 'But it's rather out of date, isn't it?' I said. 'Mimicking all those old, good, brave causes?'

I smiled. But Alice had ceased to smile. 'No. It's not out of date,' she said shortly, looking at me reprovingly, as though I was a Knight Errant criticising some glorious commission. So that by way of excuse I said to her, 'No, I meant that it was the shadow now, rather than the substance: of bravery, honour. It's not the "real thing".'

I wondered again why Alice had been so drawn to all these medieval symbols of chivalry and derring-do: these intense concepts of honour and glory. Had she been treated dishonourably once herself? Or was it just the fiction of a rich and aimless woman which she longed to enact here, another role she wanted to interpret? Was it real or false, this passionate identification with a Gothic past?

She said then, by way of answering my unspoken thoughts, 'It's all quite real to me. That's what Arthur and I fell out about. You see, I believe in all those values.'

'At face value?'

'Yes. And he didn't.'

Arthur, I could see in her mind, had betrayed the Glorious Company of the Round Table, while I had just joined it, taking his place now. I was tempted to say 'Isn't it all a little mad, in this day and age?' But I didn't speak the words in the end, for I sensed that I'd lose my place at the round table if I had. I knew now that Alice really believed in all these flawless virtues. Her shaky sanity was indeed based on this madness.

The salmon mousse was delicious. There was a bottle of slightly chilled Montrachet to go with it. But after this first course, before we went out to grill the cutlets in the pantry, I could eat no more. I pulled my chair back and lit a cigarette.

'About Clare,' I said. 'How do we get her out?'

'Well, she's in the Banbury General Hospital, we know that. In some private room there. Suffering the after-effects of that night, obviously. But Banbury's not far. Only fifteen miles or so.'

'And we just barge in?'

'No. We'll have to think.'

'And even if we do get her back here,' I shrugged my shoulders. 'It's ridiculous: Mrs Pringle will know at once. She'll hear the news. She'll know who the child really is – and that I'm not Mr Conrad.'

'Yes. I'd thought of that.' Alice fingered a tall Elizabethan silver salt-cellar. 'There's only one answer: take her back to the woods with you for the moment, until we get things straightened out. We can fix you up with a proper hideout out there meanwhile. Make it comfortable. The weather's fine enough. And there's plenty of cover.' She turned to me excitedly. 'Somewhere up in the trees, maybe. Had you thought of that?'

'A tree-house?'

'Yes. Exactly. That's something a child would like: yes, of course! A tree-house.' She beamed.

'I've made one already,' I said. 'In a big oak, overlooking the lake at the south end.'

Alice smiled. Then she laughed, her eyes glittering in the candlelight. 'So *that's* how you managed! Up a tree! I should have guessed. So that's why they never found you. I kept wondering. It's ideal! We can improve on it, maybe, but that's the answer.'

'And getting Clare out of the hospital. How about that?'

'I'll go there tomorrow. Into the children's ward I'll make some excuse – take in some old toys, some books and things. I'll find out exactly where she is.'

'Then just walk in and take her? There'll be nurses on duty twenty-four hours.'

'We'll have to make a plan,' Alice said, looking down, concentrating deeply. She spoke like a child herself just then, like a girl in a girl's adventure story, something from Angela Brazil, contemplating a raid on a rival school's dorm. So that I had to smile at her seriousness, her daring, over something, as I saw now, so essentially preposterous. But Alice believed. She was idealistic, never cynical. With all her money, real life had never touched her, I thought, and so this raid on Banbury Hospital didn't strike her as unusual. It was entirely appropriate to her chivalrous vision, a shining deed in a naughty world. But of course it wasn't something out of the pages of Angela Brazil. Alice would hardly have known that writer. It was a text straight from Arthurian legend again, out of her child's book perhaps, *In the Days of the King,* part of the search for the Holy Grail, or some other chivalrous quest, this rescue of a damsel in distress in the shape of Clare.

'Yes. We'll make a plan. We'll have to think about it,' she went on, without looking up, her dark hair fallen over her cheeks, partly covering her face, so that I could only really see the tip of her fine nose and chin.

I was so touched by her, suddenly; that she should help me thus. Even if nothing ever came of these plans... if I was caught tomorrow, if I never saw Alice again, I would have had this marvellous gesture of hers. Perhaps I fell in love with Alice at that moment. Or was it another feeling just as strong – of reverence? Of amazement certainly at her forthright generosity, at what seemed to me then to be her innocent, untroubled spirit. And it was I who kissed her now, standing up as she sat with her head over the table; it was I who gently turned her face to mine and kissed her then.

Whatever the feeling, it took us to bed together later that night, or rather onto the floor of her white, bare room with the cushions everywhere on the soft carpet and the cane dressing-table rising only a foot or so above it. The room seemed to have been decorated for life at ground level. And so we used it that way too in our loving.

The evening was hot, the big window open, looking westwards. But there wasn't a breath of wind to move the long loose-weave woollen curtains. The light came softly from a single white shade low down on the other side of her bed, and insects flew out of the night to it, through the wide mesh of the curtains, fluttering and buzzing round the bulb, trying to feed from it like a honey-pot.

I was completely exhausted after the long, fraught day. But it wasn't for this that we didn't make love. Alice, naked enough, was more unable than unwilling, and in my exhaustion it hardly mattered to me. I imagined her inability might well be part of her courtly ideals. But whatever caused it, we were happy enough just in each other's arms, and I was glad of my exhaustion.

Had I been more intent and lively I might have thought too much, too clearly, about Laura or Clare. As it was I was so tired I could barely think coherently at all. Loving Alice was more like floating in and out of sleep, where a dream stays so clearly fixed in your mind that it takes a minute before you realise you are conscious, only to find that you are asleep again by then, returned to the real dream, so that the two states are afterwards indistinguishable.

At one point, later in the evening, when I had drifted off into real sleep lying beside Alice on the bed now, I woke with a start for some reason and found how, rather than sleeping close to me, which would have been uncomfortable in the sticky heat in any case, she had moved away, a good two feet from me, asleep herself, but grasping my hand so firmly, almost fiercely across the sheet, that I feared to wake her if I moved myself at all. And so we lay like that on our backs, apart but closely linked.

I looked over at her face, in sharp silhouette against the beam of light from the lamp below the other side of the bed. Her nose was tilted in the air, as though sniffing something vital in the night. The sheet lay twisted diagonally across her body, baring one breast, covering another before running on up like a toga round her shoulder. Eyes closed, lips slightly apart, she gripped my hand as if I was leading her down a street, a blind person, completely trusting.

Alice had wanted to touch hands, I remembered, from her engagement diary in the tower. Arthur's hand, which he had denied her, I supposed. Beyond elegant dinner-parties or playing Red Indians by the lake or seeing herself as some Camelot maiden, beyond all her roles, even in deep sleep Alice wanted to hold hands more than anything else, it seemed. I'd left soon after that night and gone to my own room along the passage, for Alice had her breakfast brought up to her first thing each morning by Mary, the daily help.

When I woke, fairly late in the too-comfortable bed, someone was knocking at the door. It was Mary, with a pot of morning tea on a silver tray. Where Mrs Pringle had been gross, Mary was petite: a small woman in her thirties, with narrow features, spindly legs, bosomless and with her dank, dark hair cut dead straight round her neck, together with a boyish fringe. She might have been Irish from the last century – a famine victim. I couldn't think how she managed any strenuous housework.

'Good morning, sir,' The accent was local, north Cotswolds. She put the tea-tray down neatly on the bedside table and opened the curtains. The sun streamed in, out of an already flat, lead-blue summer sky.

Mary turned back from the window, standing awkwardly in front of the bed like a child, about to make a speech. Miss Troy asks you to have breakfast with her, sir, when you are ready. I've brought your tray to her suite.'

She spoke with an assumed formality as though she'd picked up the tone as well as these stilted phrases from a book of etiquette. Where Mrs Pringle seemed on too familiar terms with Alice and the household generally, Mary, clearly, was entirely conventional in her service.

Fifteen minutes later, shaved and dressed in yet more of

Arthur's too flattering clothes from the big suitcase, I was in Alice's white room once more, the curtains and the big French window open, giving out onto a small balcony, I saw now, with the sun blazing outside like fire.

Alice, in a long loose-weave cotton housecoat tied only at the neck, was out on the balcony, where two breakfast trays had been put on a slatted wood table. She'd started already.

'Sorry, I couldn't wait. I was ravenous! Are you?' she asked briskly, before biting deeply into a croissant. There was fresh orange juice as well, with apricot jam, a tall earthenware pot of coffee and two brown boiled eggs. I joined her on the other side of the table.

'That's fine,' I said. 'Of course, go ahead.' I was sitting directly opposite her now, both of us rather formal, even awkward for a moment. We might have been guests at an hotel. But then, just before I got the orange juice to my mouth, she put her hand across to me, stretching right over the table, and ran her index finger quickly down my cheek. And suddenly she wasn't brisk any more and we weren't hotel guests.

'Peter' she said. But she didn't continue. She just looked at me, quite still, as if she'd utterly forgotten what she was saying.

'Yes.' She broke the mood in the end, brisk again. 'I've been thinking: about Clare. I think I know how. I'll tell you. But first maybe we should take a look at your tree-house this morning, and bring some supplies down there?'

Sitting together on the sunny balcony, sipping fresh roast coffee and eating croissants in so civilised a manner that morning, I found it almost impossible to imagine living savagely in the woods again. And I thought it an even more unlikely thing to expect a ten-year-old autistic child to do.

'Alice, maybe we're both of us out of our minds,' I said. 'I want Clare back, yes. She hasn't any relations in this country. And her grandparents are a thousand miles away, one of them crippled. But is *this* the way?'

'If you want her, yes.'

'But listen, if you make yourself known to the people in the hospital they'll remember you afterwards, that you turned up out of the blue with toys for the children; and the next day that Clare disappeared. They'll put two and two together. And then they'll come up here looking for us all again.'

'No they won't. I've got another idea now. I won't go there at all.' Alice's face was bright with hidden schemes.

'You mean I'll just walk into the hospital – cold – and grab Clare?'

'No. You'll be in the hospital already,' Alice said proudly. 'You'll be there to begin with – ill in bed.' She smiled.

'*Ill*?'

'Yes! Swallow soap or something. Get sick. Violent stomach pains. Take a taxi to the hospital. Collapse! They'll keep you there for observation.'

'With a false name, and so on?'

'Yes. Why not? You said you'd trained in all that sort of subterfuge when you were in British Intelligence. They won't be looking for you up in the hospital in any case. You can say you're a tourist, staying in some hotel in Banbury overnight. Food poisoning – that's it. Well, you'll get better pretty soon. You'll be on your feet, wandering round the wards, so you can find out where Clare is. Then call me and I'll arrange to come round and wait for you both with a car sometime at night, behind the hospital maybe. We can check the place out this afternoon. Well?'

'It's possible.' I had to admit there was something in Alice's idea. If I could get into the hospital in such a *bona fide* manner that would be at least half the battle; finding Clare and getting her out would be a lot more feasible.

'Nothing venture, nothing win,' Alice said. 'Right?'

'I suppose so.' I picked my coffee up. It was delicious – not too bitter: an American blend. They knew how to do it. And I thought: I wanted Clare – yes. I had to get her. But this way would surely take me back to disaster, to a murder charge, cold tea and slops in a prison cell, if not something worse at the hands of David Marcus or Ross or one of the other hit-men in my old intelligence section. I looked at Alice and then out over the rich summer parkland. The peace, the security, the privacy of this great estate, I thought; an elegant breakfast and the love of a good woman. I wanted all this, too. But could I have both? Could I have Clare as well? That seemed like too much of a good thing.

The sun glistened on Alice's dark hair. She stood up, and taking a pair of binoculars that had been on the balcony rail, she looked out over the parkland to the west. We would hear the faint sound of an axe thudding on the morning air.

'The men are still thinning the trees somewhere over there,' she said. 'I can't see them. It's a much thicker wood on that side of the park, you know. Goes on for a mile or more: oak and beech and elm, a lot of it dead. Not been touched in years. We've been trying to clear it, but it'll take ages'

'Don't you use equipment,' I said. 'Chain-saws, bulldozers –'

She turned sharply. 'Not at all. We're doing it all by hand. There are wild flowers and things out there. You have to do it all very gently.'

'Of course.'

'Do you like that sort of work?'

'Well . . .' I was doubtful.

'I love it,' she rushed on. 'Cutting out old briars, chopping dead wood, clearing paths, planting fresh shrubs.' She looked at me hopefully, a child proposing some exciting new game.

I didn't, in fact, care much for this sort of work at all, though I liked getting a bonfire together at the end of the day and just standing over it watching the flames.

'I love bonfires,' I said, by way of showing willing.

'There's such a lot to *do* here,' Alice went on, a passionate frustration in her voice. 'I've barely started.'

'Yes. I saw the landing upstairs: that Victorian stuff lying about all over the place. You know, you should be seeing to all that, Alice, and not worrying about me.'

The moment I said this I realised I was lying – I wanted Alice's help – and that I'd hurt her again, too, for she was suddenly crestfallen, as if at some vision of future happiness disrupted. And I hated myself for disappointing her again in this way, for the predicament I'd got myself into: I wanted her help and she wanted to love me. And that was the problem: we had different priorities. Alice, looking over her half-completed world that morning, was offering me a share in it, a life with her, where together we would literally fulfil life together – thin the trees, clear the paths, sort out that long corridor of bric-à-brac upstairs and, who knows, maybe find a real use for those fabulous nursery toys one day . . .

Consciously or not, she held all this out to me that morning. Yet I held back: saw her, even, as something of a temptress, the devil on a high hill offering me everything in the world, whereas in reality I thought it was too late. I had been given a promised land already, which I had lost with Laura. The talk of bonfires just then had reminded me: of that cold blue spring evening two months before, out in the back garden of our cottage with the Bensons when I had burnt the old elder branches and the damp books from the garage and seen the pages of R. M. Ballantyne's *The World of Ice* curl and blacken in the flames.

I remembered this, and with it came other vivid glimpses of my nine months with Laura: the afternoon sun on her body in the hotel bedroom in Lisbon, the beach at Cascais, Clare on the pony; our big, too-loving dog Minty, the Easter hyacinths crushed with the grave-dirt all over the fine linen Sunday tablecloth, the disaster of Clare's eating, the potato-throwing in the bathroom – and yet the way she had slowly recovered with Laura and me. Here, in all these things created together, this was where my real future had been. And I couldn't really see my doing the same thing with Alice in this great house, which was already so much her own eccentric creation, a succession of theatrical sets where I was a latecomer, and now a prisoner held by all Alice's loving inventions.

I couldn't go back. I knew that, of course. Laura was dead. But my way forward was towards Clare. It was Clare first, before Alice, whose life had to be returned to her. That was my problem: Alice was a means to an end, not hers. Did she know this? And if she did, how long would she accept it? Those wonderful, childish traits of hers, if frustrated, could well lead to tears before bedtime.

And then, confounding all such thoughts, Alice turned from the balcony and seeing my glum face, she suddenly brightened.

'No,' she said, 'I shouldn't be worrying about you. And I'm not . . . not really. It's *me* I've been worrying about. Can't you see?'

'How?'

'You heard me the other day down by the lake – those war-whoops and beating the water up and taking those roses out to the island, not to mention playing Camelot – '

'But I liked all that. I told you.'

'Yes,' she said simply. 'You liked it. I liked it. But don't you see? I was going *crazy*. And I'm not any more.'

'I stopped you playing Red Indians, you mean?'

'No! I found *you* playing them – you forget: naked with a bow and arrow!'

'It was just that I'd had a swim that morning, before Ross arrived.'

'It was just nothing of that sort at all! You'd been up a tree for ten days as well, killing sheep and thieving the cricketers' tea.'

'I'm sorry.'

'*Don't* be. That's the whole point. You saved me: I thought I was mad, going down deep, cracked. I thought Arthur and the others were going to be proved right – Oh so right! – that I'd be dragged out of this place in a straitjacket screaming. Until I saw you, behind that shed, and heard your story. Then I knew I wasn't alone. And it's that feeling that you're uniquely crazy that makes you so.'

'I see.' And I did see.

'So,' Alice said lightly, 'I'm really saved already. It's your turn now.'

She stood with her back to the stone balustrade, no longer worried about tidying up the landscape, looking at me with a confidence and happiness that had nothing possessive about it, with no end in view apparently but mine.

'It's your turn now. You'll see!' There was a ringing American optimism in her voice. She spoke with the passion of the converted, the certainty of a prophet guaranteeing a future, offering me a miraculous world at the end of the yellow-brick road. How could I have refused her?

Alice left the balcony, going inside to dress. I picked the binoculars up and gazed out over the sunlit parkland towards the far side where the sounds of the axe had come from. Swinging the glasses round I suddenly came on Alice's two workmen, together with a third man supervising them, a little tough-looking, wiry fellow – Mrs Pringle's husband, I supposed – all of them just inside the margin of the trees. But they were not clearing the undergrowth. That had been done already. They were reinforcing the high barbed-wire fence with wooden stakes, I saw when I focused the glasses, ten feet tall, where the wire strands, less than a foot apart, made an unnecessarily formidable barrier for any animal. The fence was clearly there to keep people out of the estate. Or to keep them in, I wondered? To keep Alice in? The barrier would serve both purposes equally well. Alice thought herself sane at last. But her husband would have had no reason for thinking this, and the Pringles, it struck me then, were more likely to have been employed by him as jailers rather than housekeepers.

I turned the glasses to the south of the park. Looking beyond the cricket pitch I could just see the Pringles' lodge. Next to it were some huge iron gates, firmly shut, with the same high wire fence running along inside the estate wall to either side. Alice might be sane, but she was trapped. And so was I.

Ten

I hadn't forgotten Alice's athleticism, but I was still surprised by the ease with which she shinned up the beech branches and across to my oak tree down by the lake later that morning. The child was mother to the woman here, I knew that. And I knew she kept herself fit, thrashing the waters and playing tennis. But this was quite another sort of agility for a woman, more in the circus trapeze department. And, indeed, she was like a girl happy under the big top that morning as she hooked her legs and arms over branches, swinging upwards through the green leaves into shafts of sun that filtered through them, moving into the light above like a swimmer rising effortlessly from the deep. And suddenly, after the confines and alarms of the house, in the clear, early-summer air of the trees, the smell of wood and moss and water all around, I felt as if I was coming home again, to a kind of freedom in this hidden place.

'It's up there,' I'd said to begin with, pointing to my oak.

'Why, even you couldn't climb that.' Alice had looked at the smooth fifteen-foot bole of the tree.

'No. That's the whole point. No one could climb it. I get across onto it from that copper-beech tree, higher up there.'

And we'd gone back up the steep side of the valley, to where the great sloping beech limb came to within a few feet of the ground, giving access to my oak.

'I'll go up first and let a rope down. Then you can tie that bag of things on and I'll pull it up.'

We'd brought down two sleeping-bags from the Manor, along with blankets and some makeshift clothes for Clare to use, and some old toys, games and books as well from the Victorian nursery. I'd taken soaps, towels, a toothbrush, shaving gear and a hand-mirror from Arthur's suite. There was a decent torch and some extra tools in the bag: a hammer, nails and a small sharp hatchet.

I had taken some books from the library, for the long evenings: Scott's *Ivanhoe* and Conan Doyle's *The White Company* among them and a lot of picture magazines for Clare. In the old days this had been part of her cure, lying on the cottage floor and thumbing through the pages of the colour supplements, picking out and concentrating for an hour on some unlikely photograph – the gaudy vicious picture of a gyrating punk rocker, some bloody battlefront scene, or a skyscraper collapsing. She had found a strange solace in such violent images before; they calmed her, and I expected she might need them again now, among much else in the way of a cure, for she would almost certainly have regressed in her autism since I had left her.

Alice had given me several large bottles of soda and lime juice for Clare, along with some good malt whisky and red plastic picnic tumblers. Food had been more of a problem, since Mrs Pringle had been in and out of the kitchen all morning. We'd only managed a package of digestive biscuits from the pantry and an expensive wooden box of Harrods' liqueur chocolates which had been left in the drawing-room from the previous Christmas. On the other hand I knew I could pick up food, and anything else we needed, from the house at night, when Alice was there alone.

I pulled the big hold-all up to the top of the oak, along with Spinks's bow and the two arrows which I'd brought back from the manor. Then Alice had come up after me and finally we were both together in the tree-house.

Everything was just as I'd left it: my muddy cord suit, grubby shirt and underclothes, the billycan with the flakey remains of the boiled perch still stuck to it, the transistor, the ex-army binoculars, along with Spinks's bawdy paperback and the *Good Beer Guide* for 1979. Alice looked around, touching things, fascinated.

'You see,' I said, 'this is how I get the water, and the fish.' I let the canvas water bag over the side of the planks. 'Of course, you've got to go along that lower branch there – out over the lake. But it's no problem.'

'No. Except for a child. Maybe I was wrong suggesting you brought her back up this tree: a child in some state of shock, too, if she's been in hospital these two weeks.'

'I'd thought of that myself. I can keep her out on the island for a few days, to begin with. That's what I'd thought: out in the little mausoleum.'

'Yes. I'll put some clothes and food in there in any case, when you've gone.'

'But Clare can climb all right,' I went on. 'Probably be part of a cure for her. She was always up and down the old elder trees in our back garden. And in Cascais last summer, there was a big cork tree in the garden there: she used to get right to the top of it in a flash. These children usually have extraordinary physical gifts; I told you. Clare certainly has – climbing, hiding, running, anything like that. Maybe she got it when she was very young, out in the bush, in east Africa. She lived practically wild out there, as far as I can gather, for months on end with her parents when they were fossilling about.'

'Did she?' Alice asked vaguely. Yet she was thinking about something, concentrating on it sharply. 'All away from the big bad world,' she said at last. Then she was silent. Finally she picked up the camping gas burner. 'That's not really fair is it?' she said.

'No. But you can't have a real fire up here. And anyway, I'm not out on a camping holiday, am I?'

'What if it rains? You'll need something overhead. There's some polythene in the yard. The builders left it. That would do. I'll bring it down.' Alice gazed upwards through the topmost leaves of the oak into the burnished blue sky beyond. A breeze came just then, stirring the leaves minutely. She sighed.

'It's perfect, isn't it,' she said enviously.

'Well, for a day or two. Or a game, for a child. I wouldn't care to spend too long up here, though. I'm not exactly a hermit and it's not a tropical island.'

'You could make it bigger, though, couldn't you? You could really build a whole house up in these trees and no one would ever know.'

'I don't expect to be here that long,' I said.

'No. And maybe you won't have to. The Pringles are taking their summer vacation in a few weeks' time. Going to Spain. You could both come back up to the house then.'

'What about Mary? And the two gardeners?'

'Mary leaves at mid-day. And they're out and about all the time. We could get round that, hide you both up in the tower or something till Mary leaves each morning.'

'What about Arthur, or your son, or some other friends? Someone's bound to turn up.'

'I doubt it. And anyway, you'll probably be gone by then. You're going back to Portugal, aren't you?'

'Yes.'

'In a false beard? Or will you and Clare just walk away on the waters?' Alice smiled. She was provoking a future, provoking choices, plans in me which I'd barely thought of. She had started, as I knew she would, thinking of herself. Where would she be, where would she find a place when all this music stopped? But there was no time to think about this then.

Alice had said she'd drive me to Banbury later that morning to scout out the ground, and I wondered just how she'd manage this, given the barbed-wire fence, the closed front gates and my theories about the real nature of the Pringles' job at the Manor. Was Alice really trapped inside the estate?

We walked down a back drive, which ran through the trees behind the house, until after nearly a mile we came to a locked gate in the high barbed-wire fence at the northern edge of the estate. But Alice had a key to it.

'What's all this about?' I asked innocently.

'Oh, Arthur had this gross fence made all round the place. To keep robbers out, he thinks. But I have a car on the other side. I bought it myself, to get a little independence from him. He was always spying on me.'

She opened the gate and, sure enough, in an old tin cow-shed hidden among some overgrown bushes, was a new Ford Fiesta. Alice was trapped all right, by Arthur's intention at least, and since she didn't have to admit this, I certainly wasn't going to remind her. She thought herself sane; her husband clearly thought otherwise.

Banbury General Hospital lay at the top of a hill on the main Oxford road leading half a mile east out of the Midland town. Beneath the hill, in the old market centre, beyond the cross, was the broad Horsefair with several hotels down its length. I noted the name of one of them: the Whately Hall. It would suit me fine. I'd play the role of businessman or visitor down from London for a week, starting a Cotswold tour. Stratford-on-Avon, after all, was not far down the road. No one would question my presence in this early summer tourist season, when already there were thousands of strangers in the area.

The hospital, Victorian redbrick where it fronted the main road, had been extended by a number of modern single-storey wards which ran away behind, like fingers, into an open space of gardens and a long car-park. If I found myself in any of these single-storey wards – and if Clare was in one of them as well – getting out and away via the car-park at the back shouldn't be too difficult, I thought.

We parked there for ten minutes and looked around.

'Here,' Alice said. 'If I wait for you around here, just facing the car park entrance, so that I can get away at once. All right? When you call me I'll be here.'

The position Alice had suggested, at the end of the car park, was only thirty yards or so away from the end of one of the long ward buildings, not far from some big oil tanks and the back service entrance to the hospital. She was driving a small, almost new, black Ford Fiesta, a common enough car and colour, and speedy, too. Above all, it was just the right size for holding the narrow, winding roads which traversed all this part of the north Cotswolds, which we would have to travel on to get back to Beechwood Manor fifteen miles to the south. We studied a large scale map for the whole area.

'When the police put blocks up,' I said. 'They'll do it on all the *main* roads leading out of here and the Cotswolds first. Well, we won't be on any of them. But they'll put blocks up round the few towns in the area as soon as they can as well – Chipping Norton and Stow, which are between us and Beechwood. So we'll need to bypass them on some minor roads. Let's make a trial run back now.'

We drove southwards through the suburbs of Banbury and out into the country, marking our route on the map as we went along the smaller roads towards Chipping Norton. We avoided the town here by turning right a mile outside it at a roundabout and driving down a long valley towards Shipston and Stratford, before turning left up the wolds again towards Stow-on-the-Wold. We rode straight along a ridgeway here, where we could make good speed. And now in any case we made better time since these were roads Alice knew, nearer her home.

'They'll have the main road blocks out within about twenty minutes of our leaving the hospital,' I said. 'That will only get us as far as that roundabout back there.'

'They can't block *all* the roads as quickly as that. We'll just have to be lucky.'

I looked at Alice. She drove well. She'd been driving in England for several years. But this was the full light of day. How would she manage at night? In the dark, which would almost certainly be the best time to get Clare out, if I could get her out at all? I asked her.

'I'll *do* the trip at night, that's how, tonight, after I drop you near the hotel. I can make it several times.'

Again, I had doubts about the whole plan, which she sensed.

'Look, it'll either work, or it won't!' she said defiantly. 'But I think it will.'

'Why?'

'Surprise, that's why. They won't be expecting it. How could they? We have the surprise element, completely.'

'Yes. . . .'

'But come on, we're not nearly there yet. We'll have to stop at a call-box, just in case they're tapping the Beechwood phone, and you can reserve your hotel. And then we'd better get back and fix up your suitcase and clothes.'

'Arthur's clothes.'

'Yes. But we'll have to take all the labels out of them and get you some papers, money. Make another new person out of you.' She smiled. 'Who are you going to be this time?'

Alice was thinking of everything, and so I was suddenly determined to think up a name for myself. 'I'll be John Burton,' I said, 'and I'll come from 16 Bradford Road, London, W 2. How's that?'

'Fine. You're getting the hang of things.'

We stopped at a call-box in Stow and I made the booking that night for a single room, for one night, at the Whately Hall Hotel in Banbury. There were no problems.

I'd committed myself at last. And suddenly I felt easier, more confident as a result: the enemy was in view once more, the long-delayed plan of attack under way. There were only two choices open to me now, to sink or to swim. And since it had once again boiled down to this, to a matter of life and death almost, I felt as I had when I'd waited for Ross's vicious dog running up the valley towards me two weeks before, the bowstring tight against my cheek, just before the shaft transfixed the Alsatian: and I felt that strange surge of animal confidence as I got back into the car – something brutal rising in me, beyond thought certainly, a sort of blood-lust that surprised me. I suddenly had a vital will to succeed and I didn't know at all where that will came from.

Back at the Manor after lunch we looked out some suitable clothes together in Arthur's rooms – pyjamas, a suit, shirts, some casual wear – and carefully cut off all the labels on them.

'I'll need a dressing-gown maybe,' I said. 'If I'm to go walking round the wards.'

But Arthur had left only one dressing-gown behind – in surprising red silk, a Noël Coward affair that would surely call unwanted attention to me.

'Take it anyway,' Alice advised. 'You may need it. And don't forget some shaving things, toothpaste . . . They expect all that in hospitals.'

Alice finished the packing and then looked up at me, peering into my face. 'That scar, it's still there: a way of identifying you afterwards. We'll just have to risk that, or find you a hat to cover it.' She ran her finger gently along the mark on my temple. Then she was brisk again. 'Now: some papers. You can have one of my wallets. I got it in Florence years ago. There's nothing American about it.'

She handed me a lovely Florentine leather wallet, edged in gilt. Inside was a number of fairly grubby £5 and £10 notes. 'I'm sure they can't trace them,' she said. I counted them. There was £100 in all.

'Thank you. I'll make a note of it.'

Alice said nothing until, as we left the room, she asked: 'A weapon of some sort? Do you need one?'

'Why? I don't think so.'

'I have a small hand-gun.'

'You think I'll have to fight my way out of the place? That's nonsense. Besides, they'd spot it when I got undressed in the hospital.'

'I know!' Alice suddenly said. 'There's some old swordsticks downstairs. Arthur collects them.'

'Come on – '

'No. It could be useful. And you could keep it by you all the time. Pretend you have a limp.'

'Yes, but why bother, if they're not expecting me?'

'You never know. They might try and stop you on your way out. Besides, a limp is a good disguise,' she added brightly. 'A man with a limp . . .' She considered this conceit for a moment, as if contemplating a proposed charade in a Christmas drawing-room, before finding the idea good. But I didn't.

'A man with a limp and a swordstick and a Noël Coward dressing-gown,' I said. 'It's too much, Alice. I'd be overplaying my hand.'

'If you don't overplay your hand a bit you won't ever get into that damn hospital. Remember, you have to act as if your whole gut was on fire to begin with. Unless you really want to eat a cake of soap. And remember, too, the less you look like your old self the better. Who are you anyway? This John Burton from London?'

'Well, with a gammy leg, swordstick and that tarty dressing-gown I'd better be a London antique-dealer. What do you think?'

Alice smiled. 'You're certainly getting the idea,' she said.

Later she showed me the collection of swordsticks, kept locked up in Arthur's gun-room at the back of the house. There were half a dozen of them – silver-topped, eighteenth-century canes for the most part. I chose the least antique and ostentatious: a stout Victorian bamboo walking-stick with an antler handle and a secret release catch. Inside was a long needle of engraved Toledo steel, double-edged, half an inch wide at the top and tapering to an extremely fine, sharp point.

'I don't like the look of it,' I said.

'Nor will they if you just bring it out. You won't have to *use* it.'

I put the blade back and, using the stick as support, practised my limp across the gun-room. Arthur's suit chosen for me this time was a lightweight tweed. And I had a hat to go with it now – a tweed pork-pie that came down over my scar. I looked too carefully, too expensively dressed for an antique-dealer. On the other hand I certainly looked nothing like my real self: the man the police would be looking for.

Alice, now almost carried away by her sense of the theatrical, was pleased with the result. She looked at me from a distance, head to one side, quizzically. 'I wouldn't recognise you,' she said.

'No. Just like the first time I got into Arthur's clothes.'

Was it her wish that I should undergo successive transformations in this sartorial manner, each of which would take me further away from the chalk-dusted, badly dressed teacher I'd been with Laura, and closer to Alice – all changes which would make me more dependent on her, as puppet, as lover? In her eyes certainly I must have already fulfilled all her theatrical expectations, played the game well – changing from naked savage to tweedy countryman in little more than twenty-four hours. In my own eyes I felt less and less the actor and more the fool – who had still to assume a dangerous role. On the other hand, if Clare was to be freed... And I had to admit that Alice's ideas here, simply because of their very drama, might well work. I was dependent on Alice; it was simply this dependence that I didn't like.

'Come on,' she said, having watched me think for half a minute. 'We're ready.' She kissed me, briefly. I still didn't respond. 'I know,' she said. 'Sooner you than me. It's difficult, changing your life. But you've done it so well already, Peter, you can do it again. I've been amazed, seeing you...'

She gazed at me proudly, as on a Knight Errant about to depart on some great cause in her honour. And I saw the madness of the whole scheme once more then – but saw equally that it was an escapade which Alice, in her own bizarre mind, now relied on me to fulfil. She expected my fidelity in this cause; we were brother and sister in arms. To fail her in it would be to betray her. And I realised it was she who was dependent on me now – her life on mine, and I was ashamed at my earlier thoughts of her manipulation.

'Say goodbye to Mrs Pringle. And I'll take you to your – London train.'

She turned away, busying herself with some last-minute detail, so that I was left with an image of Alice in the great house. An image of someone I wanted to kiss now, but couldn't.

I threw a convincing fit, writhing in the hall of the hotel next morning in Banbury. I had earlier called the receptionist from my bedroom, complaining of severe stomach pains and cramps, so that this subsequent performance was not unexpected. The Manager offered me a doctor there and then – there was a surgery, he told me, just next door to the hotel, but I suggested a taxi to the hospital at once, and thus I left five minutes later, doubled up with my bamboo walking-stick and suitcase, a surprising casualty from the sumptuous Inn, stumbling out into the bright summer morning.

In the hospital waiting-room I repeated the performance, and having filled in a form, or rather dictated most of it to the receptionist, such was the imagined force of my pains just then, I was soon taken down a corridor to a consulting room where I was laid out on a raised couch and left alone.

Five minutes later a young Indian medico arrived in a white jacket with half a dozen ballpoints sticking up in his front pocket. He was a very small man, narrow-headed, with vague, heavy-lidded, apparently quite aimless eyes. His hair was dark and greased with a Disraeli kiss-curl neatly imprinted on his forehead like a bass clef.

He took one of the ballpoint pens from his pocket as if to make notes, though he had no paper with him.

'What seems to be the matter?' he asked, looking away from me towards the clouded glass window through which he could see nothing. He seemed sleepy, almost asleep. His English was perfect, almost without accent.

'Pains,' I said grunting. 'Here. I don't know – but I have an ulcer disposition.'

I had lowered my trousers and taken up my shirt.

'Where?' he asked, paying attention at last. I showed him. He prodded my stomach with the top of his ballpoint, as if keen not to sully his fingers.

'Higher up,' I said. 'And don't prod me with that pen. It hurts.'

The man said nothing. But next time he used his fingers when he probed me.

'Sick – have you been sick?'

'No. But I feel sick.'

'Have you ever had a barium meal? With your London doctor?'

'No.' The man thought for half a minute about this, his head turned away from me, dreaming again. He seemed only just in touch with life. Perhaps he'd been up all night on duty.

'It's just there, the pain, is it? The upper middle of the stomach?' He pushed me fairly hard, so that I had no difficulty in almost screaming.

'Yes,' I said breathlessly. 'There. That's it.'

'Emm . . .' he said. He took up his ballpoint again and flipped it in the air several times.

'It's as if a stake had been driven through me,' I said.

'Peritonitis, I should think, if the pain is that bad.'

'What?'

'Bad ulceration. You have an ulcer disposition? Well there's a risk of a perforation. I told you, if it really pains like that.'

'And?'

'We should probably operate. Have you signed a disclaimer form?'

'*Operate*? No, I've signed nothing.'

'I'll have one sent round. Meanwhile I'll arrange for a barium meal and an X-ray.'

'I don't think I want an operation, surely. Just keep me in for observation, no?'

'Yes. But if it bursts, well – we'd be too late,' the Indian said offhandedly.

'A second opinion? Could we have that?'

'Yes.' He turned away, in a dream again. 'You'd have that anyway. But the consultant isn't in just yet. Nor the surgeon. I'll arrange for a meal and an X-ray meanwhile. Then we can operate – or not, as the case may be.' He turned back to me. 'The nurse will give you something for the pain. All right?'

I nodded and he left me. God, I thought, an operation. I had obviously overplayed my part. If they operated. But of course they wouldn't – when the X-rays showed nothing amiss. They would then simply keep me in bed under observation for a few days. But could I be sure? Of course, I could simply refuse the operation and leave the hospital, release myself. But that wouldn't serve my purpose at all. I had to stay in the hospital and find out where Clare was; that was the whole point. I was suddenly uneasy then, all my earlier confidence gone.

A nurse arrived and gave me a pain-killing injection, and soon afterwards the same nurse helped me into a wheelchair and a porter drove me down interminable corridors to the X-ray department. I still had my stick with me, and the suitcase. I felt like a very old man, incapable of anything. The pain-killer made me drowsy.

The barium meal – a nasty, cherry-and-milk flavoured concoction – together with the X-ray took up most of the morning as I had to wait my turn in line. And afterwards I was left to wait again in a cubicle nearly an hour while they studied the results.

But eventually I had the verdict. The Indian doctor saw me again. There was nothing wrong with my gut, he said. Nothing at all, as far as the X-ray plates went.

'Just your ulcer disposition.' He smiled wanly. 'Or maybe a grumbling appendix.'

'It still hurts, certainly.'

'Well, we'll keep you in for observation anyway. Just in case. And no food, in case we have to operate. All right?'

I nodded, relieved at last. And by lunchtime, though I was ravenously hungry, I was safely a-bed, sitting up in Arthur's flashy dressing-gown, in one of the long modern wards that ran away at the back of the building towards the car-park, with my suitcase gone but with my bamboo stick still with me, as I'd insisted, leaning up against the bedside table.

I was halfway down one side of a general ward of about thirty beds, nearly all of them filled, with only two where the curtains had been pulled round in tactful silence. For the rest, the patients were a garrulous lot, when they did not hawk and cough and groan. The noise increased around lunchtime, some of the old men behaving with the excitement of predatory animals over their food. And afterwards, smacking their toothless chops, they talked to each other, loudly, often across several beds, swapping raucous notes on the past and future of their various complaints. The place was like a strange zoo, or some contemporary and unpleasant open-stage theatrical event. It was impossible to sleep.

The man immediately to my left, an elderly Cotswolds type who must have been in his eighties, swathed in bandages, soon got talking to me. He spent little enough time enquiring of my illness; his own misfortune entirely absorbed him and I was a captive audience. He was a passionate gardener, he told me, and had been out in his back patch a fortnight before where he had an old wooden-framed greenhouse. It had suddenly collapsed all over him, in a high wind up on the wolds – the same thunderstorm, I imagined, that had come up to me in the valley

– and he had been badly cut about the head and neck by the falling glass.

'I didn't know what hit me,' the old man explained. 'I thought it were one of those Yankee bombers from the Heyford base, I did.'

'Dear me,' I commiserated with him. Though I hoped not to encourage him, for I could see he loved his mishap. And sure enough, almost immediately, he proceeded to repeat the misadventure in every detail, from start to finish.

By late afternoon, the old man still talking, I could bear it no more. I asked the nurse if there was a day-room for patients on the mend. I was feeling much better. There was, and she allowed me to go to it. So, wrapped up in my colourful dressing-gown, I limped out of the ward.

Once outside and moving towards the day-room, I had free run to explore all the many corridors and wards in the main part of the hospital. And it wasn't long, wandering up and down these passageways, before I came on the children's wards. There was two of them, both on the ground floor, both running back towards the car park. The first, with its high-sided white cots, was for the youngest of the children. The one next was for children of Clare's age. The doors into both were open as I passed by. It was just after 5.30. Many relatives and friends were already inside the wards visiting, and many more were arriving immediately behind me as I walked along the corridor.

When I reached the end I turned sharply back. I decided to take the risk: just to walk calmly into the wards, with the crush of other visitors, take a look around, then walk out again. I could say I was lost if anyone stopped me.

But no one did, as I entered the first ward. Everyone, children, parents and the few nurses, was totally taken up with their own affairs. I glanced and smiled at the beds as I walked down the centre aisle. But Clare was nowhere to be seen. And then, right at the end of the ward, I saw four glass-walled, private rooms, for iller children I assumed, or private patients. Walking through another open door here I saw that three of the rooms were occupied. There were visitors in two of them. But in the third room, right at the back, at the very end of the corridor, through the glass partition, I saw Clare sitting up in pyjamas at the end of her bed. A nurse, a young Chinese girl, was playing with her, or trying to at least occupy her with some toys.

I turned away at once, in case she saw me. But I needn't have worried, for when I turned back briefly and looked at Clare again, I could see her blank face, how her eyes were quite unfocused. But it was Clare all right, with the mop of golden colour all round the top of her head; Clare alive, if not well. But physically well, I thought, at least: capable of being moved. I wished I could have gone to her there and then, my heart jumping with excitement.

As I left these private rooms, I saw a fire-extinguisher by some half-opened curtains at the end of the corridor. Beyond was a metal-framed french window leading out somewhere to the back of the hospital. I could see trees and some tired summer grass in the late-afternoon light. The car-park must have been nearby. And there was a key in the lock of the door: here was my escape.

On the way back to my ward I stopped in the main hallway of the hospital. There was a public phone on the wall here, but it was engaged, and I had to wait ten minutes before I got through to Alice. We had agreed on a code before I'd left her.

'It's all arranged,' I told her. 'I've found the present we want. I'll wait for you with it behind the station, from ten o'clock onwards, tonight.'

I wasn't given any supper that evening and I was light-headed with nervous excitement as well as from lack of food. I tried not to look at the clock at the end of the ward. I tried listening to the radio instead, taking the headphones down from above my bed. At least this ploy kept the old man next door at bay, though I could still see him trying to talk to me, his lips moving soundlessly as I listened to "The Archers".

And then, through nervous exhaustion I suppose, I must have fallen asleep with the headphones still round my ears, for the next thing I knew I was awake and on my side, with the curtains drawn all down the ward. It was 10.15 – the old man next me was still talking, I noticed, when I looked across at him.

But after a moment I saw he wasn't talking to me. With my headphones on there was still no sound from his lips. He was speaking to someone else, I realised now, someone I'd not seen on the other side of my bed. I turned.

The Indian doctor was there, together with another older man I didn't recognise, and beyond him a third figure, but one I knew: it was Ross, the man who'd stalked me two weeks before through the early mists in the valley by the lake, whose dog I'd killed and who now, much more certainly, had come to claim me.

I took the headphones off. The other man had a clipboard in one hand. He looked at it and then at my name on the end of the bed.

'Mr John Burton? he asked.

'Yes. I'm John Burton. What's wrong?'

But Ross came in at once then. 'You're not "John Burton",' he said. 'You're Peter Marlow, aren't you?' He spoke quietly, very reasonably, with kindness almost.

'I couldn't find anything wrong with him, you see,' the Indian piped in. 'There was nothing wrong in the X-ray. Nothing whatsoever. I thought there was something strange then,' he added, justifying himself.

The old Cotswolds gardener in the next bed was all ears, craning over towards us, trying to pick up our conversation. And others in the ward were awake or alert now, curious at this intrusion.

'If you wouldn't mind coming to the administrator's office for a moment?' Ross asked, looking about him uneasily at the disturbance they'd caused.

'You don't have to move, Mr Burton,' the other older man said to me, the Administrator himself, I presumed. He looked at Ross very critically. 'I'm afraid,' he went on, 'if Mr Burton denies he's the man you want, he can stay exactly where he is. He's a patient here, appropriately admitted for observation pending treatment. Your writ stops at the entrance.'

'Of course, doctor; I'd no intention...' Ross excused himself. 'I'd just like to talk to Mr Burton privately for a few minutes, here in the hospital.'

'Well, if Mr Burton agrees, that's all right. But you can do it here. We can pull the curtains.'

I'd no wish to see Ross privately here or anywhere else. He'd probably try and get rid of me at once, in whatever circumstances, I thought. But I saw that if I wanted to get Clare out I'd have to move immediately in any case. With Ross so certainly on my trail again, yet with Alice waiting outside for me at that same moment, I knew I'd never get another chance of taking Clare. The best thing was to get out of bed, prepare myself, get ready to run . . . There was nothing to be gained by staying put, that was for sure.

'All right,' I said, 'I'll come to your office. We don't want to go on making a fuss in the ward.'

I got slowly out of bed. I still had my dressing-gown on. The others made way for me as I stood up gingerly. Then I grasped my stick, taking it as support, before limping carefully out from between the beds.

The three men were moving slowly behind me now, as we all made our way towards the ward door. A night nurse had just arrived and was sitting at a table ahead of us, in the middle of the central aisle near the exit, a table which, I saw, would slightly block our progress. We would have to move past it, to either side, in single file. And if I were first through, as I would be, the three others behind me could well be delayed . . . And the sooner they were delayed in some manner the better, so that I could have the more time to lose myself in the tortuous corridors outside and reach Clare's ward without their knowing where I'd gone. There was only one obvious way to ensure their delay. I had it in my hand.

As I moved through the gap by the night nurse's table I started to release the safety catch beneath the antler handle on my swordstick. I'd have used the stick against them anyway. But Ross's words just then, as he came up behind me, suddenly annoyed me, gave me added impetus.

'A bad limp, Marlow?' he said condescendingly. 'So that's your problem. I hope you haven't hurt yourself, on the run these past weeks.'

I was through the gap now, the catch released. I turned and in the same movement I pulled out the long needle of steel and held it up, straight at Ross's chest, blocking his way through.

'Put that down, Marlow!' he said. 'I only want to *talk* to you: to explain things. With that bad leg you can't get far anyway. Don't play the fool!'

I touched Ross's shirt with the tip of the sword. 'Back!' I said. 'Back a little! Like you people played the fool with my wife.' I had a sudden urge to stick the sword in him there and then – and give the meddlesome little Indian a jab with it too. But I controlled the impulse.

The nurse, who had got up to let us pass, turned to me now and gave a short, little delayed-action yelp, like a dog. I spun the table round so that it ran lengthways across the aisle, blocking the gap almost completely.

Ross tried to vault the table, throwing himself towards me. But he came straight onto the tip of the sword, which I'd raised again. It pricked him in the arm, so that he drew back hurriedly, clutching his shoulder, amazed. I think he thought I was simply pulling his leg with these theatrical props and antics. He put his good arm inside his jacket, reaching for a gun I thought.

'Don't!' I said, moving forward towards him over the table, flourishing the swordstick at his throat this time. He withdrew and I backed away, the ward in some pandemonium now, as the shaded light on the table fell to the floor, the bulb breaking, leaving the whole room in darkness and confusion. But by then I had turned and was running furiously out the door. I was gone.

The corridor outside was deserted. I streaked along it, sword in hand, came to a T-junction at the end, and turned round one of two corners towards the children's wards before anyone saw me from behind. I had just a head start on them; they couldn't know exactly which route I'd gone. Speed was the only thing that mattered now.

And then, ahead of me, coming slowly along the next corridor and blocking most of it, I saw a prostrate patient, quite covered by a sheet on a raised trolley being wheeled by two porters. Perhaps at first they thought the building was on fire. But then, noting my flying red dressing-gown, swordstick and my pace, the two men froze with their silent passenger, and just stood there, straight in the middle of the passage.

In mounting confusion as I approached, instead of pulling over to one side, they started to turn the whole trolley in the opposite direction, as if to beat a retreat. They ended by blocking the corridor completely, the trolley stuck between the two walls.

I simply had to vault it – which I did, clearing the white-sheeted figure in one leap, while the porters backed against the walls like ambulancemen on either side of a dangerous jump at a steeplechase. At least, I thought, they might hinder the others behind me even more. And I ran on again, elated by my success, the sudden physical activity pushing the adrenalin sharply through my veins. I had that strange, sure animal feeling again: that I was going to win.

The children's ward was in almost complete darkness when I got there, only a single light coming from the far end where the four private rooms were. The children were nearly all asleep. Few of them were disturbed as I closed the outer door behind me and tiptoed quickly down to the far end.

Clare was awake again, I saw through the glass partition. A nurse was still up playing with her, and I remembered how difficult, long-delayed or irregular her sleeping could be when she was disturbed.

I opened the door. Clare looked up. But she looked past me, not at me. The nurse turned. Clare was sitting up by her pillows, constructing some elaborate edifice with delicately balanced plastic bricks on her bedside table. The nurse saw the swordstick and immediately stood up, as if to protect the child.

'It's all right,' I said. 'I'm Clare's father. I'm taking her away.'

'No!' the nurse said immediately. 'No!' But she was too stunned to say anything else.

Clare didn't speak either. Having looked up in my direction to begin, she now calmly returned to her bricks. I knew I had very little time left.

'Look,' I said to the nurse, keeping her back from Clare with the swordstick. 'I can't explain now. But I promise you it's all right. I *am* her father. She'll be quite safe.'

I simply took Clare then, quite unresisting at first, picking her up in her pyjamas, until she saw that she was being taken away from her bricks, when she screamed, a short sharp scream, so that I was forced to take away as many of the bricks as I could with me as well, stuffing them into my dressing-gown pockets. Then I made off with her, lifting her up under my arm like a parcel and carrying her out the door with one of the yellow bricks still clasped firmly in her hand.

She made no other sound as I ran with her towards the french windows at the end of the ward corridor, turning the key and wrenching the door open. Then I was out in the night.

It was difficult to move fast in the gathering darkness over rough ground, and I could hear the nurse shouting behind me now. But suddenly there was a light round a corner, above some builders' huts where they were making extensions to the hospital. And beyond these huts, right at the edge of the car park, I saw the black Ford Fiesta. The engine was running, the door open, while I was still ten yards away from it.

They never caught us. We only saw a police car once, lights flashing, tearing along the high road between Banbury and Chipping Norton, while we were half a mile away, down in the valley beneath, moving with dipped lights in a parallel direction along a winding cross-country lane. Alice had done her homework well, travelling these minor roads three times, twice at night, since I'd left her.

In little over half an hour, driving fast, we'd skirted Stow and were approaching the back entrance to Beechwood Manor, from another small by-road. There was no lodge here. The drive led to the home farm behind the Manor and there was only a cattle-grid between the stone gateposts. Turning off the drive, on to a narrow lane, we were soon hidden by thick undergrowth on either side. And half a mile further on we turned again, away from the farm, along no more than a grass track that had once been a back avenue leading round to the manor house itself. But this soon petered out, narrowing into a defile of thick brush, old elder trees and hawthorn bushes.

And here Alice drove the car into the old cow-shed hidden in the undergrowth, the bushes scraping the roof over our heads, until the headlights came up against the back wall. Then she turned everything off and we sat there, elated, exhausted, in the darkness and sudden complete silence of the deep midnight countryside.

'We'll stay here till first light,' Alice said softly. 'Then we can move. I'll open the gate in the fence for you. When you get through you'll find yourself just at the head of the valley. The sheep pasture runs away to the left: the chalk quarry on top, and the stream runs down from there to the lake. I'll come and see you tomorrow.'

She spoke softly because Clare was sound asleep in my arms, asleep at last. I told Alice then what had happened in the hospital. And finally she said, 'Well done. I *wish* I'd seen it all. I really do.' Then she kissed me gently – a sweet reward, I thought, for a crusader home from his first successful campaign.

Eleven

More than anything autistic children hate any change in the meticulous, often senseless routines they impose on themselves, with which they secure themselves to life, which makes life bearable for them. And I suspected Clare's docile sleep that night was simply due to exhaustion: a calm before the storm.

I was right. When she woke in the car that morning, in the dark just before dawn, she struggled and screamed, and she screamed the louder when the sun rose and I carried her through the heavy dew up the edge of the long green sheep-pasture and then on down the stream towards the lake. She was like a howling tornado blowing about in my arms and had we not been at least a mile away from the home farm and nearly the same distance from the Manor I'm sure it would have been all over for us; someone would have heard her cries.

As it was she didn't cease her pain until late that afternoon, out on the island in the little mausoleum, when she fell asleep, exhausted again. Even to remember those early days with Clare is painful; to write about it even more so. And several times then I was just about to pack it all in and give ourselves up.

But I knew that a return to hospital or to some special institution would only be worse for Clare. And I knew as well that, after nearly a year dealing with her problems, I was better fitted than anyone else to help her now. I had rescued her at last and I wouldn't willingly desert her again.

In the last few weeks she had obviously become attached to one of the nurses in the hospital. And I wasn't sure whether she even recognised me during those first few days. Of course I know that autistic children, in their bad times, intentionally refuse to recognise people. This is one of the hallmarks of their complaint. Since, generally, they cannot confront their own 'self', they will do everything possible to prevent any outsider recognising or promoting that same missing quality.

I knew all this from my past with Clare, when she was suffering: how not to look at or speak to her directly; to approach her in every way surreptitiously, at an angle as it were, never to confront her in any way directly, always to leave room for her mental 'escape'. And there were other tricks, too, learnt either from Laura or, more painfully, face to face with the child herself. Clare in her earlier days, in Cascais not long after her father had been killed in Nairobi, had only consented to eat from a plate set on the floor, on all fours, like a dog. And so I gave her food in the same way that first day on the island: little chunks of processed cheese Alice had bought, among other food, and which Clare adored, smeared over the digestive biscuits I put out and left for her on the floor beside Lady Horton's tomb. Clare sat against the tomb for most of that first day, sullen, hunched up, when she wasn't screaming.

'There,' I said, looking away from her. 'I eat that. That's good.'

Clare's speech had improved tremendously in the last year. But now it was non-existent. She had, for some time, come to use the word 'I' in relation to herself, and this had been a huge, a vital advance. Since before this, like nearly all such children, she had inverted the personal pronoun in order to avoid any picture of her self. Thus 'I' was always 'you' in any demand or question. 'You want some orange.' ... 'You want to go out,' she would say.

But for those first few days, more than knowing – yet simply avoiding – any word for herself as an individual, she literally, I think, had no sense of who she was at all. She survived in a continual state of animal shock alternating with panic, no more than that: a state of mere temporary survival, like a rat in a trap, with a mind closed, sullenly or viciously, to all stimuli.

She must have missed her mother. Or did she? At that time it was impossible to tell. Neither her expression nor her behaviour hinted at this emotional loss. There was a numbness in her big blue eyes; they had no depth. And her cheeks were pale, with nothing of their old bloom. She was too far gone from our world to comprehend unhappiness in it.

Sometimes her round, expressionless face would jerk in convulsive movements up and down, her chin stabbing the air, so that her blonde fringe bounced, and I would try to calm her as Laura might have done, stroking her head, offering her sanctuary in my arms; she neither accepted nor refused, simply allowing herself to be moved this way or that like a log. I might eventually cradle her, but the bobbing, craning searching motion, like a fish on dry land appealing for water, would persist, the eyes wide and blank, staring up at me. Those were the worst times, when it seemed there was no future for either of us: Clare a permanent vegetable and myself a fool holding this beautiful, broken doll in my arms.

And yet, to my astonishment, she suddenly started to improve. There was a turning point on the fourth day, a discovery that liberated her. She found the broken stonework at one end of Sir George Horton's raised tomb and saw the bones inside – the skull and shoulder-blades. And as soon as she discovered these remains she had gazed at them intently, suddenly quiet, fascinated, concentrating on something at last. And after ten minutes of this investigation she began to come alive. It was a remarkable transformation.

She put her hand inside the tomb, tickling the skull at first, before finally taking it out and holding it. I didn't stop her, for I could see from the expression on her face that here was the beginning of a cure, some miracle seeping from these dead bones in the broken tomb.

Of course, when I thought of it, I realised why these relics might hold such magic for her. The skull here, and the other bleached remains, had given her back some happy memory of those earlier days which she had spent wild in the East African rift valley, when she had followed her father about the scorching rocks, looking for just the same sort of thing: the vital fossil evidence, in just this same shape of part skulls and jaw bones, which she would have seen so laboriously assembled later, realising their importance. And so here, the discovery of Sir George's bones, in something of the same shape and condition, had given her a sense, only a glimmer perhaps, of old adventure and happiness. A sense of life itself, which she had so lost, had been returned to her.

And then I wondered too, seeing how she so obviously cared for these bones, fondling them almost, whether, in that strange upside down mind of hers, she might have thought they were the remains of her own father, whom she had apparently idolised, mysteriously returned to her here, a gift I had brought her to, and which she thanked me for by consenting to recognise me, as soon afterwards she did.

I didn't know. It's only theory, as so much must be with the minds of such children whose thoughts are so totally at odds with the logic and assumptions of our world, living as they do in their own closed universe where, like Clare, they create systems, visions, associations incomprehensible to us, roving through a whole utterly strange landscape of the mind, of which we can only see the smallest evidence, in acts such as Clare's with these bones, when they surface, as it were, for a few moments into the air of ordinary life.

Certain it is that Clare changed that day, and changed the more the day following when I carried her up, strapped to my back in a kind of rope chair, to the tree-house on top of the oak. From then on, slowly at first but with ever-increasing enthusiasm, she took to life in the trees as if she'd been born in them. Yes, for her it was much more than any child's game, a treat, something different. For Clare, I soon came to recognise, this kind of existence was the real thing. Again, I thought, a life lived once in Africa had been returned to her. A thorn tree, or a hide beneath a black rock in the Turkana Province, had become the branches of a summer oak and a wild valley hidden in the middle of England.

Clare took to this outdoor existence, the swimming when it came, the rough sleeping in the wind, fishing from the branches, the messy sticky-fingered picnic cooking and eating, as if the whole thing was a way of life specially prepared for her: as if, knowing it to be her only real cure, she had long craved exactly such a life, a life without furniture, beds, walls, roofs, plates, knives, forks: an existence totally devoid of every civilised prop, where there were no denials in closed windows, doors or other people, no timetables or duties other than those necessary for immediate pleasure or survival.

In all, and above all, she found herself in a world now so entirely lacking conventional structures and impositions that it was akin to the secret, unruly landscapes of her own mind. This life in the trees confirmed something vital in her which the people in her life had unwittingly tried to iron out. And this, I think, was precisely the reason for her cure: the valley, for the next two months, awakened in her the only 'self' she really had, a completely unconventional soul, a natural animal which prospered here, where it had withered in London and Cascais and had only barely survived with Laura and me in our cottage in the Cotswolds. Here, this quite wild balm at last gave her wings.

It was now mid-June, almost the height of a warm summer. The nights were short, starlit, rainless for the most part. Sometimes it rained quickly in the day, sudden, stormy thunder-showers from plum-bruised skies that were soon gone, leaving the air moist, steamy and filled with insects above the great bunches of cow-parsley that rose up now with a sweet rank smell, feet-high about the valley.

Clare slept at first in a sleeping-bag on the floor of the tree-house, while I slept beside her. But soon, too hot at nights, she was tempted by Spinks's string hammock, so that I slung this across the upper part of the tree-house for her, and she swayed here in the hot afternoons, head-in-air, mesmerised, the regular pendulum motion visibly releasing her anxieties, drawing the tense sullenness out of her like a poultice.

At night, too, against lightly-mooned skies and a shadow filigree of leaves and branches, I would see the string hammock move from side to side above me, shaped like a canoe wrapped around her body, as she rocked herself far out on some imaginary voyage. And then, the boat floating home on a dark sea of leaves, the swaying would gradually diminish until finally all movement stopped, and the craft berthed as she slept, held by a thread to earth.

Alice came to see us each day, usually in the mornings, out to the island first, and afterwards clambering quickly and silently up to the tree-house, so that she sometimes surprised us, like an animal rising stealthily through the leaves.

I wondered what Clare would make of her. To begin with she made nothing of her at all; she barely looked at her. I had warned Alice that this might happen, told her to take no notice of Clare, to behave just as we did, as if life in these trees, for her as well, was the most natural thing in the world. And thus Alice merged with us, with our life, imperceptibly, doing as we did in the time she stayed with us.

She had brought new clothes for Clare on the first day – cord dungarees, an anorak, socks, plimsolls. But for a long time Clare preferred her grubby hospital pyjamas or just a pair of pants. Later, in the tree-house, she hung up all these new clothes on a line of string, as if they were washing, or the sails of her grandfather's ketch, and would simply gaze at them, hypnotised, for hours on end, as they swung in the breeze.

Of course, the job I had to do here in the valley was to give Clare life again; life, and speech. So I would talk to her indirectly as often as possible without looking at her, as if talking to myself, while I tidied up the tree-house after breakfast, and she involved herself with one of her elaborate rituals or routines, placing the coloured bricks from the hospital in certain strict and mysterious patterns. Another obsessive therapy she found in stripping the oak leaves about her down to their central stem and then placing these in long opposed ranks on the tree-house planks, like soldiers confronting each other in an opposing army.

The routines were many. But each of them was recreated exactly as they'd been the hour or the day before. There was no change or development here; in these rituals constancy was all. They were her lifelines, imperative duties which licensed not only her very existence but also any attempt she might make to escape from the cage of her anonymity. And escape from this would need speech, I knew – speech as a tendril, words as antennae which would reach out and form a bridge for her to cross into full life. And speech she didn't have at all beyond mere grunts and screams; this above all I had to return to her.

So I would use words throughout the day and the tree became a babel of my voice. 'We're living here for a while,' I would say quietly as she picked at the oak leaves. 'Mummy has gone. We'll live here for a bit and enjoy ourselves. There's swimming and lots of things we can do. And Alice – Alice that comes up here – she'll bring us things we need. She has books and food too. Books you might like. That Pigling Bland book she brought: did you see that? Though I expect you're a bit old for it . . .'

Thus I would natter on, with apparent aimlessness, about this and that, about anything that came to mind, familiarising Clare with just the sound of words and thoughts again, throwing the currency heedlessly about that she might one day pick some of it up.

Though much more in those early days, besides her rituals, it was the light, the weather and the clouds that most absorbed her attention. She would climb up some way above the tree-house, almost to the top of the oak where I could still see her, and stay there for hours on end, gazing upwards into the blue sky, as if expecting something. It was some time before I realised she was waiting for the clouds which, whenever they passed overhead, she would watch intently, her head moving like a camera with them as they crossed the dome of blue. It was the same with the morning sun. She was often up before dawn, in her perch above the tree-house, waiting in the same way for the first rays of light to streak across the sky, then following the rising flood as it climbed over the rim of trees round the valley, finally cascading over the oak leaves with shafts of green-gold light.

Watching the puffy clouds roll by near to, or studying them in their imperceptible glide far up; lurking, hidden in the grey first light, to ambush the sun, Clare was like a figure for rain or shine in a Swiss weather-house, moving about the tree, alert to every variation in the sky.

Clare's life then was made up of watching. She watched the birds: the swallows as they swooped and feinted about the sky, on their usually distant aerial careers, but now almost intimate with us, feeding on the wing only a few feet above the topmost branches of our oak tree. She studied the grey and white flash of pigeons as they shot across the valley in sudden cannonades, and then glided upwards in little swoops, breasting the air like a roller-coaster before stalling suddenly, then diving sheer for a second, elated by the very medium of space. There were rooks, too, a colony of them high up on several beech trees above the valley behind us; birds that chattered incessantly at certain times of day, and which Clare would listen to, spellbound, as if eavesdropping on a familiar, long-lost tongue.

On weekends, when they were playing cricket in the park, Clare and I would spend afternoons hidden in the look-out perch on top of the big beech tree that gave out over the estate. And though I listened to the far-away thwack of leather on wood with nostalgia, Clare seemed to hear the sound much more acutely and to see the game in quite a different manner. She looked on the distant players as toys, I think, as though seeing them very close to, and would reach her hand towards them and move it busily in front of her eyes, as if she was picking the batsmen and fielders up on a board in front of her and putting them in different places. She seemed to have an equally long and short vision, like a naïve painter who shows details on the horizon as clearly as those in the foreground.

Clare watched and she listened for most of every day then, so that her sight and hearing, always fine, grew startlingly acute.

There were sounds that she heard, at midday or late in the evening, of some animal moving or crying, which I never heard at all, until, like a pointer, I noticed her sudden attentive stillness as she distinguished a particular warble or crackle in the branches or undergrowth, naming it in her mind perhaps.

'Pheasant?' I would say. 'Rabbit? Stoat? Fox?' always the man with words, tempting her with them like a bag of sweets. But at best unhappy at this verbal distraction, she would merely turn and look at me, her face blank where it was not annoyed, unable or unwilling to confirm anything for me in her own voice.

Sometimes, as another way of encouraging her with language, I read to her in the hot afternoons sitting in the tree-house, when she was swaying in the hammock above me, the bees and insects a humming gallery all round us. There was the old copy of Beatrix Potter's *The Tale of Pigling Bland* which Alice had brought down from the Victorian nursery. It wasn't the most suitable story, this account of porcine deprivation and exile. I don't know, but perhaps for this very reason it was the only book that Clare took any great interest in. Yet it wasn't the story, I think, so much as the onomatopoeic dialogue of the animals that caught her attention. Words, if no more than sounds, were acceptable to her: she had banished the coherence of plot from her life.

> 'A funny old mother pig lived in a
> stye, and three little piggies had she;
> (Ti idditty idditty) umph, umph, umph!
> and the little pigs said, wee, wee!'

My voice would rise up to Clare, like an actor's, trying to give the piglets real life for her. And sometimes she almost laughed; she reponded to the 'idditty idditties'. But more often there was silence as I ran through the saga of *Pigling Bland*: only the leaves stirring in some faint breeze as an accompaniment, Clare's hammock swaying, as she watched them, as she watched the puffy clouds float by, quite given over to some swoon in the summer greenery.

Several times, watching her growing passion for the natural world and the silent skills it fostered in her, I was tempted to give up words myself, give up trying to attach them once more to Clare. Surely, as she seemed to suggest so clearly, we lived in a place and in a manner, in a pre-human kindgom, where language was no longer necessary?

Signs would do – as they did for so much of real importance that passed between Clare and me in that time. For if Clare didn't speak, she soon willingly followed by example. She learnt to hang the canvas bag out over the lake and dredge for water, and to fish from the same branch first thing or at evening when she heard the perch rise. And later, above all, when I took her right round the edge of the valley, she learnt the limits of our safety, how beyond this hidden domain lay danger, a world where she should not go. She was particularly fascinated by Spinks's recurve bow, which I showed her how to operate. She wasn't strong enough to draw it, of course. But she would handle it lovingly, for whole mornings or afternoons, aiming at imaginary targets in the branches, miming the draw and the release, the arrow singing away in her mind and striking home, leaving her with an expression of rapturous satisfaction which surprised me.

All this knowledge she absorbed far more by my showing her than from words. So that sometimes, as I say, I was loth to educate this increasingly skilful innocence, to infect it with words. I thought Clare might well be left free of the long sad language of history. At the same time I knew that one day she would have to learn this. We couldn't live in the valley for ever. We were not animals in a pre-human kingdom. This vegetable world, this life on high formed a cure for both of us now, but at some point we would have to leave the trees and come down to earth. At some point? Day by day then I was happy to postpone it. There was so much to do, so much to keep us here meanwhile.

I've used the phrase 'vegetable world'. But that may give a false impression, as if we lacked human response in the valley, became vegetables. It was rather the opposite. Freed completely from the ties of conventional thought, from all the devious forecasts and immediate considerations which ordinary life imposes, there was time for real thought at last. One could concentrate on the essence rather than the extraneous; on matters which at normal times occupy only the corners of one's vision for brief moments: one could concentrate on looking, where one becomes so embedded in the object, so carried away by it, that self-consciousness is lost at last – corruption and mortality forgotten.

Painters work for such vision. But it came naturally to me, in that time out of life, and when it did self-realisation was complete. And instead of the hours in the day having to be filled, as I had expected, these traditional shapes of time disappeared altogether and there were only the acts and thoughts themselves, let loose from the clock, so that one was free at last. There was never too much or too little to do. There was simply the one thing to be done at that moment, without reference to past or future, complete in itself.

It's only now, weeks later, that I remember certain moments, or actions which at the time I was unaware of while simply living through them, yet which must have impressed me unconsciously, so that I can only regain them now as events in a dream brought to light long after waking.

An oak tree, as I discovered for example, supports an extraordinary variety of minute or invisible life in midsummer: bees, flies, insects of all kinds hovering up and down the long interior glades in the leaves: glades and twisting tunnels and undulating roads made by the branches, a whole stereoscopic geography which, living in the midst of it, becomes as familiar and unnoticed as the tracks or alleyways around a childhood home. Along these airy paths, shut out from the world in a green shade, the insects move, like traffic, with a constant hum . . .

And what I see – and hear – now, and had forgotten, is Clare gazing deep down into one of these leafy caverns, with an extraordinary longing in her face, as if she was struggling to resist the temptation to glide off after the insects, to actually get into and share their world with them. Instead, compensating for her inability to do this, she hummed with the insects. Yes, she 'buzzed' in different ways with her lips, miming a variety of them distinctly, successfully identifying with them in this way. And it's strange that I've forgotten this until now, for it was the first time that Clare used her lips, gave tongue at last, when she properly broke her silence.

I told Alice when she came up to see us later that day, 'She may talk again. Soon.' But Alice said nothing in reply. Perhaps, like me, she silently feared a change, any change, in this Arcadia. Of course the world outside was not entirely forgotten. Alice, together with the old transistor, kept me in touch with it. Much of central England was being scoured in a search for us. But no one visited the valley again, and no one, apparently, had traced the car, or Arthur's clothes, or Alice's money. In the middle of that warm summer, with so many people looking for us, searching all round us, hurrying to and fro with messages, rumours, tip-offs, we were a still centre in the hidden valley.

'What about Mrs Pringle?' I asked Alice one afternoon in the tree house.

'Nothing. She never mentions Harry Conrad's visit. She looks at me, that's all: rather pityingly, I think. As if I should have someone to look after me. The hell with that. I can look after myself. I'm busy anyway, preparing this fête with the local Victorian Society.'

'Fête?'

'Remember – I told you. It's exactly a hundred years ago this August when they finished building the Manor. So we're going to celebrate: a jousting tournament, a costume ball. In medieval dress.'

'I'd forgotten. But surely you'll need your husband for that?'

'Certainly not. He'll be out on Long Island all summer – watching polo, I expect. The divorce comes through in September. I never want to see him again.'

Alice was sitting on the edge of the tree house, her feet dangling in space, looking away from me, down into the green depths beneath. Clare was high above us, on top of the oak, absorbed in her vision of the clouds. It was a humid afternoon, stuffy. Something threatened. And there was another tenseness in the air now between Alice and me. This talk of Arthur and divorce again proposed a future which we both seemed unwilling to face. There were suddenly all sorts of things once more undecided, like the weather, for both of us.

Then Alice looked up at me and, as if to get away from this uncomfortable future, I thought, she said, 'I've been wondering about Clare's autism. It's curious...'

'I know that.'

'The causes, I mean, There's a book apparently, *The Forbidden Fortress*, by someone called Bettelheim.'

'Yes. I know it. Never got to the end of it, though. It's mostly case-histories. We gave up on books, Laura and I. On books and quacks and the special schools.'

Alice looked at me now, carefully this time, some big hidden query in her eyes. 'The causes, though,' she said again.

'They vary. Biological, psychological, traumatic, environmental – *ad nauseam*. They vary in each child, and in most professional theory.'

'Isn't it basically rejection though?' Alice said quickly, as if the words would dissolve in her throat otherwise. 'By the parents. By the mother. At some early stage?'

I still had no idea what Alice was pursuing at this point. 'With Clare,' I said, 'I always thought it was leaving East Africa. But the medicos and child specialists said not. I don't think I ever believed them.'

'Was Laura a cold person?' Alice asked decisively, as if she'd at last made her mind up on something.

I looked at her, surprised. 'No. Of course not. Not with me. Least of all with Clare,' I added equally decisively.

And yet, after I'd said this, I remembered Laura's initial effect on me, when I'd first seen her in the church in Lisbon and met her afterwards at the sardine barbecue on the windy hill: her apparent hauteur then, the distance she kept from people – like an insensitive Tory divorcee from the shires, I'd even thought. Yes, she could give, she had given a distinctly cold impression then. But I'd seen this frigidity as so obviously the result of Clare's tragedy and her husband's subsequent death.

It was these blows that had distanced her and nothing else. There was nothing basic in her character which would ever have made her reject Clare. Besides, I remembered the efforts she had afterwards made on Clare's behalf, the endless care and attention . . . I told Alice this and she said simply, 'People make up for things, don't they?'

'Laura never had to make up for anything. That's nonsense.'

But again, I remembered how Laura had sometimes allowed Clare to do exactly what she wanted: how, in Cascais once, she let her drive a nail through her palm, telling me afterwards that it was the only thing to do sometimes with such children. I didn't tell Alice, though.

Instead I said 'But why do you ask about all this?'

'You have a great tie with Laura still, don't you?'

'Of course. We were very happy. I've told you. It really worked for both of us, I think.'

'It didn't work with her first husband then? With Willy, the famous bone man you told me about. It didn't work with him?' she asked rhetorically.

'No. I don't mean that. I meant we'd both been very unhappy until we met in Lisbon. But she and Willy had been happy, I think. No, I *know*: she told me. He was a small, rubicund little fellow. A droll academic. A surprising marriage. But it worked.'

'You never actually met him of course.'

'No. And I wasn't out in East Africa with them either. But that doesn't mean I can't tell anything about the man, or about their relationship.'

'And his death. Wasn't that rather strange? The hit-and-run accident you told me about, how he was run over by an African in Nairobi.'

'Strange? Much more awful irony than strange. We never talked a lot about it.'

'Why?'

'Just *because* of the awful irony, I suppose. That's why. And because of Clare.' I glanced upwards to where she was still stuck in the treetop, like a weather-vane.

'But why?' I asked again. 'Why all this sudden interest?'

Alice produced a cutting from the *Sunday Times*, published almost a week before, and handed it to me. It was a long, investigative article – prompted by Laura's murder and Clare's recent abduction – about Willy Kindersley, the 'famous paleontologist and discoverer of the ultimate "missing link" in the ape-man chain' – the part skull and skeleton of the four-million-year-old 'Thomas'. But the most interesting thing about it was the unflattering picture it gave of Willy Kindersley himself who, the article went on to say, had been killed in what they described as a 'mysterious accident' in Nairobi two years before.

I read it quickly to this point, before commenting: '"Mysterious accident" indeed. He was just run down outside the Norfolk hotel by some drunk.'

Then I skimmed on through the article. There were some major paragraphs about me in it: 'An unlikely figure in this palaeontological jig-saw puzzle . . . a reputed ex-member of the British Intelligence service' and suspected killer of Laura. There was another considerable passage about Clare and her autism, citing Bettelheim among others, but finally suggesting

its origins in something that might have happened to her in East
Africa when she was very young – a ludicrous rumour of
witchcraft here, even. It mentioned trouble during one of
Kindersley's latter safaris years before, just before the discovery
of the famous 'Thomas' skeleton: arguments at a camp way out
in the Turkana Province and a raid by local tribesmen during
which several of the raiders had been killed, which had
afterwards been hushed up. In all, the article, with no hard
evidence whatsoever, built up a picture of mysterious, violent
machinations in the professional and familial affairs of Willy
Kindersley – and of subsequent mysteries in Laura's death, in
my involvement, and apparent ease of escape, and in Clare's
autism and abduction. Finally the writer spoke of an elaborate
cover-up over the whole business by everyone involved.

I suppose, given these recent sensational events connected
with Willy, this tone wasn't so surprising. It made a good story,
certainly, though little if any of it could have been true, or I
should certainly have heard something of it from Laura. The
only really hard material that was new to me, based as it was on
recent interviews with old colleagues, was a detailed description
of Willy's 'ruthless professional ambition' during his many
years looking for hominid fossils in East Africa; of how he had
'trodden on any number of toes – and bodies as well – to achieve
his ends'.

I took this to be simply professional jealousy on the part of
Willy's rivals. But I mentioned my surprise to Alice all the
same.

'Laura never spoke of him like that?'

'No. Just the opposite. She talked of his jokes, his wit, good
company. I told you.'

I looked at Alice, annoyed now. 'You're trying to tell me I've
got it all wrong, aren't you? About Willy and Laura: that I was
fooled in some way about them. And about Clare's autism, too.
That it came because Laura rejected her. You're telling me that
the three of them were all part of a lot of dark secrets before I met
them; out in Africa – and here as well. A mysterious accident,
mysterious deaths everywhere: Laura's too. You're telling me
that – '

'No, Peter!' she interrupted almost fiercely. 'That's what the
article is telling you if you read it carefully, not me. That's why I
didn't want to give it you. That's all in the *article*! I didn't invent

it. Not me.'

I sighed. 'It's nonsense, Alice,' I said. 'Isn't it surely because – because *you* want a future? All right, but you don't have to destroy their past, my past with them, to have it. A future with us, if there is one, doesn't depend on a lot of gossip like this.' I handed her back the article.

'Gossip?'

'Yes. Or at best sheer conjecture,' I went on. 'There was nothing mysterious about Laura's death, for example. I could tell them the truth about that. That would make a real story: it was my old colleagues who shot her, aiming for me. I know too much. They want me dead. That's why I took to the woods here. And that's why Ross keeps on tracking me. Why else should he bother so much? Because they want me out of the way: badly.'

Alice seemed to understand all this. Life in the valley reverted to its earlier ways after this intrusion and I forgot about the article very soon afterwards. There was so much to do. We had to have a future, not a past filled with either gossip or tragedy.

And it was immediately after this, seeing Clare's rapid improvement, that I wrote my first letter to Laura's father, Captain Warren, out in Portugal. I explained all that had happened: how Laura's death, far from being at my hand, had been meant for me, a final present from my old colleagues in Whitehall; and how Clare was safe and well, with me again now. I told him I'd understand if he didn't believe me about Laura, if he thought simply that I'd kidnapped Clare for my own selfish ends. But if he did trust my account, I told him, I planned to get Clare back to him in Cascais, when she was ready to travel, and if some means could be arranged for her to leave England with me unofficially.

I asked him, if he agreed to my proposals, to reply by way of a personal advertisement in *The Times*. Of course, he might send my letter straight to the police or, with them, set up some trap for me in subsequent travel arrangements. It was a risk. But given his long antipathy towards Britain in general, and his particular bitterness towards the secret men in Whitehall who had deprived him of his own house and lands forty years before, I thought he might well agree to any covert scheme I suggested, or even propose one of his own. His 50-foot ketch *Clare*, for example, struck me as a possible means of escape from

England, and I said as much in a P.S. to the letter. I showed Alice what I'd written. She thought it a fair plan and posted if off some days later when she went up to London.

Meanwhile we extended the tree-house, bringing up more wooden beams from the old pumping-shed and making a lower floor to the house, connected by a ladder to what was now an open terrace on top of our accommodation. We made walls for this small lower room, with strips of polythene first covered by a cross-weave of small, leafy beech branches, so that in the end the breeze was kept out and the structure still maintained a perfect camouflage.

With the same broad wooden planks from the shed, and with the tools and other equipment we now had, I extended our reach over the line of trees that bordered the lake by building a series of aerial walkways with rope handrails through the upper branches, so that in the end it was possible to move right down to the beech tree above the stream at the foot of the lake without coming to ground, always hidden in the leaves. This gave us both another access to our tree house and another escape from it, if need be. We were no longer committed to a single front door.

And besides, we now had an aerial parkland to discover and explore along these wooden tracks. No longer confined to our own too familiar house and backyard, a whole new estate was opened up for us, new trees and leafy vistas, unfamiliar branches where the coppery summer light fell in different shades and patterns. Now we could move through the trees from one green country to another, almost as if the foliage was our permanent element, like fish in a stream moving invisibly through the weeds and shadows.

With more rope I built Clare a swing from one of the lower branches beneath the tree-house, out over the lake, so that if she fell it would only be a dozen feet into the water. But she never looked like falling. Always adept physically, in every kind of acrobatics, this mild trapeze-work came to her quite naturally. And certainly she preferred it, by way of occupation, to speech, speech which was so much more dangerous for her, full of compromises, a blueprint of discipline, of a restrictive order which Clare must have believed she had now well lost. So she grabbed the swing from a higher branch where she kept it out of sight, and would throw herself out over the lake on it, skimming the water like a swallow in the evening.

With the tools from the Manor we built a rough table as well, and Alice brought us down two small Victorian chairs from the nursery, which we could eat from, both of us crouched over the wood like oversized dolls in a nook. We had a small pinewood cupboard as well to keep things in. Thus the little lower room which emerged in the tree-house, where we now slept and ate, became a cosy place. Cosy, but small. It was difficult for me to do more than stretch my legs in it, sitting on the minute chair, after supper, sipping a whisky from one of the red picnic tumblers, while Clare became involved in one of her meticulous, mysterious games on the tiny table next to me.

I watched her one evening here as a bright sunset faded slowly all about us, her golden hair reflecting a last radiance in the twilight like a halo, as she concentrated on her ritual with the hospital bricks, moving them round and about, up and down, in Stonehenge circles and pyramids.

She wasn't my daughter, I thought. But I loved her as much as if she had been. Loved her in a different way, I suppose, as someone free of me, as one might love an older woman from afar, for a beauty and an independence of spirit, who yet, without her knowing it, relied on me for her very existence. There was an unusual and comforting, a completely unpossessive intimacy between Clare and me; that of complete strangers forced together, who yet miraculously find, without words, that they share the same temperament, assumptions, hopes.

And at such times in the evening, after all the energetic activities of the day, her speechlessness no longer seemed out of place. We might have been two friends, tired together, sitting in the hotel lounge after a long day out in the ordinary world. Friends: that was it. That was what was unusual. There was an adult relationship between us, which her lack of words accentuated. We seemed, as adults, as two old friends might, to understand each other without speaking.

Two friends camping in a cosy place... We even made a shelf for books and had a basin for washing things in. The rubbish we wrapped up carefully every few days and Alice took it away with her in a bag with her swimming things back to the house. For this swimming, of course, which she had done in any case most days down by the lake, now became her excuse for visiting us.

We swam ourselves, Clare and I, as I'd done myself to begin with, first or last thing in the day, in the natural pool hidden behind the fallen tree at the bottom of the lake. And it was here one day, just after first light, down from our tree and sliding through the undergrowth, that we suddenly came on one of the deer from the parkland, a big antlered buck, head high, alert, drawing breath, its nostrils steaming in the early morning air. It was right by the edge of the water, next the ruined pier of the old boat-house.

I think Clare saw it first. Certainly she thrust her arm up at me, holding me back in excitement. But the animal must have smelt or heard us, for it suddenly turned and looked straight at us.

And it was then that Clare first spoke.

'Game!' she said, quite clearly, her face alight. And then she lifted both arms suddenly and mimed the action of shooting the buck with a bow and arrow. She drew and released an imaginary arrow several times at the animal, before it trotted away down the edge of the water. But then, like an arrow herself, suddenly released and homing viciously, Clare ran after it, fleetfoot, with an extraordinary speed and vigour the like of which I'd never thought to see in a child, so that I was barely able to keep up with her.

The buck, which before had simply been trotting away from us, now took to its heels in alarm, disappearing into the undergrowth before I heard it crashing up the slope of the valley. But Clare ran with it, keeping pace with it, her gold mop of hair flattened in the wind all round her head, before she disappeared as well.

I found her on top of the valley, leaning on the fence beyond which she knew she mustn't go, looking out over the parkland where there were only a few sleeping cows. The buck had quite disappeared. She had a pained, mystified look on her face, as if, I thought, having so obviously killed the buck with her initial flights of fancy, she could not now understand where the carcase was.

Then she turned and said to me very urgently, 'You kill it. You kill it!'

She inverted the pronoun, of course, as she had before in her damaged speech: she meant 'I' when she said 'you'. But now, so much more than a single word, she could put words together into an expressive sentence. She could speak. I was so pleased with this miracle that it was only afterwards that I reflected on the nature of what she had actually said that morning in the dew-drenched summer airs above the valley. 'I kill the deer. I kill it!'. That was what she'd said. A strange, animal vehemence which had not been there before had suddenly entered Clare's life.

Or was it so strange? Wasn't this hunting fever, more simply, a quite natural extension to her present lifestyle? A form of life in which, identifying with it so completely, she came unconsciously to mime its original foundations, in killing and pain and the survival of the fittest?

Certainly as a result of nearly two months in the woods and this developing urge to track and kill, all Clare's instincts and senses had become startlingly acute – to the point where I was disturbed by her animalism, seeing in it another and perhaps irrevocable move away from the real world I hoped she would one day occupy again.

And yet it was exactly this animalism, this heightened instinct for survival, which probably saved our lives a week later. I would never have noticed the ominous signs myself.

A footprint, a broken twig, a dead leaf where it shouldn't be? A shadow moving when it shouldn't move? Some slight noise at twilight that wasn't a bird or an animal? What was it that first caught Clare's attention? I don't know. What I do know is that one evening, returning from a late swim, Clare stopped suddenly on our path through the undergrowth and quickly drew me aside into the heart of a bush. 'Here,' she whispered in my ear, for she could put whole coherent sentences together now. 'Someone too is here.' She pointed immediately ahead.

'Alice?' I whispered back to her, looking about me in the shadows. But it couldn't be Alice, I thought. She had only left us a few hours before and she never came down late in the evening in any case.

Clare shook her head. 'No. It has been here a days,' she said in her disordered English.

'But what? What is it? A he or a she?'

'It,' she said simply.

I looked around me in the gathering dusk, straining my ears and eyes. But there was no sound, nothing unusual. A bird suddenly twittered in the undergrowth ahead of us – a long trill of mild alarm, a blackbird running over last year's dead leaves. There was a deep silence again. And then I heard another tread in the woods, not a dozen yards away, on the path we'd been on, coming towards us. It was no louder than the blackbird's run, but it had quite a different pace, slow, infinitely careful: the paws of some animal, a fox perhaps, nosing through the twilight? But it wasn't a fox, or a badger or mole, I thought then. The steps were more pronounced, and there were two of them, not four. They were surely human.

Then, in silhouette for a moment, I saw a figure pass between two trees against the flare of dying light on the lake: crouching, thin-shouldered, the skin there with an inky shine in the sunset. It was gone in an instant, flitting soundlessly away into the shadows. I thought it might be Ross again. But Ross wouldn't crouch like that, I thought, or pass so silently.

Above all, Ross would hardly be moving as the dark shadow had, naked into the night.

Twelve

There was someone else in the valley. They were sleeping rough, I assumed, and must have come from outside the estate, since they obviously weren't down from the Manor. Was it somebody looking particularly for us? Or just some trespasser, a poacher, a lone camper? The following morning we set about finding out. I explained my plans to Clare, stringing the bow and getting the sharpened arrows together as we sat in the tree house. She didn't say anything. But she was full of repressed excitement at what she obviously looked upon as a coming hunt.

We left the tree-house and, moving high up along the branches and walkways, made our way down towards the foot of the lake, leaving the trees here by the branch over the stream. My plan was to start at the bottom and work our way up to the head of the valley, carefully looking over the whole area in the half mile between.

It was very early dawn when we started, as I hoped we might surprise whoever it was, sleeping out in a tent or in the old pumping-shed perhaps. There was a ground mist in the valley again, lying in long, wispy streaks over the lake and forming heavier milky pools in the reeds by the shore. We stalked from bush to bush, keeping out of sight as much as possible. I remembered the time, two months before, when Ross and I had sought each other out in just the same circumstances. But now I had Clare and there was no vicious Alsatian. Clare, indeed, was my dog, crawling silently through holes in the undergrowth, places where I couldn't go, a pointer herself, as I followed behind with the recurve bow and the old army binoculars.

We got above the pumping-shed, looking down on it from the side of the valley. Most of the roof was gone, the planks taken for our tree house, so that I could see inside it. There was no one there. I raised the binoculars, training them out over the lake, looking up to the head of the valley more than a hundred yards away, where the mist was clearing, dissolving, as the sun rose. Suddenly a pair of mallard got up as I watched, just where the stream entered the lake, and the air was briefly filled with their craking squawks.

I saw the burnished blue and green colours of the drake flash past the lenses. And then, right behind where the birds had risen, there was another movement. I would never have seen it, I think, but for the contrast in the colours: the dark face against the remains of the white mist. I focused the glasses more exactly. It was a man, right down on his haunches by the water as if he'd been drinking there, partly hidden by a clump of reeds, a man turning his head quickly now as he followed the startled flight of the birds. He wasn't naked. He wore a loose green camouflage jacket and tan trousers. Certainly he wasn't Ross. This man had a cloche of wiry hair above a thin face. And he was dark-skinned, with a long torso and thighs, almost lanky: an African, I thought.

When I looked again at the clump of reeds there was no one there, just the sun beginning to tip over the head of the lake, melting away the mist. An African? Was I dreaming? Or had it been some trick in the early-morning light, the skin of a white or sunburnt man showing up that way, in some strange refraction coming through the mist or off the water?

Then I remembered the old Army camouflage jacket. That

detail had been real enough. It worried me suddenly. Someone, recently, had been wearing just the same thing – and it had worried me, yes. But where and why? Then I had it: the man who'd burst into our cottage and shot Laura. How could I have forgotten his dress? And the same man, a few weeks before Laura had been shot, when we'd been out walking behind our cottage with the Bensons after Sunday lunch: the man I'd seen then, in the distance, hurrying away from us along the hedge, the surprising, lone hiker in the middle of the wolds, a tall figure with a pork-pie hat pulled down so that I hadn't seen his face. He'd been wearing just the same sort of camouflage jacket; one of Ross's men, sent down from London to scout the land out before he'd come to shoot me a few weeks later.

The thought of this banished any fear I might have had, standing alone in the woods just then with a defenceless child. And suddenly I was filled once more with an overwhelming anger and bitterness – just as I'd been during my first weeks alone in the woods after Laura's death. It came to me again now, a keen, fresh sense of violence and retribution.

This man was Laura's killer, and one of Ross's men: I was sure of that. But had he found us? Did he know we were here, or had we luckily spotted him first?

I turned to Clare. 'There!' I whispered to her, pointing. 'He was over there. That man. A dark man. But he's gone.'

Clare nodded. She couldn't, I thought, have seen anything of him without the binoculars. But it seemed she had, for her body was tense now, alert. She was staring up at the head of the lake, impatient, ready to take chase against something, anything. But I held her back.

If this man had killed Laura and was hoping to do the same for me, he'd be armed. And though we might have the initial advantage in seeing him first, a bow and arrow wouldn't be much use, in any sudden encounter, against a gun. Besides, I reasoned – my first surge of anger gone – ideally I should try and take this man alive if I was ever to clear myself of Laura's murder. How else could I safely take him?

Then I realised I was looking down on a possible means: the well behind the old pumping-shed, where I'd dumped Ross's dog. The two covers were flush with the ground. If I removed them completely and put a weave of small branches over the hole, and some moss and dead leaves on top of that I would have a very serviceable man-trap. In order to get at the extra rafters for our own tree house I'd had to cut away some of the laurel behind the shed and there was a clear pathway round the back there now.

I took Clare down to look at the well, gesturing to her, explaining what I had in mind. Lifting up the two iron covers I peered down into the darkness. It was ideal. The water, in the recent long spell of fine weather, had dropped considerably and the level must have been nearly eight feet below the ground. The four sides of the well were smooth and sheer. Once inside no one could get out again without help. Yet they needn't drown, I saw, since just below the waterline there were old wooden railway sleepers, forming an original buttress all round the concrete sides of the well, which would serve as a hand-hold just below the waterline. A man could survive down there quite safely for an hour or two at least.

I hid the metal covers and Clare and I quickly started to collect sticks of old wood, placing them in a cross-weave over the hole. Very soon we had a matrix of decayed beech branches which we covered with a garnish of leaves and moss and twigs, so that after twenty minutes all the evidence of a well there had completely disappeared and it seemed as if there was now a continuous path running between the laurels behind the shed. All we needed then was a bait. And the bait, I supposed, could only be me.

The obvious plan was to make the man feel I'd never seen him, give him a false sense of security, to let him see me for a moment: long enough for him to be able to follow me, but without giving him time to shoot at me. I would then try and lead him gradually down the east bank of the lake towards the trap.

To this end I moved parts of a big fallen beech branch out across the real path between the shed and the lake shore, so that anyone coming up or down that way would be tempted to take the easier route behind the shed in their travels. I made a secure hide as well, in a hollow among some brambles about twenty yards directly south of the shed, so that I could make for this and then lie in wait, with a perfect view of the covered man-trap.

I explained everything to Clare as we progressed in the work and finally I told her that she would have to go back to the tree-house and wait. It would be too dangerous for her to come with me.

'No,' she said flatly. She could say 'yes' and 'no' well enough by now, and, as always, she meant it. I'd long ago learnt how there was no point in arguing with her when she was adamant over something. So I had to take her with me.

We walked up towards the head of the lake, moving very carefully, still keeping to the high ground, where we could look safely down into the valley. The sun was up, the mist well gone. But it was a windy day for a change. The trees stirred, the big beech boughs groaned about us, and the dry reeds by the lake shore rustled angrily in the breeze.

And soon we were stopping every half-minute, rooted to the spot, fancying some malign shape or movement in the sunny undergrowth. A sudden splash of dancing leaves or a pattern of windy shadows became a dark coppery head or a moving arm advancing on us out of the sun. As the wind blew more briskly, the placid trees and the smooth beech branches soon held all sorts of imagined danger. And I realised we were making no progress at all. Just the opposite: I felt we were at risk now. *We* were being followed, more than likely, the hunters hunted.

Two pigeons burst from a tree immediately above us, their wings beating like gunshots and I stumbled, in heart-shaking alarm, crouching down with Clare, looking wildly around. But there was nothing. Just a windy, sunny silence crowding in all round us which suddenly terrified me. I decided to go back to the tree-house, to sit things out until Alice returned. And it was Clare who had the bright idea then of how we might trap our quarry at no risk to ourselves.

'Put food in the trap,' she said.

'Food? But the man isn't an animal.'

'Put something.'

And so it was that when we got back to the tree-house I took her advice. I got the transistor out, brought it down, round the lake again, and stood it right in the middle of the layer of branches over the well. Then I turned it on, the morning music programme on Radio 3, the volume slightly up. It wasn't food, of course. But then we were hoping to attract a human, not an animal curiosity. If the man was still in the valley there was a good chance he would hear the music at some point and come to investigate. And if he trod anywhere near the transistor he would disappear with the music. The batteries were new. It would last a good twelve hours at least. It struck me as an ideal bait and I couldn't imagine why I hadn't thought of it myself to begin with.

We took up positions then, hidden in the bramble bush, and waited. They were playing a Wagner opera that morning on Radio 3 – *Tannhäuser* – and the heavy, teutonic music together with the vast guttural voices boomed and clashed out over the sunny glade like an obsessive threat. I was convinced the man would hear it if he was still anywhere up at the top of the lake, for the wind was taking the sound in that direction. But no one came. We waited for nearly two hours, and still there was no one, and we were far too cramped now in the brambles. It was time to leave, to let the man fall into the trap himself, if he would, the music still ticking away like a fuse for him in the undergrowth.

But just as we were about to move from our hide something stirred in the bushes twenty yards beyond the shed. There was a faint sliding sound then – and we were down, completely hidden again, peering out between the brambles. A minute later there was another sound, a stick cracking, louder this time, but this time from another bush, thirty yards away, halfway up the side of the valley. The complete silence. Only the brisk wind agitating the leaves everywhere under the sharp midday sun.

Finally, after another few minutes wait – we felt like fishermen at last seeing their float dip in the water – the man came into view. Very slowly at first and from quite a different direction from the last sound on the side of the hill. He came from right behind the shed itself, moving along the back wall, hugging cover. He was walking towards the transistor. Then he stopped.

And now for the first time we both got a good look at him. He was thin, just as the masked figure who had shot Laura had been. He was older than I'd expected somehow, forty, perhaps fifty. And his face was not typically African; there was no fat, nothing bulbous about it from the angle we were looking at it: an ascetic face, learned even. There was something haunted and infinitely wary about it. Then he suddenly turned towards us, startled by something. And there was the shock.

The other side of his face was brutally disfigured. There were angry scars all down one side, the whole cheek risen unnaturally, the rolls of scar-tissue like a growth leading to a half-closed, leering eye and the wreckage of an ear. There was just a hole in the side of the man's head. Here he had been hideously burnt, I thought, and the damage badly repaired. It was an unnerving vision: on one side the haunted, saint-like profile; on the other, a dark ogre from a nightmare.

I noticed Clare's face then: she had seen the man properly for the first time. Instead of expressing any hope, as I had expected, at the successful outcome to this hunt, she was plainly terrified by what she saw, her eyes staring, frozen. She was shaking with fear. She wanted to run away there and then, and I had to hold her down.

The man on the other hand was calm to a degree. He just stood there, right by the side of the shed, without moving for a minute; a calm, camouflaged, black statue. He was only a few yards from the transistor. He was bound to make another step towards it, I thought. I prayed that he would. But he didn't. He was too wary, too suspicious. He must have sensed something was wrong. He didn't even move forward a pace, where he might have slipped into the man-trap from the side. Instead he glanced at the radio once more and then retreated the way he'd come, disappearing quickly, silently into the bushes.

Fifteen minutes later Clare and I were safely back in the tree-house. And how I wished Clare had had more speech in her. For of course, in the meantime I'd been thinking; I'd had to face the fact much more clearly: what was an *African* doing in the middle of England? Could he be one of Ross's men? An African, certainly, I thought. But would Ross employ hit-men from such parts? Of course not.

At the same time as I wondered about this, another explanation for his presence emerged at the edges of my mind. Was this killer in some way connected with Willy Kindersley? – with his long fossil safaris in East Africa: a friend of his, or an enemy? I thought of Willy's death, the hit-and-run accident in Nairobi: a coloured man had been seen driving the car. An African? *This* African? This thin man who had gone on to kill Laura, and who now, for some unfathomable reason, was pursuing his revenge with us, Clare and me? It seemed preposterous.

But then I remembered the long article that Alice had shown me a few weeks before from the Sunday paper, with its gossipy intimations of evil in Willy's life, some violent unscrupulousness there, murky depths in his East African past. Could this be true? Was the African here evidence of this? I wished that Clare could have spoken more, from her memory of her life out there.

But she couldn't: or wouldn't.

'Fire,' was all she said, when I asked her.

'Yes,' I said. 'He must have been burnt. But did you ever see the man before? Did you know him? Or did Mummy? Did your father? Do you remember?' But there was no coherent reply, except the repetition now and then of the word 'fire', and a look on her face when she said it of confusion and fear. And this surprised me, for Clare, more and more in touch with life now, had become so fearless recently. But here was a memory, I felt, evoked again by this man's burnt face, that brought back an old trauma in her, a fever from her past which affected her now as it had then by closing her up like a clam. And so I wondered again if this African had anything to do with Ross at all – Ross who remained the one person I really had to fear. The African, I thought, must have had some business simply with the Kindersley family, with events that I knew nothing of that had occurred among them all out in East Africa years before.

And if this was so there was a further unpleasant corollary: one person at least would have known about any such unhappy events – Laura, who had never even hinted at them to me. Why not? Because, as the newspaper article had hinted, everyone had covered their tracks, including Laura? And perhaps Clare was now the only silent witness to whatever had happened in the past – along with the African stalking the valley somewhere beneath us. But wait, I thought – there were two others who had been with Willy in those African years: the Bensons. Of course, George and Annabelle Benson, old friends and colleagues of Willy's, whom I'd seen only three months before at the cottage. The Bensons. They might well know something of all this. But they were in Oxford. And in any case, if Laura had felt the need to cover up on this, the Bensons would surely feel the same urge. But why? What had happened, if anything, in Africa then? Or was it all a ridiculous theory of mine? And was there some perfectly sensible reason for this burnt man lurking somewhere in the woods beneath us? And was Clare's fear, for example, simply that of any child faced with such disfigurement, seeing a nightmare in the scarred face?

I spent most of the rest of the morning wondering about this uneasily, searching through my past with Laura for any incident that might explain this man's presence in the valley. But soon other events took over that day, wiping out for the time being any further thoughts.

I had dozed off later that afternoon, tired out in the heat that had come back, when Clare had woken me, shaking me, agitated. She pointed back down towards the south end of the lake.

'People!' she said urgently. 'Come. Now people are. People are!'

Her sentences were incomplete and her voice was a high and unreal falsetto, as it often was now. This was another means she cultivated of avoiding the reality of herself: she spoke as a deaf person might, not hearing herself, so the better to avoid any responsibility for what she said. But I was surprised she spoke at all, given her fears that morning.

'People? Where?' I said. 'The dark man?'

'No. No. Look. Come!'

I got the arrows and recurve bow out again and followed her silently along the aerial walkways, through the trees down to the big beech at the bottom of the lake. Until at last, twenty feet up, we were able to look down through gaps in the leaves to the ground below where the stream left the lake at its southern end near the road.

A group of campers had somehow broken into the estate through the fence, and had set up rough tents in the glade beneath us. We could only see half a dozen or so of them at that point, leather-jacketed youths and their girls, with several great motorcycles just visible to one side. But from the shouts and squeals coming from outside this space it was obvious that there were a dozen or more in the party altogether.

It was equally clear that they were no ordinary campers, but a trespassing band of Hell's Angels in their dark tasselled jackets covered with Nazi insignia. There seemed to be two rival groups of them, a second out of sight across the stream, for the youths that we could see beneath us, finishing cans of beer, would throw the empty missiles at their invisible neighbours, shouting threats and imprecations at them.

We watched their antics in silence for some time, looking down through the deep well of leaves, before Clare, sitting on the branch next me, lifted her arms and mimed an arrow shot at them. I shook my head. That was the last thing we wanted – that they should have any notion of our presence. And it was too late in the day, and too risky, to move anywhere on the ground of the valley now. We would simply stay put, on high, and ignore them. They would probably move on tomorrow.

I whispered and gestured, explaining these prohibitions to Clare, and saw the look of disappointment, even anger, cloud her face. For her, I sensed, these strangers were much more than unwelcome trespassers. They were rivals, an inferior species contesting space, and thus natural enemies. They were savages in her child's adventure-book mind, silently arrived from beyond the coral reef and camping now outside our desert-island stockade: a deadly threat to her territory, to her security, to this whole new way of life I had given her, which had released her from a clouded, nightmare anonymity.

But why had she not felt the same about the African that morning? Her anger now had certainly not been shown to him; just the opposite: she'd been terrified. And I wondered once more if the African was someone she'd known, or had seen before, in some traumatic circumstances, and who thus represented an intruder, a fearsome, God-like being whom she could not now face. Whereas these Hell's Angels, in reality and in their numbers probably far more dangerous, seemed to her fair and easy game.

They built a fire beneath us in the early evening, a dangerous, unkempt fire built too close to the trees and the dry, brambly undergrowth immediately beyond. They grilled hamburgers here and sausages and ate crisps and drank more beer. And afterwards they chanted football songs and slogans and, circling the fire, their faces livid and drunken in the fading light, shouted obscenities across to the other group on the far side of the stream.

Clare, moving silently on her haunches, restlessly changing position on the branch above, peered down at them intently, with disgust. But she was not being critical of their words or their behaviour, I'm sure. This was not the reason for her frustrated contempt, which was more that of a predatory animal, concealed in the trees above a tempting meal it cannot for the moment procure. Eventually I forced Clare back with me to our tree-house.

I woke in the soft, moonlit darkness a few hours later, the light filtering in marble shafts through the leaves. Something was wrong, missing. A branch creaked in the silence somewhere high up in the trees quite near me. But there were other louder noises coming from the end of the lake now, shouts, laughter, a faint, dangerously excited roar on the air. I turned, looking up at Clare's hammock. She was gone.

I followed her as fast as I could along the shadowed branches and walkways, for I was sure that she'd headed this way. But she had several minutes start on me and though I was well accustomed to the dark, I had never taken this way before at night. Nor had Clare. But she was smaller than I, and more supple and sure-footed, so that I was unable to catch her before she had reached the end of the line of trees. I found her at last, peering down into the glade, sitting astride the same branch we'd been on several hours before, looking down intently on the same campsite beneath.

But now there was real pandemonium beneath us. Some of the youths, half-naked and far gone in drink, were prancing with their girls round the fire, which had been built up since, with heavy old logs, so that it roared like an ox-roast in the night. But others, we saw, more sober in the company, were coming in and out of the circle of firelight, trying to interrupt the revellers, with something else on their mind. They were worried. Someone was missing. They shouted, sometimes grappling with the fire-dancers, asking for help.

'You can't fuckin' leave Hank and the others out there,' one of them said. 'They may have all bloody drowned in the lake. We've got to help look for 'em. They've been gone bloody hours.'

'Bugger off, will you?' a lout replied. 'What's it to me? You've already got half a dozen blokes out there looking for Johnny. They'll turn up.'

And they did. Five minutes later.

As we watched, like people in the dark gods of a theatre, looking down through the long clefts in the tree at the firelit glade beneath, a new group arrived in the circle of light. One of the youths here, just in his shirt and pants, was dripping wet, like a drowned but boisterous rat. And with him were half a dozen of his friends, equally rowdy, violent even, obviously the search party who had gone out to look for the stray. But the figure of real interest for all of us, both up in the tree and on the ground, was the man they had brought back with them, in the centre of the group, hands roughly tied behind his back, being threatened now with gleaming flick-knives.

It was the African, tall, stooped, a grave, inky figure in the dancing firelight.

'You wouldn't bloody believe it!' one of the youths shouted. He was taller than the others with lank blond hair. He prodded the African viciously with his knife, so that he fell forward, wounded, writhing, onto the ground by the fire. 'He bloody tried to kill Johnny here, this bloke did.'

The others, who had been dancing round the flames, stopped now, fascinated by this strange prize from the woods. They crowded round the African, who was trying to get to his feet, but without success, for each time he got to his knees someone kicked him down again.

'I was just going along by the water there,' the dripping youth who must have been Johnny said, 'When I heard this tranny blazing away out of nowhere in the trees. I thought it was one of youse buggers with a bird. But then I saw it behind a shed, and there weren't no one there. Well, I went to pick it up – and the next thing I were going down this bloody great well in the dark. I'd have bloody drowned if it hadn't been for Hank and the others right then.'

'Yeah,' the tall blond youth called Hank confirmed. 'We were just coming along the same way, heard the row in the bushes behind this shed, and then we saw this fuckin' buck nigger standing over a great hole in the ground with Johnny screaming fit to bust in the water beneath him.' He kicked the African again. 'We were onto the bugger in a flash. Put up no end of a fight, he did. But we nailed him. Didn't we? You runt!' He kicked him again. 'Well, we got Johnny out, tied our jeans together and heaved 'im out with them. And do you know what this darkie had gone and done? A real boy-scout job: he'd built a bloody *man trap* over this old well for us, lot of dry sticks and things, and put a tranny on top, so as we'd fall straight in. And old Johnny fell for it. He'd have fuckin' drowned less we'd come along. What do you think of that?'

Hank looked round, addressing the assembled company, his face shining with drunken indignation in the light. 'What do you make of that?' he added, in a tone that suggested he spoke now more in sorrow than in anger. Then he suddenly picked the African up from the ground and shook him viciously by the neck, like a chicken. 'We're going to have you, mate,' he said. 'You can't go round trying to kill British blokes like that, you know.' Then he threw him to the ground again. A friend brought Hank a can of beer, and he tore the top off, drinking deeply.

'I know what we'll do with you, mate,' Hank said at last, gasping with pleasure, his thirst quenched. 'We'll give you a taste of your own medicine. Tie him up properly, lads. Then we'll lash him to a pole.'

'What you going to do, Hank?' someone shouted in excitement.

'What these black buggers used to do to us: roast him alive! Tie him to a stake first. Then we'll roast him alive, *and eat him.*'

Hank was joking, I thought. But the African didn't think so. From what I could see of his face, squirming on the ground by the fire, it was clear that he believed Hank. The African was certainly frightened, in a way he'd never been that morning. By the fire – of course, that was it: here was another fire about to maim him again, at the very least. As for Clare, it was obvious from her pleasurable excitement beside me that she fully endorsed Hank's plans for the man. A suitable demise for her enemy of the morning.

And I thought: an end to my enemy too? Without my touching him: perhaps Willy's killer, and Laura's as well – who had then come after Clare and me with the same evil beam in his eye . . . Yet I realised I hadn't the slightest proof for any of this. But surely it wouldn't matter anyway. Hank was only trying to frighten the man.

He wasn't. They got a long beech branch from somewhere outside the clearing and dug a hole for it near the fire, pounding in sods of earth round its base with their boots. Then they tied the African to it with bits of twine and some cord from the guy ropes from their tents. They put a lot of dry brambles and sticks around his feet then, building the wood up round his legs, to his knees and then higher as the man struggled vainly, his face deformed all over now, appalled in the light from the fire a few yards away.

Hank spoke, his voice screechy with excitement and drink. He still had his flick-knife in his hand. He went up to the man.

'Before we toast you,' he said. 'Maybe we should cut ourselves a live steak or two from the ribs here.' And he opened the man's camouflage jacket and made a cut there and then as he spoke, on the man's flesh, a delicate slash across his lower chest, like a butcher suggesting a joint, so that the blood ran. 'That's what you people do, isn't it? Out in Africa. Bloody savages. Eat your mother live, you would. *Wouldn't* you?'

I still thought Hank was playing some brutal game. But this last action of his made me wonder. I knew I'd have to try and save the African, whoever he was, if this murderous charade went any further. I took Spinks's bow from my back and unwound the tape from the two arrows strapped to its belly.

Hank, having cut the man's flesh open, was a vicious Master of Ceremonies now, a shark who had smelt blood. He stood back, surveying his work, and there was silence in the glade for a moment. Was this all? Or would there be more. Surely there was more fun to be had...

Hank, sensing this silence as a vital cue, started an undulating, mocking dance round the pyre then, his blond hair flopping up and down in the light, the tassels on his Nazi jacket flying. By degrees the others joined him, mostly drunk, pleased to take up the chase again.

And together they all danced round the African, in a savage parody of jive and twist and rock-and-roll – gyrating, throwing their backsides about and clapping their hands in the air above their heads as they chanted bloody slogans and racist obscenities, the graffiti of a thousand condemned playgrounds coming to frenzied life.

But there was still time, I thought. They would calm down. Indeed I noticed one or two of the youths on the outskirts who were not taking part in the dance at all. They were trying to restrain the others.

'All right, Hank,' one of these said. 'Give it over. We'll have the fuzz here. Let the bugger go.'

But Hank took no notice. He left the circle then and went to the fire a few yards away, where he drew a long burning ember out. I knew that, even if he was only fooling, once this even touched the dry brambles round the African's feet, the man would go up in flames like a rocket. On the other hand, I thought, if I used the bow, if I shot Hank, they would find the arrow afterwards...

But perhaps I'd have no alternative. I was about twenty-five feet above the pyre, looking down at a slight angle on the African. If Hank came to set him ablaze it would be a fairly easy shot. I should be able to wound him, on the backside or leg, and take the consequences of the arrow being found afterwards.

Hank returned then, the torch in his hand, pushing his way back through the circle of dancers. He flourished the burning stick like a metronome in front of the African's face for half a minute. Then he brushed the man's good profile with the red-hot branch, from top to bottom, singeing the hair and flesh.

The African screamed.

And I could stand it no more. Hank had his back to me. I drew the string quickly, aimed for his legs, and loosed the arrow. But in my anger I drew too hard. The arrow went high. It must have transfixed Hank, going right through his chest, so that he fell forward onto the pyre, dropping the burning torch which instantly set the brambles alight at the base of the pyre.

The African was struggling now, seeing a chance of escape, Hank's body lying half across him as he slipped gradually down, smothering the flames. His friends came for him, trying to drag him away, while another, with a knife, moved behind the African and started to cut him loose from his bonds.

The others had all panicked meanwhile, for the flames had taken hold around the base of the pyre and had begun to spread outwards over the glade, along the fuses of drier grass. The whole place was suddenly empty. And the youth who had been trying to free the African had run as well, leaving his job half-done. But it was enough. The African was suddenly free of the burning post and there was only one man left in the glade who couldn't run: Hank, still sprawled to one side of the pyre.

The African had been slightly burnt about the feet. But he was still perfectly active. He should have run himself, for the flames were spreading quickly now all over the glade. But instead he stayed a moment, turned and, as a last gesture, pulled Hank's body right over the blazing pyre, so that it would roast there properly, the black leather jacket and the paint of its gold swastika already burning fiercely. Then the African was gone, running between the gathering sheaths of flame, the little fire-storm that was engulfing the tents, the motorcycles, everything that was in the glade.

But soon the flames had risen beneath us too, and caught

some of the dry beech leaves on the lower branches of the tree we were hiding in. They began to feed on the leaves, moving towards the other trees in the valley, on the very things that had hidden us happily from the world for the past two months, the basis of our security, our existence.

And there was no way of stopping it. The fire raged upwards through the trees around the glade, so that Clare and I were moving quickly back along the branches and walkways towards our tree house, the wood beginning to crackle and roar as the flames lit up the valley behind us. And suddenly we were like hunted animals in the forest, leaping from branch to branch, running from the holocaust.

Thirteen

Clare and I were back in the great house, hidden in Alice's tower, next morning: we could see over most of the burnt valley to the east. The fire had destroyed half a dozen of the trees there, round the lake, and must have burnt every remnant of our own life in the place as well – our tree-house, the makeshift furniture, the old nursery-stained copy of *Pigling Bland*, Spinks's *Good Beer Guide* and French letters, along with the ropes and aerial walkways which had been paths out of our house into a green web, a remote world hidden in space, yet where the shapes of branches, the pattern in a particular cluster of leaves, had become familiar to us as if they'd been the garden round our cottage on earth. All this must have been burnt to a cinder by now.

I had only managed to rescue Spinks's fibreglass bow, and his backpack filled with a few things that wouldn't burn and could have identified us afterwards – the army binoculars, the gas burner, the metal pots and pans. Of the rest, of all the haphazard bits and pieces which had been vital adjuncts to our life in the woods, there could have been nothing left. And I felt homeless once more, looking out on the ruined valley from the carefully arched Gothic windows in the tower, back in a contrived world, at risk again. Clare was beside me, the two of us crouching down, noses almost on the windowsill. She was sucking her thumb, bereft herself once more, looking out over the valley where there was nothing left of her content, nothing but the central trunks and a few of the larger branches of the great beech trees, blackened, still smoking in the blue summer light. I held her hand as we watched, but it was inert like the hand of a doll. The firemen were still pumping water on the smouldering ruins from the lake and the police were downstairs with Alice again.

We had escaped the flames a few hours earlier, running from the valley up the path from the lake, into the greenhouse and walled kitchen garden, and from there we'd made our way into the house by the back door, which Alice had arranged always to leave open for us in case of just such an emergency.

We met her coming down the oak staircase, half-asleep, alarmed. I told her what had happened and she had sent us at once to hide in the tower while she contacted the fire brigade and the police. And now we waited for her to come back from her interviews with the police downstairs: to hear the worst, perhaps? Had they, for example, found the arrow?

Hank, almost certainly, must have been burnt to the bone. But the arrow was made of aluminium. Besides, others in the circle must have seen the arrow: its impact, if not its flight. Would they remember the angle it had come from? From above? Or had they all been too drunk to remember anything? And what of the African? Had he escaped? Or had the police got him, along with the louts? Was this an end for Clare and me, or another beginning?

We waited. There were pots of raspberry and nut yoghurt in the fridge. But neither of us could eat. Alice's big pinewood hand loom was in one corner of the room, with a half-completed roll in the weave, a rug it looked like, or the beginnings of one of her Indian bedspreads. Clare walked over to it and gazed at the emerging cloth intently. There was a complex pattern in it, red circles and lozenges on an oatmeal background. Clare touched one of the lozenges. Then she tried to pick the cloth apart there, extract the diamond, undo the weave, and failing this she started to manhandle the shuttles, tearing them out of the loom, so that I had to force her to stop.

And she was angry suddenly, a bitter fountain of rage, the pent-up frustration at the loss and change of her life coming into her throat with a violent scream, so that I was sure we would be heard downstairs. And I knew I wanted us both to survive, so I gagged her mouth with a hand, and kept it there, cruelly, firmly, for a minute.

Then I heard steps on the stairway outside the tower, and the door opened. It was Alice. Clare and I were down on the floor, as if we'd been two children fighting, struggling. But I could hold her tongue no more. I took my hand away, expecting the awful scream again. But it never came. Instead Clare gazed up at what Alice was cradling in her arms. It was a splendid model boat, several feet long, a fully-rigged three-masted tea clipper, an East Indiaman, the hull a gleaming black with a gold band right round beneath the rails and a scrubbed pine deck with little coils of rope and meticulously detailed brass fittings. It was obviously part of Alice's expensive Victorian bric-à-brac from the top landing.

Alice saw the tears of rage, the anguish in Clare's face. 'Look,' she said, without looking at her, bending down and setting the boat up on the floor, 'there are even real tea-chests down here in the hold. You can take them out. And there are a few real sailors too, somewhere.' Alice played with the ship then, rather than in any way pressing Clare to occupy herself with it. Alice had learnt all about Clare, was as tactful in her approaches to her now as Laura had once been.

Clare didn't respond at all. But she didn't scream, though, either. And, of course, I had realised by now that all her language would have gone again in this second change of home. She was mute with this loss of Eden. And we were back again at the beginning, where I'd been with her two months before in the valley: where one couldn't look at the girl directly, explain anything to her, where she was practically an automaton, a vegetable.

Alice turned to me. 'That's one good thing about your being back in the house. There's plenty to occupy Clare with. That whole top corridor is filled with stuff, old games and things.'

'She's going to need it,' I said. 'But will there be time?'

Alice looked at me, a sudden confident surprise in her face. 'Why, of course. A lot of the wood is gone. But the fire burnt out all your tree-house as well. They've no idea you were there.'

'But what about the one I shot?'

'I don't know about him. The police didn't tell me, only that one of the boys died in the fire. They didn't mention finding any arrow.'

'And the African?'

'They didn't mention him either. So of course I couldn't bring the topic up.'

'Just playing cat-and-mouse with us,' I said. 'That's all. They must be putting two and two together down there by now. It won't be long – '

'Nonsense,' Alice interrupted. And then there was an interruption at our feet, a rending and splitting of wood. Arms suddenly flailing, her fists crashing through the masts and sails, Clare had destroyed most of the model ship before we could stop her.

The tea clipper lay like a real wreck on the floor all about us. 'It doesn't matter,' Alice said, in a matter-of-fact way, clearing the bits up, while Clare meanwhile had slunk away on all fours like an animal and hidden behind the day bed.

'It doesn't matter,' Alice said again lightly, as if Clare had just spilt some milk.

'But it *does*,' I said. 'She'll smash the whole place up. We can hardly keep her here anyway. I'm sorry. It's ridiculous. It's too much for you – '

'You're wrong. And it's not.' Alice was very firm, candid, in control. We were guests in her house now, she implied. We had come into a magic circle of her chivalrous protection, and thus all would be well. I was no longer responsible for our existence, as I had been in the valley. Alice was in charge now. I liked the idea and yet I resented it. I longed suddenly for the freedom of the trees again, where Alice had been a subsidiary visitor with us, in my world, dependent on me. Now, the chance unexpectedly emerging, she meant to turn the tables on me, it seemed. But perhaps what I really resented was the fact that in the woods, where my first priority was survival with Clare, I had not had to make up my mind about whether I loved Alice or was simply using her. In the wild, busy with Clare in the tree-house I'd built myself, the question hadn't arisen. But now, as her guest once more, totally dependent on her, I had to ask myself again what our future was. How far could I go in using someone for my own convenience, if that was the only thing which bound us together? Without love?

'I don't know,' I said weakly. 'They'll surely be looking for us again up here. We can't stay here.'

'But you *can*!' Alice was almost joyfully dramatic. 'Up here in the tower for the moment. No one *ever* comes up here but me. And the Pringles are off to Spain for their summer vacation in a few days. They'll be away three weeks. You can come downstairs then. The place will be empty after Mary leaves in the mornings. That's just it, don't you see? You *can* stay here. And wait till you hear from your naval friend in Portugal.'

I walked over to the window looking westwards, down over the formal gardens, the lines of baroque statuary and the pond with the Neptune fountain and the flat top of the great cedar tree to one side. I could see a peacock in one of its upper branches and two others pecking fastidiously along the grass beneath. The heat wasn't up yet. Indeed, the day looked set for some kind of change, for I could see huge rain-clouds gathering in the west. But this room, locked away high in the tower, was quite insulated from any change in the weather. And it was just as distant from the real world, too, which from this height and security one could view with equal disdain.

From here, on this side of the tower, one saw nothing but formal beauty, the well cut lawns, the imported eighteenth-century fountain, the ageless cedar tree, the bright blue birds who stretched their tails wide now and then in fans of dazzling colour.

On the other side of the tower was the burn-scarred valley we had left, the smoking ruins of a native happiness. I had thought in terms of alternatives. But there were none. Clare was still crouching behind the day-bed, feet up against her chest, hands over her face, living in a womb of her own making again. She was the first problem once more. She would have to be tempted back into life. I remembered the bones in the tomb on the island which had caught her fancy six weeks before. I'd told Alice about it at the time, and now I mentioned it again.

Alice said, 'There's a little sort of museum in one of the rooms off the top landing: British rock specimens, wild flowers, butterflies, as well as things from abroad. There are some bones in there, too.'

'Bones?'

'Yes. I bought them all with the place, in a locked room, a lot of bits and pieces in glass cases. The people who lived here after the Hortons. He was something important in the Colonial service, a Governor in Africa.'

'You mean *African* bones?'

'I think so. There's a broken skull. And a strange sort of shrunken head – that sort of thing. As well as spears, shields made from Zebra hide – you know.'

'Yes. I saw the big crocodile up on that landing.'

'It's part of the same collection. I don't suppose Clare would care for that. But there's a lot of other things up there might draw her out. You see? You could help her just as well here as down in the valley.'

I started to believe Alice then. This whole vast house so stuffed with Victorian treasures, in packing-cases and now museum exhibits, along landings and in tiny rooms under the eaves, all this would surely form a cure for any child on a rainy day. And what did it matter about our relationship, any ambiguity between Alice and me? We still had one thing in common, certainly: both of us remained as cut off as ever from reality. We'd both of us come to hate the present world in all its bland and mean or vicious spirits, a place quite drained of character or design: that still held us firmly together: we'd come to hate the louts and the polo-players equally, in England or Long Island, along with the sly and the craven everywhere else. And I felt our shared distaste strongly as we stood together in the warm, pine-scented room, high above the land, gazing down on the imperious peacocks and the fountain. Why not stay here, I thought, perched as high above the house as we had been above the valley? Such remote eyries had become our natural habitat. Alice had gone to the fridge and opened it. I turned to her.

'I didn't really have time to tell you last night,' I said, 'about the African down there in the valley.'

'No.'

'But your mentioning those African things in the museum, African bones . . .' I stopped.

'So?'

'Well of course it struck me: the man might have had something to do with Clare's parents when they were out in East Africa. You remember that article you showed me – do you still have it?'

'Yes. And there was another article about it in *Time* magazine last week. But you didn't believe any of it.'

'Well, what am I to believe now? What's a man like that doing here? Just a chance hiker? Hardly. And he's not one of Ross's men. So who *is* he?'

I explained my theories about the African to Alice and she said finally, 'Who knows?'

'I wonder if he got away.'

'We'll soon know. It'll be in the papers, on the news.'

'But, if I'm right, why should he be after *us*? Clare would have been too young to have had anything to do with him in Africa, and I certainly don't know him. So even if any of my theories are right – and if he killed Willy and Laura – what's going on following us for?'

The sun began to fade just then and a dark crept up over the whole landscape and there were spots of rain on the window. For the first time that summer it looked like a real change in the weather, with great cigars of grey cloud rolling up from all round the horizon.

'I don't know,' Alice said. 'Perhaps we'll find out. Or perhaps we should make it our business to find out.'

She had prepared some biscuits and covered them with processed cheese squeezed from a Primula tube in the fridge, chopping the lot up on a plate. Then she put it all down in front of Clare, still crouched by the day-bed, without looking at her, offhandedly, just as one might leave out a dog's dinner under a kitchen table.

'We'll find out about the African. Or we'll *have* to find out.' Alice repeated her ideas, thoughtful now, as if planning something vital once more, as she had with Clare's rescue from the hospital.

'There are some old friends of the Kindersleys,' I said. 'The Bensons. I know them quite well. They might help. She's an entomologist and he used to work with Willy picking up fossils in East Africa. He lives in Oxford now. Works at the Natural History museum there.'

'Can you trust them now? Won't they just think like the others: that you killed ... your wife?'

I turned away from the window. It had started to rain now, a setting-in sort of rain, the first of that summer. 'I don't know,' I said. 'They're certainly a pair of rather dry sticks, the Bensons. It could be worth trying them all the same.'

I looked covertly at Clare hunched in the corner then. She hadn't moved. But she had taken her hand away from her face.

She was looking at the plate of food at least.

'She might like some music,' I said. I hated seeing Clare as she was now, trapped, caged, like a hurt animal. It was terrible.

'There's a radio here somewhere. There, under that cloth.'

Alice went over to where rolls of variously coloured tweed were piled up on a trestle table against one wall. There was a stereo transistor behind them. She turned it on. The music was from Radio 3 again: Vivaldi, precise, dainty, remote. The sound from the two speakers reverberated perfectly about the domed ceiling of the old smoking room. But it made no difference to Clare.

'It'll be some time,' I said, 'before she improves. If ever. God . . .' I was depressed, tired. I closed my eyes against the world, against the sudden grey and rain-filled weather that was sweeping in over the wolds. I tried to let the music wash through my mind like the rain: wash thought away.

'I know!' Alice said, suddenly enthusiastic about something. But I didn't open my eyes until I heard the door of the fridge close. Alice had a half bottle of champagne in her hand. She popped the cork and poured it all out into three coffee mugs, the foam gently climbing up the sides. She put one mug down in front of Clare and handed another to me. Then she raised her own, drinking.

'I've kept it up here – for a rainy day,' she said.

I sipped some. It was good champagne, tingling cold. I drank some more. 'Thank you,' I said, looking over at her.

Alice had her hair combed severely back straight over the crown of her head, above her ears, so that the sharp curve of her jaw stood out very clearly, like a diagram in anatomy. Her eyelids flickered for an instant, caught in the rising spume of champagne bubbles. I was quite close to her.

I saw a small scar she had on one eyelid, running out a little towards her temple, which, close though I'd been to her, I'd not noticed before.

'That scar,' I said. 'What happened?' I touched her face briefly. 'Just there. I hadn't noticed.'

'Oh, years ago, I fell down some steps.'

'Yes?'

'One summer out in the Hamptons. I must have been about ten. It bled a lot.'

'I see.'

'Yes. My father had just arrived. I was running down the steps too fast. He'd driven up from New York. I remember, we were all excited. He had a new car he'd gotten himself. A British car – '

'A Rolls – '

'No – some sports car they'd just introduced. Very fast. A two-seater, long bonnet and wire wheels – and a big, sleek, rounded ass – '

'A Jaguar probably. An XK 120 – I remember them.'

'Maybe.'

'Or was it a Morgan or an MG?'

'I don't know. My brothers were all over it. And I just fell down the steps running after them . . .'

Suddenly we were both talking fast, the mugs bouncing in our hands – talking about nothing really, as if some quite unexpected sexual excitement had overcome us both which we couldn't acknowledge then.

I stepped forward, involuntarily. I wanted, I think, to kiss the scar. But instead I trod on part of the ruined model boat. A spar cracked beneath my foot and I withdrew.

She said, 'I could see the whitecaps – just before I fell – on the waves out at sea beyond the car, framing the car like a picture. It was blowing quite hard. Then I slipped.'

'That sea you wanted to swim across, all the way to England?'

'Yes. That was about the same time. I think they thought I'd fallen down on purpose to get attention, so they'd make a fuss of me instead of the car.'

'Which wasn't true?'

'No. At least . . . ' She hesitated. 'I don't think so. How can one be sure? I can see it all, the whitecaps, the car, the blood. But I don't remember the feelings exactly.'

This small mystery unearthed lay about Alice's life – a query at the end of her words, an indeterminate feeling she had carried with her for nearly thirty years like the scar: an aspect of her otherwise so assured character which she had not resolved.

It hardly mattered in itself, I thought, this childhood fall, this possible rebuff. It mattered only in that now, through this small scar on her eyelid, I had suddenly, for the first time, gained a real access to her personality. I was there for an instant myself, with her on the steps of the Charles Addams house, on that windy day out on Long Island. I could see the sleek Jaguar and the whitecaps out in the bay. And I could hear her sudden tears, the pain of injury or dismissal – it didn't matter which – so sharp and rending in childhood. I loved her then.

Alice lived for me in a real perspective now, as a feature in a map where there were clear compass-points at last. Her life could be related to some constant scale, to this scar, which provoked an intimacy between us greater than that of any sex. I could have kissed her then all right. But there would hardly have been any point. As we just looked at each other, with such candour, we could not have been closer. There was no more ambiguity.

I saw something move over Alice's shoulder. Clare's hand emerged from behind the end of the day-bed. Then she dipped a finger in her mug of champagne. She swizzled it about in the liquid for a minute so that it foamed again. Then she licked her finger.

It was a start, at least.

It was the beginning of August. I had been living wild in the valley for over two months now. But living in a house again, and sleeping in a bed now each night, inevitably brought a change of thoughts. Once more, surrounded by all the haunting impositions of man-made life, with its permanent threat of plans, expectations, decisions, I was forced to think of the future again.

If Captain Warren didn't reply there would be no future for us in Portugal. If, on the other hand, I could somehow lay my hands on the African, and if I could contact the Bensons, I might prove my innocence and stay with Clare in England.

But the news that day, and during the days that followed, wasn't helpful. In their accounts of the fracas and fire there was nothing in the media about any coloured man being involved. I supposed that the drunks had all agreed on silence about the African, and their attempts to roast him alive. The man must have got clean away, indeed, for there was no word of his turning up anywhere else in the locality, though we searched the local papers, and Alice kept her ear open with Mary, the two gardeners, and with the Pringles before they left, for any possible gossip about him in the area.

This surprised me. I wondered how any such badly burnt and highly conspicuous figure could escape detection locally unless, like me, he had holed up somewhere or had some help in the immediate vicinity.

I read the article in Time magazine, a development of the piece in the *Sunday Times*. But here, unafraid of libel I suppose, they were more free with their theories and the names behind them. Willy Kindersley, they said, in order to finance his expensive fossil hunts, had become involved in gun-running and other dubious trades with one of the warring tribes on the Kenya-Sudan border. There had been trouble for many years all over that remote northern frontier, between the Kenyan 'Shifta' – roving brigands – and rivals to the north, nomadic cattle- and camel-herding tribes in Uganda, the Sudan and Ethiopia: a traditional tale of mutual theft and pillage. But now they were having at each other with AK 47s and even portable rocket-launchers, instead of assegais and poisoned arrows.

It was an unlikely tale. Willy, I knew, had been largely financed by an oil company with East African interests anxious for such prestigious publicity, but more concerned still that Willy might discover potential drilling sites for them during his fossil surveys over the arid wastes of that Northern Frontier District. Besides, had the story been true, and had Willy thus suffered for some kind of double-dealing, why had the revenge been extended to his wife and beyond that to Clare and me? That made no sense.

On the other hand – just on the basis of no smoke without fire – it seemed to me now that something terrible must have happened to Willy Kindersley in these wilds of East Africa. But what?

'Of course even though she was out there with him Laura may never have known about any problems,' Alice said, when I commented on the article. 'You told me they were very different people, after all.'

'Yes. Chalk and cheese. But Willy wasn't dishonest.'

'You never met him, though. It's all hearsay, isn't it? Anything you know about him, you know only through Laura.'

'Yes. But one *knows*.'

'Does one? Just because one loves someone?'

'Willy was really just an eccentric academic, I keep telling you. Besides, Benson ran all the practical details on these safaris.'

'So he might know something special?'

'Perhaps. Perhaps I should risk visiting him.'

But I postponed the visit. After so long in the open I began to enjoy the comforts and surprises of life in the house. And although Clare hadn't improved with any coherent speech, still just expressing herself, when she did at all, with grunts and tantrums and in bursts of some strange language of her own, she was calm, at least, for long periods. She appeared to have accepted her enclosure. And when the Pringles went off on their Spanish holiday two days later, things were easier still, for though we kept our beds and ate mostly in Alice's tower, we now had the run of the great house after twelve o'clock each morning when Mary left. So, as once the trees and lake in the valley had been our secret estate, now the house became an equally covert playground – the long upstairs passages, empty rooms, the junk-filled nooks and crannies in the attics, which Clare and I roved up and down on voyages of discovery during the rainy, unsettled week that followed.

We took Clare downstairs, too, showing her all the reconstructed Victoriana: the great hall, the dining-room, the real tennis court at the back, the old kitchen with the lamp room, larders and laundry beyond. Yet the great cast-iron boiling tub in the laundry was the only thing that intrigued her. She assumed it was for cooking in – an African memory, I supposed, though hardly of missionaries and cannibals. She would have stayed there content all day, sitting in the big pot and poking about in the grate beneath. But it was a dangerous room for a child to be left in, since there was a great mechanical linen press at one end against the wall, a Victorian patent device with an unruly ton weight, like a great broad coffin resting above a series of wooden rollers, which you turned with a handle and chain, pressing the rollers over the fabric.

She liked the real tennis court, too, at the back of the house, built with a sloping interior roof all down one side, like a monastery cloister, where the Hortons, presumably giving up the archaic game, had built a little stage at the far end of the court. And it was this stage which Alice had refurbished, complete with new velvet drapes and Victorian oil footlamps. And here one day we set up an old nineteenth-century Punch and Judy show, which Alice had bought at Sothebys, and played rumbustious scenes for Clare, as an audience of one on a single chair beneath the stage on the vast pinewood floor. This mime, with gruff and shrill voices added, drew a response from her: a smile, a human laugh almost. She was involved, certainly. I remember looking out through the side of the little wooden proscenium at the end of an act, and seeing Clare's face, caught in a shaft of afternoon sunlight from the clerestory windows overhead: a face from which tragedy and vacancy has disappeared now, where she had escaped her past for a moment and could, I thought, have moved off there and then into a future in this house. Indeed, immediately after this last Punch and Judy show, Clare seemed to want to do just this: she tried to skate away across the huge space, thinking the old tennis court some magic place, an ice rink or frozen pond perhaps, but the floor wasn't slippery enough.

But mostly we lived upstairs in the tower and on the long, half-repaired attic corridor on top of the house, where Alice stored her costly junk. And we gave Clare a headquarters here in the old nursery further along, at the end of the landing, where there was so much we thought she could occupy herself with: the row of blackberry-eyed Victorian china dolls on the sofa, the big doll's house... There was a marvellous wooden train on the floor, too, a black-and-green engine big enough to sit in, with two open carriages behind. And a vast collection of old wooden animals, each of them paired, male and female, camels, elephants, giraffes, cows, cats and dogs, all of which had a place in a large white Ark; the deck came off the boat and the whole menagerie could be bedded down in stalls inside, with Noah, a commanding figure with a golden beard, standing by the ramp.

But none of these riches stirred Clare much. She was listless, fractious here in the nursery, where she was not totally lost, staring vacantly out into an empty world from an empty mind.

Alice, now that Clare was a guest in her house, took a special interest in Clare's problems. We often sat, all three of us, in the nursery, for the bad weather had set in for a week and we couldn't venture far outside the house in any case. Alice would look at Clare across the room, sunk on her haunches, playing repetitively with her pile of bricks: again the strange circles, with pyramids and cones inside them; and again the clear blue eyes, unblinking, as she repeated her handiwork by the hour.

'It's as if she had things on her mind too hard for her to tell us,' Alice said one afternoon. 'Or that we wouldn't understand.

Complicated things, beyond us. When you look at her eyes –
you can tell: she knows something, and we don't, and can't
know it.'

'Whatever she knows in that way,' I said, 'she *doesn't* know.
She's suppressed it. That's the whole point of her problem:
whatever it is, she can't face it.'

'I wonder. That's the usual view. I have the feeling she has
some kind of power which she knows all about. Some
extraordinary knowledge, a gift she has no use for here with us,
in this world, which is why she doesn't respond. She's
somewhere else all the time.'

'Obviously. But there's nothing *positive* about that
"somewhere else" where she is. It's just a blank. She keeps
whatever is real in her at bay by playing repetitive games.'

'How can you be so sure?'

'It's too well known. It's the syndrome: she has all the classic
symptoms. Kanner's Syndrome, it's called. That's autism. She's
not the first child to suffer it, you know. Why should you think
it's any different with her?'

'You *assume* it's autism, and that's the way you treat her – '

'Yes, of course.'

'But you won't look for the *cause* of it and treat that instead.
That's what I'm saying. The cause is something quite different,
isn't it? You're treating the complaint, the result, without
knowing the *reason*.'

'You think there's a quite logical mind there, do you, ticking
away behind the empty façade?'

'No. A quite *illogical* mind maybe. But she's thinking about
something. I can feel it. It's just that what she has on her mind
doesn't correspond with anything in our way of thinking. We'd
deny it in her if we knew about it. So she keeps it to herself.'

'*What*, though? What's she hiding? What's the form of her
thought? If it's not normal, is it paranormal? What are you
getting at?'

'At something maybe in that direction. I don't know what.
For example, have you ever wondered why she always sits like
that, always crouched down on her haunches?'

'Children often do. Quite normal children. They can get at
things on the ground more easily.'

'It's how Africans sit though, isn't it? Out in the wilds.'

'Yes, that too. She'd have seen them doing it. That's another reason why she does it probably.'

'And look at the circles she always makes with the bricks,' Alice went on, suddenly running off after some undefined theory of her own.

'Yes. What's remarkable?'

'The gap she always leaves, every time she builds it. Then she puts some of the animals, the cows usually, from the ark there inside. Then she closes the gap, with another brick.'

'Yes, she makes a sort of stockade out of it. In Kenya they call it a *boma*, a native camp, with a circular wall round it made of thorn bushes. She'd have seen that too, up in Turkana province where they were, and the other wilder places. It's just imitation.'

'Possibly. But there's one other thing: when she makes the circle and gets the animals in and blocks off the stockade, at the end of nearly every game like this, she climbs inside the circle herself, or tries to. She actually sits on the animals, like a sort of great broody hen. Have you noticed that?'

'Yes. But she's just destroying the game so that she can start it all over again. Why? What else?'

'I think there's something else. She's trying to go back and live in the place, in some place like that: a circular stockade, with animals locked in safely for the night. She's trying to get back into some security, some home of her own.'

'Maybe. She may well see it in that way. Africa, all that early life of hers out there, is a kind of lost Eden for her. I told you before: I've often thought that was exactly the reason for her autism – that she was taken away from it. There's your "cause" for you. But how do you treat that? Send her back there?'

'Maybe. Maybe that's exactly it. Perhaps that's exactly what you should do. Or it's what she *wants* to do.'

'Don't be silly. Clare hasn't the kind of reasoning to want anything so intangible right now.'

'I wouldn't be so sure.'

We left it at that. However, the following day, I wondered if Alice might not have stumbled on something.

I had gone down the attic corridor with her to look over the collection in the little museum, in case there was something Clare could safely make use of there. The room – a maid's room, I suppose – was halfway down the landing, the doorway partly blocked with Alice's Victorian acquisitions, as well as by the great Nile crocodile which crouched in the shadows, its beady eyes and vicious snout guarding the room as though it was the entrance to a Pharaoh's tomb.

The door was locked and the key stiff, so that it was some time before we managed to open it. But as soon as we did there was a strange smell, something soiled, pungent, that I couldn't identify.

'What is it?' I wondered.

But Alice could smell nothing. There was a single window low down near the floor, with an old tasselled roller blind, torn, half-covering it. The blind flapped suddenly, as though caught in a draught, though the window was firmly shut. Running down the centre of the room was a double-sided glass case with other larger exhibits littered about the place, in corners or hung on the walls.

At first glance it seemed a typical collection, picked up by some acquisitive colonial civil servant in a lifetime spent traversing the wild places seventy or eighty years before. It wasn't a big collection, and not all of it was African. There was a Tsantsas head, a speciality of the Jivaro Indians, the label said, from Ecuador in the glass case: a tiny, jaundice-coloured human head, the skull removed, with obscenely protuberant lips and nose, shrunk now to the size of a small monkey's, with a long thick tress of jet-black hair still attached to the top. And there were several dark cane blowpipes from Borneo and New Guinea, one of them not more than a foot long, like a pea-shooter or a little malicious flute, complete with barbed darts made of bamboo. There was an ordinary skull here, too, in the African section, a blackened ivory colour, with a smashed temple where someone must have killed the man years before with a blunt and heavy instrument. There were beads and cooking pots and tom-tom drums, together with a coin collection, Egyptian piastres and Indian rupees. There was the model of an Arab dhow in the case, along with an old Martini-Henry rifle and brass cartridges, with a legend in neat copperplate beneath explaining these objects as part of a contraband cargo captured by the British authorities in Mombasa harbour on July 7th, 1917. In a top corner of the case I found what looked like a minute powder-horn, the horn of a small goat, with a wooden plug stuffed into the hollow top. Inside were the hardened remains of some tar-coloured substance. I thought it must be an old portable ink-bottle, from some early missionary school in the bush, perhaps. And it wasn't until I found the label nearby, which had obviously come adrift from the horn, that I saw what it was: 'Wabaio Poison Horn for Arrow Heads – taken from Wandarobo Tribesman, Northern Frontier District, August 1919. (Made from the Wabai and Dukneya trees, found in British Somaliland.)'

The walls were covered with cracked Zebra-hide shields, long Masai spears, with decaying ruffs of red tassel just beneath the spearhead, and other native implements of destruction, all rather gone to seed now in the small, white-washed, musty room. But the really strange thing was the smell, which I couldn't find any reason for, and a collection of extraordinary tribal masks.

There were half a dozen of them in the case: African ceremonial masks, each presenting a grotesque or fearsome image, painted in vivid reds and black, with the eyeholes rimmed in white, and with dangling necklaces of human teeth hanging down in short rows at either side. Alice took one of them out. It was made of antelope-hide, crimped like a canvas over a matrix of ink-dark thorn twigs.

As I looked at it something moved behind us. Turning, I saw Clare standing in the doorway. We had left her in the nursery, content with her bricks. But she had followed us for some reason and now she stood on the threshold looking into the room, looking at the mast in my hand with an expression of strange delight. She walked forward slowly, hand outstretched.

I thought the mask too valuable or delicate for her to handle. But Alice allowed her to have it and, far from being rough with it, she treated it with delicate respect. We watched her: she held it up in front of her face with both hands and looked at it for a minute. Then she set it down against the wall and crouched in front of it on her haunches, inspecting it from a distance for a much longer time. She didn't want to touch it any more, just to gaze at it. And it seemed as she did so, as she looked into the empty eye-sockets of this hideous, livid emblem, that she had found some peace, drew some release from the violent drama in the mask. Her eyes were bright with an intelligent response at last.

Encouraged by this, Alice took the other five masks from the case and set them up against the wall for Clare, on either side of the first, which pleased her: except that something in the placing wasn't quite right. And Clare re-arranged all the masks then in a semi-circle round her, flat on the floor, so that she sat erect in the middle of them finally, surrounded by these threatening visions, inspecting each calmly in turn as she slowly circled her head, perfectly absorbed, content at last.

It was Alice who said it, though the same thought had occurred to me. 'Do you see?' she said. 'It's as if she was holding court, as if the masks were real people, courtiers, paying homage to her.'

'Yes. Something like that. Some strange game – '

'As though she was a Queen,' Alice ran on, excited by something, breathless in the closed room perched under the warm slates of the house. And then I knew what the smell in the room was: the acrid smell of old lime dust, congealed sweat, animal-hide and cow-dung, with a top-dressing, a rumour of pepper, spices. That was it: it was a faint amalgam of Africa itself, that first whiff on the quayside, or airport, or in the back streets of Cairo that I remembered now from my days in the same continent twenty years before. We were suddenly, all of us, in the middle of Africa then – even Alice, who had never been there, which was why the smell had meant nothing to her originally. The three of us had moved in time, to somewhere else, Alice and I standing over the child, onlookers at some secret ceremony. But what was it? What thing in these dead masks, what spirit in these African relics, had brought Clare to such life again? And what connection was there between Clare's mysterious recreation of Africa and the real African, with his livid scars, who'd been looking for us in the valley, and was still perhaps lurking somewhere in the area?

I had no way of finding out. Clare couldn't tell me. Willy was long dead and Laura was gone, too. Yet I felt now that she must have denied me something, some truth about their African past, which might explain all our subsequent tragedy. The only people who could help me over this were the Bensons – George and Annabelle Benson, in Oxford. And, seeing Clare's behaviour, I felt a strange urgency now, and a danger, as if something vital was at last within my grasp, and that to identify it was a matter of great urgency, against an even greater peril.

Fourteen

I took Alice's car to Oxford to try and talk to George Benson the following afternoon – disguised in one of Arthur's most distinguished Savile Row suits and with another £100 of Alice's money in my pocket, in case I was delayed overnight. I had asked Alice to keep Clare inside the house meanwhile, under her eye all the time, with the doors locked and the alarms on, until I got back. She had offered me her small automatic again, but I told her to keep it on her herself now. And I left the swordstick behind as well. The police would be on the lookout for just such an object. Yet I felt I needed something in the way of a weapon. And then I had it, a possible answer: the little horn of Somali arrow-poison in the glass case, together with the flute-like blowpipe from New Guinea and the bamboo dart. This would form a useful threat: indeed, if the poison was still active, it could form a lethal combination which Benson, given his vast anthropological knowledge, would surely appreciate.

And certainly I might have to threaten him. If Laura, my own wife, had felt unable to tell me something murky from their African past, why should Benson, if he shared this knowledge, be any more willing? Indeed, with his professional eminence as a Professor of Anthropology at Oxford University and his latter reputation on television as an African pre-history Guru, he might be extremely unwilling indeed to disclose anything improper which had occurred on those fossil treks which he had organised for Willy. All the same, I knew I wouldn't hesitate to force or frighten him into any useful admission, if he didn't offer the same willingly. Laura – and Willy too – might have died as a result of something Benson could explain. Clare might have lost her mind in the same cause, and there was a half-burnt African still lurking somewhere in the middle of England. I wanted to know about him as well.

I tested the little blowpipe upstairs in the morning before I went. At first I could make no progress with it. The darts simply fell on the floor at my feet. Then I found the technique:

one had to compress a whole mouthful of air, with puffed cheeks, and then spit it all into the tube suddenly. This way, after a dozen experiments, I found I could hit the small window in the maid's room, from the doorway on the other side, almost every time. I didn't expect to use the pipe and I imagined the caked poison in the bottom of the horn was probably inactive now after sixty years in any case. All the same, if it was to be a real threat, or if I needed it in self-defence, I might as well avoid compromise: I stuck two of the darts deep into the inky substance in the goat's horn, wrapped them carefully in a handkerchief and put them away, along with the blowpipe, into the inside pocket of Arthur's smart business suit.

George Benson, I knew, had an office in the Natural History Museum off the Banbury road in Oxford, while he and Annabelle lived only half a mile away, in part of a large Victorian house they owned in Norham Gardens on the other side of the Parks from the museum buildings. Laura and I had once had dinner with them in their flat here. Filled with dreadful chrome furniture, the walls covered in monstrous abstract paintings, it had been an excessively clinical place, I remembered, with little evidence of natural man in it. But George, despite his vague academic airs, had always been something of a go-getter: anxious for every sort of advancement, ancient or modern.

I left the car by the park railings and walked back towards the museum. It was late afternoon, hot, early August, and I'd forgotten the awful swelter and crowds of a summer city. My head began to swim and I was sweating before I'd gone ten yards. The pavements and the grass square in front of the museum were filled with mindless tourists and continental students eating melting ice cream from some rogue vendor who had his van next the kerb; they let it fall in runny coloured blobs everywhere, like diseased spittle. I suddenly disliked people all over again.

But inside the great hall of the Pitt Rivers museum it was cooler; walking the old flagstones beneath the tracery of the graceful cast-iron arches overhead, it was much cooler. The gothic revival pillars that rose up past the first-floor balconies all round the hall were moulded at every curve and intersection in the shape of leaves and fruit, with animals' heads and metal palm fronds, so that there was just the suspicion of moving along the floor of a pre-historic jungle as one walked beneath the towering skeleton casts of a brontosaurus or a sabre-toothed tiger.

Benson's museum office, I discovered, was off the first-floor gallery, near the main lecture room. Indeed, as I'd seen from a notice by the main entrance, he was giving a lecture that very afternoon, part of some summer course: 'The Hunter-Gatherers: Signs and Language in Man's Pre-history.' It had started at 3 o'clock. It was after 4.30 now. I waited for Benson, looking over a vast display-case of British Birds, some way down from the lecture room.

Five minutes later his audience streamed out and there was a crush of people, including a number of children, round the doorway, so that I couldn't see George at first. Then I spotted him, the wedge-shaped face and the fan of unruly hair above – George, in his role of television star now, signing autographs for the children.

I hoped I could get him on his own. But as I waited not far from the doorway, I felt a sudden chill in the muggy heat and my spine tickled. As I had been on the look-out for George so, I saw now, a man in the crowd seemed to be watching me. Although this time he was dressed in a smart lightweight suit, he was readily identifiable; the scar on one side of his face gave him away at once. It was the tall African from the valley, seemingly quite recovered now from his ordeal by fire two weeks before.

He was some distance away, standing behind George, and trapped beyond his admirers, so that when George came towards me, breaking away from his fans, the African was left behind and I was able to collar George at once.

He recognised me immediately and for a second he tried fiercely to draw away from me, a reflex action of fear. But I had him by the arm and his fans were pressing in behind him.

'Come quickly!' I kept a firm grip on his coat. 'I have to speak to you.' The African was still there, behind the crowd, watching us.

'What on earth's up?'

'I'll tell you,' I said. 'Your office. Let's go – '

'It's at the end of the gallery.'

I pulled George along with me, the African still caught in the crowd, but following us, I thought, as the audience dispersed. We got to George's office and I nearly pushed him into the room before locking the door behind us. The place was empty, a high-ceilinged room, with tall arched Gothic windows, half-open, giving onto a balcony, with a view of the Parks beyond.

'What's the problem?' George said calmly. 'I certainly didn't expect . . . well, after all this trouble.'

George was a deceptively mild-mannered man, I knew. Beneath the vague professorial air, the prematurely greying hair, there was a quick and decisive brain. And I could see he was thinking fast just then. But he did nothing. He just stood in the middle of the room, awkwardly rooted to the spot. There was no surprise or fear in his face, just in his stance. And it was here, in his bearing, like a badly carved statue, that I could sense his fright. And yet there was a vital interest in his eyes, I noticed, from the very beginning of our meeting: as well as the disguised alarm there was a professional interest fighting it, as though I was some dangerous, but equally rare, animal species which he wished to capture.

I took the key out of the lock and moved over to guard the telephone on the desk. 'There's a man out there,' I said. 'An African, with scars down one side of his face. That's the most immediate problem. He's been looking for Clare and me – '

'Is she all right?'

'She's fine, in some ways. That's what I wanted to talk about. But do you know that African?'

'What African?'

'A tall fellow out there with a scar. He was at your lecture. You must have noticed him.'

'No, I didn't,' George said convincingly. 'It was quite a large audience. But what are you doing? Where are you? What do you want?' he went on in a concerned manner.

'I want to know about Clare and about Willy and Laura, out in East Africa,' I said. 'Because what's happened to all of us since then I think started out there; Willy's death, Clare's autism, Laura's murder.'

'But they say – everyone says – that *you* killed Laura?'

'Of course I didn't. You'd surely know that, George. I loved her.'

'Yes. I had my doubts when I heard about it.'

'Of course you did. I think it was that African out there who shot her. And I think he may have killed Willy, too, run him down in that hit-and-run accident. And he wants us now for some reason, Clare and me.'

Without identifying the place, I explained to George how the African had tracked us in the countryside. And he said. 'I've really no idea who he is. I can't think.'

'Well, let's go back to the beginning then.' I said. And I told George of Clare's strange behaviour with the ceremonial masks. Then I went on: 'You've seen these recent articles, obviously. About Willy's fossil hunts: how there was something – something underhand about them.'

'Yes.' Benson looked up at me. He was smaller than I remembered: smaller and much more intense and in command now, as though he was on camera explaining something in one of his television series. 'All nonsense,' he said decisively. 'The idea that we were involved in some kind of gun-running: sheer malicious invention.'

'Yes.' I agreed. 'That oil company financed him. But what if we look at something else? At Willy's "professional ruthlessness" for example, which all the articles mention. I never heard about that – not a hint, not even from Laura.'

'Ruthless?' George considered the idea dispassionately. 'Yes. He was a bit. But then you see you have to be on expeditions of that sort, way out in the field, with a lot of other fossickers looking out for exactly the same sort of things. That's not all surprising. Once Willy came home he was a different man: his real self. Anyway, I don't suppose Laura knew much about his work out there. Different worlds, you know. She wasn't...' He paused, a low note in his voice, a touch of sadness. 'She wasn't in the same business after all,' he added.

'All right. But all these newspaper reports I've read, they all suggest that something strange, something violent, happened out there at some point: a raid, trouble of some sort, with some tribe way out in the wilds: bloodshed. Now come on, George: no smoke without a fire. *What* happened?'

George said calmly. '*Nothing* happened. Don't you think the press have been onto me about just the same thing? They've turned over all the same imaginary stones, asked all the same questions. What sort of raid, for example? Who's supposed to have raided who?'

'You attacked someone? Or more likely they attacked you people.'

'Listen,' George said very sensibly, sitting on the edge of his desk and wiping his brow in the sticky afternoon heat. 'If you knew anything about this fossil business, you'd understand: the local tribes, the very few of them left intact, well, yes, of course: some of them objected to our picking over their territory. But that's natural. There was no real "trouble" though. Besides, you've got to remember, we had Kenyans with us, museum and government officials, guides, all the time. We had all the permissions, from the authorities in Nairobi – '

'That's just it,' I interrupted. 'The papers say you were out on your own, on several occasions, away from the main camp, you and Willy and Laura – and Annabelle.'

'Well, yes, we were. And, as you say, more than once. We used to go in a Land-Rover, or the spotter plane, to look out for other likely fossil sites. No, you've got it all wrong, Peter. You don't really think we went round the place as an armed gang beating up the locals? That's complete nonsense. And you know it.'

'All right,' I agreed once more. 'But if everything was so straightforward, why did the press start all this . . . this muck-raking?'

'That's easy: through the jealousy of some of our professional rivals in the same line. But equally through the press's need for a good story. And there was a good story in it, I'm bound to say: once Laura was dead and they found out you'd worked for British Intelligence, Peter.'

Benson looked at me sadly, doubtfully. 'That may be the real problem, don't you think?' he went on. 'I never knew that you had those connections. Don't you think perhaps that's why Laura may have been killed, because of something murky from *your* past, not ours? Shouldn't we be talking about that, about you, and not about something that didn't happen to us out in East Africa?'

'Yes, I thought exactly like that to begin with, too: that it was my old department gunning for me. But now I'm not half so sure. There's this African. And I don't understand Clare's African obsessions either, with those masks I told you about: how she absolutely lights up, seems to recover herself completely, when she's playing with them as if she was involved in some secret ceremony.'

'Yes, that *is* interesting,' George admitted. And I could see he meant it. 'But isn't that just a reflection, some memory coming

back, of her years out there? Remember, she was with Willy and
Laura, with her parents all the time out there then, in the bush,
in the desert. But how is she? Can you really look after her?
Wherever you are?'

George was fishing. 'Don't worry,' I said. 'I can look after – '
But that was all I said. I heard a sound behind me. Looking
round, I saw the handle in the arched oak door turning slowly:
someone was trying to open it.

'Just a minute!' George shouted across the room. 'I won't be a
minute.' Then he turned to me. 'One of the cleaners probably.'
He looked at his watch. 'It's after five. The Museum's closed
now, you know. Don't you – don't you think we ought to be
getting along?'

'I don't know, George,' I said. 'I'm still not happy – I'm not
convinced. And I don't think that's a cleaner. It's probably that
African out there.'

George smiled reasonably. 'Peter, you're dreaming! Just like
the press. It's all fantasy: an African with a scar out to get you
and Clare. Gun-running in the bush, tribal battles, midnight
raids, these secret ceremonies with masks you say Clare's
involved in now. It's all like some old *Boys Own Paper* yarn.
Don't you see?' George shook his head. 'It's all something
you've built up in your mind, Peter. You've been hidden away
somewhere too long, alone too – '

But George suddenly stopped speaking. The handle of the
door was turning again. He watched it with affronted surprise.
And someone was pushing hard against it this time. I could see
the lock straining against the jamb. And I felt a spasm of fear
then, burning up my gut like a hurriedly swallowed mouthful of
raw alcohol.

There was another movement, on the far side of the room
beyond the desk. And when I turned I saw that George was
already halfway out of the open window that led to the balcony.
I ran towards him. But I was too late. He slammed the old sash
window shut just as I got to it. And it wouldn't open again, hard
as I tried. George had pulled it down so firmly that it had stuck
tight, and he was off now, down a fire-escape ladder. I could
have broken the glass. But there were iron bars attached to the
outside of the window. It was burglar-proof. The only way out
for me now was through the door behind me.

Of course, it could have been a cleaner at the door. But I

wasn't going to risk that safe assumption. I got the little blowpipe out and fitted one of the darts. Then I turned the lock, pulled the door open suddenly and stood back quickly, the pipe at my mouth.

The doorway was empty, and so was the first-floor gallery beyond and the great hall beneath. The skeleton head and neck of the brontosaurus loomed up in front of me, its great snout spotlit in a shimmer of slanting, dusty light from the glass above. Perhaps it had just been a cleaner at the door after all. I knew I wouldn't get out by the main entrance to the museum which would be closed by now. But there might be a lavatory window open, or some emergency exit I could force, at the rear of the building. So I turned and made off in that direction, moving quickly along the gallery.

Halfway round I heard the running footsteps – forceful, decisive, with nothing covert about them. The sounds were coming from somewhere behind the display cases on the far side of the gallery. But I couldn't tell from which direction – whether the footsteps were approaching me or following me. There was a confusing echo now in the empty hall. I looked ahead, then back. There was nothing. I turned back towards Benson's office, then hesitated. Then I moved forward again. The footsteps seemed to be coming from all sides of the hall now and I couldn't move. I was rooted to the spot. But I was suddenly running, for I'd seen the man, the dark shape coming from behind a case and sprinting towards me past the lecture-room.

I ran down the back stairs from the gallery into the main hall just ahead of him. And now it was a matter of hide-and-seek around the exhibits in the great hall and beneath the vast skeletal shapes of prehistoric animals: hide-and-seek with violence at the end of it, I thought, for one or both of us. For when I saw the African, just for an instant at the bottom of the stairs, I saw the piece of cord in his hand, knotted cord with stones or leaded weights tied to each end, some kind of bolas. My only chance was to lie low, and hope to surprise the man in some way – with a crack over the head or with the blow pipe.

So I stayed where I was, hidden behind the brontosaurus skeleton, down on my haunches, where I could see through the bones of the animal over to the corner of the building. The African was there: I saw his legs beneath a display case, moving out slowly into the hall. Then he disappeared, going towards the main entrance, and I took the chance of going in the opposite direction, back into another part of the museum, the ethnological section, down some steps and into another smaller, darker hall.

Here the exhibits were more numerous and the display cases packed closely together, so that the cover was far better. On the other hand I couldn't find any exit here among the Indian totem poles, South-Sea-island war canoes, and every other conceivable tribal relic and knick-knack. Indeed, when I got right to the back of the room, I found the only exit there securely locked. I was trapped. I would either have to stay where I was and try and hide, or make my way forward to the main hall again. In the event I didn't have time to make the choice.

Not finding me in the front of the museum, the African must have doubled back, and the first I knew of his presence again was a sudden sliding sound, as if some big marbles were being thrown along the floor somewhere ahead of me in the gloom. I was down on my knees, looking along beneath the display cases. And I saw what the noise was: the bolas with its round stone weights was sliding to a halt only a few feet ahead of me. Was the African unarmed now, with this attempt to set a decoy, to tempt me from my cover?

A minute later I knew he wasn't. Something – I couldn't see it in the half-light – flew through the air towards me from my left with a quick swishing sound and smashed into the exhibition case immediately behind me, breaking the glass in great fragments all about my ears. Looking up, just a foot above my head, I saw the tufted throwing-spear, an assegai taken from the wall or some case ahead of me, embedded in the war feathers of an Indian headdress, the ebony-dark shaft still quivering. But I couldn't see anybody. The African had moved away. And I ran myself then, looking upwards now. There were two galleries, one above the other, round this smaller hall, as well. But the stairway up to them must have been at the front, and I was at the back. There was no escape that way. Indeed, my pursuer could use one of the galleries, I realised, to look down and attack me from above. So I moved further back into the shadows, tip-toeing past a huge basketwork prayer-wheel, seeking cover.

There was complete silence. And so I hardly dared move. All

the same, though I couldn't be seen from overhead, I was clearly visible, dark on white, against a great snow-filled Eskimo display case where I was standing.

To one side and slightly ahead was a huge, multi-coloured Indian totem pole, rising thirty feet up into the roof of the hall. There was some cover there, I saw, at its base. I crouched down and inched towards it, finally tucking myself in to one side of the pole where I had a view once more along the floor beneath the display cases. I got the blow pipe out again and was just fitting a dart into it when the dark hand emerged from behind the pole quick as a snake's head and the cord – an ordinary piece of thick string this time – circled my neck.

I struggled but it was little use: the cord knifed hard round my throat and the best I could do was to get my feet, sliding up the totem pole, while the African held me tight against it now, my head forced back against the wood.

'The girl,' the man behind me said, 'where is she?'

I couldn't turn. I couldn't see his face. And the blowpipe had dropped to the floor. But I still had the second dart in my hand.

'Where have you her? The *child?*' The accent was more Arab than African, and the cord came tighter then. The searing pain was worse than the lack of breath, though soon there would be no breath and that would be worse still.

Using the bamboo dart as a dagger I struck out blindly behind me again and again, stabbing the empty air as the noose contracted, the man trying to restrain me while moving back from me at the same time. But at last the sharp point found a home. It struck the man's clothing first – I could hear something rip. But then it went further on: I felt the dart sink into some part of his flesh, like a skewer into a leg of mutton.

The man shouted then, a scream of agony, and he pulled the cord again viciously so that I thought I was done for. But it was his last effort against me. The cord dropped away and when I turned the African was stumbling about on one leg, trying desperately to extract the dart which the barbs held firm, deep in his thigh. There was little I could do, I thought, except run. But I stood there instead – amazed: first by the fact that this was quite a different African, a younger, much lighter-skinned man without any scars on his face, and then when I saw how quickly he subsided, his struggles dying away in a minute or so as paralysis overcame him. His leg seized up first and soon he was slumped on the floor, unable to move at all. Finally he just lay there, stretched out full length beneath the totem pole. But the strange thing was that, though he was now quite immobile, and obviously couldn't speak, the man looked completely fit. He was entirely conscious, his eyes watching me, perfectly clearly, as I moved about him – vicious, frustrated eyes, like those of a wild beast alive in a trap, still confronting its hunter. And I saw then that the old Somali poison still worked. And I wondered if this must have been exactly its intended effect: to paralyse its victim, rather than to kill.

I went quickly through the man's pockets while he lay there inertly, with a frozen gaze of fury. He had a lot of money on him, including some Libyan money, and a London–Oxford train timetable. But there was nothing else to identify him. I left him where he was. The police would find him soon enough. Indeed I was surprised they hadn't arrived at the Museum already, since George had escaped a good twenty minutes before and I thought he would surely have contacted them by now. But perhaps he hadn't phoned them. Perhaps he wanted to protect me from them, or rather to protect himself from guilt by association with me. I escaped from the museum a few minutes later myself, when I finally found an exit through a door to the side of the museum's main hall which led into a small library. And from here I was able to walk through another door, just opening the Yale lock into the street.

Then I was striding quickly off across the parks into the evening light. I was sure that George had more to offer. True, his initial explanations had been convincing enough in his office. But why had he run away? And what of the African? And now this Libyan? How on earth did he fit in? I wondered, if George hadn't phoned the police, if I might find him at home now, since his house was only just across the park. Indeed its back garden, though hidden by a line of great chestnuts, gave directly out onto the park. I could come at it that way, use the cover in the big trees first, scout the land out before approaching the house.

I crossed the big park and went into the belt of trees at the back of Norham Gardens, where I soon found George's house. I knew it was his since the detached Victorian rectory style of the building, with its fretted gable ends, tall chimneys and haphazardly placed windows made it easily recognisable out of the line of other slightly less eccentric redbrick mansions on the road. And I recognised the ugly new sliding aluminium-framed windows giving out onto the garden, which George had added, upsetting the whole mood of the place. Crouched in the bushes at the end of his garden, I watched their ground-floor flat.

The big window was partly open. But there was no human sign or sound from anywhere in the house. I moved very carefully over the fence and then across the lawn. There was another flat in the basement, I knew, and one of the top floor. But there was no sound from these either.

I waited a few more minutes just outside the sliding aluminium window, then pushed it open and walked into the Bensons' drawing-room. It was empty. The room faced south-west, so that the summer light flooded into it from over the trees, lighting up a shiny modern chesterfield against one wall and an appalling abstract painting above it. A big pot-pourri bowl lay on a table to one side of the sofa with a video machine on the other. There was a sickly, over-sweet scent in the warm air. I went out into the hall and then into all the other rooms. But the whole place was deserted.

Then I saw a half-open door leading down to the basement flat from the hall. I went over to it and listened, looking through the gap for a minute. There was no sound from beneath. I walked slowly down the stairs. The flat was empty, but in considerable disarray. It might have been a student's pad, except there were no books or papers lying about. There was a half-finished tin of baked beans and a glass of milky tea on the dirty, sugar-encrusted kitchen table. In the bedroom clothes were scattered about everywhere, expensive clothes, lightweight summer suits, fine shirts. But there were old clothes as well: grubby garden wear, a donkey-jacket, a torn pullover, a dirty pork-pie hat, an old Army camouflage jacket lying on the unmade bed.

And then it came to me. The pork-pie hat and the camouflage jacket. The African in the valley had worn just such a jacket, and so had the man who'd killed Laura. And months before, in the early spring out on the land beyond our cottage, we'd seen someone running away, his face hidden, with just the same kind of jacket, and the same pork-pie hat. It all added up: the man who'd killed Laura, who'd pursued us through the valley, was the same man I'd just seen outside George Benson's office at the museum. The only mystery now was why this African had obviously been living here all the time: in George Benson's basement flat.

I went back upstairs. There was a small room just off the hall, a study where George Benson worked, obviously, for it was filled with the books of his trade, with a typewriter and papers covering most of a large table set against a window looking out on the street.

I knew I mightn't have much time since, if George had phoned the police, he or they or both might turn up here at any moment. All the same, looking for some explanation of the African's presence downstairs, I thought I might find a clue here. I sifted quickly through the papers on the table, and I was lucky. Halfway down, hidden beneath a copy of the *National Geographic* magazine with an article by George in it, I found a letter, with the Bensons' own address die-stamped in red on top of it. It had been hurriedly scrawled, on a single side of the paper, with just the letter 'A' at the end. A letter without love or any other good wishes. It was from Annabelle, George's wife. I skipped through it quickly.

... and I certainly can't stay in the house any longer. The situation you have contrived here is quite impossible – and has been between us, in any case, for quite some time. Since you refuse to take any advice from me, or contact the police, you'll have to sort matters out yourself. I don't intend 'betraying' you now – though I should have done that long ago. It's your life – and the decisions you made in it over the years, and with Willy in the past, are *your* decisions, and you must live with them and resolve them in your own way. But until you settle things up *I* can't live with you.

The Kasters have gone on holiday. They've offered me their house and I'll be out there for the time being. But *please* – until you have made some *effective* decisions – leave me alone.

A.

The Kasters? There was an Oxford directory by a telephone on the table. I looked them up. There was only one Kaster in the book – a Mr and Mrs David Kaster. They lived just outside Oxford: Sandpit Farm House, near Farmoor. Annabelle had left George because of the African, obviously, among other reasons:

because of 'decisions' George had made over the years, decisions made with 'Willy in the past' ... Africa loomed up for me again. Something had happened out there, with all of them. I was sure of that now. Something unpleasant, to say the least of it. But what was it? The answer, I thought, might lie somewhere out along the Eynsham road, in Sandpit Farm House.

Fifteen

There was a sign on the roadside, several miles outside Oxford, at the head of a rough track just beyond the village of Farmoor, giving direction to Sandpit Farm House. The house itself was some distance away, isolated among fields, with the Thames just visible behind a line of poplars beyond. If she was in, and there were no other guests with her, Annabelle couldn't have chosen a better bolt-hole from my point of view.

I parked the car at the head of the drive and walked down towards the house in the hot evening light, a small, converted farmhouse, I saw, when I came nearer to it, with a pretty garden in front and a big Cotswold stone wall to one side, running away to the back, with an arched doorway in the middle. Avoiding the front of the house and reaching this entrance, I looked through into a deserted patio, with an empty swimming-pool in the middle. But there was someone or something in the pool, invisible to me below the level of the sides, for I could hear the sound of water, under pressure from a hose, being sluiced against the concrete.

I tiptoed through the archway and came to the edge of the deep end. Annabelle was standing right beneath me, in a bikini, her back towards me, with a hose in her hand, cleaning the sides of the pool. Tall, angular, straw-haired Annabelle, the plain, flat-chested woman. I had seen her before as a distant and perhaps troubled person, yet someone essentially hard-headed, I thought, and never vulnerable as she was now. She turned with the hose, moving to another part of the pool, and when she saw me she literally jumped in the air with fright.

'God!' she exclaimed, gasping.

'It's all right. It's only me.'

'Only you?'

She paused, shaking, regaining her breath. She tried to look over the edge of the pool, as if for help, but even she wasn't tall enough. There was a ladder to one side of the deep end. But there was no other exit from the walled patio itself other than by the doorway I'd come through. She saw she was trapped, and I helped her in this feeling by standing coldly above her, an ogre in the evening sunlight. I had no time to waste and I knew, if she hadn't been prepared to 'betray' her husband, that I might well have to threaten her in any way I could for the information I wanted. And I saw a means then, readily to hand: there was a barbecue barrow parked by the diving board, with its various cooking implements laid out on the tray. I picked up a long metal kebab skewer casually and toyed with it.

'How did you know I was here? George?' Annabelle didn't seem frightened, just very angry.

'No. I found the letter you wrote him. And I saw the flat downstairs. Where you have that African,' I added pointedly.

Annabelle looked up fiercely. 'Why can't you mind your own bloody business?'

I hadn't thought her capable of this sort of coarse talk; there had always been something refined, even old-maidish about Annabelle in the past.

'It *is* my business,' I said. 'You forget: I was married to Laura, who was married to Willy, when you were all out in East Africa together. And now I'm having to pick up the pieces of whatever it was you all got up to out there. And that's what I'm here to find out.'

'I don't know what you're talking – '

'Oh yes you do,' I broke in viciously. 'I've read your letter about not "betraying" George. And seen that African's clothes down in your basement flat. Well, that African killed Laura and now he's after us, Clare and me. So, you see, I *know*, and I want to know the rest.'

'But ... *you* killed Laura?' Annabelle looked up at me, prevaricating, I thought. And I was very angry now.

'Did I? You really think that?' I said fiercely. 'Then hadn't you better tell me?'

I sat down on the edge of the diving-board, fondling the

skewer. Annabelle sensed the violence in me, saw the violence in the skewer, too, and I could see she was more frightened now than angry.

'Where's George?' she asked, a placatory tone in her voice.

'George has run away. I shouldn't be surprised but the African is after him now. And you next. So what's this all about, Annabelle? Are you going to tell me?'

I gazed down at her intently. The sloping bottom of the pool was already several feet deep in dirty water and the powerful hose, which she'd dropped, was thrashing around like a snake. It would fill the pool eventually.

'You can stay down there and drown,' I said. 'If you don't tell me.'

'But surely you *know*,' Annabelle said. 'Surely Laura told you? We always assumed she would.'

'No, she didn't tell me. But tell me what?'

Again Annabelle was silent. And I felt a sudden stab of loss at this intimation of some vast deceit on Laura's part – Laura with whom I thought I'd shared every secret. And this made me all the more angry. I stood up.

'You better start explaining. It's too late for any more lies. *Don't you see?*' I shouted at her now, brandishing the skewer right above her head, so that she stepped back quickly.

'All right – all right.' Annabelle held her hands up, surrendering. 'I'll tell you.'

I let her climb up the ladder and we sat down on opposite sides of a wooden picnic table in the shade at the far end of the pool.

'The men lied,' Annabelle said at last. 'George and Willy. But we all had to lie in the end.' She scowled fiercely, like a caged animal, looking over at the arched doorway on the other side of the patio. She might have been expecting, daring George to enter through it, at any moment, so that he could share and suffer equally the horror and indignity of this tale she had embarked on.

'Go on,' I said. I still had the skewer with me. 'You all lied?'

'Yes. Even Laura. Though it was hardly her fault. We both had to cover up for them ... their mania for discovery, disruption,' she added viciously.

'But what about Laura? What did you expect her to have told me?'

'About Clare. That she wasn't their child. That's where it all began.'

I thought I'd misheard Annabelle. Then, realising that I hadn't and assuming some ancient infidelity out in East Africa, I said wildly, 'She was George's child, you mean? Or yours?'

'No. She was nothing to do with any of us.' Annabelle looked away, distracted, gathering her unpleasant memories together.

'What do you mean? That Clare is an orphan?'

'Yes. But more than that.'

'But that's nonsense,' I said. 'She even *looks* like Laura.'

'She does, a little. We noticed that from the start. Same fair hair, blue eyes. It made the deception that much easier. But she wasn't their child. I can promise you that...'

Annabelle's voice had that pregnant tone now, that real weight which comes with truth, the truth long withheld. 'And of course she wasn't autistic either,' she went on.

'Well that can't be true,' I said, satisfied that I knew more than Annabelle about something at least. 'Of course she's autistic.'

'The same symptoms – yes. They're very similar, or at least insofar as we have any direct experience now of such wild children. But it wasn't autism.' Annabelle was calmer, taking a precise, scientific approach to things, the ethnologist rising in her, all her old vagueness gone – seen now for the front it was. Then she added – almost, it seemed, as an afterthought: 'Clare was wild, you see.'

'Well, I knew that. She lived in the wilds, for a few years, out in Africa...'

'No. I mean she was actually reared in the wild. They found her, you see, the tribesmen in the hills, quite a long time after her parents had died. They trapped her, on her own apparently. Completely wild. But she'd survived somehow, in the hills above the valley, suckled by some animal, maybe. Who knows?'

I thought I must have misheard, or misunderstood Annabelle this time. 'You mean some kind of wolf child?'

Annabelle nodded.

'Look, this is nonsense,' I said. 'You'll have to begin at the beginning, won't you?'

'Clare must be about ten or eleven now, I suppose. One can't tell exactly. But it was nearly four years ago, I know that.' She gazed out towards the trees by the river, remembering. 'After the big rains, in Nairobi. The fossil expedition left for the

Turkana province then, four hundred miles north, making for Lake Rudolf where we had our camp that year, a place way off the beaten track, sixty miles from the last town up there, a place called Lodwar. And then we came to a village, beyond Lodwar, just a few old tin shacks in the middle of the desert.' She paused, as if suddenly unsure of her mental directions.

'Yes. It's wild up there. I know that,' I said, anxious that she should get on with it.

'It's hot. Just hot,' Annabelle corrected me sharply, remembering the heat. 'Just the long red floor of the valley. I remember coming down the one main track in the village late that afternoon: it looked like a dead dog run over in the camel-dung at the side of the road. But when we got nearer to it in the convoy we saw it was a child, mostly decomposed. The place was practically empty. There's been trouble up there for several years, warring tribes, cattle raids, border disputes. But I remember the dead child because of Clare, later: one child making up for the other in a way.'

'You wanted children, you and George?'

'No. Not after George and I fell out, at least. George only ever wanted to discover things, no matter what the cost. My job is to study things as they are: to preserve them. And of course it was George who first heard about Clare, set us all off on the trail for her.'

'Yes?'

'Yes. A month or so later he'd driven back to Lodwar where we'd left stores. And he found a group of tribesmen when he got there, exhausted, on their last legs. Not Turkana, but some Karamojong from across the border in Uganda, a hundred miles to the west, driven over the mountains by Idi Amin's army. It was all mayhem in Uganda then: the old tribes over there were all being broken up, their crops pillaged, everything destroyed. It was the beginning of the end for the Karamojong people. They were the last of the big East African tribes still intact, all their old customs, language, dress. It was all still *there*,' Annabelle went on forcefully. 'Leopard skins, assegais, war-paint, ostrich plumes, wonderful rituals, festivals, ebony-coloured warriors... They were agrarian or cattle-rearing then, but in the wilder parts, up in the Moroto mountains, there were still some nomadic, hunter-gatherers among the Tepeth tribe. The last of the old Africa...'

Annabelle paused, caught in some dream.

'So what about these Karamojong in Lodwar?' I prompted her.

'Yes. Well, George asked them about possible fossil sites to the west, back the way these people had come, across the desert or in the foothills of the Loima mountains, which straddle the Ugandan border. And that's an even wilder area, those hills. Nothing there at all, not even tracks.'

'Well?'

'Well, they told him there were a few likely river beds, dry wadis running out of the hills. Some of this hill country had seemed promising from the air – the stone formations: we'd looked at it once from the spotter plane. But it was camel country. You couldn't make it anywhere in there by road. It didn't seem possible for a fossil dig. It was too isolated. So George turned the idea down.

'But then one of these old Karamojong men – they wanted money you see: they were destitute, starving – he said he had some *real* information, not about fossil sites, but something even more interesting for a white man. So George paid him some money. And the old man told him about it then, about a white child living up there, on the other side of the mountains, with a branch of the Tepeth tribe, driven far up into the hills years before, hidden in a small valley there.'

'A *white* child? Clare?'

'Yes. But it wasn't just that she was a white child, the old man said: more than that, she was a vital symbol, an emblem for the tribe as well, because she was white and had been found alone in the wilds and couldn't speak: a Rain Queen, the old man said, a guarantee of fertility. And it was this that took the four of us there at the end of that season's dig. The rest of the team went back to Nairobi. Of course, we didn't mention anything about the child, just said we were taking a week off, looking for possible fossil sites for the next season's work.'

'You just went off on your own like that, into the blue?'

'Yes. But Willy and George knew all about that sort of travel. They'd been doing it for years out in east Africa after all. We took water with us. And there was something of a map, an old army map, and we had compasses, iron rations, several rifles – all the usual kit. Besides, Willy and George were fascinated by the whole thing now, obsessed by it all. A white child, some sort of Rain Queen, a fertility emblem, who didn't speak, the old man had said. And George was pretty sure he wasn't lying. He knew the Karamojong well. But the real point, you see, was that we hadn't done too well that winter around Lake Rudolf. Nothing of much interest had turned up. In fact, Willy had caused a lot of trouble there that year – with some of the local Turkana near Lake Rudolf. He'd dug up one of their ancestral burial places – just a strange pattern of stones, but that's what it was – and our backers were pretty annoyed too. So Willy and George both thought this might be a way of saving things, of getting the oil company to go on financing them: if they could find this strange child and bring her back to civilisation. Instead of a lot of old fossil bones, a white Rain Queen to a lost tribe . . . well, that would make better publicity back home.'

Annabelle paused. She was angry, derisive. A lock of her hair had fallen across her cheek. She brushed it away slowly. 'Of course that was the start of the whole problem; why the tribe attacked us afterwards,' she went on, reflecting. 'George and Willy's problem . . . they could never stop digging up and destroying things, like all the other white men in Africa. Old bones or a strange child, it was all the same to them. Africa had to be dug up, torn apart, and all just for the sake of publicity or money or professional advancement back home. Anyway, to be fair, we were all of us intrigued by the adventure to begin with. So we set off. . .

'For the first two days west of Lodwar we were on a hardened camel track, quite straight, like a road, so that it should have been easy going. Except for the heat. This was the start of the really hot weather. And even though we moved mostly at night, it was killing. Flat as flat could be, just the baking red floor of the valley. And though we could just see the hills twenty or thirty miles away, shimmering in the distance ahead of us, we wondered if we'd make them . . .

'Well, we did. On the fourth day. The ground rose fairly quickly then, up the old stream-beds, and the going was easier. It was a little cooler and there was some shade in the rocks. But it was just sheer chance we ran into the old Volkswagen in one of these dry wadis where it had conked out years before.'

'A *car*?' I asked.

'Yes. Almost entirely covered in a sand drift, beneath the ledge of the wadi, just a front bumper and a wheel showing.

Well, when we got the sand away we saw the end of the car had been lifted up on rocks a few feet clear of the ground, and beneath it were the two skeletons lying side by side.'

'Skeletons?'

'Well, they were partly mummified. Strips of flesh, then the bone. The sand and the dry heat under the ledge had preserved them side by side there, close together: a man and a woman, trying to find some shade beneath the car, obviously. The woman had a lot of hippie beads round her neck and there was a ridiculously small plastic water bottle between them. That was all. Except for the child's stuff.'

Annabelle eased herself on the bench, sighing in the evening heat.

'We found that inside the car: some tiny clothes, a teddy-bear I remember, a few other toys. But there was no sign of any child – of Clare, in fact. I suppose she must have been about two years old when her parents died. She'd probably had the last of the water . . . and she'd survived, somehow. Quite soon, higher up into the hills, a little vegetation started. There was some water, a few animals. We saw jackals. So maybe that was how she survived. And then these tribespeople found her, the Tepeth from the other side of the mountains.

'Anyway, it was clear what had happened before they found her: those flower children, the hippie generation of the late sixties – here were two of them, and their child, out in Africa, searching for some paradise out in these empty hills. They'd taken a Volkswagen, knowing little or nothing about this sort of country, and had run out of petrol, food, water. Or all three. And that was that. They paid the price.'

'But who were they? They must have had families somewhere back home. Someone must have been looking for them. Didn't you let them know?'

'No. As things turned out, we didn't. But now we knew the old Karamojong had been telling the truth. There'd been a white child in the car, and it must have been this same child, living further on up in the mountains.' Annabelle had become excited in the telling of this story, which she had withheld so long, her voice reflecting the excitement of the actual reality. I no longer had to threaten her. I was excited myself.

'Well?'

'The valley the old man had talked about was on the far side of the mountain, beyond the main peak. And it was hard going, dragging the camels up through the dry scrub. You see, we were on the wrong side of the mountains for rain. That came in on the other side, blowing from the west, from equatorial Africa, over the lakes.

'It took us a whole day just to get round the scorching peak. And then suddenly we were down the other side and in another world. It was almost lush near the top, pale spring green slopes, with old cedar trees on the ridges way beneath us and a thick rain forest below that. But there were wild flowers up where we were. And the air was marvellous, the sky huge, pale blue, violet, with a few great puffy clouds sailing in from fifty miles away. I remember it all exactly. There were proper animals on this side, too. Mountain antelope, colobus monkeys further down, and a leopard we saw. And it was all untouched, that was the point. Just the sort of wild paradise those two flower people had been looking for.

'We were at the top of a long valley at that point, running straight down to the plain fifteen or twenty miles away, empty. And the old man had said this tribe lived in a much smaller valley, to the side, high up. So we looked around all that day. Finally there was this craggy defile we found, hidden to the south along the range, which looked a possibility. And that's where they were. We got there just before nightfall, up on some big stones that formed a kind of dry dam before the hidden gorge dropped away beyond. We made camp there – and that's when we first saw them, looking down over the rocks, about half a mile away, at the bottom of a small saucer-shaped valley, small fires glimmering in the half light, blue smoke, stars coming out.

'And there was this smell in the air from the fires, the cedar wood from the ridges. And a small waterfall from the peaks to one side, and some maize and banana planted out on the flat ground in the middle outside the stockade which enclosed the dozen or so big thatched huts – '

'A stockade?'

'Yes. A round *boma*, made of stakes, thorn bushes.'

I remembered Clare's endless circular games with the bricks and how she put all the animals from the ark inside.

'There must have been fifty or sixty people in the settlement. We watched some of them that evening through the binoculars.

They were bringing in the animals for the night – cows, goats. Then they pulled a gate of thorn bushes across the entrance and that was that. It was perfect, like a nativity scene.'

'All untouched, up in these mountains?'

'Well, not quite. The men were just in loincloths when we saw them; a few of the older ones in monkey skin cloaks. But I don't think they were a virgin tribe. They'd been driven up here – years before: by Idi Amin's men or before that by some other rival tribe. The Karamojong have always been fighting among themselves. But this lot were something different, certainly, in that they were totally isolated now, hidden, had reverted completely to a pure subsistence living. They'd gone right back into the old Africa, before the strangers came. This was how Africa *worked*, do you see? As it all used to before we came. And I remember, from the very start, how George and Willy were sort of . . . salivating over it all, as we watched from up on the rocks, like vultures.

'Of course, the problem was, if they had this white girl hidden with them, and especially if she meant something important to them, as soon as they saw us they'd assume the worst, that we'd come to take her away. They'd put up a fight. And Laura and I, at least, assumed we didn't want that.'

'So what happened?'

'We let them find us. We made a fire first thing next morning, on our side of the rocks. And they saw the smoke rising. A group of them came over the boulders half an hour later. There were half a dozen men with assegais. Fierce. Or they could have been.

'George spoke to them. But he didn't know much of their dialect. These were part of the Tepeth tribe, entirely mountain people, not Karamojong proper. He could barely understand them. But he managed to explain that we were only looking for fossil sites, rock samples – that we'd come from the other side of the mountains and were going back that way. Their leader was a tall, intelligent-faced middle-aged man. He had trousers and he spoke some English, so he'd obviously lived down on the plains once.

'Well, we mentioned nothing about the child of course. But we asked if we could stay for twenty-four hours to rest before we went back. Willy offered them some money. But they wouldn't touch it. And they weren't at all keen on our staying.

We asked if we could come into their camp for water. But they said they'd bring us some – they *certainly* didn't want us in their camp. We'd hidden our rifles – and there it was: a stalemate. We could stay until the afternoon, they said. But after that they wanted us on.'

'But you didn't leave?'

'No. And that's where the trouble began. We stayed there, camped on the rocks that night. Laura and I wanted to go back. But the men were determined to stay. They thought they could do some deal with the tribe over the girl: offer them one of our guns or more money, corrupt them properly.

'In the event, we didn't have a chance to make any offers. They came for *us*, when we hadn't left, early next morning. Laura and I were asleep, behind the hobbled camels. But the others had been taking turn about all night as look-outs. And there was a terrible fight. The warriors had crept up to attack – all round beneath us, over the rocks. But George had seen them first, and we had all the advantage of the high ground . . . and the two sporting Winchesters. They had only their spears and machetes. It was something of a massacre.'

'You mean they shot them *all*?'

Annabelle looked at me angrily, as if I'd been responsible for the disaster.

'Half a dozen of them, I suppose. The rest, the other half dozen, got away, back into the hills to either side of the settlement, because by that time George and Willy had moved down the gorge into the valley, getting between these stragglers and their camp. But the others meanwhile, the women and children, had barricaded themselves into the stockade, closing the great thorn gate.'

'You got in, though?'

'Yes. Willy simply set the stockade gate alight – set the whole thing on fire.'

'I don't – '

'It's true. He thought he'd just burn the gate down. But the flames spread at once, kept us all away – until most of the front of the *boma* was burnt down. Then Willy was inside, running among the huts, looking for the girl, with the women and children and old people panicking everywhere, screaming, because some of the grass huts had caught fire too. Well, Willy found the girl, in one of the huts at the back, next to the chief's hut. She was lying on the ground, terrified, curled up like an animal, he said, in with a lot of chickens. But it was a grand hut, there were zebra skins and blankets on the floor. The chickens must have been for their witchcraft, used as a poison oracle probably.

'Anyway, Willy picked the girl up – I was with him by then. But then this head man, this tall African suddenly came in through the doorway of the hut. He hadn't been shot and he'd come back into camp – and of course he went for Willy, tried to spear him, missed. George jumped in. And the three of them were struggling about the floor among the chickens for a minute. But the thatch behind them had caught fire – the grass walls. Laura grabbed the child. And then the headman found himself losing against George and Willy. Finally they pushed him into the flames at the side of the hut. And that's why – '

'That's why that African has scars all over the side of his face,' I interrupted. 'That man, the one you have living downstairs in your house, the one who killed Laura. It's the same man, isn't it?'

'Yes,' Annabelle admitted. 'It's the same man. He killed Willy. He ran him down later in that car in Nairobi. But I don't know about Laura.'

'But it's still really only the beginning, isn't it?' I said, starting to shout once more, angry again. 'An illiterate African from some hidden tribe in the middle of Africa: how the hell does he come to be living in Oxford?'

Annabelle moved on the picnic bench, as if trying to avoid my attack, her long bronzed body angled sharply at her waist, leaning away from me now. 'It was only the beginning for us, too,' she said earnestly, 'after we'd got the girl safely back to Nairobi. We thought we'd hear no more about it, you see, because shortly afterwards the drought came to Karamoja. The rains failed that year and each year afterwards. The people starved, died. And Amin's scavenging army did for the few that were left. They even got up into those mountains. Though most of the Tepeth people up there had been finished off already. Their crops had failed. They were in no position to complain of Willy's depredations. What with the drought and the pillage it was the end of the Karamojong, the Tepeth, the end of all the other hill tribes.'

'Yes, but the African?'

'He survived. Didn't he? Obviously. With the help of the Libyans. And George.'

'What?'

'Oh yes. The African was no fool. And he wasn't illiterate. He'd lived on the plains, been at a missionary school. Anyway, a year later, just after Willy had found the "Thomas" skeleton, that four million-year-old wonder man, the African turned up in Nairobi among thousands of other refugees from Uganda. Of course he thought he had us where he wanted. And he was right. He wanted justice, compensation, all that. And he wanted the child back, too. You see, that was exactly it: Clare *had* been a vital emblem for that tribe. A Rain Queen. As a child, as someone who'd miraculously survived in the deserts on the other side of the mountain, she was a symbol of generation for them, a guarantee of the land's continued fertility. It all made perfect sense. And you can see why – since of course as soon as we'd taken Clare away the rains had failed out there everywhere.'

Annabelle looked at me wide-eyed, as if I'd denied something obvious, though I'd said nothing. 'It stands to reason, doesn't it?' she said, almost shouting. '*Their* reason. The African knew Idi Amin wouldn't last. So he wanted the girl back. And he wanted the legal and financial compensation he knew he'd get, too, if the whole thing came to light. He wanted to set his tribe up again. He saw a future for the old way of life in Africa – their ways, not ours. And of course he thought Willy was particularly vulnerable just at that point.'

'To blackmail?'

'If you could call it that. Everyone was wild about the "Thomas" skeleton just then. Willy and George were top dogs in the bone business. They'd beaten all the field. Fame at last. There was a lot at stake. Because if the world heard how they'd shot up and burnt this tribe in the hills, it would have been the end for both of them, Rain Queen or no.'

'But where *was* Clare?'

'Laura had taken charge of her right from the start, and held on. You see, after the massacre in the hills it would have been too risky making any professional capital out of the girl. So we all kept quiet about Clare. But the Kindersleys had a big bungalow outside Nairobi. Servants, a big enclosed garden. It was ideal for Clare. They had several nannies, African women, though Laura looked after her mostly. She brought her up. She and Willy had never had any children . . . that was one reason.'

'Yes, but what did she tell her friends out there? Her parents in Lisbon?'

'Oh, that was easy enough. She told everyone that she'd legally adopted the child, in Kenya. That Clare was an orphan, a retarded child, the only daughter of a white couple, missionaries, killed up-country in Uganda by Amin's rogue army. And at the time, since those people were killing white and black out there quite at random, it was a perfectly possible tale. Anyway, everyone believed her. And everything that had happened up in those mountains – well, all that had blown over, we thought. Until the African turned up.'

'Willy paid him off?'

'No. Just the opposite. Willy said he'd deny it all, everything that had happened, the shooting, the burning. He told us no one would believe the African anyway, in the present circumstances in Uganda. He said everyone would believe *his* version if the business ever came to light: that the tribe had been set upon by Idi Amin's men. Soon after that we all came back to England.'

'But even that wasn't the end, was it?'

'No. But you've been involved in most of the end, haven't you?'

'But how did the African get *here*, to your house?'

'He caught up with us again. A few months ago, just after you'd left your cottage.'

'I can see that. But *how*? And what the hell was George doing sheltering him? Why didn't he tell the police?'

'Yes. Well, George had a reputation now you see, as well.'

'Yes, and I had a wife.' I was furious.

'I told George that . . . he'd probably killed Laura. But George said there was absolutely no proof. He came here several months ago. The Libyans helped him, that's how. He'd told some of the newspaper people in Nairobi – that's where the press rumours of what happened first started. They didn't believe him, just as Willy thought. But the Libyans there did, or pretended to. He met them in the refugee camp. They were pro-Amin, of course, Moslems, revolutionaries trying to stir up trouble in Kenya by supporting these refugees. And what this African had to tell them was ideal: evidence that Amin *hadn't* been behaving badly to the other Ugandan tribes, that it was *white* people who'd shot this tribe up. And, more than that, it had been the famous Willy Kindersley and George Benson who'd done the damage. If they could prove that they'd have some real publicity for Amin's cause. So they brought the African to Libya first, then over here. They had to find the child, to have *real* proof of the whole thing – that was the point. It took them a long time to trace what had happened to Clare, where you were living in England. And when they found out, the African went off on his own after you. That's my opinion. It was more personal revenge for him now. All right, he must have killed Laura. But he lost you and Clare. And that's when he turned up here, looking for help. He wanted somewhere to live in this area. But above all he thought George might come to know where you two were hiding, that he could get to you both that way. And he was able to blackmail George then – about the shooting in the mountains. You see, when the British press got onto the whole thing a month ago – when they found out you'd worked for British Intelligence, when Willy's East African business blew up all over again, the African thought people here would probably believe his story now. And they would have done, I think. So George agreed to put him up.'

'While he looked for *us*?' I said, my anger rising bitterly again.

'I told George that. But he said if half the police in the country couldn't find you, the African wouldn't be able to.'

'So he was just going to let him live here indefinitely?'

'I don't know. I just don't know. George thought he could work the thing out . . . given time.'

'He thought the police would get me for killing Laura. That's what he thought. And that Clare would be locked up safely in an institution then or sent back to Lisbon. He thought he would get out of it all that way, didn't he?'

'Probably. But the African doesn't know where you are now, does he?'

'No. But he's been close enough – a few weeks ago.'

'He has a car. There's been another man with him helping him. A Libyan, I think, from London.'

'I don't have to worry about him. But if the African is on the move again I think I know where he's gone: back to where we are.'

And I was on my feet then, moving off, thinking of Alice and Clare alone in Beechwood Manor. 'I'd better hurry,' I said. 'It's not the end yet.'

'No. I'm sorry it ever began.' Annabelle called after me.

I turned, half-way across the patio. 'Sorry? Is that all?' I said bitterly. 'I wish you'd told someone about all this before. What a lot of trouble you'd have saved everyone.'

'Yes. But I thought Laura would have told you all about it, long ago.' Annabelle looked at me sadly. She had a point there, I suppose. I turned and left.

Sixteen

On the drive back to Beechwood I wondered how I could have been so wrong about Willy Kindersley – and about his wife Laura. Though perhaps that was unfair. Clare's abduction hadn't been her fault. Rather the opposite: with her subsequent care she'd probably saved the child's life. And yet she had never told me anything about it all. Had she intended to – one day? And I thought again of all the days we'd never had together. Or maybe, more likely, when she married me, she had wanted a clean slate over the whole thing, to start afresh, as if this frightening past had never happened. She had wanted to forget Africa, forget the African. And the tragedy lay in his wanting, so insistently, to remember her – and Willy and the other two, and Clare. His revenge had caught up with almost all of them. And the one thing I had to ensure now was that it didn't catch up with Clare.

With his Libyan friend out of the way, I couldn't see that the African had much chance of ever getting her back to his own country now. And so I could only assume that, at this point, driven by bitterness and anger in the whole matter, he simply wanted Clare dead, along with any of the white protectors or guardians he found with her. The African wanted his own simple revenge now on a white world that had dispossessed him of his home, extinguished his tribe and sent him into exile. That made sense. I could well understand that. But meanwhile the search for this natural justice had probably deranged him, which was why he'd been haunting our valley a few weeks before: not as rescuer but as killer.

There was also the matter of Ross to think about. Since it hadn't been one of his hit-men, I realised now, who had killed Laura in mistake for me, Ross must simply have been pursuing me on his own account for any damning facts I might yet publish about my time in British Intelligence. Ross, as well as the African, was still to be accounted for.

Suddenly, as I drove along through the Oxfordshire lanes, I wanted to be out of England, away from the Cotswolds. I wanted another fresh start, just as Laura had, a year before. I wished I could have been in Lisbon again, on top of one of those windy hills, or in the old Avenida Palace Hotel, or out in Cascais – anywhere away from these threats, these imponderables.

But of course this was just what Laura must have felt, before she met me, when she first came back from Africa. She had wanted to forget it all too. And yet the past had caught up with her and with Willy. And now with George Benson as well: the past in the shape of this canny, ever-persistent and now explosive African.

When I got back to Beechwood that evening Clare was asleep upstairs in the old nursery, safe and sound. After Alice had let me in through the back door we had gone up to her at once. I saw her sleeping then, just a sheet pulled half over her small body in the dry heat under the slates of the old house. She lay sprawled on her stomach, face down against the bed without a pillow, head sharply profiled, arms outstretched, with one leg raised like a hurdler about to jump.

I looked at her face as carefully as I'd ever done, remembering how often in the past I'd seen something of Laura's expression there – a sudden narrowing at the corner of each round eye, the very slight, snub-like cast at the tip of her nose, the same fine, peach-coloured hair and skin. But I'd been wrong about all that, too. She wasn't Laura's child. And for the first time I realised I'd nothing left of Laura now – nothing of her flesh and blood, which I'd cherished in Clare in the months since Laura's death. An inheritance, as I'd seen it – something of our love together commemorated in Clare – had been snatched from me. This child was a total stranger, reared in the African wilds, who had just happened to share some of Laura's physical traits, that was all. And for a moment the realisation of this seemed to invalidate my life with Laura. It had been based on false premises. For Clare hadn't been autistic either, but simply a child brought up without others of her kind who thus never received human affection or the language which comes to underwrite that. I had been wrong about everything, among them these things which Laura could so readily have explained to me. And again, I felt a sharp discontent – no, more a sense of exile: that Laura had kept me outside such vital places in her heart.

But watching Clare just then, lost so calmly and completely in sleep, I saw how vulnerable and thus how human she was. In such sleep, at least, she lost all her wild animal qualities: her speechlessness, her physical excesses, that worry in her eyes where she seemed to search for some ultimate horizon, a dream of a fair country where she could no longer live. In sleep now, she was an ordinary child in an old nursery, surrounded by animals as toys and not as sole companions and supporters. She was supported here by all the traditions of an essentially human childhood. And suddenly I saw another reason why Laura had kept me in the dark. She had wanted to give the child just such an ordinary background, a conventional future in a world which we had both hoped Clare would one day enter. And so she had kept Clare's real past hidden from her as from me, so that the girl – with her disabilities or her wild gifts – could live a life in civilisation as easily as she might, and at least be unencumbered with African ghosts.

That made sense: Laura had been protecting Clare, as much as herself. She had been offering Clare a future by erasing her past as a happy savage. Yet had Clare really been happy in that wild valley, lying on the earth among the chickens? I remembered with what fear she had looked at the African, when she had first seen him again, in our own valley a few weeks before. But she had loved the African masks in the little museum along the landing. They had brought her to life again. There were contradictions here that I couldn't follow. Though perhaps that was the whole point: they were exactly the contradictions inherent in Clare herself, part animal, part human, and she could not reconcile the two. Clare both loved and hated what she had lost, and Laura, from the very beginning, had sensed this: how much human hurt as wild happiness there was in the life of this child. In any case people have an enormous need to bury or deny such savage imponderables, the pain of such contradictions, and thus prevent their spread like a contagion among the human tribe. And this was surely what Laura had done.

But the disease, for so long dormant, had come to light again: with an African in the moonlight of an English valley, in a ceremonial mask, an empty basement flat in Norham Gardens. The wound of the 'past had opened again years later, like a dragon's egg, offering a gaping vision of human folly and disruption. It was my job to close the wound now, if I could. That was all. Clare might no longer be Laura's child. And yet exactly because of this, because she was so completely an orphan, I saw how much more she belonged not to one, but to both of us. And if before, by Laura's deception, I had felt something vital in our marriage had been taken away from me – I realised now, watching Clare, how, in this new-found truth, I had been given the chance of properly commemorating my love for Laura, by ensuring that what she had wished for Clare would come to pass.

Later I told Alice all that had happened that day in Oxford, as we sat on chairs outside Clare's partly open nursery doorway, on the top landing. Safe and sound, I thought... Yet now every creak and movement in the old wood of the Manor, as the fabric cooled after the long hot day, made me uneasy. The house was well locked, with the alarms set, and we had checked through all the rooms – the basement, the tower and all the other nooks and crannies – for signs of any intruder. But the African had been so like a ghost before, coming out from the Great Rift Valley to Norham Gardens, stalking through our woods by the lake as easily as he'd moved through the busy streets of Oxford, that I felt, with such apparent magic at his command, he might surprise us at any moment even in this stronghold – suddenly sweeping up on us, borne on some secret wind, through the walls or the roof of the house.

So we sat there, quietly, on the top landing – Alice with her small automatic and I with the old pump-action Winchester .22 across my knees. After what I'd experienced that afternoon, I wasn't going to bother with Spinks's bow, or the swordstick or the poisoned dart. Now, if it came to violence, I aimed to fire first. It was time to put away native things.

But it didn't come to it. Nothing untoward happened that night. And the only news next morning was good news: along with an account of the Oxford fracas, there was an answer from

Captain Warren at last in the personal column of *The Times*. Under the code name 'St. George' which I'd asked him to use, the message ran:

> 'Assume you are still in central
> England. Thus will wait for you, with
> suitable transport, at Tewkesbury from
> week beginning 1st September.'

'That's clever of him,' I said to Alice. 'Tewkesbury is way inland. Only about twenty miles or so south-west of here, on the river Avon, where it joins the Severn and runs out to sea at Gloucester. Obviously he knows he can get the ketch that far up-river. He won't have to risk staying in any port, with police or customs about. And with all the summer boats around on the river and in the Bristol Channel, he won't be noticed either.'

But Alice was not so enthusiastic. 'It's probably a trap. And how can he sail over here alone in any case, all that way? An old man? All the way from Lisbon and back?'

'Why not? He has a man to help him, and he was a captain in the Navy himself. He did it before, too, when he first took the boat out there.' I was elated. 'The first of September,' I said. 'That's in ten days time. We should be able to get to Tewkesbury from here easily enough.'

It all seemed suddenly possible just then – my escape, Clare's escape. I'd forgotten the African. I'd very nearly forgotten Alice. We were sitting, the three of us, having breakfast up in the tower, with the windows open. Mary, the daily help, was downstairs doing the rooms. The Pringles were still away on holiday and the two gardeners were still clearing the wood, but round the lake now and the valley to the east where we had lived, cutting out the burnt trunks of beech. The weather was hot again. But it was a muggy, flyblown, mid-August heat, with low hung cloud overhead and little black thunderflies in the air even at that time in the morning.

Alice stood up and went over to the fridge. She was wearing a thin, short-sleeved cotton shirt and she reached round an arm now, trying to scratch the small of her back where something had bitten her. I got up myself, following her, and scratched her back for her. Clare meanwhile had returned to the floor where some days before she had started trying to re-assemble the model of the old tea clipper she had destroyed a few weeks ago. It was as if, unconsciously, she already sensed a maritime departure in the air.

'I'm sorry.' I still had my arm on Alice's back. 'It's just that yesterday left its mark. I was hoping I could be out of all this: the African. Not you.'

'But why bother about him at all now? Why not tell the police yourself in any case? About everything, from the beginning?'

'About that Libyan in the museum? And what about that Hell's Angel I shot – apart from Laura, who they'll still think I killed. There's an awful lot of mayhem I still have to account for.'

'Well, you can't run forever. And you can certainly prove self-defence in the museum. And what you did in the woods could have been an accident. Besides, it was the African who pushed that lout onto the fire. And you *didn't* kill Laura.'

'Maybe. But while I was proving all that the police would be bound to hold me for quite a time. And what would Clare do meanwhile? No – I have to try and get her back to Portugal, where the Warrens can look after her. So I can't tell the police now. Don't you see?'

'Perhaps.'

I could see how Alice clearly foresaw an end to things between us now; a possible future let go by default. She opened the fridge and bent down, and her shirt slipped up her back a few inches, showing her narrow, bronzed waist and the sharp bones in her vertebrae. A sense of other life – ordinary life, domestic life, loving life – suddenly moved in me.

'What about your divorce?' I asked.

Alice stood up, three yoghurt tubs in her hand. 'September,' she said. 'The settlement is all but agreed in New York. Not that there was much to settle. The house here is mine, of course.'

I thought I knew what she was thinking. 'Would you live with me? Would you really want to?' I asked.

'Yes,' she said abruptly, impatiently. 'What else could be so obvious? It's you, though. Do you want to?'

'Yes,' I answered, but more slowly.

'You don't seem so sure.'

'Just it's never been so easy, for me.'

'Nor me. I told you. With anyone. But we could probably get on together. We've plenty in common.' She smiled. 'We don't get on with other people after all. That could be the main thing!'

She stopped smiling then. But there was something even better in her face – hope, and a wry, calm amusement: the reflection of a future between us, offered up and jointly accepted.

'I love you,' she said. 'But if you're going to be running all over the world soon – '

'Let me get Clare safely to Portugal.'

'*Safely*?' she said, suddenly angry. 'But the boat could sink. Besides the old man may have set up a trap for you in Tewkesbury. He probably told the police here as soon as he got your letter.'

'I'll have to take that risk. But if I get to Portugal, and leave Clare, I'll come back here and we can start afresh. I'll tell the police all about it then. And later maybe we can get Clare back, and she can live with us.'

Life sprang up before me then, another life, another chance with Alice and Clare. Perhaps I didn't deserve it. But it was there all the same, waiting for me.

Then we heard the car drawing up, crunching round the gravel in front of the house, and I felt threatened once more. 'Don't worry,' Alice said. 'It's nothing. Just those Victorian people – the Society. They're coming this morning to start fixing things up. This weekend it's the hundredth anniversary of the house, you remember? The fête, the jousting tournament, the cricket match, the costume ball. Had you forgotten?' She smiled now, that active smile of hers, where she suddenly became a decisive person, intent on life, with all the gifts for living. Indeed, I saw how our being together these past few months had so encouraged both our better qualities. She no longer acted without cause, a mad Ophelia in a Camelot outfit, spotlit among the greenery of the conservatory, or gave Indian war-whoops without answer down by the lake, or brought roses to a crumbling tomb. She had a live audience at last, a sounding-board with me – and her mimic vigour, her quick laughter, her idiosyncratic renovations about the house were no longer masks in front of some awful despair, but the true face of appropriate passions. As for me, where there had been an equal despair, she had given me a similar hope. All the same, I wasn't living with Alice yet.

'Well, I won't be involved in this fête,' I said.

'Why not? The police aren't going to bother to look here again.'

'That's nonsense.'

'You could just be a guest.'

'Disguised, you mean?'

'Yes. Exactly. Just like you've been before, as Harry Conrad and that antique-dealer in the hospital. This cricket match they're playing – that's your game, isn't it? You told me how much you like to play it. Well, now you can. It's all in nineteenth-century costume. The Society are arranging it. Or what about the jousting tournament? You could get dressed up for that. They wouldn't recognise you got up in a lot of armour either, would they?' Alice was suddenly very happy. She saw a future between us: a future of all sorts of fun and games, a future of disguises.

'Me – in the jousting tournament – ' I said incredulously.

'Yes. Why not? The riders are coming from all over: even some real knights – '

'But I can barely ride a horse, Alice, let alone poke people with lances from one going full gallop.'

'No?' She seemed genuinely surprised, crestfallen, at my reply. And I saw then how much she wanted to believe in me, as a Sir Galahad or Launcelot reincarnate. She wasn't cured of that sort of heroic delusion, I realised. Indeed, by my helping her achieve some sanity, I had encouraged her all the more to think of me as some shining knight errant, a worker of all sorts of miracles on her behalf.

'Alice, you must be joking.'

'Nothing venture, nothing win,' she answered very seriously.

It was now Tuesday, the 20th of August, and there was more than a week to fill before I could think of leaving for Tewkesbury to get there after the 1st of September. The fête was due to last two days – starting the next Saturday afternoon, with stalls and sideshows in the immediate manor parkland, and the re-created nineteenth-century cricket match to be played further down in the grounds. On the Saturday evening a medieval Costume Ball had been arranged, with appropriate food to go with it – tickets at £40 a pair – to be held in the great Baronial Hall.

Sunday was the day of the great jousting tournament, with visits for the public round Beechwood Manor and gardens as well. There was to be a Mrs Beeton cooking competition in the morning, held in the old kitchens, and a selection of other treats later on: a vintage bicycle race round the manor drives, an exhibition of Victorian farm equipment in the yard, excursions about the estate in a coach and four, dog-and-donkey-cart rides for the children, together with short aerial trips for the more intrepid in a tethered hot-air balloon which was to be chauffeured by a man dressed up as Passepartout from *Around the World in Eighty Days*. Since the proceeds were all to go to the Victorian Society they were arranging everything. It seemed a fine programme and many hundreds of people were expected. But there was no place in it all for Clare and me.

I had other problems. For example, although Alice would be able to drive Clare and me to Tewkesbury easily enough, taking the small lanes over the wolds and perhaps travelling by night, I couldn't leave for the river town before the Friday of the following week, to arrive there on the Saturday, which would be the 1st of September. I would have therefore to spend this coming busy weekend hidden in the Manor with Clare. And further, since the Pringles were due back from their holiday on the coming Saturday, Clare and I would have to spend the last week after that incarcerated up in the tower. It was not a happy prospect, especially since the weather, which had been quite cool and overcast for a week, had now turned brilliantly fine again, the start of an Indian summer.

The days were noticeably shorter, but they were burnished Mediterranean days now, with a shimmer of blue heat in the air almost from sun-up, while by early afternoon the temperature was intense, the sun a slanting fire in an ever-cloudless sky. We searched for shade, Alice and I, about the house. But Clare became restless. She wanted to be out in the open, to swim, above all, to cool herself down by the lake in the hidden valley where she had been happy. But this she could not do – for apart from the African, whose sudden violent presence loomed from every bush now, Alice's two men were still clearing the burnt trees away from the shoreline there.

Nor could Clare play outside in the parkland or in the formal gardens down by the great Neptune fountain, for the volunteers from the Victorian Society were active everywhere in the grounds, preparing the fête. Thus we were confined for most of the day to the top landing or the tower and both places, so close to the sun, became unbearably hot.

So it was that I had brought Clare down one afternoon to the wine cellar in the basement, where it was deliciously cool and safe – bringing a chair and some rugs and Clare's toys with us, the ark and its animals, with a book for me to read by the light of the single bulb above the pyramids of old wine bottles.

Yet when I got down there, I found I'd left the book behind, and more importantly that day's newspaper, which I'd put aside somewhere with an account of that week's test match in it. Clare seemed completely bound up with her animals on the rug next a bin of Gevrey-Chambertin. So I had left her, explaining what I was doing, and gone back upstairs, closing the cellar door. When I returned less than three minutes later the door was open and Clare had gone.

She had either run herself, I thought, or the African had taken her: the African, ghost-like again, who'd been haunting this dark, unused basement area, waiting for just such an opportunity. And though it was cool in the cellars I was suddenly drenched in sweat, mad at my stupidity in leaving Clare by herself. And worse, since Alice had gone far down into the parkland with one of the men from the Victorian Society, I would have to search for Clare alone.

First I stalked from door to door along the shadows of the basement passage, a bottle in my hand ready to smash it in some dark face. But all the old, unused rooms here, with their creaking doors laced with cobwebs, were empty.

I went upstairs. She could not have come into the big hall, or gone up by the main staircase, since I'd just been in that part of the house myself. She could only have left by the back door into the yard via the kitchens. Then I thought – the old laundry room, with its huge copper cauldron and the dangerous linen press: that was where she'd probably gone, where she'd once before played so happily in the grate and in the big tub itself.

I rushed out to the yard and into the laundry. She wasn't there. But she'd gone this way, I saw then, for on the cobblestones, next the gateway leading down towards our old valley by the lake, I found one of the wooden animals from her ark, a big tawny-maned lion.

I went back to the house and fetched Alice's Winchester from the gun-room. Clare must have gone down to the lake. But had she gone there of her own free will or had she been taken? I took no risks myself, pumping the stock, priming the gun as I ran out of the yard gateway. Luckily there was no one about on the eastern side of the house where the covered laurel pathway led down to the back drive and then on to the orchard, and beyond that to the ridge of beech trees and the hidden valley below.

The sun cast fierce shadows through the bushes as I sprinted along beneath them. I crossed the back drive and then took a short cut through the orchard, stalking from tree to tree now, moving towards the hedge at the end which would bring me out near the top of the valley. Early Worcesters hung thickly on the branches and wasps hummed at my feet picking among some already rotten windfalls. But otherwise there was complete silence in the baking afternoon heat. I wasn't far from the lake, yet the sound of the chainsaws and the axes, which had echoed up from the valley there for weeks past, was gone. The silence was unnerving. Then something moved beyond a row of apple trees – a gathering movement, as if from many feet, swathing steadily towards me through the dry grass. I raised the rifle.

A flock of white geese, big birds, striding through the dappled shade of the orchard, came into sight. And suddenly their loud and outraged cackles, when they saw me, broke the silence. A few of them pursued me as I moved away from them as quickly as I could, down towards the hedge at the end of the orchard, where I could get over onto the pathway on the far side which led down to the bathing-place at the northern end of the lake. But when I got to this hedge, hiding beneath it, I heard another sound: footsteps, human footsteps this time, coming slowly towards me along the path on the other side. I raised the gun again, trying to peer through the briars, hoping to get a clear first shot if necessary. Through the hedge I saw Clare coming up the path, hand-in-hand with one of Alice's workmen, a middle-aged man, burnt a deep bronze, wearing a singlet. Clare wasn't happy.

'Why can't you swim?' she asked petulantly, reversing the pronoun as usual, wanting to swim herself. Of course the man didn't understand.

'Oh, I can't swim down there now, Miss. I've work to do, see? But I'll get you back to your Mum up at the house, you don't worry. See, you can't be down there with us with all those trees and branches falling about the place. Not safe. But you'll be all right now, you'll see. You have your Mum with you up at the house, I expect, won't you?'

Clare didn't reply. And there was nothing I could do. Clare's existence here had been discovered. But perhaps the trusting gardener would think nothing of it – just a stray child belonging to one of the people from the Victorian Society. He would look for Alice now, who would take her over, having invented some suitable excuse for the girl's presence. The man would make nothing of it. Why should he? There were a dozen people about the estate that afternoon. So I shadowed the two of them, keeping behind the hedge, back up the pathway to the Manor.

They went into the yard first and it was there, hidden behind the gateway pillar, that I saw the small car parked right next the kitchen entrance. It hadn't been in the yard ten minutes before. The boot was open so that whoever was taking something out from the back was invisible.

Clare and the man walked over to the car. Then the boot slammed shut and I saw the gross figure of Mrs Pringle looming up with a load of parcels in her arms. At the same moment the gardener spoke.

'Hello, Anna. Back sooner than expected. Not 'till the weekend, we thought.'

Mrs Pringle came round to the front of the car. 'Billy, hello. Yes, we came back early. Half the Spanish hotel went down with some tummy bug. Terrible. We were offered the chance of an earlier flight home. So we took it. How has Miss Troy been – safe and sound, or mad as a hatter? We were worried. We phoned several times, heard about those thugs down by the lake. But she's been all right, has she?'

The gardener nodded. 'Yes, indeed. Mary and Alec have been keeping a firm eye on her, no problems. Apart from that mad lot down by the lake. Broke in through the fence they did, and then set the whole place alight. But we've strengthened the fence now. Miss Troy won't get out of the place, leastways, that's for sure.'

Mrs Pringle looked at Clare then. 'Who have you got there, Billy?' she asked, peering over her packages.

'Don't know. Some kid. She came down to the lake just now. But it's not safe. We've been cutting back the burnt wood. So I've brought her back up here. Don't know who she belongs to.'

'I'll bring her to Miss Troy. She'll know. Must have something to do with one of all these people come to fix this fête. But doesn't the child know who she is herself? She looks old enough.'

'Doesn't seem to. She talks kind of funny, too.'

'Well, we'll soon find out. Come here, child. What's your name?' Mrs Pringle, her great body towering over Clare, had the air of the Beadle in *Oliver Twist*. Clare didn't answer her. So Mrs Pringle bent down and tried to wheedle Clare towards her, calling to her as though she was an animal.

'Come with me, child,' she said eventually, in sterner tones of her indeterminate London accent. She put her parcels on the roof of the car. Then she held out a very pudgy arm. She'd obviously been doing herself well in Spain before the tummy bugs set in. 'Come on. Don't be afraid.'

'*You* don't want to come,' Clare said suddenly, staying where she was.

'No. *I* don't want to come, but *you* do, don't you? Come on, we'll go and find your Mummy or Miss Troy. She'll know.' Finally Mrs Pringle had to lead Clare away, in through the dark passageway towards the kitchen, like a child being taken into an institution.

And again, there was absolutely nothing I could do. I could only hope that Alice, with all her quick inventions, would find some sudden inspiration here, when she saw Clare coming towards her with the dreadful Mrs Pringle.

She did. Half an hour later Alice found me, on tenterhooks, up in the tower. From one of the turret windows I'd seen Mrs Pringle and Clare moving out into the parkland, and had seen them all return some time later, Alice walking easily, holding Clare's hand, chatting to Mrs Pringle. Was it all over? Or just one more beginning?

'It's simple,' Alice said when she had started to explain to me. 'You're Harry Conrad again. Remember? Our friend, Arthur's lawyer friend from London, the man you were before, when Mrs Pringle found you locked in the wine cellar. And Clare is your daughter. Harry has a daughter anyway, just about Clare's age. And you're both staying with us – come down for the fête. What could be more natural?'

Alice smiled. I sighed.

'Now don't start thinking up objections,' she went on. 'It's done. I've explained it all that way. And Mrs Pringle accepted every word of it. She doesn't suspect a thing. Why should she? Just the opposite. She was pleased you were here again. You see, she thinks you're my new man, my next husband. And she *wants* to think that, don't you see? So that there'll be a future for her down here: that I'm not going mad all on my own, talking to myself, before being dragged off in a straitjacket – which would mean the end of everything for Mrs Pringle here. Don't you see? So she's *pleased*.'

'Yes. I see. We're back to the theatricals.'

'So all we've got to do now,' Alice rushed on, 'is to get you down to a spare bedroom again, have some suitcases out and some more of Arthur's clothes. And Clare can come downstairs too, into the next bedroom. It'll make everything easier. The two of us can stay here quite openly, until I take you to Tewkesbury next week. And you can join in the fête now – why not? You won't have to stay cooped up in the tower anyway. It's *ideal*.' She emphasised the word sharply, brightly, happily. And when I didn't reply she said, 'Isn't it?' even more sharply, but less happily.

'Yes,' I said finally. 'I'll start getting my make-up on. And the costumes.'

'Why, I hadn't thought of that. You could play your cricket now – '

'And the medieval costume ball,' I interrupted. 'That's even better. That'll suit me perfectly.'

Alice wasn't sure whether my irony was real or assumed. She came towards me, undecided. 'There wasn't anything else I could think of saying to Mrs Pringle,' she said. 'I don't see why – '

'No. I'm sorry. There wasn't anything else. My fault for letting Clare out of my sight.'

'Besides,' Alice broke in, suddenly enthusiastic again, 'What better than spending a weekend down from London with me?'

'What better, indeed,' I said, kissing her.

And so, as Harry Conrad, on that Saturday afternoon, I finally got my game of cricket. Certainly no one could have recognised me – as either Marlow or Conrad. For I was the perfectly dressed late nineteenth-century cricketer now, complete with rather moth-eaten old flannels riding high above my ankles and secured at the waist by a yellow and purple tie, a cream shirt and a minute Tweedledum cap, striped in various faded blues, with an even smaller peak perched high on my head. I had heavy sidewhiskers, blossoming like rampant ivy round my ears, and a handsome bandit's moustache curling down round my chin, which Alice had fixed up for me, together with a bandana handkerchief, like a stevedore's, knotted against the sweat about my neck.

The rest of the equipment, gathered together by the Victorian Society from old pavilions, schools and houses about the country, was equally in period – stumps, bats and pads. Only the ball was contemporary, along with the players beneath their beards, among them half a dozen well-known cricketers. I had secured a place on one of these celebrity teams purely as Alice's house-guest.

Of course, I needn't have taken part. But I couldn't resist it. My disguise seemed overwhelming, Clare was being looked after nearby by Alice all the time, and the air of pleasurable anticipation down in the old log-built pavilion where we all assembled for drinks before lunch, was immense. It was all worth the risk, I thought. The food was cold, a sumptuous buffet with whole hams and pâtés with a great deal of chilled Frascati to go with it, slaking already rising thirsts, for the day was brilliantly fine and hot again. The captain of my team was a distinguished ex-England cricketer, a batsman from Gloucestershire, a classic stylist in his day, tall and still supple and now unsuitably got up to look like his great predecessor in that county, Dr W. G. Grace. The poor man had to remove part of his huge beard before he could get near the Yorkshire ham.

But I was put to sit next another player, at a back table out of the way, someone, like me, quite unknown in the game. Middle-aged, with thin hair cut short, a very conventional-looking fellow ill-at-ease in his disguise, as well he might, since it was composed of a most rapacious growth of mutton-chop whiskers. I didn't press myself on my neighbour here. On the other hand I couldn't remain entirely silent. And nor could he, though he seemed no great talker either, even encouraged as we both were with repeated draughts of iced Frascati. But I explained vaguely that I was down from London, and more vaguely still that I was a lawyer.

My companion perked up at this information. 'Oh,' he said,

trying to extricate a piece of the salad that had lodged in his rampant whiskers. 'I used to see a lot of lawyers. I'm with the Police. The South Riding. I'm Alec Wilson. Chief Superintendent, for my sins.'

My stomach turned over. 'I play a little cricket,' the man went on. 'But I'm really interested in the history of the game. That's why they invited me here. I've written a bit for the cricket magazines – mostly about overseas tours in the nineteenth century: that's my speciality. Those American and Canadian tours, for example, in the late nineties. There was quite a bit of good cricket over there then, did you know? Surprising.'

'Oh, was there?' I tried not to look at the man uneasily.

Luckily, shortly afterwards, the Chief Superintendent became engrossed with his other neighbour in some long and arcane tale about an early Indian tour, games against the great Ranji some time after the Great War. Meanwhile, I studiously occupied myself with an innocent young man to my right – beardless, in a peach-coloured blazer, who turned out to be an Oxford scholar doing a thesis on Sport and Society in nineteenth-century Britain.

The lunch passed off without further alarm, and with a good deal more cold Frascati, so that by the time I was fielding in the blazing heat out on the mid wicket boundary half an hour later I could barely see the game, seventy-five yards away, what with the sun in my eyes and the drink running to my head. Thus when one of the celebrity batsmen, an old English wicket-keeper rarely noted for his circumspection, clouted the ball mightily in my direction, I never saw it at all. It sailed right over my head and into the cornfield, not yet cut, which lay behind the pavilion: the same field which, starving in my tree nearly three months before, I had stalked through on my way to steal the cricketer's tea.

I went after the ball, vaulting the fence before wading into the edge of the tall corn. And it was then, less than twenty yards away to my right, that I heard something rustle in the stalks, deep down, and saw the corn move – agitated by some fairly large animal, I thought, since there was no wind at all that afternoon. I found the ball. And then it suddenly struck me: what sort of animal, in such broad daylight, near such crowds, would be lurking in a corn hide? A hare perhaps, or a fox? Or a man? An African?

I was uneasy for the rest of the match. Of course we were all being watched – by three or four hundred spectators round the ground. But increasingly from then on I had the feeling that I particularly was being watched, especially when I went out to bat, much later in the afternoon, when the sun had come to slant right down over the big chestnut trees on the western perimeter of the park. It may have been nothing more than sheer nerves or imagination of course. But I became convinced that someone was watching me as I walked out to the middle: someone from above, I thought, from one of the trees beyond the boundary. Someone, hiding, had their eye on me, just as I had spied before on the weekend games here from my own look-out post on top of the huge copper beech.

The fierce glare of the afternoon had gone now, replaced by velvet shades of blue and violet in the sky, and the long spiky shadows of the fielders crept across the wicket like Gothic spires and pinnacles as I took guard. And now I felt completely exposed, at risk, especially since the fielders were crowding in all round me, hoping to finish the game quickly and get back to the pavilion for some long drinks, for I was a tail-ender and our team still had forty-odd runs to make to win.

I wanted to get back to the safety of the pavilion myself, to see if Clare was all right. I was extraordinarily jittery. I looked round, checking the field, before the first ball. What was that sudden flash of light, I wondered, something reflected from the low sun in one of the trees? That movement of a branch in another? Why that sudden murmur from the crowd, riding on the evening breeze now? There was something malign in the air, in the thick trees round the boundary. I wanted to get out of the game as soon as I could, out of the firing-line. The ring of close fielders gathered round me, threatening me with their great beards. The bowler began his long run.

Of course, as happens in cricket, when one wants to get out one fails. And I failed miserably that afternoon. I swung viciously at every ball, the old ebony-coloured bat with its twine handle making perfect arcs down the line, carving the air with a tremendous swish, so that even if I'd not connected with the ball the impudent fielders would, I think, have retreated. As it was, they were all soon out on the boundary. I couldn't get myself out at all. Instead, with fours and sixes sizzling back over the bowler's head like cannon-shot, we won the game in less than twenty minutes.

Head down and running, I tried to escape the applause when I returned to the pavilion. One of my sidewhiskers had come loose. It was time to disappear back to the house. But I couldn't see Alice or Clare as I walked through the crowds gathered now outside the log hut. Then I was inside the pavilion, among the other cricketers, offering their congratulations. And then I saw the tall, lanky, dark man with a fuzz of wiry hair, in the smart tropical sports jacket straight in front of me: the African. He was coming towards me, smiling. I raised my bat – as if to strike or protect myself, the sweat from my exertions falling in my eyes, almost blinding me, as I waited for the blows to fall.

But it wasn't the African. I heard the voice of the Gloucestershire captain: he was introducing me. The man I was facing, shaking hands with now, was a West Indian, one of the great cricketers of his time, who, invited but unable to play in this charity match, had just arrived on the scene, making a courtesy call at the end of the game.

I shook his hand. 'You surely got to the pitch of the ball there, man,' he said dryly, remarking on my unexpected innings.

Then Alice was by my side, adding her congratulations. But for her, since she understood nothing of the game, seeing it at best as some dull version of baseball, the praise took a less restrained form. She jumped up and down like someone cheering a victory in a World Series.

'You see?' she exclaimed. 'Nothing venture – I *told* you.' Then she looked at me more circumspectly, from a distance as it were, her rumbustious praise suddenly changed to a speechless admiration, where the joy lay only in her eyes. There was nothing of the baseball fan in her then. It was much more as if my mild success out on the cricket-pitch had been for her a battle won against the infidel, and I a crusader home to her arms at last.

By the time the medieval costume ball got under way in the great Gothic front hall that evening I had become quite used to my disguises. This time I appeared as a fifteenth-century Albanian nobleman, with a villainous moustache, wearing a velour doublet embroidered with crescent moons and stars, with woollen hose, soft leather boots and a fur-rimmed turban surmounted by a splendid ostrich feather. No one could have recognised me from Adam.

Alice's pre-Raphaelite features and hairstyle went perfectly with a more conventional medieval costume: a long off-the-shoulder Elizabethan gown with high ruffed shoulders and a velvet overdress and some sort of crinoline beneath, for the whole thing came out like a bell round her legs, right down to the ground. On top she wore a conical hat, like an old wizard's cap, with emblems of the zodiac on it, and a long fine muslin drape falling away from the peak. Perhaps the gown didn't entirely suit her. She was a little too short in the leg and long in the torso to carry it perfectly. But her natural athletic grace made up for this: she moved in it beautifully, making it a dancing veil where, though the body was invisible, you could so clearly sense all the supple lines beneath, a perfect force controlled, withheld.

'It's funny dancing in this,' she said, flushed with excitement, as we took a turn round the floor before supper, with Clare always in our view, dressed as a page, just a few yards away, on a seat by the great fireplace. 'My legs – it's like moving them about inside a big tent. I can't really feel the material. It's as if I was dancing with nothing on below the waist!'

The small orchestra, equally in period dress, with Elizabethan harps and horns and other suitably odd instruments, played quadrilles. Great firelit braziers and huge candles glittered all round the hall, the wooden floor had been polished and chalked, and the couples moved to and fro in their courtly dance, increasingly amazed at their prowess, with a passion for the dainty steps either invented or re-discovered. The air was full of memorials, the contents of theatrical costumiers and old cupboards revivified: breaths of French chalk dust, a hint of starch and mothballs, of warmed silk and fine scents. An elaborate medieval buffet supper waited for us in the long dining-room next door, laid out on a full complement of old plate, with silver goblets, cuts of roast venison, whole pigs with apples in their mouths and tall crystal jugs of mead.

Filled with these costumed dancers, the huge Gothic house, for so long an empty shell, now at last displayed its true colours. Something of the gallant love and theatricality of its original creators – the Hortons now entombed down on their Avalon in the middle of the lake – had been returned to it. It was impossible not to share in this regeneration. And for long moments, as I danced with Alice then, though immersed in this reflected past, I was equally convinced of a future: of a time between us where this evening's impossible theatricality would naturally give way to an appropriate contemporary life between us.

Alice, on the other hand, had entirely given herself over to the moment. The evening perfectly fulfilled all her craving for the chivalrous gesture, for disguise, for wild adventure, for a life of marvels. She was released by her costume and the heroic mood onto one of the many stages in her mind which before had been dark, frustrating her imagination. Now she could play one of her hidden roles in public, entirely appropriately, without the scorn of her husband or friends. I had freed her from that stigma and this evening's nostalgic requirements gave her complete theatrical licence. She could live fully at last, by escaping completely into an imagined past, where she had always wanted to live, without doubts or the accusation of dottiness. Here she could justify her fantasies, her long isolation from the real world: here, in this recreated medieval dream, she saw reality.

It worried me. In the future, would she always want, *have* to live like this, a life so far removed from the ordinary? If I lived with her, one day she would find me ordinary enough, and I could come to be just another outworn prop in her ever-touring company. I foresaw a time when I might need her more than she needed me, since, after my own years of adventurous stupidity with British Intelligence, I had learnt to thrive on ordinary life with Laura and with Clare and with our dog Minty. Alice in the long run might offer, and require in return, far too rich a mix.

True, I had been mad enough myself, more recently, living wild, killing sheep – and living with Clare in Arcadia. And it had been my example in all this which had at last rescued Alice from her mad despair. But I had no great wish to carry on the game. And perhaps she had.

Yet if she did, I saw then that I would have to help her all the more. I loved her and thus my life, I realised, had come to be framed by her needs – and by Clare's. Without their problems, disabilities and obsessions, I would have no real existence myself.

Suddenly Alice said, with great happiness, quite unaware of any of these thoughts: 'What luck we've had meeting, you and I.'

'We'd never have met at all, you know, in ordinary circumstances. What could you have had to do with a schoolmaster from a fourth rate boys – '

'That's what I *meant*, idiot! Since the circumstances *were* so extraordinary. We *had* the luck. We earned that, don't you see?'

'We both of us really live a bit off the map you mean.'

She smiled and nodded. 'We were meant for each other!' she said with light irony. Then she added, serious now, 'This is the real thing.'

Perhaps she was right. But again there was such a way to go between the dream and the reality here. For the moment I was Harry Conrad, masquerading as a medieval Turk. But in reality I was Peter Marlow on the run, pursued by the police, by a vengeful African – and by Ross, too, I suddenly remembered. I'd lost all my past. And my future, if I had one, hadn't even begun.

Yet Alice, all the while that evening, had clearly seen at least one of my future roles. When I walked into my bedroom that night, after the ball was over, with Alice and Clare just behind me on the landing, I was suddenly confronted by a great suit of shining black, medieval armour – facing me like a threat on a stand by my bed, complete with a plumed visored helmet, long spurs, chain-mail gauntlets, and a white, heart-shaped shield, dazzlingly quartered by a red cross.

'There you are,' Alice said. 'You can try it out tomorrow, in the tournament.'

My head started to swim. I was hot and sticky already after a night at the ball in my Albanian outfit: the idea of being enclosed in this monstrous straitjacket, even for a minute, appalled me. But Clare thought it a good idea. She was fascinated by the armour.

'Yes!' she said firmly, brightly. 'Yes, yes!'

'No,' I said, just as firmly. 'No.'

I turned to Alice. 'I told you I can barely ride a horse. You must be joking.'

But Alice wasn't.

Seventeen

'You can't be serious, Alice,' I told her in her own bedroom later, when Clare was asleep. 'It needs practice. You can't just suddenly start jousting at my age – and that's an understatement,' I added smiling, hoping to treat the matter lightly, hoping to unearth the essential joke I assumed Alice intended.

But she said firmly 'You could practise tomorrow morning. The others will be doing just that. The tournament doesn't start till the afternoon. Besides, you don't have to *kill* anyone, you know. It's just a game.'

'I wish you really believed that.'

Alice was over by the window, starting to get out of her elaborate Elizabethan costume. The wizard's hat she had worn, with its lovely zodiac patterns, was on her bed. I picked it up, fondling the swathe of light muslin that fell from the peak.

'What do you mean?' she asked abruptly, and I realised I was on delicate ground. But I was annoyed with her now, that she should continue so wilfully to insist on this unnecessary charade.

'That you really believed it was just a game: all these costumes and disguises, and now this bloody great suit of armour. You said I'd helped you, cured you even, by sharing your madness by my living wild in the valley first, and then with all the roles I had to play myself. That's what you said, and that's fine. But we can't live this sort of theatrical life forever, these dreams of chivalry and whatnot. Perhaps now and then. But if you live it all the time, well, that puts you way out of touch with reality.'

Alice was about to step out of her heavy dress. But now, at the last moment, like an actress refusing to relinquish a part, she decided not to, hitching it up on her shoulders again. She walked over to me.

'Reality?' she said brightly. 'I can afford to disregard it. And so can you.'

'We can't,' I said. 'That's just silly.'

Alice came right up to me then and put a finger on the tip of my nose, touching it reprovingly. 'It's nothing to do with money, Peter. What I mean is I'm just like you. You despise the real world as much as I do. I know that. You're just as much a stranger to reality as I am.'

This was true enough. And yet I avoided the truth of it in my next words to her. 'But I've had to leave the real world,' I said. 'I've been on the run. You don't, since no one's looking for you.'

'That's simply convenient argument. I'm talking about basic personality. Long before you met me you hated the common lot – you isolated yourself from it, from them. And so have I, yet you blame me for it now.'

'No. I just said I didn't think we could make a lifetime's performance out of it, that's all.'

I was well on my way to disappointing Alice, I could see that. But there was nothing for it. I could no longer acquiesce in her every fantasy. I was sure I'd damage Alice then, as much as I'd helped her before by identifying with her dreams.

Alice turned away. 'You're just suiting yourself now. You forget: you played all these "games", as you call them now, to your advantage before. They were the saving of you, too. Don't you remember? Living wild in the wood. That saved you. That wasn't a game. And when you were Harry Conrad and that London antique dealer in the hospital those roles saved you – and Clare as well. And the cricket match this afternoon, dressed up in that little cap and side whiskers, and being an Albanian nobleman this evening – you enjoyed all that as well didn't you?' she added bitterly.

'Yes. But now – '

'Now you're becoming like Arthur. Just like him: full of refusals, dull care, the common lot.'

'No. It's just that I don't want to break my neck tomorrow with a barge-pole on a galloping horse.'

Alice turned to me again with a slightly malicious smile, like a teasing child. 'You've just lost your nerve, Peter, that's all.'

I could see now how, after all my other impersonations, she had contrived a last testing hurdle for me in the shape of this jousting tournament: finally, to succeed with her, to deserve her, I must actually appear as a shining knight in armour, tilting victoriously in her cause, with her favour, a little ribbon or red hanky, tied to my lance. It was an absurd dream. But I could not think of any other reason for her insistence in this obviously and unnecessarily dangerous nonsense.

'Alice,' I said, trying to make things up with her. 'it's not really a question of nerve – though that's part of it, I'll admit: it's a question of *sanity*. It's an unnecessary risk. Can't you see that? If I was injured and had to go to hospital what would happen to Clare? And they'd find out who I was then, so I'd just be locked up afterwards. There'd be no future for us.'

But Alice, this dream so nearly within her reach, was quite unwilling to relinquish it. 'You could at least *try* it,' she said. 'It can't be all that difficult.'

'I should think it's bloody difficult, especially if you're no great horseman. And I'm not. But what's the point, Alice? What's the point? That's the real question.'

'It's *life*. Don't you see?' she answered simply.

'It's death, more likely.' I thought even then that I could rescue the situation with a joke, by taking Alice in my arms. But when I touched her she withdrew, unable even to look at me. And I sensed then that her madness went back much further than I'd thought; that the games she played at Beechwood were not the result of her marriage or of her isolation in the great house but had their origins in some unresolved trauma way in her past, that I knew nothing of, which I could never unearth or cure. I had failed her in this last event, this charade of courtly valour: I was thus no fit person to accompany her on her golden journey through life. I would not be that ever-daring, valiant knight from her child's story book, *In the Days of the King*, who would rescue her from the dark and brambly wood. I wanted to rescue her with sanity, not by injecting some continual drama into our affair.

She turned and looked at me now from the far side of the big divan. 'You've really been using me, haven't you? As long as you were in a fix, I was useful to you: my money, this house. But now – '

'Alice, that's not true, I'm *still* in a fix. And besides it was always your suggestion that you help me, that I came up to the house in the first place, for example. You forget that.'

We were arguing now, prevaricating, accusing, objecting, denying. All the angry emotional grammar we had never known before we seemed to know by heart now. And that was nonsense, too, I suddenly decided. I was becoming like the schoolmaster I'd been, treating Alice like the child she was. There was no future there, as Arthur had so obviously found, who had treated her in the same way. Yet I was determined not to give in, not to be bullied in the matter of the tournament: there was equally no future for us in that either.

'I'm sorry,' I said. 'Let's not fight any more about it – can we not?'

She didn't reply. I picked up her wizard's hat. 'You looked marvellous this evening, you know,' I said.

She turned then, smiling at last. She took the hat from me and put it on again, setting it at an angle rising back from her dark hair, so that the long swathe of silk spun round her body as she swirled about for a moment on the far side of the bedroom. 'Tomorrow I've another costume, for the tournament: it's a surprise, as the Queen of Beauty.'

'Queen of Beauty?'

'Yes. There was one at every tournament in the old days: I'm to be the Queen of Beauty tomorrow. The Victorian Society suggested it. So why not, I thought? It should be fun.'

She let me kiss her then, lightly on the cheek. 'Great,' I said. 'I'll look forward to it all.' Then I turned back, halfway to the door. 'Of course, they were quite right, the Society – there couldn't have been any other choice.'

It seemed we'd made it up then as I looked across at her and we smiled at each other. But out on the landing I had that last vision of her as someone quite isolated again, as she had been when I'd first seen her apparently talking to herself in the conservatory – isolated now, madness creeping up on her once more in the shape of her Elizabethan gown and wizard's cap. I had somehow lost her. She would sleep with these props next to her that night, and not me, I thought, dreaming of another even more elaborate disguise on the morrow. I had lost her, and she had lost all those happy, decisive connections with real life which my predicament had given her. And yet all my problems remained as great as ever. Could I overcome them without her help? I was tempted to go back and tell her then that I'd take part in the tournament after all. But when I got to my own room and saw the great mass of black armour looming up at me, still confronting me like a brutal foe about to attack, I thought better of the idea. I picked the crusader's shield up. And I saw then that it wasn't real – that none of the armour was genuine. It had been made quite recently, in some light metal, as a theatrical or movie prop. So much for Alice's Arthurian legends, I thought: Camelot and all the Knights of the Round Table were just as fake.

And yet on the following afternoon I had to admit that the whole medieval recreation looked real enough: startlingly real – a dream come to genuine life in the brilliant sunshine. There was a Grand Procession first, Alice leading it side-saddle on a white charger, of all the Knights and Officers of the tournament, all of them moving on dazzlingly caparisoned horses from the Manor to the lists on the far side of the cricket pitch. A dozen small candy-striped tents for each Knight had been set up here, with individually coloured pennants snaking out in the slight breeze above them.

Nearer the centre of the park a line of wooden hurdles had been set up, like an endless tennis net, along which, down either side, the Knights would charge each other. Further across, facing the middle of the hurdles, a gaily decorated stand had been built, with a long striped awning overhead and the rest festooned with flowers, in swathes of cloth and coloured ribbons, all contrived to form Gothic patterns of slim arches and rose medallions which successfully hid the basic metal scaffolding beneath.

At either end of the hurdles tall lances had been stacked in cones, one against the other, stiletto pennants flying from their tips. A large crowd meanwhile, freed from their morning sports and balloon rides about and above the Manor, had gathered all round the boundary ropes, and there was a buzz of incredulous expectation in the air. Clare and I, dressed again in our costumes of the previous night, had seats in the main stand, not far from where Alice was to sit, right in the front, in a flower-bedecked loggia, with the President of the Victorian Society. In front of us at that moment, a medieval jester, complete with cap and bells, was entertaining us. But this archaic amusement was well forgotten when the long procession came in sight. Each of the Knights was surrounded by their own little retinue of grooms, armourers and supporters, while interspersed between them walked a colourful assortment of archers, halberdiers, standard-bearers and men at arms. At the very head of the procession the musicians of the previous night doubled now as strident trumpeters, announcing the tournament in long high clarions.

I was suddenly lifted by the magic of it all, by the great winding line of armoured horsemen and attendants, chain-mail glinting in the sun, with all the other colours in their shields and pennants – the reds and golds and blacks – turning the procession into a vision from some medieval Book of Hours, a crusader's army setting forth on the vellum of the green sward.

Despite the flimsy veil she wore I could see Alice's face clearly when she arrived to take her throne. Dressed in a long white gown with vast billowing silk sleeves, in a tight, almost wasp-waisted gilt embroidered velvet bodice, she was in seventh heaven – in the midst of an incredibly extravagant dream now at last perfectly realised. I was sorry in a way that I couldn't share it with her. I envied her invention then. And somehow I think she sensed this, for when she finally sat down in the flower-strewn box at the front of the stand, she turned to me for a moment, to where I was sitting a few rows behind her, and, having first looked at me with surprise, for I'd not seen her all that morning, she went on to smile at me with an expression of extraordinary triumph – triumph with an element of spite in it: she had moved finally, with this glorious procession, into a vital world of colour and light, into a promised land where I, through my lack of faith, could not join her.

Yet when the jousting itself actually started and the darkly armoured knights, like evil machines, their plumes flying, thundered down along the hurdles at each other, I was glad I was no part of it. Clare was on her feet most of the time with excitement. But had I been on one of the horses myself, I would almost certainly have ended up in hospital, or worse. One of the well-practised Knights, indeed, took a fearful tumble, jolted violently out of his saddle by a padded lance, to be rescued by St John's Ambulance men suitably attired in striped doublets and hose.

I thought the whole thing comic for a moment, as well as dangerous. And yet what a lot of energy and imagination had been given – by Alice particularly, I knew – to organising the vastly elaborate charade. And I was amazed then at the intensity of Alice's dream, the tenacity with which she had pursued and successfully realised this pageant of archaic valour. I had to admit now that there was something wonderful about her obsessions, something that was not madness. Perhaps it was a particularly American quality, extinct there as everywhere else now, which she still possessed and had brought to life again here: a quality of reaching out, far beyond the boundaries of ordinary hope, towards an imagined light – of risking the infinite, sure of its promise. Alice certainly had this continuously available generosity of spirit, a romantic vision which I, in my sanity, had lost years ago, if I had ever had it. And I felt ashamed of my tardy, careful nature. I was a prisoner of my wishes – someone always at several removes from the real action – a spy by nature as well as by old profession, who could only really see the world through binoculars.

And it was through these, towards the end of the jousting, when the flags and pennants began to dance in long, snake-like shadows across the parkland in an evening breeze, that I noticed the man walking down from the Manor towards us. He was immediately, blatantly noticeable as he came among the costumed spectators in the stand, dressed as he was in a dark business suit, a smallish, almost elderly, rather common-looking little man. I noticed his hair, too, dank, dark tufts of it plastered down with some stiffened dressing over his ears and collar. He searched the stand for someone, gazing about him with an air of great self-assurance and superior concern, as if such costumed nonsense and all the jousting was nothing but a dalliance for rogues and vagabonds.

I had seen this man somewhere before, I thought, seen just that same expression of contemptuous dismissal. But where?

Then I remembered. Months before, in the conservatory, when I had first seen Alice, dressed in a Camelot outfit, apparently talking to herself, she had in fact been talking to this same man: her husband Arthur.

I had forgotten Arthur. I'd been worrying about the police, the African, about Ross. I'd quite forgotten him – forgotten that we had another, and in the present circumstances just as dangerous enemy, who had now walked in on us out of the blue, a pallid ghost, the bad fairy come at the end of the feast. He was looking for Alice, of course, but hadn't seen her yet.

I realised we couldn't run. Clare and I would get nowhere in our costumes. We would have to bluff it out somehow. Alice no doubt would have ideas. At least, I hoped she would.

She did. When the tournament came to end, and Arthur had finally recognised and approached his wife, she immediately

called Clare and me over to her little loggia in the front of the
stand, where she calmly introduced us to Arthur.

'My friends,' she said. 'You don't know them: Bob Lawrence
and his daughter Belinda. They're staying here – down from
London for the celebrations.'

Alice introduced us in her most gracious social manner. But
her husband replied in quite a different manner. 'Oh, are they?
Well, I guess that's fine, for them, I'm sure. And you too, Alice,
Just fine.'

He spoke contemptuously as well, a harsh, grating American
accent, a common tongue, quite unlike Alice's. There was
power in his voice, but not the educated power of any East-
Coast attorney, I thought. This was much more the tone of a
brutal success derived from the Chicago stockyards.

We shook hands. Clare looked up at me and smiled, enjoying
these fictional introductions, which she saw as no more than a
continuation of the day's brilliant theatricals. Then she looked
up at Arthur. And she stopped smiling, for Arthur wore a
steady expression of weary disgust. I saw him properly for the
first time. I was surprised by how much older he was than Alice,
twenty years older at least, I thought. He must have been in his
mid-sixties. There was a chilled, blue look about him in the
warm twilight, as if he'd just come out of a cold store. The
crown of his head, together with his brow, was over-large,
protuberant. But the cheeks hollowed out rapidly and his chin
was small, pointed, decisive. His head was like an inverted pear:
there was the sense, almost, of some deformation in it, while the
dark, moist tufts of unruly hair were widely spaced, I saw now,
showing clear patches of skin beneath, like the scalp of a new-
born baby. There was the sense of someone who had got his
own way with life, in every matter, at the cost only of his
appearance which alone reflected unpleasant failure. I was
surprised that Alice could ever have come to marry such a cold,
elderly fish.

Yet it seemed as if Clare and I had successfully passed this
initial test with him. But how would it be when we were back in
our own clothes, as ordinary guests in the Manor? Could we
sustain the fiction then? Arthur had such a wary look in his eye
for all three of us that I feared for the future.

And I was right there, too. I was unable to speak to Alice
alone before we all trooped back to the Manor, where another

smaller buffet supper with cooling drinks had been laid out in the great hall for the sweating contestants and the costumed guests from the stand.

Quite soon after the exultant merry-making had begun here, when the band of musicians, now well laced with mead and ale, had started out on some jaunty trumpet themes, Arthur cornered all three of us where we had been standing by the great fireplace at one end of the hall. He was fidgeting, frustrated, clearly with something pressing on his mind, which wouldn't wait.

Alice, brashly inventive as ever, gave him the opportunity to unburden himself. 'Bob Lawrence, here,' she said with happy charm, 'is an expert on medieval armour...'

She had hardly finished speaking before Arthur replied softly, urgently, with barely suppressed vindictiveness. 'Don't for God's sake play the fool any more, Alice,' he said, sorrow equalling the anger in his rough American voice. 'You've caused enough trouble already – but this time you're really playing with fire.' He stepped between us then, as if to protect Alice. Then he turned to me, foreknowledge and a dismissive arrogance crowding his face. 'This man is Peter Marlow. And his daughter Clare. He killed his wife a few months back, then abducted the girl from hospital – helped by you, as I understand it. The police have been looking the whole country over for both of them ever since.' He turned back to Alice now. 'Don't be such a damned fool, Alice. This is real madness.'

An angry brightness had come into Alice's eyes as she listened, something sharp and fierce in her expression: hatred for this man. And yet, more than looking at Arthur now, she seemed to be gazing straight through him, focusing on something behind him or lost in some huge new bitter thought of her own. She smiled then. And it was the same overblown, unattached smile, now touched with real madness, that I had noticed in her expression the first time I'd seen her down by the lake, months before, when she had yelped in the wind, floating great Indian war-whoops out over the water.

'Who told you?' she asked.

'Why, Mrs Pringle did, of course. She called me a few days back in New York, when she was certain of the matter. I came straight on over. This time you've really gone too far. But we'll see what we can do.'

He tried to shepherd Alice away, with cold consideration, as the madwoman he so clearly considered her to be. But Alice resisted.

'No! Leave me! We'll all go together.'

And we did; all of us moving off in a rather awkward procession through the costumed throng, out of the great hall and into the porch of the house.

And it was here that Alice suddenly drew her little automatic from her velvet bodice, before levelling it at her husband's back.

'Don't look round,' she warned him. 'Just go on walking.'

Arthur was unaware of what had happened. Then he half-turned, saw the gun. She prodded the weapon into his back.

'Go on!' she said, like a cattle-drover. 'Out the front, then left. Round to the back.'

Clare was excited by this turn of events in our living theatre. I wasn't. I had no idea of the script. Clare said 'Good!' in a considered voice, like a circumspect judge at a flower show. Then she repeated the commendation. 'Good! Good!'

'What are you doing?' I asked.

'You'll see.' Alice didn't look at me, concentrating on her work.

We walked out of the porch, down the wide front steps of the house and into the warm still airs that had come up with the night, no more than a strolling family group, it would have seemed – to the few people, chauffeurs and others, who were grouped around the cars parked everywhere about us, on the drive and over the lawn surround that gave out onto the dim parkland beyond. Our feet crunched on the crisp white gravel that lay faintly all about us, like a thin fall of snow in the half-light, and Alice trod the pebbles lightly, gun in hand, like an avenging angel in her long white Queen of Beauty costume, intent on retribution, pushing her husband forwards into the darkness.

'I don't know where you think this can get you, Alice,' Arthur spoke lugubriously, as if he had quite lost interest in everything.

'It's getting *you* somewhere. Not me.' Alice replied with tart efficiency. 'I've really had too much of you interfering in my life. This is *my* life, *my* house. Not yours.'

'I gave it you, though: your life *and* this house. You forget that. I thought this house, for example, when I bought it for you...' Arthur hesitated and there seemed a touch of genuine sadness and regret in his voice when he spoke again. 'I thought it might ... cure you? If that was ever possible. All this Victorian craziness, that and all the other madness. Yes, a cure, if that was possible. Improve you at least.'

'*Improve* me?' Alice was angry again. 'Like some reform school? But you're my madness, you know that. Not me. You – with your... Well, every single stupid thing: possessiveness, meanness, bad temper, your *ugliness*. Was I to have nothing then before I got this house? Just a toy of yours? Cooped up like a – ' she couldn't find the word, 'like some fancy cake decoration, running your gracious social life out in the Hamptons or the Drake Hotel in Chicago or your New York apartment: just decorating your life, while the others *worked*. You gave them a life. But you took mine. You gave them everything that mattered. While I had to fight beyond fighting – that was my madness – just to get this house, to get away from you.'

I couldn't follow this conversation at all. Who were these 'others'? I assumed Arthur must have been married before and these 'others' were earlier children of his. We had walked right round the house by now and were coming up the covered laurel path, the old tradesmen's entrance, where the branches arched overhead, blocking out almost all the light which came from the few lighted windows above us.

'I told you when we spoke last time here three months ago.' Arthur's voice was faint, absorbed by the thick foliage above him. But the righteous anger in it was still clear enough. 'I told you that you'd never make it here on your own. Go from bad to worse; dressed up in all these circus outfits, playing Red Indians or a bit-part from *Camelot*, living in the past – some damfool golden age of yours, with all those old crocks and platters, those cockamamie Victorian things. And I was right, by God. Now you've got yourself hitched to a killer. But if you give me that gun, maybe we can still get you out of it.'

'This man has already got me out of it. I *am* out of it. Free and sane. And you're not going to put me back – anywhere. I'm going to put you away this time.' Alice spoke with the relish of a child now, winning at last in some long-running nursery antagonism. I was holding Clare's hand tightly, walking along behind, more than uneasy. 'But what can you do?' I asked Alice. 'Mrs Pringle knows everything. She's probably called the police already.'

'She has,' Arthur intoned ahead of us.

'We'll see,' Alice said brightly, firmly.

We'd come through the big stone gateway into the yard where the light from the tall back windows more clearly illuminated the enclosed space around us. We heard the trumpets spilling out from the great hall in front, some merry dance.

Alice was just ahead of me, Clare right behind, pushing forward, anxious not to miss the least development in this midnight charade.

'We'll lock him in here for the moment,' Alice said, gesturing towards the old laundry, where the door was already half-open, blackness beyond. A moment later she had pushed her husband into the darkness and promptly locked the door on him, turning the heavy Victorian key with all the satisfied finality of a hanging judge.

'We'll find Mrs Pringle now,' Alice said, 'and do the same for her – the fat sneak.' Again, the tone of Alice's voice was high and childish. And the words, too, I felt, came straight out of some long-ago world of hers, from a childhood battle with her brothers perhaps, or from some Edwardian adventure book which she had read at the time, embarking even then on her golden age: a world of chivalry and derring-do. Alice, with the arrival of Arthur, seemed to have dispensed completely with all her new sanity and returned to a life of myth.

'You mean – put her in with your husband?' I asked.

She turned and I could see the startling glints in her eyes, even in the half light. 'My husband?' she said incredulously. 'My *father*. Yes – he's my father! Don't you see?'

I hadn't begun to digest this startling information before we heard the first thin scream coming from the old laundry a few yards behind us, more squeak than scream, like a rat's first complaint in a trap. But it was Arthur's voice, I realised, first this startled little whine, but suddenly rising then like some untuned wind instrument going wild until it reached the high strident pitch of a steam whistle. Then the shriek stopped, cut off in its prime only to start up again a few seconds later. But now the pitch was much lower, intermittent, as if someone was playing violently on an already broken instrument, punishing it, destroying it. There were scuffles after that and the sounds of heavy things falling about and being dragged along the floor inside. It was just as if Alice had unwittingly pushed the man into a cage where some wild animal had torn him to pieces and was now quietly devouring him.

We ran back. I turned the key and opened the door.

'There's no electricity here!' Alice called out as we both tried to push our way through the door at the same time. 'Just an oil lamp on the shelf, to the side there.' I cursed Alice's meticulous Victorian re-creations then. But I found the lamp almost at once, on a shelf next the diamond glassed windows, and lit it.

The old laundry was a longish, fairly narrow room, with the big copper boiler to the right, set slightly out from the wall, wooden draining-boards behind that and the huge Victorian linen-press running down the other side, its big wheel, handle and chain – which pulled the great coffin-like weight along the wooden rollers beneath – just visible in the dim light. But I could see nothing amiss anywhere. The room appeared quite empty, like a cave with its arched ceiling and heavy chocolate-brown paint, a cave or a freshly opened tomb filled with mysterious utensils, patent Victorian devices, strange grave gifts from a long-vanished civilisation which loomed up now, taking even stranger shape in the flickering shadows cast by the lamp.

Then, moving towards the boiler, I saw a single smart brogue shoe sticking up in the lamplight, over the rim of the cauldron. Arthur was slumped inside, lying like a banana, curved out round the bottom, his head rising up the other slope. His business suit still clung to him neatly like something dumped in a laundry bin before its time. But Arthur's head had gone all astray. It was badly twisted, turned ninety degrees to the side, so that while he gazed straight over one shoulder, the rest of his body faced resolutely forward. It was as if his head had been a bottle-top which someone had wrenched open far too violently. He was dead. Yet he could hardly have killed himself in such a manner, I thought.

I lifted the lamp, searching out the other shadowy distances and corners in the room, looking for someone else. And as I did so, the wavering oil flames illuminating the spaces beyond, I saw the African – just for an instant – crouching beneath the draining board. It was certainly him. I saw the camouflage jacket, the long thin face a golden mahogany now in the lamplight, the ridges of scar tissue to one side, the eyes deeply inset, intent, vicious – exactly those of a trapped animal about to spring.

And in the next instant he did so, releasing himself like a sprinter from his blocks, rushing towards me. Yet it wasn't me that he wanted. Clare, curious as ever, had come right into the room behind me, and in the darkness I hadn't noticed her. But the African had, and he grabbed her now before I could do anything to stop him.

Then, putting the lamp aside, the three of us were on the floor, struggling beside the boiler, with Alice standing helplessly above us, flourishing the gun. But she could do nothing with it.

'Don't!' I managed to shout up to her, as I tried to pin the African down. And she didn't. The man, holding Clare with one hand, could only fight me with the other – while fear and vast anger gave me a second small advantage. Yes, just as I had when I'd shot Ross's dog in the valley and battered the lamb to death afterwards, I found a fierce strength then, a strange, vicious physical supremacy. I had the African by the neck, with two hands round his sinewy throat. I think I would have squeezed the life out of him, as we twisted and turned, if he had not decided to cut his losses and struggle free. He pushed me away, his fingers driving fiercely up into my nostrils so that the pain became unbearable. Then he was on his feet, dragging Clare with him into the dark recesses of the room.

I picked up the lamp again. Alice had come right next to me now and together we stared into the gloom. Clare was crying. I could hear her, somewhere in the darkness ahead of me. I handed Alice the lamp.

'Here! Hold it – up high – and follow me.'

I took the automatic from her and walked forward. We saw the African then as we both moved to the end of the room. With his back to the wall he was holding Clare, like a shield, high up, right in front of his chest, so that she covered almost all his torso. I couldn't use the gun. I noticed how near he was to the end of the great oak linen press, the half-ton wooden coffin filled with stone, which faced his thighs and midriff, while he held Clare at a level above it. He obviously had no idea what the machine was for, or how its great weight could be made to slide towards him. Yet I couldn't use it against him in this manner unless I was sure that, while I did so, he would keep Clare out of the way.

He answered the problem for me. Since Alice and I were now to one side of him and thus only the press blocked his escape towards the door, he let Clare go and stepped up onto it, before starting to walk over the top of the machine.

I had my chance then. I rushed for the handle as he towered above us. Grasping it with both hands I turned it viciously, so that the great box began to move, slowly at first, but with ever-increasing momentum.

The African, feeling the machine slide beneath him, lost balance, stumbled, righted himself – and then as the rollers began to spin faster, he found himself walking a treadmill, a journey he couldn't sustain, being pushed back inexorably on the great box towards the wall. He panicked then, jumping off the moving press as it sped towards the wall, springing off the end of it, as from a diving board.

But the great weighted box was running like a battering-ram now, the handle at the side spinning round unaided. The African, landing on the flagstones, was immediately caught in the gap between the end of the press and the wall. And when the vice closed on him, it went on closing, without resistance, ramming into his back, first gathering all his bones together in a fierce grip, before squeezing them brutally like a car in a metal-compacter, driving the breath out of him. In the end he had no wind left to scream and all we heard were his ribs cracking, the vertebrae in his neck breaking, so that his head, now the only part of his body above the level of the butt end of the press, nodded first and then keeled over suddenly, unanchored now, like a dark fruit released from its branch.

I stood there horrified for several seconds. The man seemed to have been dispatched by some elemental force, a fly crushed on a windowpane. Yet I, in fact, had dispatched him – and I was horrified at the result: this death's-head now caught in the flaring oil light, lying on its side at the end of the press, as after some violent beheading.

Nor was this the only madness of the evening. There was Arthur lying behind me. Arthur: husband or father? And it suddenly seemed to me more than likely, given his age and that touch of the old mid-West in his voice, that this man was her father, the rough tycoon and Chicago meat-baron, Arthur

Troy, creator of the family fortunes. And I saw then how Alice had gained no sanity with me at all in the past months. She had come to tell the truth perhaps, here and there. But she had lied all the time about the real things. She had never been married to any New York attorney, never had a son by a previous marriage. There had never been the 'real thing' for Alice, and all this reality she had told me about was sheer invention, fictional replacements for life, dreams of living.

Long ago, something must have led her to think of this man, whom latterly she had come to despise, as her husband. Long ago, for some agonising reason, she had turned her father into a husband: and so, before this present hatred, she must have loved him once. Loved him to distraction? Perhaps. It was certainly madness. Anyway, father or father-figure – it hardly mattered any more. She had destroyed them both.

Clare was quite unhurt when I picked her up, while the trumpets from the great hall, with the attendant hum of excited talk and laughter, had obviously prevented anyone in the house from hearing our battles down in the old laundry. The yard was still empty when we looked outside.

Alice had regained most of her icy control, at least, if not her sanity. She took her little automatic back, then locked the door on the two corpses with nerveless competence, hiding the key.

'That's that,' she said easily, as though completing some tiresome shopping expedition. 'They won't find them in there for quite a while.'

I was angry suddenly at what I felt to be her sheer callousness in the matter.

'My God, Alice, you just told me he was your *father*. You can't leave him in there like that. *Is* he your father?'

'We've not the time,' she called back tartly over her shoulder. 'And yes, he is.'

'Why didn't you tell me?'

She didn't reply. I was carrying Clare in my arms, as we threaded our way between the parked cars towards the kitchen entrance to the house.

'No time?' I whispered back angrily. 'No time? For your *father*?'

'Later. Afterwards!' She dismissed her father as curtly in death as she had in life. 'We need Mrs Pringle now,' she went on.

Suddenly, longing to be away from all this mayhem, I said, 'She must have told the police already. Why don't Clare and I just try and make a run for it now – in your car?'

Alice stopped in her tracks. 'No. I'll come, too.'

'Why? You've done nothing. Let us go alone. We can get to Tewkesbury and wait there.'

Alice was looking at me closely. I could see her face quite clearly in the light from the big windows above us. And now, just beneath the veneer of calm and control in her expression, I saw a great fear, fear for what we had just done, perhaps, of what we had both witnessed. I'm not sure. But I knew I couldn't leave her then. She needed my help now as badly as I had needed hers, months back, when she had first surprised me naked in the valley. I couldn't leave her then, someone I loved – and so I was perfectly willing to give ourselves up to the police. I was ashamed at my idea of leaving her.

I said, 'We'll stay. Of course we'll stay. And wait for the police. Mrs Pringle is bound to have called them.' It seemed an end at last.

But Alice, her faith renewed by my change of heart, now had other ideas. 'She may not have told them,' she said brightly, suddenly decisive again. 'Let's find out.'

We surprised Mrs Pringle a few moments later in the old kitchen as we came through. She was sitting at the long pine table, her back towards us, a huge tin of fancy biscuits open in front of her, nibbling at them furiously, nervously, like a great mouse. Her husband, Arthur's chauffeur, a small ferret-like creature whom I'd not met before, was with her. They had a bottle of Ruby Port between them – unopened, though. Obviously, knowing my real identity now as a wife-killer, and that I was roaming about somewhere in the house at that very moment, the party mood had not blossomed in either of them. Recognising me, even in my guise as a fierce Albanian, Mr Pringle stood up in some alarm. His wife turned then, a chocolate biscuit stalled halfway into her great jaws.

'It's quite all right,' Alice said gently. 'Go ahead, Anna – it's hundreds of extra calories, but go right ahead, relax. You needn't worry at all. It's all over. My father's gone out. He's gone to get the police.'

Mrs Pringle looked greatly relieved. 'Oh,' she said nervously. 'He . . . he needn't have bothered. He asked me to call them myself. We wondered where you – '

Alice interrupted her graciously. 'We were just talking together, outside. And now we'll wait upstairs, I think.'

She had already begun to shepherd Clare and me forward, through into the main house. The Pringles stood aside, letting us pass without a word. But just as we reached the doorway of the kitchen, Alice suddenly turned back. I never saw her reach for her little automatic – only saw the gun itself as she levelled it at Mrs Pringle: and heard the shots. She could hardly have missed the woman with her great bulk, standing by the kitchen table. And she didn't. The bullets whipped into her like little darts, puncturing, burying themselves in the meat of her body. Not one bullet, but two, three. I couldn't stop her, though I tried.

'There!' she shouted as she fired. 'That's for sneaking on me: you fat sneak, you spy!'

Alice found these archaic expressions again in her anger, like a character in a *Boys Own Paper* adventure, while pumping the life out of this contemporary glutton, this cunning modern woman who had betrayed her – phoning her father in New York and now the police – finally destroying all her too honourable dreams.

Mrs Pringle keeled over the table like a huge top-heavy ship, scattering the fancy biscuits and the bottle of Ruby port, which broke on the old flagstones, the wine spreading like early blood, before the woman's own wounds opened.

Again, the sound of the trumpets and the other raucous entertainment in the great hall drowned the shots from the automatic. No one moved for an instant. Then Mrs Pringle's husband was down on the floor, tending his wife, while I stood there by the kitchen dresser, confused, appalled, the gunfire still ringing in my ears a certain end to things, to any future.

I turned to her. 'For God's sake!' I shouted. But before I'd finished Alice swung round to face me, still holding the gun, levelling it at me now, as another who had betrayed her. I can't be certain if she actually intended to fire at me, since I never gave her the chance, throwing myself violently to one side down behind the dresser. And when I looked up again a few seconds later, she and Clare were gone from the room, their footsteps beating on the corridor which led up to the great hall.

When I reached the entrance to the hall there was no sign of either of them. They'd been swallowed up by the crowd of costumed revellers, and it was almost impossible in any case to distinguish anybody in their various courtly disguises. All I did see was the two black-and-white chequered caps of police officers over by the hall door, bobbing about among the other more colourful headgear. Avoiding the police, I circled round the hall in the opposite direction, pushing and shoving among the ragged, jolly Knights and their women, the trumpets still blaring. For a moment I thought I saw Alice, her dark hair and bronzed shoulders, over by the hall door. But when I eventually struggled over to it, there was no one there. Alice and Clare had disappeared – out of the house perhaps, for the hall door was open. But where?

Outside on the gravel surround I saw the flashing lights of two police cars, parked some way down the drive, blocked by other cars parked all over the verge. They could hardly have gone down that way, I thought. I looked out over the dark parkland straight ahead of me. If Alice and Clare had left the house, and I felt sure they had, that would have been the only safe way for them to go: out into the darkness, beyond the ha-ha which divided the front lawns from the park. I moved off in that direction in any case, jumping down in the ditch and going on towards the cricket pitch.

Clare – as if the evening's events were all part of some large joke – was laughing in a strange soundless way when I found the two of them fifteen minutes later sitting on the cricket-pavilion steps: knees tight together, head swaying up and down, hands clasped round her ankles, her face was full of smiles, as though Alice had just come to the end of some very good story. Alice was sitting next to her, breathing hard, puffed with her run across the long field.

I'd approached them warily enough, thinking Alice might draw her gun on me again. But when I asked her about it she laughed, as if she'd never levelled it at me.

'I threw it away,' she said. 'No need for it now.'

She seemed to have forgotten the mayhem in the kitchen. She had already removed her shoes and now she started to take off her Queen of Beauty costume. There was a thin moon behind a filigree of clouds; it was bright enough, at least, to make things out. The night was still warm.

'This is nonsense,' Alice said casually. 'This great outfit. I'm sweating.'

She took her velvet bodice off, then pulled the arms of the silk dress down from each shoulder before starting to release the catches at the back of her waist. Then she stepped out of it, leaving just a slip on beneath.

'Cold,' I said. 'You'll get...' I really didn't know where to begin. I was sweating myself. I shook my head. 'Alice,' I said finally, 'I don't see the point.'

'Does there always have to be a point?' she said. 'Besides, there *is* a point,' she went on suddenly. 'We're free.'

'Yes. But –'

'We're still *free*,' she insisted.

'What can we do here, though? Just postpone the inevitable. The police –'

'Why not? They can wait till morning.'

Clare spoke then, seemingly equally unaffected by the recent events, which I supposed she must have seen simply as a continuation of the two-day-long drama of the fête, the cricket match, the costume ball, the jousting tournament. 'Are you playing again now here?' she asked, 'That game you had here before?'

'No. It's too dark, sweet. It's too dark.'

I sat down beside Clare and picked her up and put her on my knee, holding her round the shoulders lightly in one arm. I thought this must be the end of things between she and I. And I wanted to make the most of it with her, without her knowing of my sadness. At least, I saw now, Alice was right in one way: there was some point in this last folly of hers: it had given Clare and me time together once more. We were both headed for separate institutions now, just as Alice was.

'Clare,' I started, thinking how I could tactfully explain my imminent departure from her life. 'I thought I'd tell you –'

'Story?' she burst in brightly. 'Iddity, Iddity story? The one of the pigs?'

'Well, but I don't have the book –'

'Yes!' she said. 'The book in your head. Go on.'

And so instead of the slightest grim news, I started out on *The Tale of Pigling Bland* again, inventing what I couldn't remember, the three of us sitting quietly on the pavilion steps in the dark.

'This is the story of Pigling Bland...'

There was no noise in the night, far down in the parkland where we were hidden: except, after five minutes, the faint sound of a siren in the distance, just when I had got to the point in the tale where Pigling Bland, released from bondage, is stopped by the local village constable on his bicycle.

Later we slept fitfully on the pavilion floor, in a corner, on batting pads and among stumps, waiting for the police to find us: the three of us together in a line, secure in the dark, breathing the night air in the pavilion still warmed by the day, a faint smell of leather and willow, touched with linseed oil and old grass cuttings.

Clare fell asleep first, with my velvet Albanian doublet over her: fast asleep, quite at ease, it seemed, as if Alice and I were both shepherding her, between us, through the night towards some exciting new adventure, the world of some other lake in a valley or hidden African paradise, where she would wake in another miraculous landscape. To begin with, in the complete darkness, all we knew of her existence was the easy rhythm of her breath: small waves, an echo of her journey, her transformation between light and dark, the only worldly sound, beyond which lay deep sleep or the noise of her fantastic dreams. But then Alice and I, moving towards each other, gently closed the gap between all three of us, so that we came to shield the girl like leaves round a bud and we felt her life then, heart-beat as well as breath.

Alice touched my face in the complete dark, stumbling on an ear, an eye, my mouth. She had forgiven me, it seemed, for what she had seen as my earlier betrayal. Whatever anger she had felt for me in her bedroom the previous night, in the kitchen, had dissolved. No, not dissolved; it was more than that. It was as if some whole new person had taken over Alice's mind – her body even – as a substitute does for some injured person in a game. Alice had re-invented herself, taken on another role, that of pliant mistress in my arms, a woman without any knowledge now of her murderous disruption, her violence and hatred. It was a strange feeling: I was touching some other woman in the dark.

I had thought to ask her about her father. But it wasn't the moment – the answers could only have come from the woman she had been and was no longer – and there wasn't time. And then I thought again: husband or father, what did it really matter? She had seen Arthur as both: as lover and enemy. That was clear enough. The rest, for answer, could only lie on a psychiatrist's couch. And I, with Laura, had given up on all the quacks and specialists a long time before with Clare, in what we had seen as her tragedy. But was it such, I wondered now, with either of these two, Alice or Clare? Was it not simply their way of looking at life, a way as valid as ours, in which they saw things hidden to us and made associations which lacked all our dull logic? And if their strange visions gave them a disadvantage among ordinary mortals, that vision, that madness even, seemed to me then an inviolable gift, as much a part of both their characters as any other of their attributes I loved. Without it, I realised, Alice and Clare would have lacked their most vital dimensions, that quality of fierce excess in a bankrupt world, bounty amidst impoverishment, swift imagination riding over every mean thought.

How shortsighted I'd been to look so hard for sanity in everyone, in Alice or in Clare. After all, I saw now, the bizarre was Clare's particular gift too: that untutored wildness in her which, whatever disadvantages it might bring, would always free her from the mundane. A cure for such people could well become a life worse than the disease, I thought, when they would lose all their strange stature, as we would miss their passionate example.

So I loved Alice that night without reserves, without queries or judgements: and loved her the more since in any case there would be no world between us tomorrow where such reservations could have any effect. And thus, an end so certainly in view between us, we were both quite free at last.

Eighteen

Next morning a thin, almost translucent blanket of mist lay everywhere, low down, hugging all the parkland: the sun rose above it, trying to force its way through, with patches of blue sky just visible here and there, promising another brilliant day in these last days of summer.

I'd woken early and gone to one of the pavilion windows, the others still asleep behind me. Then I'd opened the door a fraction. Finally I stepped right outside. The manor was completely hidden, nearly half a mile away. It was difficult to see more than twenty yards, and there wasn't a sound on the muffled air. Nothing penetrated the soft, pearly stillness. The police, until the mist cleared, would be handicapped in their search for us – and the tracker dogs would be at a disadvantage, too, with so many confusing human trails to follow after the fête. We had some time left.

I shivered in the cool, early air, still just in my thin costume shirt and woollen tights, a foolhardy reveller about to face the police courts. And I felt another stab of regret then – looking out on this magic shroud, this safety curtain touched with coming sunlight, beyond which the day lurked, full of promise, that I would never be free in.

The mist was already beginning to clear as I watched, the sun warming. Suddenly I heard the muffled sound of a dog barking and then another: up by the manor. I went back inside. Perhaps there'd just be time to brew some tea before they found us – on the gas ring in the little kitchen to the side of the pavilion where the cricketers had their food prepared. I lit the gas, gazing vacantly out over the cricket pitch where the mist was thinning quickly now.

Then I heard another noise above the sound of the gas in the small kitchen, a much stronger rush of air, a great whooshing sound, like a jet-engine starting up. I looked beneath the sink, at the canister of propane stored there. But there was nothing amiss. This new sound came from outside the pavilion, I realised, from somewhere in the mist.

I was very tired, so that at first I thought what I saw a few minutes later must be an illusion, a projection on my mind of a last suppressed longing for freedom. Less than fifty yards away, as the mist cleared, I saw a big square box on the ground, a sort of wicker basket it seemed, and above it, swelling up into the air like an effect in a surrealist painting, a huge pear-shaped object, striped in vivid reds and golds, grew in front of my eyes, suddenly reflecting the rising sun like an orb of fire. I wasn't dreaming.

It was a balloon.

Of course: it was the hot-air balloon they'd used all yesterday morning at the fête for tethered trips with Passepartout into the sky. I'd quite forgotten about it. The men had returned this morning and were starting it up again, about to take it away.

I went back into the main room of the pavilion. Alice was awake when I got there, with Clare, both of them standing spellbound at the window.

'Quick!' Alice said when she saw me. 'Here's our chance – we can take that balloon!'

Alice was off her head again, I thought. There were two fairly burly men tending the balloon, we saw now, one of them on the ground unleashing some of the tie-ropes, the other inside the basket manipulating the gas burner, so that as we watched he pulled a lever, like a beer tap, beneath the fabric and there was a sudden dart of flame and another great roar of sound as he maintained the great balloon, now almost fully expanded, in a stable position above him.

'Take it?' I asked. 'But how? We can't – '

Then Clare, still half-asleep, interrupted. 'It's a magic!' she said. She smiled easily as if this vision in the dying mist was something entirely expected, the balloon a transport arranged by us, in which she would shortly continue her dramatic life at the Manor by soaring into the sky above it. Alice had just the same optimism. She stood beside me in her slip – shivering, but from excitement more than from the early chill in the misty air.

Yet even as we stood there the mist was clearing ever more rapidly, all the blue and white horizons above the parkland coming into focus. We could see the Manor now, half a mile away to our right, and I heard the dogs bark again. And then I saw some dark figures, spread out in a long line, approaching us. The police were just stepping down across the ha-ha.

Alice saw them too: and suddenly she had the little automatic in her hand. She'd hidden it, not thrown it away at all.

'Alice,' I shouted. 'No!' I tried to take the gun off her. But I was too late. She raised it, pointing it at me. She had that great glint of adventure in her eyes once more, on the rampage again, determined on a last rash throw where she would finally turn the tables on her fate.

'Well, are you coming?' she said. 'We're going.'

'Alice, it's crazy. We can't control it.'

'I can. You just pull that thing.'

'But where will it get us? It could blow us anywhere.'

'Exactly. The police will never know where.'

I tried to stop her again. But before I had the chance she had grasped Clare by the hand and was out of the door running furiously down the pavilion steps towards the balloon. I ran after them.

The police, I saw, were moving towards us in a huge circle, round three sides of the park, not more than a quarter of a mile away. But though they must have seen the vividly coloured balloon through the dissolving mists, they hadn't seen us yet. They were still walking slowly across the grass.

'No!' I shouted after Alice, gaining on her. But she was still well ahead of me. The two men, both of them on the ground now, releasing the last tie-ropes, didn't know what hit them – a child dressed as a medieval page a woman in a slip flourishing an automatic, followed by a man in a velvet doublet and hose – all three of us streaking towards them. And Alice ran fast, with the child in tow, for the police had just seen us now, and were running towards us.

Alice flourished the gun at a fair-haired young man who had been tending to the gas burner, and who looked at us all when we arrived by the basket as if he'd seen ghosts.

'Out of the way!' she shouted at him. Then with her free arm she lifted Clare off the ground, putting her in the basket before starting to climb in herself.

'What the bloody hell – ?' The second much older man spoke now, standing up on the far side of the basket where he'd been tending the ropes. He was a big swollen middle-aged fellow, gross with good living, with an adventurous old 'Wizard Prang' RAF moustache. He stepped briskly forward now, coming to eject Alice and Clare from his machine. But he hadn't seen the little automatic.

Alice raised the gun over the edge of the basket and fired. The man stopped and looked about him wildly as the sound echoed round the park where the sun had bathed almost all the mist away. 'The next one's for you,' Alice shouted. The big fellow retreated, as did his fair-haired colleague on the other side.

I stepped forward myself then. 'Come on, Alice,' I said. 'This is nonsense. You can't get anywhere. Come on out of it.'

But Alice had pulled the lever already, igniting the gas-burner again, starting it off with another roar, so that the basket, already just free of the ground, began to drift slowly upwards.

There was nothing to do then but jump into it myself. But as I did so, I noticed that one of the tie-ropes was still in place, pegged to the grass.

The big man noticed this, too – and saw his opportunity, running quickly forward before clinging to this rope. Meanwhile the police were closing fast, all of them running hard now, little more than a hundred yards away.

Alice had her hand on the lever, activating the gas supply continuously, the snout erupting in a great sheath of flame above us, so that in moments we were ten feet above the ground. But the man had firmly grasped the last tie-rope and was hanging on to it for dear life as the balloon rose very slowly upwards, dragging the rope through his hands. The first of the police were only fifty yards away.

I leant out over the side of the basket. The man beneath was coming to the end of the tether, was almost airborne with us now. If the police got to help him before the rope ran out, their combined efforts would keep us on the ground. Already we were almost at a standstill. But the balloon, gradually filling with the hot air, won the battle, inching upwards. And in a moment the man was airborne, rising with us.

In the end he saw it was no use and suddenly he let go, dropping ten feet like a stone, sprawling over on the grass. Immediately afterwards, free of his great weight, the balloon surged upwards, the last tie-rope dangling just above the heads of the police as they arrived beneath. One of them had a revolver out; others shouted up at us.

But we couldn't hear their voices. Already we were fifty feet above them, a hundred feet, rising fast in an upcurrent of sun-warmed air, the gas burner still on full charge, drowning all other sound. And soon all the men were far below us as we climbed through the last streaks of mist, a huge red rose in the brilliant morning air, the sun rising well above the line of trees to the east, burning my eyes, blinding me, so that I could see nothing.

But Alice had certainly managed to escape: there was no doubt about that. We were rising like an express lift, as if some great hand had snatched us up from the earth, and I could feel that, could feel all the pits opening in my stomach as we shot upwards. And despite my horror at the event, I suddenly felt a huge elation then as well, embraced by this sheer miracle, the giddy weightlessness of rising thus in space, the Manor and the parkland falling away, the green countryside just beginning to form a relief map beneath us with model animals and other toys on it.

I was blinded by tears from the rush of wind in my eyes, as well as by the sun, so that when I finally managed to look at Alice I saw she was laughing, laughing fit to burst, as at some fantastic joke. Yet I could hear nothing of her laughter against the great blast of gas that was propelling us up into the pale blue dome of sky. She was like the butt of some joke in an old comic silent film, a crazed woman caught in nothing but her slip, lost to the world.

We must have been about a thousand feet up when Alice suddenly released the lever and the gas flame died. There was an extraordinary silence then. And now that we were apparently suspended in mid-air without reason, I felt nervous for the first time, even afraid. There wasn't the slightest turbulence, nor the sound of any wind through the wire lines of the balloon – nor the murmur, the faintest echo rising from the ground beneath. I looked over the side of the basket. A bird, a big seagull, glided past some hundreds of feet below us. But we were quite stationary, stuck in the air, trapped in space, in a vast, early-morning silence from which, like dangling puppets, we should never find release. Yet Alice looked at me then with triumph: a woman at last embarked on a long-postponed vital journey.

'You see,' she said. 'We made it! We're on our way.'

'Yes,' I said gently, determined not to antagonise her at this height, for she still had the gun in her hand. 'You made it.' And though we very obviously weren't on our way and were going nowhere, I didn't mention this.

Alice looked over the side of the basket, gazing down at the Manor and then at the parkland on the far side of the cricket pitch where all the little candy-striped jousting tents with their flowing pennants were still in place, the flower-strewn stand and the line of hurdles in between. The early sun, behind the tents and banners, casting long sharp shadows across the grass, gave these remains of the tournament a vividly fresh, three-dimensional effect from this height, like a field of battle, empty at first light, the warriors asleep under canvas, a field where the glory, far from being over, had not yet begun.

Alice gazed lovingly on this site of her dream, taking no

notice at all of the reality on the other side of the park, the crowds of police by the cricket pavilion gazing up at us. She had no idea, beneath this heaven in a gilded orb, that her dream was behind her now and all Camelot laid waste.

She said, still looking over the side, 'You see, there's nothing you can't do if you really try. And there's so *much* we can do now. That big brambly wood over there,' she went on, looking westwards, 'We can really clear that, let the flowers breathe – and pull down that ridiculous barbed wire fence. Don't you think?'

She turned to me, intense, suddenly ecstatic, just as she had been with me before, offering up some brilliant project which we might share in the future.

'Yes,' I said. 'We can do that. That fence is ridiculous.'

Alice, I saw then, acknowledged no defeat. Her land, her great house and all the myths she had created there, though hundreds of feet away were now at last near enough for her to reach out and fully possess them.

Clare, who had been gazing rapturously over the side as well, suddenly said 'Pigs? Sheep down there. We can have pigs,' she added very definitely.

'Pigs as well,' I said. 'I hope so.'

'I want to sort out the books in the library, too,' Alice went on, pushing further ahead into all the lovely caverns of her dream. 'And the top corridor, all that Victorian stuff: I've left it far too long. That crocodile for example, the big beady-eyed monster upstairs, should we put it in the hall porch and scare the guests?'

Freed from the earth there was no longer any restraint whatsoever on Alice's fantasies, no barrier at all for her now between illusion and reality. Both were one, the same bright flame, sustained by every frustrated longing she had ever had.

'And the people, of course!' She spoke again. 'They can come now. All the people.'

'Who?' I ventured.

'Why, the real people, of course.'

'The people like yesterday, you mean? At the tournament.'

'Yes – *yes.*'

She looked away from me. She was calmer now, distancing herself, as if studying long guest-lists in her mind, sorting out the wheat from the chaff, the quick from the dead, selecting the real, true people who, now that all the calculating cheats and liars had been vanquished, would finally make up the round table with us in the great dining-room. Alice, in her successful ascent from the world, had struck a decisive victory over the infidel, finally dispensing with all the earth-bound, common lot.

But there was one element in her fantasy still unfulfilled, a holy grail of sorts almost within her grasp but yet to be achieved. And that was me. I could tell from her eyes when she turned to me again just then that she still doubted me, doubted my full consent in her plans, doubted that I would share this glittering future with her, this coming world which lay all about us in its infancy, as clearly mapped as the real earth beneath us was just then, deeply etched in dark and misty greens by the long shadows of the morning.

She spoke with the gravity of a bishop before a marriage or confirmation. 'You do believe me?' she asked.

'I do,' I lied.

'Everything?'

'Yes. Everything.'

I moved across to her then and held her in my arms. 'Everything,' I said again.

And in those moments, when she was so close to me, I suddenly found, against all my better judgement, that I did believe her. It was as if, in touching her and making these promises, I had transformed all her folly into lovely inventions and happy devices, genuine articles of faith which she returned to me now and which I could thus no longer deny. I believed her. She let her belief run through me, like the lovemaking we had never managed, so that the sensation was physical and I was suddenly giddy, my head singing, struck by this passing miracle.

In those moments, and as she stood away from me, her face caught in the rising gold of the sun, Alice was transfigured. She had justified her life at last, with all its preposterous flaws and startling visions. The flaws were forgotten peccadilloes now, erased mistakes in the design, as in some great church window, where only the faith remained. Alice had come into her real estate at last, a place entirely of the spirit. At last, in a balloon instead of on a white charger, she had been rescued from that dark and brambly wood. Yet I was not her saviour: I knew that now. Forsaking the world, she had saved herself with her own great fidelity. And she was that chalice with the wine, not I – I who had simply had the luck to taste it briefly.

A small breeze had come up as the sun rose, and now suddenly we were moving, as well as falling in the sky.

Alice said, 'There! We're off. We'd better get some height again.'

She pulled the lever, but nothing happened. The gas snout, rising above us from a coiled pipe like the worm of an old pot-still, was silent. Alice tugged the line again. But again nothing happened. The mechanism that lit the gas had failed, or else there was some trick or process in the ignition which we knew nothing about.

'Do we have any matches?' Alice asked.

'No,' I said. 'Nothing...'

'Maybe you could climb up?' she queried.

'Why?'

'See if something's stuck in the pipe – ' There was an urgency in Alice's voice, and with good reason, for we were falling now, beginning to descend quite fast. And without the gas, with the air cooling all the time in the fabric above us, we were likely to hit the earth with quite a thump.

I tried the lever myself, but it was no use. The life had gone out of it. I checked the pipes leading up from the two big gas cylinders in the basket, shaking them, thumping them, before switching the supply from one cylinder to another. But it made no difference. There was plenty of gas, I realised now, for we could hear it each time we pulled the cord, hissing up into the great gold throat of the balloon. It was the spark which was missing. The magic had disappeared. And now we were dropping faster, in a long angled glide, moving over the cornfield beyond the cricket pavilion, falling towards the ring of tall beech trees above our hidden valley with the lake beyond.

'God,' I said. But I kept my voice down. We were gaining speed and losing height all the time, as we dipped down into the cooler airs above the moist valley where we could see the mist still lying all over the lake in the middle.

I wanted to say something. But there was nothing to say. My throat was suddenly bone-dry and all I could do was fight the panic. The police, meanwhile, I saw, had doubled back, running across the park following our disastrous flight. The

wind, which had been nowhere before in the balmy morning
sky, blew past my ears now, and I could feel the dead weight of
the balloon growing all the time as the warmth died inside it,
and we fell to earth, helpless puppets in this great child's toy
gone wrong. We all knew we were going to crash then. Yet
Alice was suddenly very angry, not afraid.

'Why us?' she shouted, above the wind, her eyes wild with
defiance. 'Why? We've done nothing wrong. It was the others!'

I didn't have the words, or the time to reply. The bronze
burnt tops of the old beech trees were rushing towards us now as
if we were on the steep slope of a roller-coaster. I gripped the
side of the basket, protecting Clare, bracing myself, Alice next
to me. It seemed as if some down-draught had caught us, that
we were being sucked into the tall trees on the rim of the valley.
I couldn't see how we could miss them.

But at the last moment we had just enough height to smash
through the topmost branches, twigs cracking beneath the
basket, and then we were headed straight for the misty waters of
the lake, straight for the island in the middle, where only the
little Gothic pointed roof of the Hortons' mausoleum stood
clear of the milky pools covering the water. There was nothing
we could do then, except wait for the crash.

'Get down!' I yelled. 'Below the sides, arms over your heads,
back to the water!'

We were all of us down in the bottom of the basket then,
bracing ourselves in a huddle, Clare between us – just a moment
before we hit the roof of the mausoleum.

If only we had hit the water. But instead the basket jack-
knifed upwards against the slope of the roof while the balloon
rushed onwards, so that suddenly we were on our side, being
dragged across the slates, and then I was falling, pitched from
the basket, falling into the milky envelope beyond the
mausoleum, before the sudden intense cold as the liquid beneath
gripped me. I was still holding Clare as I fell. But I had lost
Alice.

It was chaos then. Something in the crash had hit me on the
temple, a great glancing blow. But I was still conscious as I went
under the water, struggling for what seemed like minutes in the
depths, with Clare gone from me now as well. And when I
reached the surface I could barely see a thing through the white
shroud that lay all about me.

Someone was screaming. It was Clare: I knew that thin voice. And finally I saw her, bobbing up and down in the mist a few yards from me. She seemed unharmed. We swam towards each other. But there was no sign of Alice.

I looked round for her wildly. The roof of the mausoleum had fallen right in, and the basket had come to rest on its side in the water several yards away with the squashed gold fabric of the balloon itself just visible in the mist beyond. The water had begun to calm all around us and I heard shouts from invisible people on the shore. But Alice?

I shouted for her as I reached Clare, holding her up in my arms, treading water.

'Alice!' I screamed. But my voice seemed faint, choked. And I realised it was from the blood that had trickled down my cheek and into my mouth. I would have dived for Alice then. Perhaps she was trapped beneath the basket or the crumbling shroud of the balloon. But I couldn't leave Clare.

Eventually I turned, making for the shore. But as I did so I heard a splash behind me and looked back. Over by the balloon, ten yards away, I saw Alice's head rise for an instant in the water, a sudden dark, glistening sheen of hair. Was it a trick in the deceptive misty light? No, it was her, that head and naked shoulders, half her body rising sheer from the depths for a moment with an arm raised high, like a missile, just as she had risen from this same water three months before when I'd swum with her here after we'd first met. I turned back, swimming towards the rippling circles. But I was weak now and Clare was struggling. It was no use, we would all of us drown.

I tried to dive back into the water when we got to the shore by the old boathouse and I had handed Clare over to the police who had arrived all along the banks now. But that was no use either, for the men held me there against my will and I finally hadn't the strength to resist.

Several police swam out into the lake themselves, looking for Alice, as the mist began to clear, and I sat shivering on the stone pier, the remains of my Albanian costume in damp shreds all about me.

Someone came up to me and put a coat round my shoulders. I looked up. It was Ross: Ross – who had stalked me through this same valley months before and through the hospital corridors in Banbury. He had got me at last.

'There,' he said. 'You'll be all right now.'

'What did *you* want with me, Ross?' I said to him eventually.

'To save you – from yourself, Marlow,' he replied at once. 'Rushing off like that from your wife. You see, I knew you hadn't killed her. And I knew you were holed up somewhere in these woods, you see. I just wanted to save you ... all this trouble.' He looked round him, at the debris on the lake.

'But I left Intelligence years ago,' I said. 'Why should you bother with me?'

'We always look after our own, Marlow.'

I knew Ross was lying then. He had wanted rid of me – under lock and key at the very least – when my old department had got wind of my memoirs. He would have his way now, but I hardly cared.

I still had Clare in my arms. I was stroking her wet hair, holding her to me. Ross tried to take her from me then. But my strength came back and I resisted fiercely.

'It's all right,' he reassured me again. 'Her grandfather's here.'

I saw the little procession of people arriving then, sliding down between the burnt beech trees into the valley: Captain Warren, sprightly as ever with his boot-black hair, being helped down the treacherous slope by a group of police officers.

Clare saw him as he walked up to us: and there was a flicker of recognition in her eyes. But she pushed herself deeper into my embrace and stayed there, crushed against me like a threatened wild animal again. When the Captain came clearly into view, standing above me, I looked up at him coldly.

'It was never going to be any good,' he said, shaking his neat head. 'I couldn't have got you out on the boat, all the way here and back to Lisbon. It would never have worked.'

I didn't say anything. But then something struck me, as it had so often struck Alice. 'You could have *tried*,' I said with annoyance. 'You might have trusted me. Nothing venture – '

'But why should I?' the Captain interrupted, his own anger suddenly rising. 'Why should I have done anything for you – after what you did to Laura.'

He saw me as a murderer too. He was wrong. They were all wrong. They lacked faith. And I remembered Alice's shouts, as we fell to earth in the balloon. 'Why us? We've done nothing wrong! It was the others...' And I believed her then, all right.

I turned away from the Captain, and found myself rocking Clare in my arms, looking out over the lake where some of the police were still diving about, vainly searching for Alice as the mist finally cleared and the sun rose high enough above the trees to dip in over the copper-coloured water, fingering the valley with gold. I had lived for months, I thought, in this burnt-out Arcadia – and that, at least, would always count . . .

Months before, a body had risen like a sword, sheer from the lake, happy in the sun – and the same body had appeared for an instant in just the same way, minutes ago, desperate for survival. Alice had disappeared. But wherever she was in the water she remained a promise I might one day redeem. Ross joined me again and we both looked out on the fruitless search.

'Of course, she was so much her own worst enemy, too,' he said. 'Inventing things all the time. Crying wolf.'

'What do you mean?' I had hardly any anger left, even for Ross. But I did my best.

'She wouldn't be drowned out there somewhere, Marlow, if she hadn't been such a storyteller – '

'You're the liar, Ross – '

'Oh yes, the local police would have believed her then – when she phoned them two nights ago, saying you were with her, right there in the house with her, she said, in the next bedroom in fact. But they didn't believe her. Just thought it was another of her fantasies. It wasn't the first time she'd taken them for a ride, you see. Ever since she first came here, apparently – she's had them on the hop over something or other, calling them all hours of the day and night: she was being raped or the Martians were landing out on the cricket pitch. That sort of joke. Besides, they'd been through the whole house and the estate with a fine comb, twice before, looking for you. So they didn't believe her when she called them late the other night, after that fancy dress ball. They did nothing about it – till that nurse of hers called them yesterday afternoon. Saved a lot of trouble, wouldn't it, if she'd been the sort of woman you could believe. But she was crazy. And that's that.'

Ross looked grimly over the sun-streaked water.

'You're lying, Ross,' I told him confidently again. 'You're the storyteller.'

He turned and smiled. 'So she fooled you too, did she?'

And I couldn't answer him then.

They took me to the police station in Stow first, where they charged me with Laura's murder, and then to the cells and the court in Oxford the following day, where I was more formally charged: and afterwards held in custody, pending trial. That was over six weeks ago.

Later I was also accused of manslaughter – the African in the old laundry; of causing grievous bodily harm to a Libyan in the Oxford Natural History Museum and of killing a youth with a stolen bow and aluminium arrow...

Ross must be pleased. I'm not likely to betray his department with my 'memoirs' now. Or not yet, at least. No: I've written all this instead. This will be my defence. My lawyer thinks that with any luck, when all the contrary evidence comes to light, I'm likely to be cleared of all or most of the charges. With any luck? I don't believe much in that now.

On the other hand I've had so much luck already. In meeting Laura and Alice, in loving them. And I don't doubt it now, as I did when I was first living up in the trees like a savage in the hidden valley, that quality, not duration, is the significant thing in love. Or do I believe this now simply because I have to? The women dead, myself incarcerated in a prison cell. A gloomy thought. There is the bright side, however. I'm bound to be freed sooner or later, proved as innocent as Alice was: and Laura, all of us victims of a vicious, mendacious world.

But then comes the awful doubt: will I ever be released by such a world? In prison one's thoughts swing wildly between extremes of hope and fear. Only one thing is certain. Clare, I've heard, is alive and well, living again by the long Atlantic rollers with her grandparents in Cascais. She has certainly escaped all the lies and every other mean human scheme, escaped back into her own wild landscapes. And I can see her now, as she was when she rushed up to the top of the cork tree that evening in the overblown summer garden by the sea – when she perched in the topmost branches there, against the blue Atlantic sky, gazing like a look-out towards another world – a girl in the crow's nest of a ship, blonde hair running in the wind, absorbed in some secret voyage.

She's free. She's going somewhere. I'm certain of that, at least.